The Edge of Chaos

Also by Pamela McCorduck

Familiar Relations (novel)

Working to the End (novel)

Machines Who Think

The Fifth Generation (with Edward A. Feigenbaum)

The Universal Machine

The Rise of the Expert Company
(with Edward A. Feigenbaum and H. Penny Nii)

Aaron's Code

The Futures of Women (with Nancy Ramsey)

The Edge of Chaos

A novel

Pamela McCorduck

SANTA FE

Lines from the poem, "From the Hymn to Inanna,"
from *Women in Praise of the Sacred,* edited by Jane Hirshfield,
HarperCollins, New York, 1994, are used by permission of Jane Hirshfield.

Book and cover design by Vicki Ahl

Sunstone books may be purchased for educational, business, or sales promotional use.
For information please write: Special Markets Department, Sunstone Press,
P.O. Box 2321, Santa Fe, New Mexico 87504-2321.

Library of Congress Cataloging-in-Publication Data

McCorduck, Pamela, 1940-
The edge of chaos : a novel / by Pamela McCorduck.
p. cm.
ISBN 978-0-86534-578-2 (alk. paper)
1. Complexity (Philosophy)--Fiction. 2. Santa Fe (N.M.)--Fiction. I. Title.

PS3613.C3823E35 2007
813'.6--dc22

2007022271

WWW.SUNSTONEPRESS.COM
SUNSTONE PRESS / POST OFFICE BOX 2321 / SANTA FE, NM 87504-2321 /USA
(505) 988-4418 / ORDERS ONLY (800) 243-5644 / FAX (505) 988-1025

For my husband, Joseph Traub, always there for me

For Judith Gorog, in lifelong friendship

Preface

The Santa Fe Institute exists, and is devoted to research in the sciences of complexity, but I've taken a novelist's license to restructure it slightly. Some who make cameo appearances in these pages are real scientists, and their words here are words they've spoken to me, or published. But the main characters are, of course, entirely of my own imagination, and bear no resemblance to people living or dead. The ancient city Benito dreams about is Çatalhoyuk, at present under excavation in southern Anatolia, Turkey.

A study guide can be found at the end of the book, helpful not only for book groups, but also for the individual reader who wants to reflect upon the reading.

—Pamela McCorduck

Winter 1993

He asks to speak to his daughter, but the German voice sternly insists that she cannot be called from class. He admires how clear the Germans are about priorities, but explains why he must speak to her directly.

Oh, the voice says, more conciliatory now. I am so sorry. Perhaps it's better if one of the teachers informs her—more personal than the phone? He's briefly tempted. Immediately suspects the temptation, less an urge to ease things for his daughter than a convenience for himself. Perhaps, he concedes, but as her father, I'd prefer to do it.

He waits for a very long time. The connection is tenuous, and he feels a slight anxiety rising, that it might simply go dead. The phone system here is unreliable. As he waits, he makes plans to reroute the call if they're cut off.

"Papa?" They've told her it's him.

"Nikki?" He hasn't exactly rehearsed, but whatever words he thought he had desert him. Does she have any privacy where she is?

In the silence she says, "It's mama, isn't it?"

"Mama died last night, babe." He will not use the euphemisms.

She gasps, but doesn't cry. This death isn't entirely unexpected.

"I'm in Istanbul. I'll fly to Munich and pick you up. We can go to New York together. Stevie's coming down from school. Char's arranging the funeral. For Tuesday."

"Was she alone?"

A good question. With no answer he intends to give his daughter. Their daughter. "Millie found her late last night."

"Millie?"

"Your mother hired her a few weeks ago. A nice lady." He doesn't know that; hasn't cared to get past the self-protective courtier's smile of the Filipina nurse-companion the two or three times they've encountered each other in the hallway.

"Was she alone, papa?" Nikki doesn't mean a nurse companion.

I don't know. The truth. Harsher in its way than yes, she was alone, or no, she was not. He says nothing. He hears his daughter breathing hard and fast, repeating a word softly: no, no, no. "You weren't there?"

"I'm in Istanbul." Indicting himself as he says it.

"Could you not have been there just once for her? Just once?"

No point in answering. He's sometimes thought this child, always so angry with him, so quick to blame, must have conceived this fury before she was born. Coiled under her mother's heart, stirring to life, somehow she perceived her father's plea to destroy her before it was too late. Then it was too late and she's paid him back in rage and accusation ever since.

Suddenly her grief pours into his ear like acid. It surprises him. His wife has been dead to him so long that he's failed to anticipate his children might grieve their mother. He must have expected his daughter to be relieved, forced as she was from the beginning to be a parent to her own fragile mother. He reminds himself: the girl is only sixteen. He reminds himself: it's his duty to love and cherish her. He wishes he could also like her.

"Does grandma know?"

"Char tried to tell her, but doesn't think she really understands. Maybe just as well." These women who've surrounded him, furious daughter; dead wife; aunt who's been mother to him and not; mother-in-law long ago senescent—though they live off him, and very well, he's been perpetual supplicant, he thinks, to every one of them. This is not what he hoped love would be.

When he hangs up, he wonders if he and his daughter have spoken in German or English.

Winter 1996–1997

Mutualists, Competitors, Hosts and Parasites

It begins simply. By chance a man and woman meet at a dinner party. The woman is momentarily, mildly curious; plays a game at the threshold of consciousness, what if this man instead of another? The man—well, the man is in the habit of masking himself.

Then it's past. The woman is distracted. Others at the table make claims on the man—his hostess wants his gratitude, his dinner partner wants his attention. No wonder. Down the table he sees her husband, the face of a fanatic, distrustful and famished.

No, it begins even more simply than that. A single-celled seed, one of millions, penetrates, is engulfed by, a single-celled egg, also one of millions, to exchange and recombine information, set up possibilities. But only possibilities. What happens isn't inevitable. The outcome depends on so much: it could all have turned out differently. Played a second time, it would have.

He makes his first appearance at a dinner during that festive week between Christmas and New Year's, when you need a four-wheel-drive to get through the foot of snow that's fallen on Christmas Day in Santa Fe. The guest of honor, the new man in town, Molloy sits at the table quietly, his black eyes absorbing. Very early he's trained himself to learn by watching, has cultivated an expression of polite attention that can mask anything from acute yearning to utter boredom.

Conversation down the table drifts in fragments to him. From a woman:

"Really rigid. Into calorie reduction, so eating between eight and twelve hundred calories a day, migod who needs it. Can't he wait until telomerase?" A man: "Most of the universe might be influenced by energy whose force is actually repulsive." Another woman: "Thai kickboxing. My niece in L.A. It's replaced aerobics." Another man: "He does VC and is very high on MEMS, the next big thing."

He watches the Texans, new to him. He's talked to a couple of Texas women earlier, overly made-up, as southern women always are, exaggerated talk, almost caricatures, but conveying that they know this, are laughing at themselves and their own over-the-top performance as Texans. "Why, they're just big ol' darlin softies. Sweet natured as can be. You have to shoo them out of the petunias, is all." It takes him a moment to understand they're talking about their longhorns.

His dinner partner, apparently a gallery owner, apparently placed next to him because he's known as a collector, has been speaking of a conflict between supporting authentic Indian arts and encouraging the next step in their evolution. Even serious collectors hesitate at the new. She winks. Is she flirting? Politely, Molloy offers his attention. "What do you tell them?"

"The artists themselves are torn. They'll gang up on a potter who throws a pot instead of hand-coiling it, but then overlook kiln firing instead of firing in an open pit. Or the opposite. If her spirituality is in order, they'll forgive everything."

"Order," Molloy muses. "Order's much over-rated." He hears one of the scientists down the table.

"All that geometrical foundry dreck, the twentieth century's version of national hero on horseback," she says. "*Hofkunst*. That's why it always ends up on the lawn in front of city hall. It won't make you nervous by taking you someplace you haven't already been."

The German word, *Hofkunst*, court art, makes him study her with particular interest. Too old for conventional prettiness, but she's radiant with self-confidence, accomplishment, experience. A blueblood. He's dealt with more than a few in his life, the real thing in Europe. With the bluebloods, you must first discover their vulnerabilities. Not so much to gain advantage but to get a better map of the territory. Hers? They'll come clear, they always do; he's a patient man.

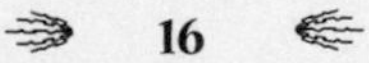

A brief image comes to mind, a woman in a full skirt on a wooden bench, her big hat, her boots, her laughter. Little cause, big results. He's not superstitious, but.

He turns back to the gallery owner, mask in place. His thoughts drift to his hostess's house, a place acclaimed for its charm, even given the considerable charms of Santa Fe's old historic district. The house is pictured on a best-selling postcard, appears in countless coffee table books: tourists risk life and limb leaning out to snap pictures as their sightseeing tram labors past it. (True, a small number of the more skeptical guests resist its charm. They think the house tries too hard, that its 1915 Pueblo style, more faithful than the real thing, borders on the precious.)

At cocktails Molloy has stood beside the editor of a slick arts journal, watching him appraise the living room clotted with Belter. The editor leans over confidentially. "One does so hate it when people come here, cart everything they've ever owned to Open Hands, and order up whole housefuls from Southwestern Spanish Furniture Company. Like they have no personal history."

Across the continent Molloy has left behind an apartment full of personal history and is glad of it. "Other houses here have antiques."

The editor nods. "Hauled God knows how down the Santa Fe Trail, like this stuff; humped up on carts and mule back along El Camino Real from Mexico City; shipped over from Barcelona or Cadíz. Not the incongruity, Molloy, the—overbearingness. It's our hostess, Miss Maya, announcing that her most important asset ain't her money, but her history. Not that money's nothing, but it's just not enough any more, is it?" The editor helps himself to an olive and, old hand at cocktail parties, spits out the pit discreetly, drops it in what would have been an ashtray if anyone smoked any more. "Poor Maya. Born a few decades too late to be merely an heiress, a socialite. Respectable calling not so long ago. These days we're oppressed by the aristocracy of accomplishment, so Maya needs a job. Maya's chosen vocation, you may have noticed, is social curator. Clever, and, give her credit, some flair, connecting the right people with the right people. So no one's surprised she's the first to snag you here. We're part of an exhibit, you and I, Molloy."

Molloy recognizes and rejects the assumption of fraternity. "Don't you like her?"

"You don't have to like her to come to dinner. Just know that the whole thing's a transaction; you'll get something useful out of it and so will she. Say this for Maya, she thinks charm is best confined to architecture."

"A view you share." By half-questioning, it just evades insult.

"I thought you were a New Yorker. The home of plain talk."

"We're not always the barbarians people say."

"You'll feel right at home, Molloy. Santa Fe is just about one of the outer boroughs these days."

The New York apartment, a memory palace, a riverside godown of objects from where and who he's been. A kind of tomb, actually, the highest three terraced stories under the roof of one of New York's fine old apartment ziggurats, the top floor his, the floor below his children's, the floor below that public, so to speak, where a decorator's impersonal hand is contradicted only by family photographs. A young bride and groom coming down the steps at St. Ignatius; formal portraits of a mother and her two infants; pictures of the family on skis that might be anywhere. Later he'd studied that wedding picture, wondered if he could read in the couple's faces something of what was to come. He'd thought himself happy that day, he remembered that much.

When he closed up the memory palace the last time, he wondered who would open it next, what they'd make of what they found. (Not literally—the children come and go, followed by the cleaning service, followed by the estimable Celeste, who bikes uptown from the office on what she calls Trigger to make sure everything is properly done.) No, he wondered who'd eventually enter with curious, penetrating eyes, intent on reading meanings in all these objects, their placement, that moment when everything froze, a spell cast by a malevolent spirit. He hasn't brought anything to Santa Fe except some pictures.

This much he knows: the individual formed by a chance meeting of two cells grows, differentiates, changes, evolves, learns (or, God help him, doesn't) from everything that life flings at him; seizes the initiative, only to be pushed down unplanned paths to learn and change again. A matter of simple survival. Yet through everything, his sense of himself has persisted stubbornly. He's not who he once was, and yet—he is. Change at every level in response to yearning, to learning. But something endures. The central paradox. He'd like to understand that; has heard they know something about it at the Institute just up the road.

Despite his general reticence, Molloy claims attention that first night because he's a novelty. Because Maya Sinclair has anointed him as worth having a dinner party for. He certainly claims the special attention of one or two at that table with a dark and Paleolithic energy that stirs and disconcerts them. With one question he gets everyone's undivided attention.

Gossip forms the integuments of human society. They'll later tell each other that Molloy rode the market in the eighties like a stunt pilot, and when the 1987 crash came, picked himself up, brushed himself off, and started all over again. No, he was a careful student of just-in-time, and sold out nanomoments before that crash, walked away with dust on his shins, a few cuts and bruises. But walked away. Wrong. He was one of the eighties corporate raiders, his only product takeover threats, leveraged buy-outs; his profits obscene. No, no, emphatically no. He'd managed one of the great hedge funds, high risk, high payoff, and bailed out as the market soared upward, knowing it couldn't last, leave 'em laughing. But against almost all predictions, the market's lasting, this long boom of the nineties, at least in the United States. So wrong here too. Molloy's still in the market, and on intimate terms with money old and new: an advisor to governments and supra-governments, like the European Union; an advisor to the great multinationals and their half-brothers, the World Bank, the International Monetary Fund. A tight European connection. Maybe all of the above. Nobody really knows.

However he'd got it, Molloy's stashed his loot who knows where; he doesn't say. But you never forget that he's got it. At auctions, he'll soon be seen casually bidding on twenty-thousand-dollar Navajo rugs in lots of four and five. It's understood that he wants the rugs, that he wishes success to the benevolent societies sponsoring the auctions. But more than the rugs, the benevolence, he wants to win. Auctions were invented for men like Molloy, competitive to the kill. His edginess is sometimes abrasive; maybe the edge of the self-made man who's raised his fortune from nothing (once? twice? more?) and fundamentally doubts its permanence. JAWS, an observer finally shrugs. Just Another Wealthy Shithead. Santa Fe crawls with them.

That loot (and Maya's blunt telephone calls) soon brings Molloy invitations to seats on half a dozen important boards—art museums, the opera, charities. In these ways, Santa Fe is no different from New York or Dallas, and he's known this intuitively. Molloy will protest that he doesn't mean to do anything in Santa Fe but tend his investments, maybe begin good works. He's more or less retired now, he'll explain diffidently, though the few gray hairs at his temples are more cosmetic than credible.

This is an early answer as to why he's here. Which is the question he puts to all the dinner party that first night, the question that gets everyone's undivided attention: *Why are you here?*

The Domain of Attraction

The woman, Judith, who has played and promptly forgotten the game of what-if with this stranger Molloy; the woman of strong opinions on geometrical metal sculpture, from whose tongue has tripped the dismissive *Hofkunst*, court art, is no stranger herself to dissembling. While her radiant smile makes her own dinner partner imagine that no one's ever listened to him so attentively, so appreciatively, meeting each point with little nods of encouragement, with eyes that widen to the telling detail, a thrilling confirmation to him of how clever he is, brilliant really, one could fall in love with such a discriminating woman, she is in fact preoccupied with the mortal illness of her dearest friend Sophie, sliding ever closer to death.

As Judith sees it, this oldest of courtesan's tricks isn't dishonest. It simply permits her to retreat undisturbed to her own thoughts. Inside that retreat she's even been known to find proofs to theorems.

Tonight her thoughts fix on a dazzling autumn morning, searching for mushrooms in the cool woods beneath the peaks of the Sangre de Cristos. "Good pickings today," her friend Sophie had said. Overnight in Judith's side garden, stinkhorns—mushrooms the size and shape of a human penis—had pushed themselves up, comical and vulgar, and Sophie had agreed: good harvesting up in the mountains. On the phone, Sophie had laughed self-deprecatingly. "It's been so long since I've seen an erect penis that it's barely a fond memory. Whereas you probably saw one just last night." To this, Judith had murmured ambiguously. She didn't mind Sophie's vicarious longing, but she felt she owed Benito some discretion.

"How's El Gran Conquistador doing?"

"Just fine," Judith said. "He saw, he conquered, he came."

"And the Norwegian?"

"Been back in Oslo for a week. What kind of a slut do you think I am?"

"A safe-sex slut, I hope."

"You're a biologist, you know sex is never safe. But I do my cautious best, Soph. The Norwegian's a better fantasy than reality. Yo? Lars? Two of us in this bed, hon. Nordic *joie de vivre*."

The stranger's question brings her back to the table. *Why are you here?* It penetrates her meditation on death, focuses it, but she doubts this Molloy is asking a metaphysical question. Present now, she hears her fellow diners answer.

They're here because they can be. They've arrived recently, most of them, and they've come from anywhere else. They might be tethered to their distant origins by fax lines and e-mail, they might saturate the broadband, but in the flesh—in meatspace, somebody jokes—they're in Santa Fe. They consider themselves post-journey: no longer pilgrims but the arrived, no longer questing but at rest, come home.

One or two of them have always been here.

None of them says what Judith thinks, that the city of Santa Fe murmurs to them in a seductive archaic tongue. Cities were like this in the beginning; the private walled off from the public for protection, for seclusion, for marking the clear distinction between what outsiders are permitted to know and what they aren't. An ancient Sumerian from the city of Ur (the ur-city?) magically transported through five millennia and ten thousand miles wouldn't be astonished to find himself in a town of mud-colored one- and two-story buildings, their backs to the narrow public thoroughfares, their hearts a central courtyard. A town surrounded by canal-watered fields would reassure him.

Judith plays with Molloy's question. "Why here? The work, of course. First and foremost, the work. Then—the possibilities. Like garden gates. With luck, a gate opens, reveals a garden, even a front door. I lived in New York for many years, as guarded about its private life as Santa Fe, but my childhood was in a European country of garden gates. Gates have possibilities."

Molloy listens, putting things together.

"To a timid child, a gate always seemed less"—she seeks a word—"*forward* than a doorway. A gate lets you only part way in. You can always back out if you're not welcome." She smiles. "I see you fail to imagine me as timid. I was. In some ways, I still am."

She gazes at Molloy. What if this man and not another? What if Sophie weren't dying? What if, what if, what if? In compensation for evading Sophie's questions about Benito, she'd stopped in the middle of the trail and said to her good friend that autumn morning:

"Soph, did I ever tell you how I get through those mind-numbing meetings where I consult? Okay, I'm at the conference table, yellow pad, MontBlanc pen, power suit, the whole works; some weenie's droning on about asset allocation. Me, I'm looking around for the target guy. Pretty soon I find him, way buff in his perfectly-tailored Brioni, rich silk tie, and very starched shirt—target guys are almost all in the legal or the financial departments; they find the laundry from hell for that starch. Even better if the shirt collar is just a tiny bit too tight. I'm telling you, this outfit does for me what fuck-me heels and garter belts are supposed to do for the average guy. Well, no wonder. It's all evolutionary biology, right?" She puffed her chest, extended her arms. "The so-called broadside display, the looming effect, striking fear into the hearts of enemies and lust in the loins of potential sexual partners."

Sophie was crouched down, her hands spread on the forest floor, pushing aside the fallen pine needles, pretending not to listen too carefully. But the pause provoked her. "Yeah?"

"So I slip off my shoes, do a gentle belly flop onto that mirror-finish table, wiggle down on my front like a grunt under enemy fire." Sophie was rapt; the body English was too good to miss. "Real careful past the water carafes, the stack of yellow pads. Past the weenie, still droning on: nobody pays attention to me. Finally I reach target guy face to face. Whoa! He knows just what's coming, a who-me smile and shyly drops his eyes. I reach over and loosen the tie first. Then the buttons, one, two, three. That starched shirt parts, like opening a registered letter from the priciest law firm in the world, like the top coming off a box from Harry Winston. I reach inside. Maybe the chest is smooth as a baby's ass, maybe he's all yummy chest hair; it's always a surprise."

Sophie was sitting back on her heels, eyes wide.

"Then I either drag him up on the table with me like this, or I just slide down and straddle his lap. Bingo!" A perfect *plié* topped off with a little shimmy.

"You—are—kidding—me."

"No. You have no idea how boring meetings are in corporate America. Oh you mean—trust me, Soph, people see exactly and only what they expect to see. Since they don't expect to see the wild thang in a boardroom, I might as well be invisible. When we're all done I boogie back down the tabletop to my chair. Nobody's even noticed. Target guy's all crisp, spruce and buttoned up again, a contented little smile on his face. The weenie drones on, we're moving twenty percent of assets into discount bonds for the following maturity. If the meeting's really long and boring, I find another guy and do it all over again. It passes the time, you know what I'm saying?"

Sophie had smiled, shook her head. "I always knew you didn't consult for the money."

At the dinner table, Molloy waits impassively for her to go on. Target guy in his starched shirt, beautifully cut suit.

"Our gates, our doors, our window trim—usually turquoise blue, hmmm? Adopted from the local Indians say the guidebooks, a talisman against evil spirits. No, it came with the Spaniards, who learned it from the Moors, those African Arabs who've left such deep marks on Santa Fe. Turquoise. Nice word, French for Turkish. Oh, we were multicultural before the word was invented."

But not multicultural, Molloy thinks, before the Turks were. Whose territory was a trading crossroads, including for turquoise, mined in the Sinai, traded into Europe. He's sometimes taken holidays devoted to following old trade routes. An eccentric passion, all in all: he's had to do it alone. One crazy winter even the old caravan route across the Sahara from Fez to Timbuktu. Four-wheel drives, not camels, and a crew of ten to get him there. "The Moors?"

"We were African here before the first black slaves arrived in Jamestown," Judith says. "Éstevan the Moor explored here early on. Adobe came from the

Moors. The locals were building mud huts, but puddling mud, not baking bricks. Adobe. Like our word daub."

Molloy thinks back further, imagines he could almost name the people in Asia Minor who'd taught the Moors. History here, long by the standards of the Americas, is still brief. He raises no objections.

"People say the *acequias*, the irrigation ditches, also came from the Moors, but that's not quite right. The Pueblos knew how to irrigate. What we got from the Moors was the word itself, *al-Sarqiya*, and a governance system to make the ditches work for four hundred years or more. Longhorn cattle, the horses with Arab bloodlines. The *curanderas*, the local herbal healers, a lot of their lore comes from the Moors. You see it in the names of the herbs, *albacar*, sweet basil, good for childbirth and straying husbands. *Alfalfa*. *Alhucema*, lavender."

Another fleeting image comes to Molloy, a bottle on a bathtub ledge, *lavendelöelbad*, a woman's hand reaching for it. He sometimes grieves more now than he had at the time. The woman called Judith is naming further Moorish legacies, jewelry, dance, even flagellation. "Practiced, or—" she smiles skeptically, "*formerly* practiced by the Penitentes. Supposed to originate in old Muslim practices."

"It could've come from the Aztecs," somebody says. "Aztec priests whipped themselves with cactus thorns."

Judith nods. "Another convergence in old New Mexico."

She's at her half-century of life. No, past it, he knows. She seems sculpted herself, of a scale and self-possession to wear her massive silver jewelry negligently, setting off her silvering hair. As she addresses each member of the party in turn, low-voiced, confiding, they fall silent and bend forward, but Molloy imagines the story is for him alone. He's taking it in on multiple levels, the story itself, abundant with amusing but significant facts (a woman who could solve the problem of what to talk about the next morning) and then the first vulnerability, a streak of intellectual vanity. He answers her silently, adding, amending, gifts he'd like to bestow, but isn't yet ready to. At last she returns to him, smiling slightly. "From the Moors, I think—but this time via Provençal, not Spain—comes Santa Fe's deep, abiding eroticism."

The phrase lingers in the silence. Molloy's black eyes never leave her and he feels the beginning of something so long absent he hardly dares believe it. Hardly dares name it. Hope. Life. Desire.

"Not that this has ever been an easy town to live in," somebody finally says. "Getting a crop out of this land was always backbreaking. Acequias or not, you get wholesale droughts some years. The Santa Fe so-called River is a joke. The Rio Grande ain't so grand, and is thirty miles away. We're at seven thousand feet here, the last frost could be June, the first one September; the storms in July and August—what the Indians call the male rains—could ruin a year's crop then and there. No gold, no silver, not even coal."

"Or, thank God, uranium."

Molloy persists. "Why did people stay, then?"

Judith answers. "Because Santa Fe is *tierra santa*, holy ground, and if you're open to that you begin to think you can't live anywhere else." She stops, and a kind of mischief lights her face. "Of course it's all a colossal fake. But an effective colossal fake. You see right through it and love it all the more. The whole is really more than the sum of its parts."

Lock-In

Mischief can backfire. Yes, she'd entertained Sophie that autumn morning, and they'd moved on, focused on the forest floor, collecting quickly. Sophie instructed, Judith listened, a professional lifetime's habit for each of seeking, sharing, speculating, raising questions: surface skepticism that camouflaged the intense joy of learning. In between, they talked of nothing special; recipes for the mushrooms, gossip about their friends.

Both unmarried, middle-aged; both scientists. They'd known each other first in college, then in graduate school, though with a sentimentality that would have surprised them if anyone had pointed it out, they exaggerated to friends, even to themselves, how well they'd known each other then. At Berkeley they'd ground away on required courses, prelims, qualifiers, laboring over dissertations, no time for anything else. Knowing the same people counted as friendship. After the Ph.D., Judith went to Columbia and Sophie took a post-doc at UCLA; even Christmas cards stopped after a few years. Yet they'd found each other here in Santa Fe, resumed their friendship tentatively, found harmony, become close.

Sophie, a year or two younger than Judith, was small, muscular, and exuded competence. You wanted her on your Nepal trek, your fieldtrip to Borneo, your bushwhack through the rain forest. She'd done those and much more with elegance, economy, a refreshing lack of fuss. She was as compact spiritually as she was physically, and when she and Judith found each other in Santa Fe after all those years, the doubts she'd entertained as a graduate student resurged.

To Sophie, Judith still seemed flashily brilliant but unsound. That marriage: anyone could've predicted it would fail. The speculative science that only sometimes paid off. An unseemly delight in jewelry, pretty clothes, in the attention of men. Judith took her vacations in big European cities, spending hours in museums and concert halls, meeting over coffee and cream-laden confections with a network of friends that seemed boundless, so must be superficial. Sophie took her vacations backpacking alone in the San Juans. (Judith also hiked in Europe, but did not admit this to Sophie, ever. Judith's idea of a good hike was when a sun terrace or mountain hut appeared at the end of three hours' ramble to reward her with tea or garlic soup before she started back to clean linen sheets and a featherbed.)

Yet as Sophie came to know Judith, she began to allow that Judith's glitter and performances might be a legitimate personal style, that sometimes, even in science, it paid off; that Judith's joy in personal adornment was in fact an enviable gift for delighting in the small things of life. In Sophie's opinion, that included men, whose universal sense of entitlement simply irritated her. Judith might flirt at dinner parties, glow in professional meetings, tell tall tales in private, but she was steady in ways that Sophie valued; she cared about the same things. From that, Sophie permitted friendship to resume and grow.

In an hour they'd reached the ridge, their paper sacks full. They sat down for lunch, surveyed the valley below, dappled with cloud shadows, the stunted *piñon*. "Bury me here," Sophie said softly. "I'd like to feed the 'shrooms."

A silence. Then Sophie resumed. "Jay, the burial may be sooner rather than later. Those stomach problems? I was sure it was gastroenteritis. It isn't. I got the diagnosis yesterday. It's ovarian cancer. Stage three. Treatable but not curable, as they say."

A cave-in, a sudden sweat, denial: let this be a joke, though Sophie didn't joke like that. People they knew were beginning to stumble and fall, but up to now it hadn't come so close. Both women understood the gravity of the diagnosis.

"Why didn't you call me? How could you live with that overnight by yourself? How could you let me—go on like that just now?"

"Because last night I figured you were otherwise occupied. Because just now I could use a laugh." Sophie's hand scrabbled nervously in the dirt, betraying the effort it cost to control herself.

Judith took Sophie's free hand, looked away, afraid to exhibit her own face, too naked with mixed feelings. The news was a rodent chewing in Judith's belly, her chest; an intimation, a suffocation, side by side with a momentary but genuine and shameful relief: it had been Sophie's diagnosis, not hers. Then something ground up against her brainpan—her jaw, part of a contraction that threatened every soft tissue in her skull. She shivered. The sun was no longer warm.

She glanced at her friend, staring off stoically at the valley below. Sophie had at first seemed a type. Judith was sympathetic to women who'd been bruised by the battle to get into the international men's club called Big Science, ruefully aware that her advantages—the accident of her own looks, the fact of her former husband—in some ways eased the battle for her. (Made difficulties in other ways that she often forgot until they undermined her yet again.) Both she and Sophie had trespassed upon, and worse, excelled in a male preserve, but Sophie had been decorous enough to exhibit penitence, which Judith would not. If Sophie wanted to wear a hair shirt of denim every day of her life, buy underpants in plastic packages at three for ten dollars, reward herself by carrying on her back everything she'd need for two weeks in the wilderness, fine; but Judith couldn't regard it all as somehow morally superior.

Judith was first to see that she and this spiky biologist had parallel values, that they were both exacting connoisseurs, herself of civilization, Sophie of nature. In the realms they loved, they sought the best. With effort she'd brought Sophie around to seeing that staying in a five-star hotel could be compared to studying Kurt Gödel, Albrecht Dürer, each the very best that civilization, a product of the human mind, had to offer, and each to be cherished for that alone. When Sophie grasped that, she was open to friendship.

"What will you do, Soph?"

She'd fight it, Sophie said simply. She'd try everything and anything. First surgery, remove as much as possible of the cancerous organs, then chemo and radiation. Ovarian cells tended to seed their cancer all over the abdominal wall, seeds too small to be seen and removed surgically. "They've just identified the genes—the mutations—that cause this," Sophie said with grim satisfaction. "Really good therapy can't be far behind, can it?"

"Are you scared, Soph?"

Sophie nodded slowly, deliberately. "Not of death. But scared of pain. Scared of being helpless, which you always are. And then—somehow it seems a little early for the Grim Reaper to come calling." Judith squeezed her friend's hand. "Of course," Sophie went on almost pedantically, "the chemo's much improved. Remember when they had to cut down those endangered trees to get taxol, and there we were, trading off women's lives for rare trees? They can semi-synthesize it now from clippings of the common yew. Of course it's now capital-T Taxol, registered trademark. A story there."

It was obscene for death to intrude in the midst of all this sweet life pressing around them, the trees and shrubs, chipmunks darting cheekily; the wildflowers, the birds. Yet Judith saw that the birds were mostly crows, plump and noisy, funereally black. Sophie followed her eyes.

"What is death?" Judith asked the universe stretched out before them, the green valley dipping to rose-gold desert beneath a violet sky, the mountainside under their haunches, the fragrances of the pines carried on the well-mannered breeze. It was rhetorical, but Sophie answered, as Judith knew she would.

"The end of order." A pause. "But only locally. When I die, I return what I owe to the biosphere, the stuff of me. Never really mine in any long-term sense. Although," she added sardonically, "it damn well felt like mine, I must say. A small and probably useful delusion." Sophie picked up the paper sack full of mushrooms she'd collected. "Bless the fungi. They're the brokers who'll redistribute the stuff."

At last Judith had the courage to look directly at her friend. The years had transformed Sophie's cropped hair from blonde to gray, but her skin was still smooth, her body taut. It was not so much the battle to get into the international men's club as generations of tough American rancher women who'd shaped Sophie, endowed her with her lack of pretension, her mild but perpetual mistrust, which shot from her tongue like little darts, stinging and disconcerting men who wanted something cozier from a woman. Sophie had bent over too many books, too many instruments; she had a small perpetual hunch. She'd

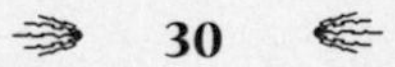

never married, and seldom entertained lovers, unlike Judith, who was long divorced but experienced in love.

"You're being very brave, Soph. You don't have to be."

"I'm not brave. I'm a biologist." Sophie returned Judith's direct gaze. Judith the well beloved. Sophie had come to envy that about Judith, though not ungenerously, she hoped. She could admire Judith's softness of shape and voice, a voluptuousness that seemed to attest to being lovingly touched, caressed, the sharp edges melted away by the grace of passion. Judith's blunt bawdiness had amazed Sophie (she never saw a certain pompous physicist at the Labs without remembering Judith's nickname for him, Needle-Dick the Bug Rapist). It made her secretly wonder if one of her own problems with men had been a species of puritanism. If so, she thought, that was an amazing contradiction in a biologist. Whatever. Love was a kind of wonder that, for some obscure reason, she hadn't been permitted to know.

"Sounding pretty mystical there, Soph."

"That's what it takes to be a biologist these days."

Sophie looked away, withdrew her hand from Judith's, the first in a long series of steps she'd take on her journey away from life. She mused aloud for a moment about cancer itself, why this one and not another. Judith was struggling against tears. "Don't die yet, Soph. I love you, girlfriend."

"I hope not to, Jay." The old nickname. Nobody used it who hadn't known Judith before she was twenty-five. "I'm not really ready. And I love you. Though I have a harder time saying what love is than what life or death is. How about you?"

Judith blew her nose and dabbed at her eyes. "I'm in complexity, my Aya Sofia, so maybe I could tell you what love is." She smiled through her tears. "But you really don't want to hear."

Emergent Phenomena

Two weeks after she's met him at Maya Sinclair's dinner, Molloy stands at Judith's office doorway at the Institute. She's on the phone and waves him in, amused that he's forced to step high over the old threshold, duck to get under the doorframe. He stays slightly hunched to avoid hitting his head on the low ceiling.

"Yeah," she's saying, "I think this does have a nice economic interpretation." She studies Molloy boldly. A guarded man, giving away nothing. Reserve born of confidence? Or fear? Hand over the mouthpiece. "Have a seat." Hand away. "We've got an economist at Yale who's promised to think about exactly that."

Molloy hasn't yet shed his eastern armor, though that will happen soon enough, she thinks, especially when he walks those bench-made shoes through Santa Fe's winter muck a few more times. "Yeah. Could be a nice paper with apps in finance." She sees Molloy's attention sharpen subtly. "I'm thinking option-pricing problems are essentially equivalent to optimal-stopping problems, and these are just special cases of the general DP problem. Can you? *Ciao*. Sorry to keep you waiting."

He grins, runs a hand over his tight black curls as if to reassure himself that he hasn't bumped his head after all. "Molloy," he says. "We met at Maya's. I heard you were interested in financial applications."

Ah, Molloy: hardly recognized you without your mirror shades and shoulder holster. "Financial apps just fall out of some other work I'm doing. Not really central to my interests. Still, it's always nice to do something useful. Pulls in a few bucks from a consulting firm here called New Business. You know about them?" Of course. Santa Fe, such a village. "And it's a gesture of search-and-rescue for the economists who seem to need it these days."

But when all's said and done, she adds, it's only incremental research, grants and laurels work. You'd never get a grant, or into the National Academy, for anything really outré. "Believe me, Molloy, it's chilling to watch the geezers being inducted into the Academy for work that now seems seminal, but when they were doing it, was too wild to be considered."

"You do both, then." He makes himself right at home.

"I do both." She doesn't tell this Molloy that she admires the people who can blaze their own path without caring what the world thinks. She blazes her own path, but always has a good cover story. How old is he? Mid-forties? Older? What's he doing in Santa Fe?

His eyes are drawn to the whiteboard, a messy plane of unproved theorems. "It looks like a Twombly."

"Should I explain?"

"Should I?"

"I know Twombly," she says evenly. "Do you know functional analysis?" Though it's meant to sting she can see he's pleased. She can't imagine why. *I know Twombly*. It's unseemly to enjoy a win quite so much, but then you aren't a scientist because you hate competing.

"Give me version lite." Arms folded over his chest in tacit challenge, he follows her through the visitor's version of her work, which is to explore and define the limits to science. "There's been a hidden message inside the roar of knowledge overload, and that message has been *limits*. Science, Molloy, is the most powerful way of knowing humans have ever devised. But some things can't be done in science; some things can never be known. To identify those—the known, the not-yet-known but someday knowable, the forever unknowable—is my own sweet game."

"Damn," he says. With approval. Almost envy.

He's come from the president and is now free, so they have lunch on the Institute's sunny patio, protected from the January winds. "You've been in the big time," he begins, "so how—?" Her brow forms the silent question, and he interrupts himself. "The president gave me bio sketches of all the senior researchers." He declines to add that he's also read her home page. Plus a further dossier. "You left the Ivy League to come here. You don't find the isolation too much?"

"Interesting question." Is he already having regrets about leaving New York? "We're famous for being far away. *Far, far away, my lords*, as Cabeza de Vaca once said." Though it's January, she's protected by sunglasses and a floppy straw hat.

"Which was when?"

"Fifteen twenty-eight, fifteen thirty. *La Villa de la Santa Fé de San Francisco de Assisi* was nowhere, mud huts, the most distant northern outpost in the Americas. Flash forward a few hundred years; it's someplace all-American called Sanna Fay, though plunked a bit awkwardly over the old Spanish town. Still nowhere—civilization's center of gravity has simply spun to the northeast. This is a town fated to be on the outer edges."

He's quiet. She licks the yogurt off her spoon thoughtfully. "In nineteen thirty-two, Aldous Huxley designated all this the Savage Reserve, the last place on the planet, according to *Brave New World*, where people were born, mated, and died the old-fashioned way. No escape from the Savage Reserve. The margins have their advantages. Passions and fashions of far-off capital cities never quite make it to Santa Fe in their most pressing forms."

"Until Georgia O'Keeffe. Until Santa Fe Style. Until the sciences of complexity." He looks around at the Institute, making a name for itself these days at something new.

A thug's face, but quite beautiful teeth inside that bust-of-Apollo mouth. At Maya's party she hadn't noticed. "Minor and passing Molloy. For all we know." What if this man and not another?

Though he's sitting in full sunlight, the planes of his face shadow each other stubbornly. His brows could've been applied with a *sumi* brush, and beneath them the oversize black eyes are unsettlingly intense. The nose asserts itself; the full-lipped, almost pouty mouth is Mediterranean. At ancient margins, Celts had once mixed with Greeks; anyway, many a southerner had stopped by Ireland and left his genes, if Irish Molloy is. "Your work?" he asks. "Your work seems important. The Institute's fame is growing. A center in spite of itself."

Work yanks her back from erotic Arcadias. "Like all scientists, I'm a gambler. My work, my pseudo-Twomblys in there, all very high risk. I lay a bet my work's important, even crucial. High payoff if I'm right. By now *les jeux sont faites*, and as usual the house has the odds. I could, for one thing, be wrong. Good chance out here on the scientific margins, the edge of chaos. I end up on the trash heap of history despite—" she crushes the yogurt cup "—despite my very best efforts. Or, suppose I'm right, but the world doesn't see it until years from now, when somebody else re-invents what I once did and gets all the credit. Either of those, the house wins, and I lose. It's a rough game."

"Not unlike investing."

"Or, I'm ahead of my time, premature, nobody pays attention. It happens in science. Mendel and his garden peas. Maybe worse, I'm postmature, another kind of discontinuity. Could've been done earlier, but everybody was looking the other way."

"Again, not entirely unlike—"

"Then there's the worst, most common outcome of all. My idea, somebody else waltzes in and takes credit. The times I've actually protested that, it got me exactly nowhere. Any parallels with investing in that? Don't think so. We all play our games. But here's the difference, Molloy." She takes off her sunglasses now to make sure he gets it. "You win your bets, and you have money. Money makes the world go round; I don't despise money at all. But I win my bet, and I have something really consequential."

He slaps his knee loudly. "Thank God! I can't tell you how tedious it is, always getting sucked up to for your money!"

The mortification rises to her face, only partly relieved by the fact that he can make fun of her. She retreats contritely behind her sunglasses. "Very bitchy. I'm sorry. No offense intended. Hang around scientists long enough and you pick up their uncouth manners." She looks away. "Explanation, not excuse. It was quite inexcusable."

He shakes his head with amusement, says nothing, takes a bite of his sandwich.

"Give me a break, Molloy. Compared to physicists, mathematicians are the soul of intellectual humility. For this work I'm doing, I was trying to understand

the markets, sat down with an important managing director on Wall Street, trained as a theoretical physicist, big-time quant."

"All managing directors are important," Molloy says with a slight smile.

"Is that why they refer to themselves as MDs?" For an instant she thinks he might actually laugh. "Part of my brain is listening to him explain to me why physicists are God's own gift to derivatives trading, and part of my brain is asking, how do they do it? How do they inculcate these guys with such magnificent self-confidence, such swagger? It isn't exactly reality—every time I submit a paper to a physics journal, I'm asked to dumb down the math, please. Anyway, he goes on and on, physicists so action-oriented, so uniquely able to deal with the real world *and* models of it. Finally I plant my tongue firmly in my cheek and say, oh George. Murray Gell-Mann couldn't have put it better himself. Does George take offense? Does he even get the joke? No. He blushes slightly, and thanks me. Murray Gell-Mann, he confesses sweetly, is his hero. I told Murray the story and, to his everlasting credit, he laughed like hell. Still, this might not be a tribe you want to get very snug with."

He says nothing, keeps chewing, watches her.

"When I first got here, I cherished the distance of Santa Fe from the rest of the world. Let me gamble outside the spotlight, please, preserve my pride. Like O'Keeffe, who called this place the Faraway Nearby. Also like O'Keeffe, I get back to New York as often as I need to. Get the hair done, checkups, some kind of theater, the roar of the crowd. New York, the perfect Zen city, always in the moment and only the moment."

He's fixed on her with a focus that disconcerts her. To break that spell, she looks away to a nearby adobe wall, dappled in the sunlight. Few men know how to ask the good questions. Even fewer know how to listen. She tries reconstructing the conversation to seize what's provoked her self-revelations, but it's not in his words. In hers? Herself on the trash heap of history? A commonplace phrase. But never before has that seemed so menacingly possible. "Oh, mountain climbing," a very brave woman once said. "For a few minutes you stand at the summit and then the wind covers your footprints."

"Let's stretch our legs." They move back through the building, the clack of a copier counterpointed by somebody pleading on the telephone, out to the

Institute's grounds. Though they're only a few hundred feet higher than the city, the *piñons* are already taller, thicker, than those below in Santa Fe. Patches of snow linger from the Christmas storm, but the path is dry.

"Good. Your nice shoes won't get trashed. I always laugh when I get instructions to dress for a conference 'business casual.' They don't mean this." Sweater, jeans, athletic shoes. He only nods. Off-balance, and still she keeps talking, a failing defense against that subtle siege of his. Later she'll understand that he's a master negotiator, with a perfect grasp of tactical silence.

They emerge from the woods, Santa Fe below them, low, flat-roofed, hand-rounded buildings the same color as its soil. "Santa Fe," he says softly, as if he can't quite believe he's here. "A fine fusion of dwelling and landscape."

"Santa Fe's deliberately buried its real, very complicated, very ambiguous history under brown stucco, fake adobe. I'm not knocking that. Santa Fake has much to be said for it. The little-town-of-Bethlehem look is not only a nice human scale, but dwellings that seem a part of the earth remind you that you are too. The artificial is the deepest, most human of gestures. Who tells the truth about his own history?"

A long silence. The obsidian eyes glitter, watch her, not the city below them.

"But I liked it better when the Institute wasn't quite so much a part of intellectual central. Santa Fe was both a good and a bad place for the Institute then. Fanta Se, as the locals say with such charming self-deprecation. Santa F-E-Y, as my elderly mother always writes me. It still pretends to be the faraway nearby—faraway from Los Angeles, from New York City, from Chicago and Dallas, faraway from Harvard and Columbia, Berkeley and Stanford. But here we are with all this electronic medulla oblongata, so nearby too."

"A colossal fake, you said the other night."

"An invention of real estate agents and the Chamber of Commerce; a fantasy for wealthy Anglos to buy into; Fanta Se offers us whatever we've lost or maybe never had; sheer nostalgia. A very effective fake, to repeat myself. Greater than the sum of its parts. Maybe because it wasn't just boosters, but historians and scientists and artists who made the myths."

Whether he's content with what he's heard or bored by it she can't tell.

The carnal presence he carries with him is both inviting and slightly sinister. Slightly irritating. "We're here because we can be. Why are you here, Molloy?"

He takes his time replying. "I will tell you that," he says with a curious precision. "I will tell you. But now I must go." And excuses himself gracefully.

Path-Dependent Behavior

The same sunny January day, across town from the Santa Fe Institute on an old estate now housing an archaeological center, Benito Jiménez stared down at sherds spread out on his desk by a husky young man. Beside him was a slender woman he'd introduced as his sister. "Are these like, interesting?"

Benito examined the sherds thoughtfully. "Where did you get them?" The couple was casually but expensively dressed. Not the usual pot thieves.

"Our folks just bought this new ranch outside Albuquerque. This stuff is like, all over the place."

Benito knew every site in the basin and was dubious. The young man picked that up. "The ranch was in this old family for like, forever. The grandpa finally died, a hundred and three or something, thirty people lined up to cash in. They decided to sell, our folks bought."

The young woman was scanning Benito's office appreciatively, the hall beyond, the gardens beneath the brilliant winter sun. Private archaeological institutes dotted the southwest, often begun by wealthy easterners who'd come out early in the twentieth century and fallen in love with the sun, the air, the vastness, the history. Some were discreetly hidden, but the Center for Archaeology was too central to town to be overlooked except by the dullest of tourists. Wealthy eastern amateurs too had founded the Ark early in the century, two women who'd come west to live the way they wanted in Santa Fe's easygoing sexual climate. It had gradually become a serious scientific institution.

Benito's face was altogether polite. "Your folks?"

The Váldez family, he learned, owned a chain of convenience stores attached to gas stations all over the southwest, ready to expand to Montana and Wyoming in the fall. Not the usual pot thieves at all. Benito asked to see the site.

They pulled off the interstate at an isolated gas station, the kind that sells more carbon in the form of sticky sweets than fossil fuel, one of the few in the southwest to escape being owned by the Váldez family. Benito followed the Váldezes' green Jimmy along a two-lane blacktop that faded into gravel, then dirt, then tracks, the winter grass brushing the undersides of their vehicles. Across a cattle guard, a sign warned that they were passing through tribal lands. Beyond a gate, a craters-of-the-moon track led to a derelict ranch house, a couple of SUVs parked outside.

Harry Váldez waved toward a rise and his sister Mimi invited Benito up behind her on the back of her all-terrainer, something between a motorcycle and a lunar exploration vehicle, with extra-large wheels and forgiving axles, for what turned out to be less than half a mile along a rutted trail to the site. Benito kept his mouth shut. He'd done his share of long hikes to remote digs. Then too, the Váldez family had made its money by respecting the internal combustion engine.

Now he remembered this site after all, known throughout southwest archaeology as Black Crow. But everyone knew that Black Crow was picked clean long ago. Benito thought of the sherds spread across his desk and then rethought, the archaeologist's art of retelling anew the story of the evidence.

Who'd claimed the site was empty? Malcolm Ryan, one of the brilliancies of southwestern U.S. archaeology, a man who'd laid out great tracts of the field's intellectual property. But Ryan's heart was too restless, his demon too greedy, his fear too carnivorous, to settle only for credit earned. Already the first, the best, he craved an insuperable distance ahead of the runners-up. His ethics were notoriously elastic, and he was too arrogant to cheat with subtlety. Thus he'd been caught seeding sites with pieces from elsewhere to make a point, buttress a hypothesis (which might, in the main, be correct); he'd been caught insupportably stretching the dates of human remains he'd found. Detected, he blustered denials, went quiet, let it drop. No one was going to arrest and try him; archaeology wasn't a court of law. He'd been right often enough, he pointed out to his detractors, to permit him a mistake or two.

Lyin' Ryan. Maybe the site was intact after all, and he'd spread the rumor because he hoped to hoard it for himself.

"What do your parents intend to do here?" The ranch was too far out of town to be useful for convenience stores, cattle were a loss, and there were no apparent mineral possibilities.

"They just wanted it," Mimi said, as if the value of owning thousands of acres of sagebrush, chamisa and cholla out in the middle of nowhere was self-evident.

Benito made the hundred-plus mile round trip from Santa Fe to Black Crow every day for a week. What he found there stunned him. It might be the last undug southwestern pueblo of significance. Probably settled around 1100, the Coalition Period, and deserted two hundred years later for unknown reasons, though everyone in the field, Benito included, had theories about why. He walked methodically over the desolate site (osha root in his pocket to keep the rattlers at bay) examining sherds, possible ruins suggested by subtle rises in the earth. Did the inhabitants of Black Crow just overpopulate themselves out of food? Did climate change lead to drought? Did they lose faith in their leaders? Were they stressed by hostile tribes? All of those?

The southwest was full of sites where Puebloans had settled for a few hundred years, moved on. "Not *abandoned*," a Pueblo woman had once said testily to him. "We could always come back." Evidence said that people reoccupied sites, left them again. No one knew why.

Black Crow, a peak population of several thousands, had been a trading crossroads—patterns on the potsherds suggested they'd originated all over a giant crescent reaching northward into Colorado and southward into Arizona and Mexico. Even more distant trade items might be unearthed—shell beads from the Baja California coast, turquoise from the Sonora and Nevada deserts, decorative bells cast in central Mexico, feathered ornaments from tropical birds even more distant.

"Who were they? Anasazi?" Harry Váldez had caught Benito's excitement and came out from Albuquerque to the site for an hour or more every day during that first week.

"Not polite," Benito said, "though everybody says it. *Anasazi* is a Navajo word, hung on the locals by the newcomers, the Navajos. Roughly equivalent to trailer trash. Ancestral Puebloans is the preferred term."

Benito guided Harry along the pueblo's perimeters, explaining that without serious investigation he could only guess it was one of those elaborate communities with clearly defined habitations, four and five stories high; ritual community halls. "Not kivas, strictly speaking. We have no provable idea of what these great rooms were for, though they resemble modern Pueblo kivas. Here. This was probably a field house, established outside the city limits for workers to stay when they worked and guarded the fields." Harry saw nothing but pebbles, tufts of dry grass harped by the wind. Benito brushed dirt away, drew outlines. Okay, maybe. A stretch.

Harry was canny enough to be the chief of his parents' convenience store empire but nobody, himself included, would have described him as an intellectual. Yet something about the old pueblo caught his imagination. He followed Benito around eagerly, asking questions, taking notes. Unaccustomed to the sun, out of shape, he turned red under his straw hat.

No, Benito answered patiently, pottery wasn't invented by the Puebloans; it probably came up from the south around two hundred BCE. Late on the world scale of things, but not late for the Americas. This pueblo was probably built when the climate was stable if not exactly benign, predictable enough to farm, raise children, elaborate on the social structure.

But fifty years after its founding, new construction stopped. The tree record suggests prolonged droughts. Chaco Canyon, maybe the seat of a central government, or the home of an elite priesthood for all this part of the world (a predatory, even cannibalistic gang of thugs in one fringe theory) ceased to be central. Population and trade began to decline. By the time the Spanish arrived, the tape had been running in reverse for 400 years. Big agglomerations, almost cities, had broken back down into towns, then villages with walls, implying external threats. Abandonment, finally massive desertions. Benito didn't add that he worked with a team at the Santa Fe Institute to simulate all this, thinking the ebb and flow of this civilization might be explained by theories of complexity. The Artificial Anasazi.

Harry surveyed the desolation. "What did they live on?"

Corn, Benito said. In good times and bad, corn for breakfast, for lunch, for dinner, for bedtime snack. Some beans and squash, prickly pear, *piñon* nuts. The very occasional piece of game. "Typically, two years' worth of corn would be stored on the roof, just in case. A child would start to produce a surplus—more than the kid ate—after age nine, and would be a big-time contributor by age twelve. Since children were a net positive for the family, the whole population grew steadily in the thousand years before European contact, though we can't say for sure how many lived here at any one time. From the number of sites you'd guess a lot, but we can see that all the large sites were occupied and abandoned sequentially."

"Why?"

Benito shrugged. He hadn't taught formally for years, and it came back to him, the pleasure of instruction. The simple and obvious questions from a novice that sometimes stopped you in your tracks, re-ordered your assumptions. Harry had probably been the class cut-up, couldn't wait to get out of school, didn't need to swear he'd never crack another book because it didn't occur to him to pick one up. Who'd now discovered the deep human joy of learning. He was the right age to be Benito's son.

"Lots of reasons. Climate change—it's the end of what in Europe they call the Little Ice Age. Severe drought. Even if the climate had been stable, people would've run out of firewood, exhausted the soil, depleted the game, moved on."

"I thought these noble guys were supposed to be full of lessons for us to live wisely on the land."

"Right," Benito said. "I do a little lecture called 'Popular Fallacies about the Native American.' I'll send it to you sometime."

For many more questions, Benito could only shake his head. "We'd have to investigate more. Even then."

Home, his head full of the week's discoveries, somewhere between waking and sleep, the ancient city came to Benito as it often did at that hour, not quite a dream, not quite willed. It brooded on a low hill, over a long-gone riverbank and wetlands. Below the city lay the central Anatolian plateau; in the distance, the snow-capped mountains. As always, he approached at sunset when the city was almost invisible, its walls the same mud as the hill, more geology than artifact. Only closer would the hill's irregular top reveal itself, man-made structures twenty meters high, reminding him for a moment of the Hopi dwellings on First and Second Mesas.

The ancient city covered more than thirty acres, and humans—as many as ten thousand of them at once—had lived and died here for a millennium. But as he'd pass through the dark silent alleyways, he was alone. And fearless. He'd always preferred cities without people, the chambers of the dead. Sometimes he imagined a figure had flitted behind a corner into the deepest shadows, but when he pursued it, he found no one. Sometimes he thought he heard a flute, but knew it was only the wind playing through the ruins. Humans had left only signs—and their bones.

He saw wall decorations the first time he came. Images of bulls, heavy-horned, perhaps a bearded god astride, thought to be symbolic in those days not of masculine power but of the female reproductive organs—later, he'd see a bull's head and horns explicitly composed within the female figure, just where the uterus and fallopian tubes should be. The bull was everywhere on the walls, and within shrines he found bucrania, the decorated skulls of bulls, generative and destructive aspects simultaneously. Nearby, the image of an erupting volcano, and then a vivid mural, a band of hunters pulling the tongues and tails of wild deer. He'd also discovered an image of vultures with great fringed wings systematically attacking headless men. Even in the falling darkness, he could see that the vultures were ochre red. Flocks of human handprints on the walls overreached and occluded each other, a disquieting sign of crowding.

He once tripped over what he thought was a stone, picked it up, a clay figurine, an immensely fleshy woman, perhaps a fertility image. He'd found several more since, smooth and evocative.

Tonight he turned a corner and confronted something new. Before him was a wall, covered with dozens of life-sized human breasts, molded out of clay.

The vision took his breath away. He stepped close, touched them tentatively, stroked them. Some nipples were inverted or open, as if bitten. After a moment he pushed his fingers into the holes. Inside the breasts his fingers found the beaks of vultures. Horrified, he fled the city and into troubled sleep.

Vicious Cycles

On the same day that Molloy showed up at the Institute and had lunch with Judith, and across town, Benito learned about the Black Crow site, Nola Holliman got on a plane for Houston with her eleven-year-old son. In Houston he'd undergo a bone marrow transplant, a desperate last remedy against his recurring leukemia.

The boy would deliberately be sent to the edge of death, drugged to the inanimate, marrow sucked out of his bones by monstrous needles, cleansed, replaced. It was, she thought, a strange bargain that life made with death: let me come as close as possible so that life might prevail again. If he lived through this, didn't tumble off that precipice into death's arms, just one more datum on the learning curve, then he must endure at least forty days in isolation, so weakened was his immune system. Nola closed her gallery and left her husband Ernie in Santa Fe alone.

She'd learned much in the two years since the initial diagnosis. "Acute lymphocytic leukemia," the doctors had said. "ALL—the most common, the most curable, of childhood leukemias, cancers. Not an easy road ahead, but of all the leukemias, the best one to get." As if there was a best one to get.

She'd slowly learned how to deal with hospitals, to anticipate that though they called you in, they were seldom ready for you, as if, instead of being the parent of a desperately ill child, you were a guest stupidly trying to get a room at a luxury resort before check-in time. She'd learned that charts got misplaced, mixed up, confused; that the all-important counts—white blood, platelets, hemoglobin, neutrophils—were best left to weekdays, because nobody trusted the weekend lab staff. She'd learned an ever-changing set of terms: stem cells, pherisis, marrow harvesting, kidney metabolites. She'd learned about blood donation credits versus blood to a designated patient. She'd learned that careless technicians, some of them physicians, could wound her boy, add even more to his pain, and set him back by their indifferent techniques, their heedlessness. She'd learned that sometimes she must exert herself to keep the doctors comfortable, so that they, in turn, would make Pete comfortable.

She'd learned that she couldn't count on her husband.

"Everyone but me seems to know what to do," Ernie said glumly when Pete's diagnosis was made. No, she protested, I'm learning, Pete's learning, be there with us and learn too. No rehearsals for this.

"He only wants you. He cries for you when he's in pain. I can't help him. You can comfort him, I can't. I'm no use."

He's your child too.

At first she took it to be his profound shock, that his cherished boy, whom he'd loved so deeply as a baby, kissing Pete's toes playfully as he changed diapers, whom he'd loved less demonstratively but surely just as much as the boy grew, became a soccer player, a skateboarder, this child was in mortal danger. The threat, the helplessness: at some level Ernie knew and could not admit that except for holding him in the light of their hearts, Pete's fate was out of their hands.

Later, she wondered.

Nola also learned about her son. He was both more exuberant and more self-contained than he'd ever been. He did not deny death, but he defied it. He insisted on normalcy when normalcy was impossible; he took chances, and she could not, would not stop him, forfeit his childhood any more than it already was. He was heartbreakingly brave. She admired it and wished he had no need for it. He was growing in wisdom, and when the chemicals made all his hair fall out and he looked small, wizened, and elderly, his simplest words took on the resonance of a great sage, weighted with meanings she could barely decipher.

He enjoyed remissions. He looked blessedly healthy then, went to the movies and video arcades with his friends, skateboarded with his best friend

Alejandro, did science projects at school, started learning French. She had to drive herself to punish him for peccadilloes when her heart exulted that he could be so normal.

She learned, above all, about herself. She learned that though she might fall asleep bargaining with fate—make this an erroneous reading, oh please; let this be a mistake; let these new numbers be the first sign of the real turnaround and not another letdown; let this new drug do it—she woke up to the reality that the problem hadn't gone away. It breathed as she breathed, it pissed and shat as she pissed and shat; it lodged in her stomach, her head, sank itself into her shoulders, swam into every capillary, crept along every nerve of her body; not just her companion but her possessor.

Sometimes she challenged it directly. What if something happens to me? Then what? Not impossible, her friends stricken with grave illnesses of their own. She hadn't been a young mother when Pete was born. What if something else claims me?

Nothing else claimed her. Her mother died, she rushed to Chicago to arrange the burial, tie off the loose ends, and was back to Santa Fe in less than five days. No time, no place, to grieve an elderly mother who'd been privileged to live a full life.

Nola lived daily with the fact that though others wanted to help, and often did, it was not their problem. Their child was not mortally sick. Hers was.

Little children of suffering parents had died unexpectedly, unjustly, throughout human history, and somehow those parents had survived, she knew. But she also thought bitterly that parents of the past had endured hours, perhaps weeks of crisis, and then, however great their grief, knew resolution. Her crises had gone on for two years, up and down, lifted, dashed, dazed. Now she knew families who'd lived through five, seven, even more years of this. "We just try to stay ahead of the meds," a weary mom had said to her as they sat waiting for their children to receive yet another transfusion. "If we can keep her alive through this one, next month—well, something might turn up."

She'd learned humility. Though she'd gladly have given her life for her sweet son, she discovered that she and his father couldn't even donate bone marrow. "We don't think it will come to that," the oncologist said, "but it doesn't hurt to be prepared." Not his parents, in one sense too close to him, in another too distant. If he'd had siblings. If it came to that—it probably wouldn't—a stranger might match, donate bone marrow.

First, however, they'd use his own bone marrow, extracted and cleansed of leukemia cells. They hoped. Some might get through. Interferon just in case. They would nearly kill him to cure him.

At Maya's dinner the night Molloy was welcomed to Santa Fe, it sat beside her, an obscene guest, its shape growing more distinct, to see and to dread. It was not Death, majestic, hallucinatory. It was some evil minion of Death's, a practical joker, a demon, whose grotesque behavior would hardly be noticed, much less matter, to its master, Majestic Death. She'd babbled stupidly, compulsively to the new man; probably bored him; he thought her a fool; she didn't much care; forgot about it.

As she settled into a Houston hotel room, called room service, left the food untouched, she knew she must deal with Ernie one of these days.

Phase Transitions

"Tell me your story," Judith said, elbows on the tile counter where Benito, in a tee shirt that said *My Life is in Ruins*, was fixing dinner. A new *retablo*, a painted saint's image, had gone up over the kitchen fireplace since she'd last visited. "God, Benito. I do love your art. Do you lift it from the Ark?"

"No. Not because I'm so honest, but because they'd miss it. The downside of superb inventory control. My story, *querida*, is strange enough. Last week a couple came into the Ark with a bunch of potsherds."

The story emerged in the lilting English of the native New Mexican, a melodic tongue that could stop Judith and swivel her head if she heard it in Los Angeles or New York, instantly calling up the autumn smell of roasting chile, summer intensity of the sky. Benito's ancestors had come up the El Camino Real on horseback, not foot, erect in full armor and plumed helmets despite the punishing desert sun. They'd bequeathed him a carriage so upright it seemed unnatural, a head of hair once coal black but now silver, and deep blue eyes that seemed to be the battlefield between a tragic and a vastly amused view of life.

"Incredible," Judith said at last. "You have the money to dig?"

"Yeah, staving off contract archaeology for the highway department for yet another year. Not enough long-term. Maybe an in-house grant from the Ark. I'll call Heinz down in Austin; he might have some underemployed graduate students. Diana up at Colorado. Nice thing about archaeology. Time is, as we say, on your side."

Pass by Benito's house on Canyon Road, a little east of the galleries, and

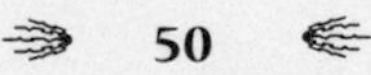

you'd guess the family was just making ends meet, the small windows cloudy with age and grime, their trim peeling, the metal *canales* that drained rainwater off the roof bent out of shape by vans or other tall vehicles that had tried to tuck themselves next to the wall to keep from blocking the narrow road.

Old Santa Fe style, it abutted the house on either side, which made it impossible to tell from the outside where Benito's house left off and the neighbors' houses began. It might have been Benito's house that Judith had in mind during her discourse on gates at Maya's dinner party. Behind Benito's gate was a different world. The courtyard was sheltered and welcoming, shaded in summer by century-old cottonwoods, the sound of the hidden *acequia* running close by. Through the front door was a wide hall, once an important room of the house, whose ceiling Benito had opened up with skylights to cheer and brighten, shedding a most untraditional light on an old Mexican altar he'd hauled up from Jalisco state. Nothing was worshipped at that altar now but junk mail and the daily *Santa Fe New Mexican*.

From her own house, Benito's was a short walk down the old goat path and then west on Canyon Road, and she made the walk weekly, a bottle of wine in her string bag if Benito was cooking.

Benito was clearly pleased this evening, his violet eyes for once unambivalently glad. "I'm happy for you, Benitole. Very. Let it lead to something big."

"Not too big, *querida*. It shouldn't interfere with the good life."

She smiled. He was making a little fun of himself, more of her, her ambition. Dear Benitole, whose own ambition fell so short of his abilities. He could tell you that human history was a lovely instance of a complex adaptive system, emerging from the interactions of many seemingly independent but in fact interconnected elements (human volition, the global climate, technological invention, to name only a few) that had their greatest significance as an ensemble, interacting dynamically, over time. But he was unenthusiastic about going further. Though his reputation was respectable, he lacked the fire that made others aim at the grand and history-changing theories. He couldn't be bothered. Maybe this explained his bachelorhood too: marriage had simply been too much trouble. In all this, she believed, he was still an aristocrat, deterred by anything that suggested exertion, not because he was lazy, but because effort was unseemly.

"Me, I spent the day with a crank."

"Ernie Holliman."

"Right the first time. Told him I'd read one of his proposals. Oh my. But I don't rush to judgment. Over this ever-longer lifetime of mine, I've befriended many who seemed to be at the fringes."

"Present company?" he asked dubiously.

"Some stayed at the fringes, but others—others the world now recognizes as brilliant. Junk science, pseudoscience, pathological science, so easy to define in the abstract, so hard to tell in real life. So I share my doubts only with you, beloved."

"The very story of my calling," Benito said with a cheerful resignation. He'd been thrashing around his kitchen, putting together salad dressing, now shook it all in an old jam jar. "Archaeology crawls with nut cases. Don't get me started."

"Oh, start. Nice to think I'm not the only one up against the whackos."

"Your Anglos-were-here-before-the-Indians guys. This says the primeval Anglos were wiped out by invading Asians who brought nasty diseases. Your Hopi-legends-have-it-right guys. This says they didn't get here by the Asian land bridge; they got here on rafts from Polynesia. Ancient Negroid remains in Brazil, dating from at least fifteen thousand years ago, and what does *that* mean?" He stopped, then went back to shaking the jam jar. "Show me the DNA, the blood-type evidence, please. Hey, some of this shit will turn out to be true. Okay, I say; so long as the Hopi prophecies don't have it right. Not to mention the Tibetans. You know this from one of the Tibetan holy books, eighth century? *When the iron bird flies and horses run on wheels, the Tibetan people will be scattered like ants across the face of the earth and the dharma will come to the land of the red men.*"

"So I've heard." With interest she watched his long fingers pick over the salad before he dressed it.

"The nut cases are lively. But for every one of them, you have your ten archaeo-drones, so obsessed by the bits and pieces that they can't look up from their dust brushes long enough to wonder what it all means."

"Think of your archaeo-drones as simple agents following simple rules. The complexity will emerge."

He glanced at her, unsure even after all these years whether she was joking, or lapsing into her slightly earnest pedantry. In fact, she was grinning at him; he grinned back. She picked up a pot lid. "Mama's *mole* sauce? An occasion, that's what it all means." Benito's mother had been an herbalist, a *curandera*, famous throughout the southwest. And an exceptional cook.

"Ernie still going on about the connections between phrenology and brain science?"

The nonsense she'd read earlier this day, phrenology proving to be correct in principle if wrong in the details. Ernie threw around the right jargon, was jubilant about new kinds of scans that detected localized brain behavior—counting, naming, reasoning, thinking about sex. But to show a place was associated with specific behavior didn't tell you how the signals were encoded, or that the locale had actually caused that behavior.

Yet something larger puzzled her, and over supper she thought aloud. "I ask you, Benitole, to a non-scientist, how is Ernie's stuff any different from worrying about the limits to science? Or speculating about parallel universes? The accelerating expansion of this particular universe? String theory? Self-organizing systems? Jumping genes and retroviruses? Flat earth is out, flat universe is in. Universes reproduce like rabbits. To the untrained eye, everything looks woo-woo. The trained eye too." She looked up, arrested by a painting over the living room couch, an image of the martyr St. Agatha, about to have her nipples sliced off by what looked like pruning shears. "I love your art, but that one—"

"You tell me the difference, real science from woo-woo," he said softly. "But not this very moment. *Querida*." He held out his hand. "Let's go celebrate in the nun's bed."

Having made love with an energy and finesse that exceeded even what their most envious friends imagined, they lay stroking each other affectionately. "I can't see how Nola, with her refined taste in art, lives with all those kitsch phrenology heads."

Benito chuckled. Then got suddenly serious. "Doesn't bother me in the least. I tell you what does. Ernie has tuned out. It's like he's not even on the same planet with his own kid. When things get harder with Pete, and they probably will—you ever seen anyone go through childhood leukemia? Not pretty, *querida*. Not movie stuff. Nola's going to erupt. She'll be entitled. She's the one carting that kid back and forth to Albuquerque for blood tests and chemo this winter, icy roads and all. Just the effort in that alone—she's worrying herself sick about Pete and on the road every week, plus running the gallery out of her back pocket, while that *pendejo* sits there with those damned heads, spinning theories that, excuse me, are quackery. Pisses me off, even if she doesn't care. Which reminds me, how's Sophie doing?"

Dear God. Was it their age? Their time in life? Sophie had done well through the initial surgery to remove her ovaries, uterus, and fallopian tubes, along with her appendix, half her large intestine and omentum; bravely endured four months of chemotherapy and been rewarded with a remission. Had even gone back to work. But twelve months later, the symptoms returned, markers were rising. She'd resigned from Los Alamos once and for all.

"The chemo's a killer. But then so's cancer. She's hoping to get into an experimental program at the University of Denver. Very high-dose chemo, followed by a bone marrow transplant. For now she has more good days than bad. She's already lasted longer than average. Whatever that's worth." They lay in silence, thinking of a child's mortal illness, the mortal illness of their friend; inevitably, their own mortality.

"Her expertise help?" Sophie had spent the final part of her Los Alamos career researching first, the effects of radiation on cells, and then helping to map Chromosome 16 for the Human Genome Project. She'd even been on the team that identified the human telomere, the protective cap at the end of the chromosome that prevents the chromosome from degrading or shortening during DNA replication, a cap possibly crucial in preventing cancer. Certainly implicated in human longevity.

Judith reached over to the bedside table, swallowed the last of her wine. "Just in the irony column."

"Tempo perdido los santos lo lloran."

With effort she translated. "Lost time—the saints weep over lost time." She reached out to hold and be held, let comfort turn to desire once more. "The chaste women who originally slept in this bed. All that pent-up passion for only their dear Lord. We do it for you, ladies, sorry for the joys you missed."

"You don't know that, *querida*," he objected softly. "The women in those convents had their favorites, male and female. Who knows what went on in this bed before us? But let's not make the saints weep."

He was a man of many moods when he made love, never the same twice. He could bull ahead, gratify himself, her pleasure a polite afterthought; other times, teasing about her intensity, he claimed he just went along for the ride. He'd just been playful and energetic; now he moved slowly, deliberately, conferring a blessing upon her, a beneficence, a veneration of the sweet brevity of flesh.

More is Different

A week after he visits Judith's office, Molloy calls her late one night. It's been a hard day and she's stretched out on the couch reading trash, staring into the fire and morphing into the vegetative.

"Can I come over for a nightcap?"

She looks down at her old robe, grimy with morning newspaper print, a few frontal stains of unknown breakfast origin, the rag socks recycled from hiking. She'll have to get dressed. Put in her contacts. Damn.

He's there quickly—doubtless called from nearby on his cell phone—and boldly appraises the room, stops at a table where pots are clustered. Aloud, he begins an inventory. "That one's Cochiti. Zuñi. Santa Clara. Another Santa Clara. Acoma, but not the usual stuff. Since I'm going to be a Santa Fean, I'm learning. That one—"

He's exchanged the bench-made shoes for custom boots. The shirt collar's open but still white, still starched. Jacket and trousers still Manhattan somber though no longer pinstriped. He shakes his head: no nightcap after all, not even coffee. This'll be, she thinks, a mercifully short visit.

He's fixed on the mystery pot. "Old. Really old."

"Well done, Molloy." A good eye. Amateur collectors are always fooled by the peach-colored clay slip, the black horizontal bands, the waves coming back on themselves. Even experts have tripped. He frowns, shadowed chevrons between his dark eyebrows.

"North central China," she says finally. "Somewhere between twenty-five hundred and twenty-three hundred BCE."

A small grunt of triumph. "China. Okay. A ringer. And this?" He's turned to see a human skeleton, almost life-size, carved of pale gray aspen, and seated on a small chair in a wooden-wheeled cart.

"A *muerta*. A local figure. *Doña* Sebastiana. The man who carved this can only do one every couple of years. It takes too much out of him otherwise."

He studies the skeleton. "I can believe that. The lady's energy is formidable. Death and I aren't unacquainted, but I'm not sure I could live with that day in, day out."

We live together peaceably, Judith thinks. Death and I aren't unacquainted either, and *la doña* stands for the pity. The mystery. The inevitability.

He's moved to the paned windows flanking the fireplace, hands behind his back. Outside, the Sangre de Cristo range rises dramatically in the east, five thousand feet above Santa Fe's own seven thousand foot altitude. A new snow has fallen. With the storm past, the moonlight on the slopes, the wild peaks dazzle the eye. "How can art compete with this?"

"Pretty, isn't it?" she agrees.

"Pretty." He utters the word scornfully. Uninvited, he pulls open a french door and walks out on the long covered wooden porch, the *portal*. She follows; pleased the view gives him pleasure, an impulse to claim credit. "Approaching from the front, you don't see it," he muses, "that something like this'll be waiting for you. No need to ask you again why you're here." He looks at her directly for the first time since he's arrived. "You're cold. Back inside?"

In the lamplight he sees he's tracked snow onto the Saltillo tile floor, seems momentarily dismayed. Someone, she thinks, has house-trained him. "Worry not. It'll evaporate in minutes."

He picks up a book from a side table, gives a self-deprecating little snort. "I cracked my skull over this for an entire summer once. All in a day's work for you, I guess." Merton's classic, *Continuous-Time Finance*. Part of what earned him a Nobel.

"No," she says softly, "that one's hard for everyone. Worth the effort, though. You're very ambitious, Molloy." A brain behind that thug's face. No, not a thug. But—a desperado. Always an air of menace.

"Ito calculus. Wiener processes. Stochastic differential equations. That's about where I crashed and burned."

"Ito did that work in the early fifties, post-war Japan. Studying rocket thrusts. The original rocket scientist. Utterly unappreciated till Merton saw how it applied to finance."

"You admire that."

"I admire that."

Firelight plays across the planes of his face, softens the warrior's helmet look she saw in the sun's glare a week ago. Still, here because he wants something. What? She lets him break the silence.

"You consult."

"For New Business, mostly. Some government work."

"The problems?"

"Anything they hand me. Finance, mostly. Sometimes strategic planning. I'm known for being a worst-case analyst. I can always dream up scenarios to curl your hair. Well, maybe not yours." A little joke, Molloy, laugh already. He remains reproachfully solemn. "In fact, I seldom have answers. But I'm very good at asking the right questions."

From barely looking at her he's now appraising her as boldly as he had the room. "Finance. Handle your own assets?"

"God, no. Neither time nor inclination. I have a professional."

"Mind saying who?"

"A guy in Boston." She names him.

Molloy nods. "Good choice. Nice guy. Powerful performer. Collects American impressionists."

"You know Michael? I bet you know his minimums. A lower bound on my net worth. Clever, Molloy."

He shakes his head; for the first time something like a smile animates his face. "Easier ways to find that out. No, I'm curious that you consult on problems you don't have the patience to work on for yourself."

A challenge and close, she thinks, to needling. "Sorry I didn't make myself clear." Which is: You don't get it. Plus, who needs this at ten o'clock at night? Plus—but the fact is that she's surprised to see him again. After the lunch it occurred to her he might have arrived that morning all dewy-eyed with idealism, imagining the scientist as Parsifal, and instead she'd given him low-down truths of the trade. Which doesn't nullify the Parsifal aspects, but science isn't as simple as grand opera. "The level I consult at offers me nice test-beds for my work. At the level of keeping my nest egg fat and happy—money for its own sake isn't very interesting to me."

"So you mentioned."

He can bite, and she flinches. "Did I tell you things you didn't want to know? About science? About scientists? This scientist?"

"Illusions are always a nuisance in the end."

She closes her eyes, wishing to put things right. "There's enough—enough Episcopalian Girls' Friendly Society left in me to feel bad about disillusioning anyone, Molloy. It must've sounded grubby. Parts of it are. But in my calling come moments of great beauty. Even holy moments. About me—please know this too. In the presence of the sacred, I know enough to be humbled."

He nods slowly, stares into the fire, thinking whatever passes behind those intense black eyes.

Handsomely booted ankle on the knee, arms spread across the back of the couch, he should look altogether relaxed, but he gives off a palpable tension. The American stance, she thinks; Nazis fingered spies who sat that way, because only American men ever did. What's he here for? Apparently not to be reassured about his illusions. Or even about her.

"This is confidential," he begins at last. No, she contradicts silently, or you wouldn't be confiding. "I've been approached to be on the board of the Institute. To make an informed decision, I need to know more about what you do there."

Matters suddenly clarify. Such men have come her way before. Too sophisticated to talk about cost cutting and efficiency, they snap out crisp little phrases like *managed research, return on investment, rationalized planning*. They always fail. They're always made peevish by that failure, and by the scientists who fail them.

"The Institute is devoted to the sciences of complexity."

"And your work?"

"Sorry. I can tell you about complexity or I can tell you about my work.

Which, for your purposes, may not be mainstream enough. Other people at the Institute with a more general take on it—"

"Your work. Complexity in general. Either one." A voice of quiet authority, just as he'd moved around the living room, on to the *portal*, a man used to his own way, unused to asking permission. A slightly arrogant desperado, then.

"I hear you collect pictures. Wouldn't you be better off doing your good works at one of the art museums?"

He takes a long moment, his face unreadable. "I'll assume you're asking me a civil question and not just blowing me off." He's offering her that at least, and now she guesses his exasperation isn't solely with her. "Most art right now—painting, architecture, opera, maybe music generally—is trapped inside a monotonous dialogue with itself about its own history. But science. Science actually sheds its skin and moves on into the future." He adds pointedly, "Which is my strongest desire."

"Yes. No. It's complicated. Very, very complicated."

This is more interesting. Much more. Slouched across her couch, a bearing that verges on the insolent, the desperado is given to thought. Has a good eye. Has attempted Merton by himself. Desires the future, not the past. She's mellowing. It could be worthwhile in the end. His hands, hirsute down to the first knuckle, lie stiffly across the couch-back cushions. Belying the body's slouch, they're tense, would finger-drum if he'd let them, but he's a man under unsparing self-control. Maybe, she thinks, she's witness once more that unstable blend of deference, suspicion, fear, and envy that people who long for the life of the mind show professionals who actually make a living at it. What to do when chasing a buck has lost its savor? It would explain the desperado. Maybe the menace.

Who knows? Would it hurt to have a friend on the board? She gazes down at the book on the table. "This won't be easy."

"It's never easy." He seems to be thinking of other things. Sits up now, all urgent attention, almost enthusiasm. Still tense. "Teach me all about fractals, chaos. Show me some holy moments."

She examines him for sarcasm, even irony, but can find none. Shakes her head; let's begin right. "Chaos is a special case of complexity. Fractals—well, *fractals*. Remember when the pope divvied up the globe between Spain and

Portugal, half to each, so they wouldn't keep warring over territory? The pope's about to announce another division—half the universe to complexity, half the universe to fractals. It's the only way we can keep Mandelbrot from eating everything in sight. Fractals are complicated, not complex."

It takes him too long to smile. She shrugs. "So long as we're being upfront about money, how much does it cost to be on the board these days?"

He's finally relaxed enough to grin. "One makes a modest pledge, according to one's means. Money's not the issue. The issue is time. Infinite opportunities, finite time. I need to choose."

"Be careful where you invest. Like everything else, organizations have life cycles. The Institute is already some ten years old. We may be past our prime. Maybe the revolutionary science is done and all that's left is the mopping up."

He doesn't reply.

After a while she says, "I'd like to do it by e-mail, this tutorial." His face shadows, goes neutral again. But she always saves her freshest self for real work in the morning, prime time: speculating, building models, proving theorems. Secondary time, afternoons, are for preparing talks and papers, going to seminars, writing referee's reports and recommendations, doing e-mail. (A concept, a young classicist once assured her, shared by the Greeks. Aristotle's rigorous *Organon* was well known to be morning work; he'd tossed off the *Poetics* in the afternoons.) Tutoring a neophyte, even if he might end up on the board of her institutional home, is way down on a long list of priorities. "You do have e-mail?"

Molloy hesitates—maybe the only time he's ever hesitated in his life, she thinks wryly. A keyboard, and all that this implies, never mind the irritations, the limitations of electronic conversation.

"Okay." He's up, hands clasped behind his back, staring out at the moonlit mountains again. "Good skiing tomorrow."

"I was thinking just that. Thinking I might get a few runs in before work."

"Let's go together. No point taking two cars up."

She balks, feeling crowded. "No. It might not look that way, but I was working on a problem, and if I crack it overnight then I'll want to go straight to work."

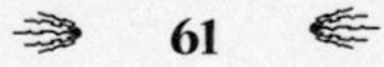

"I could call you first thing in the morning." He picks up on her resolution, backs off.

But when she arrives at the ski basin lodge for breakfast, there early to beat the lift lines, the Texans, to be first on to the fresh powder, she sees him at once, smiling knowingly at her as he eats a breakfast burrito. "No luck on the problem?"

She puts her tray down across from him. "A blood rush to my brain might help. Ski here much?"

"Not here. Before I ever came to Santa Fe I used to ski Taos. I still prefer it if I've got the time. Or Alta."

"Alta. You have good taste in skiing, Molloy."

"You know Alta? I used to come all the way from Europe."

"But the Alps—?" When did you live in Europe? And why?

"Snow's much more reliable in Alta. Powder up to your crotch. Plus, I prefer my animals in zoos. Ever tried to deal with a European lift line? Something comes over those otherwise remarkably courteous people, the same thing that comes over them on autobahns. Brings out the very worst in them." He adds with a grin, "Unfortunately, in me too." Looks up. "Lift's running, let's go."

Outside, stepping into their bindings, a heavy man, awkwardly out of control on his skis, bumps into Molloy and, in distinct Texan, excuses himself effusively. "No harm done," Molloy says politely. "But if God had wanted Texans to ski, he'd have made bullshit white." The Texan looks stricken, torn between laughing and being offended, not even sure he's heard right. Judith has to turn her head to hide her own laughter. It's an old New Mexico joke.

As the Texan poles clumsily away, she shakes her head at Molloy. "These people pack heat."

He grins up at her from where he's making an adjustment to his boot. "Good thing I didn't think of that. It might have given me pause, at least for a moment. You think he'll ambush me on the bunny slope? Or will my disguise fool him?" Dark goggles down, ear band, New Yorker black from head to toe, he's indeed incognito. He's seemed helmeted, a thug, a desperado, but now, looking up at her, grinning, he surprises her with his appeal. You've broken hearts, she thinks suddenly. Not mine, babe. Not mine.

They ride up without speaking, savoring the silence, the freshness of the early morning, the newly groomed trails below, cottony snow bowing the pines under the radiant blue sky. With Molloy's skis swinging out ahead of him, his boots, his fine gloves, she can see he treats himself to the best of everything. At the top of the lift she starts right toward the blue and black trails, but he goes left, toward the double-blacks, the steep and deep. "Don't hit a tree," she calls. He waves a pole and disappears. A modern satyr would appear silently from the woodlands on skis, make mischief and ski off like that, she thinks. She doesn't see him again that day.

Lessons in Complexity

To: jrg@santafe.edu
From: molloy@newbus.com
February 1, 8:34 p.m.
So. Just what is complexity?

Start with the obvious and fundamental, he thinks. Will she simply send along a reading list, e-mail me if you have questions? She might already know that the rich don't bother to read when they can call on tutors. She won't expect that, by now, he's read a lot. From the ID she'll see that he not only knows about the little consulting firm called New Business but has an affiliation. Actually, a financial interest.

To: molloy@newbus.com
From: jrg@santafe.edu
February 1, 8:40 p.m.
Complexity is: interaction, aggregation, and adaptation by a system that nevertheless maintains its coherence. The rest is commentary.

Is she kidding? He plays the game patiently.

To: jrg@santafe.edu
From:molloy@newbus.com
February 1, 8:45 p.m.

Perhaps you could say more. Like the difference between the complicated and the complex.

He moves over to another lively screen. The Hang Seng is whiffy. He hits a button and speaks into his headset. "Marty? The Hang Seng? Yes, I can see that. So what are you doing with my money, Marty? Shall my children be paupered thanks to you? No, not a straddle. Not now. Yes, my eye is ever on the sparrow." Numbers fly past, trades ten thousand miles away where it's already tomorrow morning. The numbers sing to him in patterns. He leans over, puts on some music. Wonders what he's really doing here. Escaping the past? Embracing it? He's promised himself not to ask. He's not who he once was, and yet—he is. The central paradox. *Interaction, aggregation and adaptation by a system that maintains its coherence.* A beep tells him a message has come in. Perhaps the lady has deigned to answer.

To: molloy@newbus.com
From: jrg@santafe.edu
February 1, 9:03 p.m.

Okay, commentary.

We distinguish between complicated and complex like this. An airplane is very complicated but can be completely described in terms of its individual components. But describe the air traffic system, and you have to include interactions between its parts—commercial, general and military aviation, Piper cubs to jumbos, main and secondary airports, interactions with the environment, everything from air quality to politics in the oil-producing nations. Those *relationships* shift over time and their shifts are contingent and nonlinear—small causes, big results. That's complexity.

Put it another way. Some things are predictable—what goes up must come down, the earth orbits the sun, hydrogen always bonds with oxygen two to one. Not really simple in concept or execution, but we understand it well enough to make confident predictions, to teach it to schoolkids, so we think it's simple.

Other things are utterly unpredictable. Evolution, for example. We can look back and see how it happened—how this step led to that, and how this event—a meteor, or a change in the climate—permitted one kind of life to thrive, even prevail, and drove another into extinction. But run the tape again and it wouldn't be the same, ever again. We might know the laws, but they express themselves in such a complicated way that we're left only with probabilities. We're starting to get pretty good about climate—the macrosystem—but weather, the microsystem, eludes us. We can see how storms arise, but we can't tell very far ahead of time if they will, or where. The famous butterfly effect and all that. You could run the same exercise on the key events leading to the European renaissance.

This is the beginning of complexity. We'd like to understand why a system takes one kind of step and not another. How does novelty occur? Novelty is a big issue.

Phil Anderson—you should get to know him when he's here next time, Nobel laureate in physics—likes to say about complexity, "More is different." That about sums it up.

Did you enjoy your runs yesterday?

Not bad, he answers her silently. Not great. *You could run the same exercise on the key events leading to the European renaissance.* Could you run it on the entire history of Western art, Madame Genius? Or on the life of one small casualty of the late twentieth century? Cure? Ross had asked with one of his rare and gentle smiles. Begin with a simple human connection. Then we'll talk about a cure. Molloy types again with surprising two-fingered dexterity:

>More is different.

I don't get it.

She's still on-line so they go into chat mode.

Judith: Changes in quantity lead to changes in quality.

Like pornography, we think we know complexity when we see it, but nobody can propose a definition that everybody likes. Of course I'm hoping that *unlike* pornography, this will not be a moving target. We need a crisp and stable definition. Maybe an oxymoron, a crisp and stable definition of complexity.

A complex adaptive system: Orderly but not too orderly, surprising but not completely random. (BTW, funny how "random" has become adolescent slang just now?) Assimilating the fact of randomness—that people can contract diseases or be lucky in love or make a fortune (isn't that a nice word? derives from the Latin fors, chance) is one of the great psychological and philosophical tasks of our time. We're pattern-seekers by nature. Randomness repels us.

Sorry to get so free-associative on you. It was a long day.

An appealingly earnest woman when she puts her mind to it, he thinks. Taking this tutorial seriously now, anyway. He'd skied partway down yesterday morning and waited in the trees until he saw her coming down her own trail. An experienced skier but not aggressive. She saves that for other things.

Molloy: Sounds like theology. Fortune. For a woman who disdains money, you mention it often enough.

Molloy sighs to his terminal. Only people who've been able to take it for granted disdain money. He's not such a man. He'd been partway through a third-rate education at a second-rate religious college in western Pennsylvania when his natural feel for numbers (the lifetime stats for every member of Pittsburgh's Steel Curtain, stats for the Pirates when they'd really been a powerhouse, all effortlessly at the tip of his tongue) had magically transformed into moneymaking. In a course where students simulated investing in the commodities market, he did so well with his scrip that he quietly gambled his scholarship money on the Chicago Board of Trade. It paid much better than poker. He lived comfortably for the next two years, and rewarded himself with a graduation trip to Europe. It was the only graduation present he received. It changed his life.

He gets up to the other screen again, hits a few keys. Through the open line: "Marty? The yen is toast, Marty. Put your own money there, pal, not mine." He imagines a trading floor, a few hundred sweaty male bodies screaming, finger signaling, turbo-charged by the blended funk of fear and aggression, a distinct subnote of polecat. No, ancient history. It's hand-held wireless like every other trading floor these days. And women.

Judith: >Sounds like theology. Always the case early on in science. Let me only live long enough to watch it go from theology to the real thing.

In the 18th century, Voltaire skewered poor John Needham for claiming that matter could self-organize. Needham was not wrong. He just had the wrong level of organization. Voltaire was completely wrong. Self-organization is a significant principle in complexity. (Remember V. also skewering Leibniz for claiming this as the best of all possible worlds. When I was an undergraduate my professors were contemptuous of Dr. Pangloss. How's Candide taught in this era of multiple universes and the anthropic principle? Poor old Leibniz, an example of premature arrival in science.)

The anthropic principle. He pencils a note to himself on his ever-present yellow pad to look that up.

Fortune. I'm a word freak. As Robert Graves said, there's no money in poetry. Of course, he added, there's no poetry in money either.

Is that Graves or the woman herself? Neither she nor the poet have thought very much about money, he muses. There's poetry in money, all right. Art, anyway. With some asperity he replies.

We should take that up some time, the poetry/money connection. Maybe I could change your mind.

Usually when people allude to his money he says deprecatingly, "Who starts these irresponsible rumors?" Which eventually leads to his quiet assertion that he's certainly comfortable but that he makes money for others, is not himself particularly well off. A necessary gesture of self-protection. He doesn't pursue that now. Instead:

Something I'm missing. General principles of complexity?

Judith: General principles.

That complexity evolves out of simplicity—simple agents, simple rules, give rise to great complexity.

That this evolution is a dynamic process, full of give and take, feedback loops, learning, what we call co-evolution, systems pushing on and shaping each other reciprocally and producing novelties.

That on many fronts, a complex adaptive system evolves toward a regime poised between order and chaos—LIFE exists at the edge of chaos, the compromise between order and surprise.

The whole is greater than the sum of its parts. Collective properties, emerging out of the interaction of many levels of components, are unpredictable but very real, very much worth our attention. The anthill. Intelligence. Life itself, probably. These collective properties don't reside in any single component of the system, but emerge from their interactions, from the behavior of the whole system itself, and only emerge when the whole system is in action.

But this is science, not dogma. We could be wrong.

It begins simply. By chance a man and woman meet at a dinner party. Simple agents, simple rules. Great complexity emerges. The man types:

Still don't get it entirely.

He thinks he does, but is loath to let go of a friendly human voice in the middle of the lonely night. All nights are lonely, but he hasn't always minded. Complexity, a piece of cake compared to, oh, mastering the convoluted order of precedence of the Germanic nobility. Bad enough the titles themselves, *Herzog, Fürst, Graf, Markgraf, Pfalzgraf* and the like, but on top of that, apparently equivalent titles were not at all equal if the family had been ruling rather than non-ruling, if the title had been created before or after 1800, if it was only Austro-Hungarian and not actually German. Jürgen being for once serious: "Does a *Grossherzog* outrank a *Fürst*? It depends on the family history."

Both screens are still lively, but his attention is fixed on the monochrome words of one, not the polychrome graphs of the other.

Judith: A concrete example. An infant is born with some behavior wired in, its genetic endowment, but how it behaves is also specified by the environment—nutrition, stimulation, affection, whatever. Many responses are possible to a given stimulus, but some are more successful than others, get reinforced, become patterns and survive.

A baby is born to an unstable mother, a phantom father. What happens to that child? Those children? He's tried not to be a phantom.

A kid isn't just passively receiving experience, but it doesn't have the power to change much, either. It's part of a larger dynamic system that includes other people, includes its environment, includes its physiology, includes its past. Notice—the physical *and* the symbolic domains.

Things better off not exhumed can still pain him. Pain is preferable, Ross would say, to anesthesia. He himself reserves judgment, prints the message, thinking he'll study it later.

Molloy: Okay, it's getting clearer. What if something new, something unexpected, happens to this kid?

Judith: An infant—any complex adaptive system—has an inventory of solutions. Does this look like anything else I've come across? How did I solve it before? The richer the repertoire, the better the system can cope with novelty. It finds something appropriate, or invents something new by recombining elements of the old patterns. Baby bricoleurs.

Baby bricoleurs. Though he hasn't been feeling exactly sunny for the past few minutes, his brain, if not his face, smiles. He changes the subject slightly, a maneuver he isn't entirely proud of.

Molloy: Is this something new under the sun? And what do computers have to do with it anyway?

Judith: Excellent questions, both. No more tonight. Go to bed, Molloy. It's late. I can't even type any more. We'll save it for next time.

He won't go to bed for a while, having other business to conduct. On the sound system, a Nüremberg cowboy laments *ganz allein, ganz allein*. The Germans and their sentimentality. Hell, his own. Why do this? He's seen enough privilege to know that golden girls glide across a serene sea, impervious to rusted hulks, old storms.

Get a grip, he tells himself. Notes the irony. He isn't the first man in his family to work the graveyard shift.

Random Events

Judith knew how some teenagers talked, at least some of the time, because of Alejandro next door. Alejandro was eleven and fascinated by all things. He remembered everything he heard, saw, or read, though not always with complete accuracy.

He'd read somewhere and thought about it every time he peed: if the flush toilet hadn't been invented in a climate where water was abundant, no one would have dreamed of wasting water that way. In protest he sometimes declined to flush. (His mother protested in return.) He knew that *pueblo* was a cognate of *people*. He puzzled over the idea of someone much older described as handsome in his prime, or a great beauty in her day. With snapshots of relatives, he'd work to map the old face he knew now onto the image in the photo. Then he had to take a second step, try and ignore the old-school clothes, hairstyles, cars, and think how that person would look in hair, clothes, cars that were really cool. He probably spent too much time watching the fractal generator on his PC, but he really got into it. His mother scolded that he spent too much time playing Doom, but now he was hearing about Pokémon, which he totally wanted to get.

He too was occasionally Judith's student, but with Alejandro, she asked as many questions as she answered.

"Why do you kids say *like*? As in, *And I'm like...*"

"You don't think it's good English?" Alejandro had dropped in after school and they sat comfortably in the kitchen, drinking hot chocolate. Judith did not ask him to explain the meaning of his clothes, oversize trousers to the knee, bony legs protruding, which made him look like some goofy wading bird. She was more or less used to the wholesale adoption in Santa Fe of fashion statements from the South Bronx, Pueblo and Hispanic kids in hip-hop clothes; though once, when Alejandro brought over his pal Jim, whose family had come from Tibet (Jim the closest American equivalent to his Tibetan name) his appearance was odd enough to evoke the whole issue of teenage-boy fashion once again in her mind.

"You've got school on the brain. I'm just trying to figure out what *like* means. Same with, so he goes, and I go, when you mean so he says, and I say."

Alejandro swung his stick legs back and forth. "Well, you act like you totally know what it means. It means *He says*, or *I thought and then said*, or *I didn't think, I just said*. Like, you know." He laughed, his teeth still too big for his mouth.

Judith laughed too. The technology. Things are like, because this is above all a world of simulations. Molloy goes, his words on a screen; that's not really saying. She goes, she doesn't really say either. The kids' language has picked it up exactly. Their declarative statements framed as questions: *My name is Alejandro?* Nothing is certain in this world. "How about random. Like, this random guy—"

"You know," Alejandro said. "Random."

"Use it in a sentence."

Alejandro squirmed. "Oh, that's so random!"

"What is?"

"Asking me about random. It's, like, unexpected."

"Outside the pattern?"

Alejandro nodded, relieved, across his face the expression of genes from many places, eyes that must have wandered across the Mongolian plateau, cheekbones that appeared in low-relief Mayan carvings, a mouth from a conquering Spaniard (who'd got it himself from a full-lipped African ancestor).

"Your generation might be the first to really get it, that randomness happens."

Alejandro sipped on his hot chocolate and nodded, unsurprised. "Why not?"

"Some people believe in grand and perfect plans, even if we don't understand the details."

"Do you?"

"It's complicated. Very, very complicated." Hadn't she just said something like this to Molloy? "I'm a randomness person myself. It unties the knots."

She told him a few mathematician jokes, a bit dopey, a bit instructive. He rolled his eyes in mock agony but laughed; he got them. At last he picked up his skateboard, heading for the park. She loved him in his skate-rat mode; cheerfully read articles he marked for her in *Thrasher* and discussed them with him.

"There are three kinds of mathematicians," she called after him. He stopped. "Yeah?" "Yeah. Those who can count and those who can't." It took him a moment, then he laughed. She wanted to stop time. In a year or two, or three, Alejandro would have exchanged the skateboard for light wands, the skateboard park for a place to rave, or whatever the fashion would be by then. God knows what he'd be reading. Porn websites, probably. "How's your buddy doing?"

"I get e-mail from him. So he can do that, at least."

"You worried about him, Alijo?"

Alejandro gave an eloquent shrug that said it all.

"Alijo." What did she want to add? That death was shocking enough at her age, impossible at his? Apologize that here she could not instruct nor protect him? That they were on this strange journey together? She'd have hugged him to her if she could, gamey boy-smell and all, but he stood apart, resistant. So she blew him a kiss as she always did when it was time to part and watched him run off along the dirt road.

Perturbations of Small Amplitude

To: jrg@santafe.edu

From: molloy@newbus.com

February 6, 11:04 a.m.

Where were we? Okay, no definitions of complexity everyone agrees with. Are there measures of complexity?

To: molloy@newbus.com

From: jrg@santafe.edu

February 6, 4:39 p.m.

Yes, but different things get measured in different domains. We'll take it up later. Gotta run.

She was on her way to a bodywork session. She'd resisted Santa Fe New Age woo-woo, but a pulled muscle had compelled her to try bodywork—a kind of superior massage, she'd supposed.

So it was. Music, incense, rubbing oils, even a view out the window into a small, enclosed garden, but above all, touch—informed, strong, evocative. For someone who dealt all day every day with symbols, being forced to attend solely to sensation was a singular experience.

The florid dramatics of the first session receded; effects became subtler. Released from her muscles, her tissues, unfamiliar feelings swarmed through Judith's body, and sought to represent themselves as stories. She didn't understand these stories, but knew they were important, the book of her life, narratives demanding recognition. Sometimes they left her ebullient. Sometimes they left her deeply sad.

They emerged first as images—gates, for instance. Gates floated through her imagination, old wooden garden gates like those around Santa Fe, unpainted, slightly battered where people with full arms had kicked them open carelessly. In contrast, the tidily painted garden gates of her years in Germany. Formidable gates, to fortresses, to cities, to empires themselves, the gates in the walls of Istanbul, the Great Wall of China. Iron portcullises, stone archways, hatchways, moon gates, *toriis*, turnstiles, wickets, *zaguans*, pergolas; gates to corrals, with their high posts and lintel; more modest gates to sheepfolds and pigpens; stiles; gates as memorials like the Brandenburg, gates as bridges, like the Golden; gates as barriers across railroad tracks, into tennis courts. Gates carved and gates plain; gates painted and gates naked; gates mullioned and gates railed. The Pearly Gates. They rose in her mind's eye as she was being rubbed, pulled; resisted easy analysis, haunted her.

Then maps. Old highway maps, as if through a high-powered magnifier, the red and black threads tangling (lines in an age of the nonlinear; wires in a wireless time; snakes when snakes were endangered species); contour lines; relief maps, globes and projections; legends, scales and keys; maps that showed populations, linguistic groups, weather patterns, water; isobars and isohels; ancient maps marked with "Dragons Bee Here" or Baja California thrust crudely into Alaska; maps of the human brain, the human genome; maps of long-gone empires, the Austro-Hungarian, the Roman, the Alexandrian, the Napoleonic, the Ottoman, the Soviet. Shifting on the massage table from back to stomach she saw the foot chart on the opposite wall, Chinese reflexology (Footpath to the Body); thought of Ernie's skull maps, subway maps, Madrid, New York, Paris, Munich, Budapest, multicolored tangles, the potent names of the lines themselves (the A train, the Bakerloo line) and the stations (Port Royale, Isartor).

My life is mapping. But more?

Vivid and persistent, the images made of her head a ridiculous theater. She'd try to make sense of it all and fail.

Sometimes under Jill's hands she imagined the chain of human souls who, since ancient times, had practiced and yielded to the power of this technique, this wisdom—the Chinese philosophers, the Buddha himself, the Homeric heroes, the countless, nameless women in labor, whose pain had been softened, focus sharpened, mind clarified, lives made whole again by the careful, informed hands of the gifted.

This time of the year, late winter, Judith could lie on the table watching the sun set behind the filigree of a bare Russian olive tree. The room's walls were painted the same muted greensilver of the olive leaves, and so were the *rejas*, the narrow wooden spindles that barred a small opening in the sand-colored adobe garden wall outside. Thus the Russian olive shaded, filtered, conversed with its inanimate neighbors, and with the watching eye.

"The left side. Always the left side with you." Jill was working over a knot in Judith's shoulder.

"The private side," Judith responded dutifully.

"Be kinder to yourself. Ask yourself why you're starving that private side. No need to go hungry with all this abundance."

"No. I guess not." Pathways opening from the sacrum sounded like ice fracturing, but she held back, fearful.

"My job," Jill had said a long time ago, "is to disturb the old patterns, introduce new frictions, new pressures, new movements in your body that will let you know, let you feel, that you're not obliged to follow the old patterns permanently. You have a choice." Like a complex adaptive system, she thought. People had known about such things in a common sense way forever.

Today Jill's hands moved down Judith's back. "Let go of that ideal you. The real you is just fine." No, Judith thought. It is not.

"Have you cried?"

"No. I grieve, can't cry."

Jill sighed. "How's she doing?"

"About how you'd expect. I'm grateful for every week."

At home Judith ate a quiet supper, and pondered the pathways she hadn't yet got the courage to explore. *The real you is just fine*. Whoever that might be. At her age.

When the moon swung around and shone directly on the bath, she ran water and slipped in, at peace and distant from the world. A few lines of poetry forced themselves on her, a fierce prayer chanted four thousand years ago by Sumerian worshippers of the ancient moon goddess, Inanna, queen of heaven and earth:

> *You, Inanna,*
> *Foremost in Heaven and Earth*
> *Lady riding a beast,*
> *You rained fire on the heads of men.*

Fire on the heads of men. The moon an impact event, in the jargon. Something unthinkably colossal had collided brutally with planet Earth, splashing matter into the heavens. Most matter would have returned to earth, fire on the heads of men, but orbiting the planet, always within a tantalizing, even melancholy view of home, a swarm of small bodies was permanently exiled. A century or so, no time at all as such things go, they pulled themselves together to form the moon.

It could all have been otherwise. A slightly smaller body hits the Earth and there's no moon at all. (She scrubbed her legs, scrutinized her torso, sprinkled now with a constellation of little red moles that multiplied with each passing year.) Without a moon to slow it, the earth's rotation might've continued through five-hour days, as at Earth's beginnings. Or, a larger body hits the earth and there's two, a half dozen moons. Two moons would probably have collided eventually, sending all that fugitive matter back home to Earth, though no fun to get caught in the storm of a lunar collision. Fire on the heads of men. (She raised herself out of the tub, stood in the moonlight and dried herself slowly, lovingly, still in the light of the familiar silvery disk, dazzling in the clear winter sky.) This world without a moon was unthinkable. Life itself impossible without a moon, if life had risen, as maybe it did, in the tidal zones—moon's gift to earth.

The Sumerians had the right idea, the moon as queen of heaven and earth. Moonlight, moon goddesses, the long history of it all, cosmic and human; the moon regulating populations the way it regulated women's organs. It all preceded and would outlast a middle-aged scientist lying languorously, gratefully, alone in her cool white bed.

So it was only late the next afternoon that she found Molloy had responded nearly twenty-four hours earlier.

To: jrg@santafe.edu
From: molloy@newbus.com
February 6, 5:10 p.m.

Am I a slow learner? You can say more.

To: molloy@newbus.com
From: jrg@santafe.edu
February 7, 4:35 p.m.

You're not a slow learner. I'm a slow teacher.

A tiny difference in the plan can make a big difference in the outcome. Our genome versus the genome of the chimps. Tiny differences in how genes switch on other genes that switch on still other genes—a cascade of switching that allows rich complexity to unfold from simplicity. Our moon.You asked about chaos, which I said was a special case of complexity. It's a case of extreme sensitivity to initial conditions, the so-called butterfly effect.

But Ed Lorenz was much more subtle than popular myth allows. Yes, he said, a rogue butterfly in Brazil flapping its wings might set off a tornado in Texas, but so might all the previous flaps of its wings, or the wing flapping of millions of other butterflies, not to mention more powerful agents, such as us. If a flapping wing can set off a tornado, maybe it can also prevent one.

Maybe the butterfly's influence spreads in turbulent air, but not in calm air. Maybe it only affects the southern hemisphere, and can't cross the equator. Maybe it affects the tropics but not the temperate zone. We can guess; we don't know. Whether we'll ever know is what I think about.

It was two days before Molloy answered.

To: jrg@santafe.edu
From: molloy@newbus.com
February 9, 3:37 p.m.

Sorry for the delay; been out of town.

I think I get it. Complete order is dull. Frozen. So is complete randomness. I mean complete chaos, which isn't the same thing as randomness, right? Chaos is deterministic, patterned. Randomness is—just random. I'll try and be more precise. Anyway, it's what's in between order and chaos that's interesting, right?

To: molloy@newbus.com
From: jrg@santafe.edu
February 9, 9:16 p.m.

Are you back in Santa Fe now?

What's interesting is not quite in between. More toward chaos than order. You've got it: chaos looks like randomness, but operates by deterministic rules; randomness does not. The key area is what we like to call the edge of chaos. At the edge of chaos, a system is open to new input, to learning. It can't learn anything at all if it's in frozen order, or at the other extreme, in chaos.

To: jrg@santafe.edu

From: molloy@newbus.com

February 10, 10:03 p.m.

Still on the road. God I hate hotel rooms.

The edge of chaos is where you learn. Interesting. How does the Institute fit into all this?

To: molloy@santafe.edu

From: jrg@santafe.edu

February 10, 10:35 p.m.

How does the Institute fit into all this?

Right, you're thinking of coming aboard. Okay, to produce a mighty book, said Melville, you must choose a mighty theme. Same with science. On any given day at the Institute, gathered around our grand table to talk are folks who've chosen the mightiest themes.

We share those beliefs I mentioned earlier. (Pop quiz, Molloy: name them.) We think we can rub up against each other and make sparks. Even fire, maybe.

Officially, we are cross-disciplinary, looking for classes of complex systems that share structural and other features across fields, across levels of nature. Including human activities of course.

He answered the pop quiz and wrote, perhaps a shade boastfully, that since he was still on the road, he hadn't looked it up in his notes. Then added that he'd been on the edge of chaos himself the last few days: he hoped to God he was learning something.

Judith studied those last lines on her screen. Normally she'd have ignored such a personal opening. But pity and curiosity moved her. Pathways she'd lacked the courage to explore. Was this one of them?

To: molloy@newbus.com
From: jrg@santafe.edu
February 10, 11:20 p.m.

>I've been on the edge of chaos the last few days.

Because of complexity, or something else?

To: jrg@santafe.edu
From: molloy@newbus.com
February 10, 11:23 p.m.

Both.

Tell me where your own work fits into all this.

The evasion both disappointed and relieved her. She resumed impersonally.

I'm not sure my own work fits into all this. Let's say it's yet to be mapped out. This is a young field. Everyone's still learning. Edge of chaos. We may drop over. Or fall back and freeze. Be careful where you spend your money. Your time.

One more thing. No, complexity isn't new. My masseuse, an exceptionally intelligent woman to be sure, intuitively understands what we're calling complexity, though she wouldn't call it that. She knows that with effort (hers, then mine) systems (her clients like me) can change, adapt, as the environment changes, and those changes in turn feed back to and transform the environment. So she works at changing patterns in my body, energy flows, the way I hold myself, which, you won't be astonished to hear, affects my feelings. I roll off her table a kinder, gentler, more open soul than when I climbed on. This k.g. soul goes out into the world, and you can actually see it—the guys in the grocery are sweeter to me; I smile easier (the Buddhists might say I'm more *with* them, but the truth is, I myself have evoked this by being *with* them). Different transaction entirely from when I'm my usual preoccupied self. (Actually I go look at art after I've finished with Jill; see it in a fresh way, but that's another story.)

She'd started to write that she hoped Jill would unblock whatever had dammed the creative work. But decided against it. True enough about the art.

What we do at the Institute is study in a scientific way what some smart people have always felt intuitively. Science made feeble attempts earlier, in pre-computing days, but always studied systems with known and fixed constituents. Now we know that adaptation matters. Matters big-time. The system we begin by studying won't be the same a little while later. Adaptation not only changes the system, but it changes the system's environment. Me in the grocery store. Sets the stage for a system's reorganizing or restructuring itself, for novelties to emerge.

HOW DOES THAT PROCESS WORK? THE BIG QUESTION WE ALL WANT TO ANSWER.

To: jrg@santafe.edu
From: molloy@newbus.com
February 11, 12:06 a.m.

I'd still like to hear about your own work. What about explaining over a dinner with me? I owe you that.

Judith smiled. Then she laughed out loud, went to bed, didn't answer until late the next day.

To: molloy@newbus.com
From: jrg@santafe.edu
February 11, 4:30 p.m.

Here's a better idea. Saturday I'm going with friends to El Bosque del Apache, a major bird refuge south of Albuquerque. Probably the last weekend before they start heading north. You'll see all sorts of complexity in action with the birds. Will you be back in town by then?

Jumping Across Landscapes

It's three hours in the car from Santa Fe to El Bosque, and Judith has time to regret her impulse. Should she have told Molloy her friends are a gay couple? Don't ask, don't tell? Or is it that she and Ron have a long, if interrupted history together, while Molloy—not even a friend yet really—is stranger, outsider? For the first hour things are somewhat stiff.

"Ron and Gabe have the Cholla Bookshop and Cafe," she says as they pull on to I-25. "Ron and I went to high school together—"

"About the time of the Albigensian heresy." Ron interrupts from the front seat.

"We more or less lost touch until we ran into each other here."

Ron's locker had been just beside hers at the American School in Munich, a youth bending over her worshipfully as she wrestled with her books, him purring nonsense, voluptuous Venus, words he'd just found in the dictionary. Ron's father was helping to revive the postwar German film industry at Geiselgasteig; her own father was at Radio Free Europe, pitching American propaganda over the Iron Curtain, take the A train to freedom. Ron and Judith had been thrown together mainly because they shared little with their fellow students, who lived to hear Elvis on the Armed Forces Radio Network, and whined endlessly about spending the best years of their lives away from home.

Ron and Judith had loved Munich, taken off together on long walks inside the city and out, practicing their German, thrilled to be taken for locals so they could concur with the snide anti-Americanisms of waiters and bus drivers. They'd been swept up, she saw later, in a romanticism that was already long out of date, revived then thoroughly discredited by the Nazis: the redemptive power of nature, the superiority of long walks in the wilderness, singing and reciting poetry aloud. Her natural preference was somewhat different, but the fling with German romanticism hadn't done either of them any harm. After some tentative and eventually failed physical fumbling between them, they moved on with relief to friendship. Then they'd each left Germany for American universities, and drifted apart.

Munich was where they'd met European high culture, opera and concert halls, classical poetry, painting. Ron had simply added these to the mélange of so much that he loved with joyous generosity (including Elvis) but Judith would look back to regret that she'd failed to be equally open. Caring only for what she discovered at fifteen, sixteen, seventeen, had foreclosed her from much that was vital and American, had made her, in her own later eyes, a trifle stuffy and old-fashioned, at least about popular culture. However, it had prepared her perfectly for life with Jonathan.

Ron hadn't disagreed when they finally re-met in Santa Fe and were sizing each other up, how elapsed time had shaped them. "But you meet rock as a kid or you don't meet it at all," he'd said. "You watch the tube out of habit or you don't watch it at all. Likewise movies." He'd looked at her reproachfully. "You never saw a damn thing I did?" "I didn't even know you were making films. You could screen a few for me." He shook his head. "What Ron's trying to say," Gabe had added, "is that the work was of its time and place. You can't appreciate how well he caught the Zeitgeist." Especially if you didn't even get it at the time. Then, queening: "No *wonder* you don't get half our jokes." "No eternal verities in your art, Ron?" she'd pressed on. "Stuffed like a Christmas turkey with eternal verities," Ron had retorted, "but you'd have to see the films in a hundred years. Today you'd be too distracted by the sideburns and bell-bottoms."

"A bookshop," Molloy says thoughtfully. "You don't worry that you're a dying breed?"

"Oh, we are a dying breed," Ron replies cheerfully. "But someone has to cater to that other dying breed, the gentle reader."

"You don't worry about Amazon-dot-com? About the mega-stores?"

"We offer lattes instead."

Then a long silence. Perfectly framed in Gabe's rearview mirror, Judith sees her own disembodied chin and throat. Long past voluptuous Venus. Denial, a small and useful illusion, in Sophie's phrase, is still denial. Barbie Turns Forty. One of those pieces of electronic folklore that made the rounds—Bifocals Barbie, Hotflash Barbie ("Press Barbie's bellybutton and watch her face turn beet red while tiny drops of perspiration appear on her forehead; comes with handheld fan and tiny tissues.")

She closes her eyes, casts cast about for any subject she can think of. "I don't think I know how you guys met."

Gabe dismays them by turning from the driver's seat to answer. "In the gym. Banal? Banal. I didn't even know that word until I met Ron. Just a surfer boy, buffing myself to the max, and you could see he was struggling." He smacks Ron sharply on the thigh. "Nice quads, dude. So I leaned over and helped him with the weights. Here, ninety-seven-pound-weakling, do it this way. He was so—"

"Grateful," Ron supplies quickly.

"Grateful. One thing led to another. We hung in L.A. for a long time. I learned from him—a lot, really a lot—but believe it or not, he learned from this surfer boy too. If that isn't the recipe for a long-term relationship, tell me what is. Whoa, I learned more than the word banal. Get high on a book. That's way weirder to me than Ron getting high pumping iron, okay? He's producing TV movies, doing real well. We're not thinking too much about the future."

Judith leans back, glad to let the words fill the close air inside the car. Imagines this unlikely romance in the gym, this encounter between an overly cultivated and an unformed mind, the two of them co-evolving.

"Then one day I get wiped out but good on my board. It's like over for me. Or it will be real soon. I get home, and that guy, he knows without asking. He also knows something I don't; the best thing for both of us is to get the hell away. So to Morocco for a few years."

They've dropped down La Bajada from Santa Fe, moving toward Albuquerque at what seems like the speed of light. Molloy shifts uneasily in his seatbelt. Judith suspects not fear of speed but that someone else is driving. In this she's wrong. Molloy has been used to drivers for many years in many places, has learned to abide by practical sumptuary laws, never the biggest, most conspicuous car, but always a solidly built one, at times armor-plated; and the men up front have been not only drivers, guides and interpreters, but sometimes bodyguards.

Ron glances at the passengers in the back seat. "Gabes, this is way cool, but Molloy looks like he's queasy about doing a face plant on the dashboard."

"Nothing a Prozac drip wouldn't cure," Molloy murmurs. He has a man's face, the skin stretched tight over bones planed sharp as weapons; nothing about it underdeveloped or juvenile; nowhere visible the boy's face it must once have been. His jaw line is all business; by noon he always needs a fresh shave. Over lunch that day at the Institute, the play of shadows across the moquette of his midday beard had oddly distracted Judith.

She's glad of this man's face, its planes and angles, its gravity, even vague menace. Science, and even more, technology, is so much a refuge for the unendearingly boyish that you could forget grown-up men existed.

Gabe ignores his partner. "Me, I could've stayed in Morocco forever. I learned some French, a bit of the local Arabic. I'm thinking, hey, I'm talking a foreign language. You college grads, this is not exactly thrilling stuff. But for someone who barely got a courtesy diploma from Encinitas Regional High School."

Molloy hears the yearning in Gabe's voice and feels a rush of sympathy. Another who discovered a self he preferred abroad.

Ron says, "When I see him slipping into his *djellaba* and brewing mint tea, I give him his space."

"What brought you back?"

"Molloy wants to know why people are where they are," Judith says.

"Not money. Your old schoolmate's a shrewd investor, Jay, and we did well in the market. Still do. Everything isn't sunk in the shop."

"Things fail," Ron adds. "Learn to diversify."

"Sound strategy," Molloy agrees. The desert has now lost even its *piñons*, is bare of vegetation except for the leafless cottonwoods he can see in the distance, along the Rio Grande.

La jornada de muerto, the journey of death, he's just read. Could you ever love such bleakness? Men and women have died terrible deaths here, throats parched, their last earthly vision the eager quadruped, with a million years of instinct to tell it exactly when the tipping point was, when it could, with impunity, tear into and gorge itself first on your softest, most vulnerable parts; then later, sated, dismember and scatter you all over these lands, leaving the vultures to gather and pick at what was left. Did you roll onto your back and invite it to be mercifully swift? Or did your own million years of instinct curl you up protectively, however futile that was in the end? The predator has loomed over him more than once, but he's never yet rolled onto his back. Never will.

"Anyway, we came back," Gabe says, "because it was his turn. He needed to hear his mother tongue. But not L.A., okay? So we came to Santa Fe. It reminds us a lot of north Africa."

Santa Fe reminds Molloy of places he's been too, but not the dark Allegheny hollows of his childhood, not the flat, obsessively groomed fields, the German-orderly forests he'd soared above so often at another point in his life, coming and going to Frankfurt.

"Santa Fe's another one of those lost cities whose real bricks are nostalgia—like Jerusalem, Fez, San Francisco," Ron says. "And just like North Africa, you have to get on a plane for decent medical care. We hadn't intended to do anything in particular, but then the bookshop op came along, and we said, hey we can do this."

Gabe grins into the rearview mirror. "Sometimes I think of showing up at my class reunion and there it is on my name-tag: co-owner, bookshop. They're thinking, oh, you do gay porn, and I'm saying, we sell more Hegel than anyone in the southwest."

Ron adds, "Not that that's such an achievement, all things considered. Have you read Brother Hegel, Molloy?"

"Not since—oh, around the Albigensian Heresy." He turns the phrase over in his mind, trying to remember who they were and the nature of their heresy.

"Yeah," Gabe says not unkindly. "You look more like a Schumpeterian kind of guy." Schumpeter, Judith thinks. Ron, what have you done? Molloy pauses, smiles, rubs his chin in that offbeat way he has. "Creative destruction. Could be."

Flocking Behavior

They stand in a brilliant setting sun, warmly dressed against the wind bite, while above them, immense numbers of water fowl arrive to settle in for the night. By the thousands birds float down from the rosy gold skies in remarkably orderly fashion, each somehow finding a spot on the lagoon, though the birds scold each other crossly as twilight encroaches, and the lagoon gets more crowded. Ron thinks of World War II newsreels, parachute invasions. Judith thinks of a public swimming pool in Japan. Molloy thinks about flocking behavior.

The birds are voyagers from the Canadian Arctic, wintertime guests gracing this all but treeless stretch of the New Mexican desert, this wide marshy spot in the Rio Grande, a place cold for humans, but suiting the sandhill cranes, the snow and Canada geese perfectly. In the hyperthermic summer the birds would perish within a day, but of course by summer they're long gone back to the Arctic.

As the cold and darkness creep up, the avian scolding swells. Judith wants to get back in the four-wheel-drive and continue along the observation loop in warm comfort.

But in a few minutes, Gabe stops the car, reaches for binoculars. "Whoa, do I see an eagle on that snag, pal?"

In mock exasperation Ron turns to Judith and Molloy in the back seat. "He suffers from *folies de grandeur*. Lovable, but exhausting." From behind his own binoculars, "No, Gabes, that is no eagle, man. A pretty big hawk, I grant you, but no eagle."

Good-natured argument, consultations with the field guide. Judith sides with Ron that it's only a hawk after all. Molloy says, "I've only seen pictures."

"On greenbacks?" Gabe asks. The question is light but Molloy doesn't reply.

"You aren't a birder, Molloy?"

Bird watching, Molloy has thought, is something earnest vegetarians in sensible shoes do in the late afternoon of their lives. He's surprised to find himself here at all. "No. Not a birder. I'm here because Judith promised me complexity in action."

Ron nods. "Flocking behavior. Swarm systems. Yeah, you'll see that sure enough."

Wild turkeys waddle to the car for handouts, bold as any Yellowstone bear, while ringtail pheasants, grouse and crows stroll the dirt roadways like *flaneurs*. Flocks of sandhill cranes, elegant as garden ornaments, step daintily through the marsh water.

"Brought back from the brink," Judith observes. "Less than twenty alive at the time of Pearl Harbor. Now tens, hundreds of thousands at this refuge alone."

"From under twenty? Isn't that kind of a monoculture, genetically speaking?" Gabe's movie-star looks are going into soft-focus, but you can still see the surfer he'd been.

Monoculture. Judith notes that. Gabe's received a real education from the University of Ron these fifteen years. Or maybe he knows this stuff from serious gardening.

"Didn't somebody try to imprint whoopers with an ultralight plane and lead them down here?"

Judith makes a face. Bad science perturbs her. "A failed experiment, I'd say. Not that you can't learn from failure. My most indelible—my most poignant—learning experiences are usually failures." Molloy watches her, awaiting a revelation. "So much work to get a handful of whoopers and their sandhill pals imprinted with the plane as leader, parent. Then a whooper got tangled up in the plane somewhere over Colorado. Right after they arrived, a coyote and a bobcat got another two. A couple of adults and an immature are supposed to be hanging in, but frankly, it worked better for the geese."

"Life is so fragile."

She contradicts Molloy silently: no, life is surprisingly robust. Don't be fooled by the special cases. Thinks of Jonathan in the nursing home; the phone call she'll make to Sophie before dinner. Special cases each of them. Random events, Sophie calls them. "Of course it's my random event, which makes it more interesting," Sophie had said. "To me, I mean."

They move slowly, giving way to other birders, stopping at choice viewing spots. Judith glances at Molloy discreetly, wondering if such slow pleasures are to his taste. Her impulse to invite him, but he must've known what he was getting himself into.

Gabe waves his well-toned arm, encompassing the horizon. "It looked better before the fire."

"It looked better before people and their livestock got here," Ron adds. "Albuquerque as grassy savanna with oak trees, not the desert it is now. Some claim the town wasn't named after the Duke of Alburqurque at all, but from *alba*, white, and *quercus*, oak."

No, noun then adjective, Molloy thinks; says nothing. They're in the habit, he sees, of giving each other these little gifts, odds and ends of facts. Entertainment for them. He tries to imagine the desolate landscape they've just driven through as former savanna, blessed with oak trees. He himself seldom leaves Santa Fe unless it's to go north, where he can count on seeing green. East to the Pecos Canyon. "Will we get to see the cranes dance?"

Judith seems puzzled. "Do cranes dance? Ronnie?" Ron shrugs.

Molloy smiles slightly, offers his own small gift. "Theseus knows the secret of the Labyrinth is encoded in the dance of the cranes."

"Theseus," Ron says thoughtfully. "Theseus."

Gabe lifts his binoculars. "Is this one of those whoopers?"

"Bird brain," Ron says affectionately. "That's a great blue heron and ain't it a beaut?" A noble bird of lush, bluish-gray plumage stands splendidly isolated and aloof in a pond, moving its head slowly on its long S-shaped neck, waiting for a snack to come swimming by, waiting for a mate, or just waiting for the fulfillment of its heron days. The sun has fallen now behind the Las Gallinas range (Judith notes that name, will bring it up at dinner) imparting a fine and fiery glow to the sky, which sets off the bird dramatically.

Molloy breaks the long silence. "About complexity."

Judith nods. The man's goal-driven, say that for him. "Let's get along to the north end." They go north to vast flooded fields, where birds large and small arrive in groups of a dozen or more. "You see the formations? So far as we know, they aren't communicating in any depth. Danger ahead, food here, look out for the kids, but not much more. They act from a small set of wired-in instructions. First: *Keep a minimum distance from the neighbors, or from anything else*. Second. *Copy what the neighbors are doing*. If the guy next to me is turning right, then I'll turn right too. If he's settling down for the night, I'll settle down for the night too—probably over-determined by another wired-in instruction for a bird that says if the light begins to fade, start settling down for the night. Finally, *Keep trying to move toward the center of the flock*.

"But what if the guy on one side of me is settling down, but the guy ahead of me isn't? Then I have to choose, and I do it randomly. Meanwhile, my neighbors are watching me, keeping their distance, trying to move to the center." She was acting all this out, turning her head, flapping her arms, furtively shuffling sideways. "Three simple rules. Yet rich and complex behavior arises. Look at that, just beautiful. Easy, fluid adaptation to the unexpected. Flocking behavior." She catches Molloy's amused smile. You asked.

They train on great flocks of birds wheeling in elegant spirals overhead, some dropping to the water, others moving on mysteriously to further ponds and lagoons, still others hesitating, circling, then descending slowly. Now the snow and Canada geese arrive by the hundreds, jabbering petulantly at each other, while the sandhill cranes come down delicately in threes and fives, sometimes a group of a dozen.

"Such elaborate patterns—they delude us that some kind of central intelligence is present. Not so," Judith says quietly. "A-life. Anthills. Robots—fast, cheap and out of control. Human cultures, civilizations. Same thing. You'll see more in the morning when we watch the fly-off."

"No one's in charge. But it happens anyway." Molloy thinks of markets, electronic blips passing at the speed of light across borders, time zones, beyond understanding. The birds are like traders, watching each other warily, doing whatever their neighbors do, rising and falling in some intricate dance.

"A little more complicated than that. Not much. That's life."

"What's life?" He's buried the dead, grieved, is still alive. He examines her face, seeking something. Her merry blue eyes seem direct, and yet. Then he has it. A slight but perpetual sideways tilt to her head, the oblique gaze of the born skeptic.

"What—is—life? A property of carbon we used to say when I was just starting out. Then we'd say, oh life. A verb not a noun, a computation, a concentration of order, the inevitable consequence of self-organization, an emergent phenomenon—" She waves it all away. "Now we know we don't know."

He tries something simpler. "Where do the geese go when they take off?"

Gabe can't resist. "On wild goose chases, of course."

Molloy smiles; he's asked for that. The original wild goose chase, Zeus in horny pursuit of Nemesis.

Judith gazes out over the lagoon, the settling birds. "We're still groping. Life. Hell's bells, we don't even know what water is."

"H-two-O." Ron says, puzzled.

"Steam, okay. The molecules are loosely coupled. But liquid or ice, tightly coupled molecules, it's a mystery. We can't calculate from first principles—quantum physics—the freezing or boiling points of water. Someone will get the Swedish prize for that one of these days. So if we don't know what water is, it keeps me humble about trying to tell you what life is, Molloy. Is a virus living or not? Who knows? Who cares? We talk instead about varied aspects of molecular biology. The boundary between living and non-living seems meaningless."

"The boundary between living and non-living is not meaningless," Molloy says decisively. "Not to me."

Swarm Systems

They have dinner that night at a Socorro steakhouse sealed in the 1950s, red flocked wallpaper, men only at the tables, ill at ease eating in public, their feet wound awkwardly around chair spanners, table legs, napkins falling out of their laps or tucked dorkily into their shirt fronts.

"Did you reach the Aya Sofia?" Judith knows Ron asks for her sake, not Sophie's, and is touched.

"Her machine. She could be sleeping." Or didn't feel like answering when the world was too much. Judith takes in their fellow diners. Engineers and other assorted geeks from the Very Large Array, or maybe the northern part of White Sands. New Mexico Tech. All exiled to where women won't live. "Cherish me, guys, I'm a rare bird here."

Molloy says, "A veritable whooper."

Judith challenges Ron. "Whooper."

Ron holds up an index finger. "Silent W, derived from the Middle English, *houpen*, to call, to shout; the French *houper*, to shout, probably originally Teutonic, *hup*, up, related to hubbub, maybe even hubcap."

"*Hupe*, German for car horn." From Molloy. Judith looks at him with new interest.

Gabe marks scores on the paper tablecloth. "Extra credit?"

"I believe everything but the hubcap part," Judith says.

A game now begins that they leave Molloy to figure out for himself, though he sees his *Hupe* has somehow earned him a tally mark. Conversation resumes, but then a word is suddenly emphasized. (Ron lifts his wineglass. "My companions." "With whom you break bread," Judith says quickly.) The idea, Molloy sees, is to supply an etymology. Not necessarily authentic, only plausible. Challenged and found to be fiction, you forfeit points. Extra credit means citing the word in a line of poetry or bringing in foreign language cognates. Anybody can play, but it's clearly Ron's and Judith's game. Ostensibly a competition. for Gabe keeps score, the real game is to produce etymologies of such cleverness that in some sense everybody wins, everybody has a prize. Molloy will remember that night vividly, especially the laughter. Laughter, and *poppycock*, which through elaborate definition is agreed to derive from very ancient tongues, and means baby shit.

Next morning at four, dark except for occasional other birdwatchers whose headlights pass by looking for a viewing place, they park again at the shore of a wide lagoon, sip coffee from a thermos, await the dawn. As the mists lighten, moving shadows transform themselves into tens of thousands of geese and cranes, nudging and observing each other, a few following each other in awkward goose step for a yard or two through the shallows, all preparing for the day's work of foraging.

Yet they seem hesitant to leave the pond this dawn. As the sky slowly turns from pearl to gold, the noise rises, the birds mill restlessly. Occasionally a few snow geese struggle out of the water, flapping inked wingtips. But without followers, they fall back again.

"Lacking critical mass—" Ron begins, interrupts himself. "Who eventually does lead? Do the alphas carry more weight than any old guy who tries to struggle up and out?"

"Good question," Judith says. "I'll ask Murray." To Molloy: "As it gets going, pay attention to the patterns. These little groups of three and four start up, aren't followed, go back to the water. First attempts to respond to a message that's whipping around: *Time to fly*. You almost see them saying, *Time to go? You going? I'm going. Well, if you're going—nah, nobody else is, forget it*. But the idea's still pinging round the bird network, time to fly. Another group tries, this time the feedback is positive; more groups start up.

"It's the Institute all over, only with us, it's ideas. Those guys—" she points to a couple of snow geese, honking at each other and struggling off the lagoon's surface, "they're Stu Kauffman and Brian Arthur. *You think this? Yeah—could you go along with it, follow it? No.* Everybody settles down again. That's Chris Langton over there, trying out another idea. *How about this one? Yeah, you go! And I'll help because I know what you don't.* That lone bird over there—that's Murray. He almost knows enough to do it all himself. But hey, he needs colleagues, pals, collaborators too. Something emerges from a collective effort that's beyond, transcends any individual's capabilities. You could argue a brain works like that too."

"Like we're standing here inside a big brain getting ready to fire up," Gabe says.

"Possibly. You're half asleep; ideas are floating around, struggling for recognition. Forget that one, absolutely nuts. Your internal editor beats it down and it disappears. Another idea comes along, same process. All this maybe half a dozen times. Then comes another, and the internal editor says, yo, can't think of a reason to be against that one. So it takes hold, is taken up, claimed, by one, two, then a bunch of neural sites, and pretty soon everybody joins in. We're watching a system move between phase states. Fly or float? Solid or fluid? Dinner at El Farol or stay home? That's what these little two- or three-agent fly-ups are, attempts to push the system from one state to another. Compelling in its own right, but applications are very useful—telephone network routing, robot control, financial data analysis."

Ron yawns. "In my review, I'll have to say the second act could use a little tightening."

"Be patient," Judith says. "It'll be worth waiting for."

"Cold?" She nods. Molloy encloses her from behind in his arms, sheepskin-clad and cozy. They sway slightly, keeping the circulation going. She's sharply aware of the oddity of this stranger's embrace: warming, yes, and also slightly perilous. He bends down to her ear, his unshaved face scraping her gently; she can smell the coffee on his breath. "We should—" But he doesn't finish.

"Is this disappointing you?"

"No, not really."

"No-not-really is code for damn right."

"No, I mean it," he murmurs behind her, thinking she doesn't yet know him well enough to understand that he always means what he says. Or shuts up. A grace he gives himself these days. "Never done anything like this. It's nice to be doing it first time, maybe last, with you." He knows at once he's misspoken, the schoolboy awkwardness has caught her off-guard, irritated her. She moves out of his arms and away reproachfully. But all this is lost in a surge of noise from the lagoon. A phase transition begins.

First dozens, then hundreds, thousands, tens of thousands of snow geese, Canada geese, and sandhill cranes take to the air, a blizzard in contravention of gravity, lifting in majestic homage to the sunrise. Wings flutter like bunting, a familiar snap and strut, yet amplified a thousand times and so distorted into something else, God's own sail luffing, prayer wheels set by all the pious in the world at once, a lodi implected with unearthly cries of grief—and they're gone. A few feathers drift down to the lagoon elegiacally.

Gabe claps. "Fucking gorgeous! Wow! Where you gonna see something like that on your workstation, hey?"

Molloy nods agreeably. "I've seen flamingoes rise off Lake Nakuru in Kenya like that. The difference was that the birds were flame-colored, it was about four in the afternoon, and I'd just finished a nap. Plus the temp was about seventy-eight Farenheit."

Judith watches him. How much has he learned? Here they are, the sciences of the complex, all laid out for him in this strange landscape, if he sees it. Do you? she queries silently. He glances at her across the reproachful distance, looks away.

"Let me get this straight," he says at last. "Why are the birds here?"

"The Bosque needed to be hospitable." Ron replies. "For years it wasn't. Salt cedars had sterilized the ground, destroyed everything the birds needed up and down the food chain. The Army Corps of Engineers had done a number on the wetlands."

The dark Molloy seems suddenly, momentarily alight. His arms are fixed tightly across his chest as if struggling not to stretch them out, address the dawn like some ancient shaman. Low-voiced, his words are still an invocation, a blessing. "But it's all coming back, the great web of the Rio Grande watershed, farmers working with miners, with government agencies, big birds working with little ones, fish and snakes and mosquitoes; each going about its business, yet acting collectively at their appropriate levels." He stops, as if made shy with pleasure. "What *emerges* at the next level is unpredictable. Puny individuals doing their thing, yet together—together achieving something grand. The whole is greater than the sum of its parts, and up till now, till what you people call complexity, there was no scientific way of expressing that, understanding it, exploring it. Now. Here it comes." He's fixed on the sky, not needing their assurance; self-confident in, pleased with, his understanding.

"We're getting there," the woman says softly.

⁂

Ron pulled her bag out of the four-wheel-drive. "What's happening here?" They'd already dropped Molloy off at the condo he was renting.

"Nothing. He's been getting a tutorial in complexity for the last few weeks, e-mail. I thought it might help to see a little complexity in action."

"All this weekend," Ron said carefully, "one could observe what's known in zoology as the copulatory gaze." Gabe rolled down the driver's window and leaned out. "Not even you, clueless one, could've missed the point that he's dying to jump your bones."

She shrugged. "More like my spider veins and my too, too sagging flesh. He's new in town, lonely. He'll find someone his own age to play with."

"That's okay with you?"

"That's okay with me. Look, a guy like that. The first time a little snuggly bunny comes along, I'm history. This woman is no man's history."

Gabe burst out laughing, but Ron said calmly, "Be careful. He's afraid of you. Don't, I'm right. Judith, Judith. Still the girl in Frau Klein's tenth-grade German class." Hands on both her shoulders, he searched her face. "On this planet of the apes for so long, and you don't understand that aura of yours. Are you really so oblivious? From the very beginning you've had it. Take responsibility. For a girl to be unselfconscious is delightful; for a woman, it's inexcusable. Be careful. People have odd ways of dealing with their fears. This is no guy to have as an enemy."

She considered it. "Not my enemy, not ever." She didn't know why she knew that. "Skiing a few weeks ago, I saw him take off down a double-black like a jackrabbit. Whatever that man is, afraid is not it."

"You're deliberately misunderstanding me, fair Judith. He's afraid of you. You."

"Molloy's afraid," Gabe added softly, "but damn, he's sad too. The saddest human being I've seen in years. Last night over dinner we're all laughing our asses off, he smiles, he even gets off a chuckle or two. But I never once saw him laugh, just let go and laugh."

"That's the difference between you and me, Gabes," Ron said. "You see sadness. I spent the weekend wondering who rammed the stick up his butt. I like you better than I like me."

Strange Attractors

Sophie lay stretched out on the daybed, a book on her lap. She'd lost so much weight that her clothes swamped her, though her face glowed luminously, perversely, inside the frame of her collar, a false sign of vitality. She'd gone through every bottle on the shelf, each one promising, each one finally letting her down. At least she had the dignity of her own hair back, a nimbus of dandelion fluff for the first time in months.

Judith stood over her. "Have you been able to eat anything at all?"

Sophie shook her head. The cancer had caused another abdominal blockage, and along with being hungry, she endured a pain that called for morphine, though so far she resisted.

In Sophie's ordinary, healthy years, their friendship had been built like a coral reef, a cell at a time, events and laughter, a few tears, cultivated slowly into something that did not ask to be examined. They were both private women, not given to genuine revelation except in self-deprecating anecdotes suitably embellished to amuse each other, stories that signaled pain or pleasure only to the informed listener. Which they were for each other, in delicate and tactful ways. They understood each other's professional struggles, the endless task of discovery, innovation, persuasion; and parallel to those, the personal struggles, what being a woman in science meant in the twentieth century, nothing simple. Above all, they could read each other's silences.

But when Sophie's diagnosis came, and would not go away; when the markers resisted dropping; when their hearts had lifted at the idea of a bone marrow transplant, then been shattered; when hope was reduced to staying alive from month to month, and finally, to no more than achieving comfort, then they'd begun to teach each other to express the inexpressible.

Once a shy, almost inarticulate woman, who found delivering a professional talk a kind of torment, Sophie now phrased what had once seemed unsayable, arabesques of excess, a humor she'd always had, now magnified. She seized upon the essentials (what else was left to her?) and insisted on the same from her friends.

"I don't ask why me," she said to Judith once. "After all, why not me? We all owe a death to the universe. What's absent is meaning. A random event isn't a meaning. The joy of my life, the central organizing principle, has been finding patterns where other people missed them." But impending death, whether random event or final element, forced her to look for new patterns, for what had been overlooked as she was forced into a retrospective, explaining her life to an audience of one, herself.

Examining, explaining, sometimes provoked a rage. "What I don't get," she said to Judith another time, "is the ovaries. Damn, damn, damn. Never any use to me. I had horrendous cramps when I started my periods, the Midol queen. I never wanted children. So what use—? Or maybe use 'em or lose 'em? I've watched you with men, Jay. You absolutely light up, textbook bio-iridescence. You are truly a man's woman. Oh, no *particular* man's, but you glow in their presence. Your ovaries send men some chemical message that tells them they'll love every minute of it, and whaddya know, they do. They take that glow, that chemical message, as tribute to their own personal, ineffable masculine charm. They can't wait to get you into bed, and they're jubilant when they succeed. They don't detumesce in your presence. They stick around the next morning, want to fix you breakfast and go back to bed and play some more. They keep calling up, leaving pathetic messages on the answering machine; send candy, flowers and slender books of poetry; ready to desert the mothers of their children and the mates of a lifetime, just say the word; they entertain hopeful, detailed fantasies about you in hotel rooms, in traffic jams, under the blankets in first class. They bring up your home page with your picture and do unspeakable things in front of your key theorems. No man has ever stood you up, has he? Of course not. You're the biochemical dominatrix, and they'd gladly die for the privilege of being whipped around by your pheromones. You've had more proposals of marriage than I've had orgasms."

Judith interrupted the tirade with laughter. "Maybe it sometimes seemed like that to you, my Aya Sofia, but—"

"Not seemed. Was. Still is. Men *want* you. Ordinary women your age have already gone into retirement, become sexually neutral senior citizens, ankles *this* thick with edema, hair in finger waves from the specialist in geriatric hairdos, but you! Men still follow you around with their tongues lolling out. Sheesh, even Ron, who has no sexual interest in you whatsoever—I assume—gets all avuncular, looking out for you, *just in case, what if, don't mention I was checking up on her*."

"Ron checks up on me? With you?"

Sophie's face registered utter disgust. "Oh, yes. No secrets on a deathbed, girlfriend. Ron's appointed himself *in loco parentis* for you. Any other woman, I'd throw up. I might throw up anyway. Women like you need ovaries. Women like me do not. Yet I have them, and they turned on me. Self-sabotage. My sexual organs have always been a burden."

"Body chemistry. A hypothetical question, Soph. You're getting ready for a party and the urge suddenly comes on. You could just take care of yourself, but what chemical message does self-help send to potential partners later? Don't get up; it's all taken care of? Or, here's a lady who just enjoyed it and would like it again? Big difference. What's the best strategy, pheromone-wise?"

"Do you want to get laid, or just want relief?"

"Depends on who's at the party."

"I'd have to research it. Your experience is?"

"Inconclusive, Soph. Tried it every which way."

"How often do you—?"

"Per week? Per day? Per hour?"

"I don't believe you."

"You probably shouldn't."

Sophie laughed as she was meant to, then groaned. "This one has the ring of truth." So Sophie's rage passed, and she seemed reconciled to how she had lived her life, what she had missed, had chosen to miss, and now would never have.

Judith began picking up sickroom items, old magazines, empty water glasses. "How was the day?"

Sophie smiled wickedly. "I watched cooking shows. No, really. I take a prurient interest. You can watch them all afternoon. Bread—bread being kneaded makes me faint with desire. I cream over chopped onions sauteeing in a skillet. Whip egg whites in front of me and my mouth goes slack, St. Teresa in ecstasy. Garlic swells my loins; grill a sirloin and my pelvis aches. Bacon makes me rapturous; I'm ravished by mousses. Mashed potatoes. I'd betray my nation for mashed potatoes in my mouth, so soft, melting, yet so firm, so commanding, in their integrity. Even you would blush to see me respond to stuffed zucchinis. A chicken leg and I'm a slut. Pan-fry it gently, sensuously, its juices oozing: oh, stop me before I plunge again! I'm the Mary Magdalene of lamb chops, the great red harlot of tofu, the whore of Babylon for split pea soup. And corn on the cob—my teeth, my tongue, my fingers, my God! Chard raped me this afternoon, but oh, chard knew I was asking for it and I confess, I wept at its feet afterwards in gratitude. I surrendered utterly, again and again, to vegetable soup. Freshly peeled shrimp tossed carelessly into a hot wok—oh God! *Yes!* Red lettuce! You make me forget my God! Cheese, cheese, so soft, so runny, so fragrant—so late in my life, and I finally understand multiple orgasms. At the end, at the very end, a macaroon must have its way with me, but by then it meant nothing: I was spent, done in, the sheets had to be changed. Tell me about work." Sophie closed her eyes.

After that?

Sophie opened her eyes. "I care because it's important to you, sweetie." Because it's a drag being regarded only as sick.

"Work's fine. Caltech wants a talk. I'll do it in winter when I need some warmth, add on UCLA or Santa Barbara. Said yes to a keynote on the island of Rhodes next spring. The perks are always nice." Judith did not say that an article had been blocked; the referee's report clearly the work of Feydor, or one of his associates. Why drag him here?

Sophie smiled her congratulations. Her hands, always so slender and finely shaped, now lay on her blanket like mummified claws. Yet for the first time in her life, her face was radiantly beautiful, newly glorious, having shed years and worries and everything else inconsequential. Why hadn't she looked like that in the healthy part of her life? The act of dying as beauty treatment seemed beyond irony. But Sophie's small luminous face suddenly contracted in pain, and Judith leaned over her. "Tell me what I can do, Soph."

"Talk. Tell me a story. The strangest sex you ever had. Aha, you laughed."

"The strangest place? Or the strangest guy?"

"Don't dodge."

"It's—it's not a story for laughing, Soph."

"Tell, tell. I told you I'd die with your secrets."

Judith began reluctantly. "Summer in New York, hot as hell. Fifth Avenue, near the University Club. I saw this enormous crowd. Turned out they were gathered around a guy making chalk drawings on the sidewalk. A good copyist—doing a repro of 'The Naked Maja'. He was in one of these brief little swimsuits European men love, not much more than a thong. An absolutely beautiful young body. You just admired it from head to toe. Absolutely beautiful except—except he had no arms. He was drawing with his toes. The arms were—thalidomide arms, those little flippers. Heartbreaking. But he was wonderfully agile, moved around in a little half-crouch, legs extending, retracting, just like arms. Only they weren't." She stopped, wishing she hadn't begun, torn between the imperative to speak honestly, the hopelessness of conveying what had really happened. She wasn't sure she knew herself.

"*Way* weird," Sophie said. "I can guess the rest."

"No, Soph. No, you can't. Hear me out. He had to be German. They'd had the worst problems with thalidomide babies in the sixties. So I said something to him *auf Deutsch*, and he answered back, a real wisecrack, I don't remember what. After a while I took him for an iced tea, which he managed very unselfconsciously with a straw. We talked about painting. The repros were for the tourists; he actually did his own stuff, had a gallery that represented him in Berlin. This was a *Wanderjahr* for him. He was in some fleabag on West 43rd Street, so I told him I had a spare room and he came home with me. Don't smirk, Soph. I was almost old enough to be his mom; all admiration was well within bounds. But once at home. No, no details on this one. No details. Just that—just that it

wasn't the usual one-night stand. For one thing, it was more like a week."

"With his toes?"

Judith looked away. "Yeah, sure, with his toes. With his well-endowed manly parts. But most of all his voice. The voice of a mystic." She stopped. "He made me understand how people drop everything and follow one of these guys to the ends of the earth. He'd talk about the hands he didn't have, what they were doing—'my ghost hands' he called them. The word for ghost and spirit is the same in German, my spirit hands. I could feel them, I swear it. Just like real hands on my body. I was probably in a state of mild hypnosis. Not so mild. I cried when it was time for him to go."

"You make it sound serious." Sophie still wanted this to end as something to laugh about, was disappointed.

"He turned the most ordinary, most spiritually numbing Episcopalian childhood upside down. He showed me—Soph, this is hard. Showed me, trained as a scientist, skepticism my middle name, that I was capable of a spiritual experience. In the Hindu tradition, the *Gitagovinda*, even some of the *Mahabharata*, it's the act of love—that ecstasy—that's the closest we humans can get to an encounter with the divine." She shrugged. "So then I came here."

"Why?"

"Looking for—an encounter with the divine." She said it with a deprecating smile, then lifted Sophie's shoulders gently in one arm, with the other, fluffed the pillows. Sophie had become appallingly light. "Let's talk about something else. How I misspent my life?"

"Yes. Good. What would you have done differently?"

"Ignored my fears. Got over my timidity. Taken more chances."

"You! You were never afraid, never timid. You fucked freaks for fun."

"No freak, Soph. With him I thought . . . so this is what people call magic. Enchantment. A spell. Always wondered what happened to him. What if. Not my path. But I've always wondered. Has anything like that—not the sex, a spiritual kind of thing—ever come your way?"

"No." Sophie's face again contracted; she clutched the bedcovers, breathed uneasily. "I've got all I can fucking well deal with on this plane, never mind any other."

Life on the Edge of Chaos

Molloy chooses an expensive restaurant, one that will go out of business a few weeks later, felled in the long dry stretch between Christmas and the summer tourist season, Santa Fe's contemporary *jornada de muerto*. He doesn't drink, but Judith does, a medicinal glass of wine. And then another.

"You have strong opinions on art." He has too, ever since, on that graduation trip gift to himself, hair to the middle of his back, flared jeans; he'd stood awestruck in European museums, seeing art for the first time. (And also fleabags. Literally. When he protested the red welts on his torso to his landlady, the night marauding of the bedbugs, she replied with Parisian suavity, Parisian cheek: "M'sieu, one must avoid the second class carriages on the Metro.")

Awestruck, and completely ignorant. It hadn't even occurred to him to get a guide, human or written, to tell him what to do, see, think; leaving him to wander through dusty galleries, squandering precious hours trapped with old coins—old coins!—when he really wanted to see pictures. But this way he saw for himself that the early Renaissance painters had painted with feathers—in their hearts if not in their hands. It moved him to inexpressible joy. That summer he learned to have complete confidence in his eye.

The woman across from him smiles. "I have strong opinions about most things."

"Geometrical metal sculpture, she said, this century's version of national hero on horseback. Most damningly, *Hofkunst.*"

"Did you hear me say that? It means—"

"I know."

"Hope you don't own a garden full. You can take the girl out of New York. Dumb concept, dumb art. That's how I feel about most geometrical sculpture."

"That's how I feel about most art. It's mostly dumb ideas. But the art that embodies a great idea—that I cherish."

"Necessary but not sufficient, as they say in my game." She tucks eagerly into her dinner. "I hear you collect."

He's noncommittal. "You'll have to see what I've got sometime when I've pulled it out of storage." He pushes his food around, aware he's hungry for something else. Observes her, wondering what simple rules have led to this complex woman, what give-and-take has shaped her. "Learning about swarm behavior at four thirty in the morning makes an indelible impression. I like your friends. They're easy to be with. They seem to have a lot figured out."

"Ron and I go way back."

"To the Albigensian heresy."

"Forgive us." She's smiling.

"No problem, I looked it up."

"Then you got his little joke. Maybe not. Ron and I found each other because we were both living double, multiple, lives without knowing it. But we could see it in each other."

"He was gay when gay was a hanging offense. You?"

"You like little jokes yourself, Molloy."

Though he probes again, she says nothing more about whatever multiple lives she once led. Leads. A patient man, he can wait, appreciates some fakes all the more for their fakery. He asks instead about her work, assumes a practiced expression, curious, slightly doubtful, a face for countless presentations by eager entrepreneurs. As a rule it masks—well, not this, whatever it is.

Like a mature person, she begins, a mature science eventually begins to seek and appreciate its own boundaries. Not the end of science, in the catchphrase, but a redefinition of what's worth pursuing. It's showing up in odd nooks and crannies, physics, mathematical logic, economics, computing.

All guardedness, all worldly sophistication, seem to fall away from her, releasing an enthusiasm so endearing, so—American. She grows radiant, expansive; generously includes him in. Here's where she lives, heart and soul. He suppresses a smile, the impulse to touch that luminous intensity, to reveal his enchantment; forces himself to attend to her words. Since the universe began, she's saying, some light might be so distant it hasn't yet had time to reach us. The universe might well be infinite, but if we can't see it, we'll never know. A limit. We're locked, moreover, inside our own universe; if other universes exist, they're forbidden to us. Yet another limit.

Then there's the old philosophical problem, which is to distinguish between knowledge of the world and knowledge of our mental models of the world. "Less the limits of science than the limits of scientists," she says playfully. "If a deep Theory of Everything in fact exists, it might be too deep for us to grasp. No reason to think the universe was constructed for our convenience. Our minds evolved for other purposes. Aren't you going to have that? Can I taste?" She's already reaching to his plate, approves, digs back into her own dinner cheerfully. "Stop me if this is too much. God, Molloy, are you one of these tiresome guys with no weaknesses? Nothing to excess? Except tone your abs?"

"I control my abs as a favor to my shirt maker. No, it's not too much, not so far." He evades the question of weaknesses. "I do want to say that I like a woman who enjoys her food."

"Was I wolfing? Talking with my mouth full? Using the wrong fork? Fusing with my food instead of eating it, as Stu Kauffman would say? This is awfully good."

He shakes his head, feeling benign, provident, afloat on a warm lagoon of well-being and good will. "No. You were enjoying it. Good for you. Fusing?"

"We didn't cover that in Complexity one-oh-one? *Why do we eat our food instead of fusing with it?* I know, I know; it sounds like one of Stu's corny jokes—anyway, why?" Eyes bright, fork at her mouth, she bites the meat delicately with even white teeth that exhibit, he thinks, all signs of professional alignment, thus a responsible and loving middle-class family. What was she like as a child, a proto-scientist? Did she collect bugs and butterflies? Did an amiable dad guide her first mathematics? She radiates glorious warmth; a woman who's learned very early to trust the universe, and therefore feels entitled to understand it. He envies that warmth and trust; he admires her glow, her

American enthusiasm. He yearns to—fuse with it.

"If we fused?" Her face is again transformed; not the impertinent teasing of other times, but something new, a broad smile, generous with promise. An invitation to respond. "If we fused?"

He's suddenly at a table in Germany, a clever but badly educated young man vaulted by his cleverness into exclusive company, and smart enough to keep his mouth shut, absorb with those onyx eyes everyone's smallest gesture. From assorted hereditary German princelings, barons, counts, eldest sons, Junkers, the odd archduke or two, and other members of the aristocracy, he's learned table manners. More or less lost his first name. Learned further useful things: to walk on the left of his seniors; the power of kidney punches, crotch kicks, cleats raked down a bare thigh on the soccer field. And elsewhere. It had buffed his German too.

Not a muscle's stirred, yet his entire body has somehow shifted straight into the cardio training zone, pulse up, nerves taut, verging on breathless. In a moment he's going to need mouth-to-mouth, life support, God knows what. He can barely speak. "If we fused?"

"If we fused . . . we'd explode."

He drops his eyes to the table. It's the strongest erotic jolt he's felt in years, and he's not too old to flush.

She's laughing. "We do not *fuse with*, but *eat* our food, because the biosphere is supracritical. Our cells, on the other hand, are just subcritical."

He struggles to control, to bring reason to bear, on what batters him, relief, desire, joy, gratitude, fear, a contradictory torrent his skin can scarcely contain. "I'm—I'm lost."

"If we fused with our dinner, the molecular diversity this fusion would create within our cells would unleash a supracritical explosion. Va-voom! Lethal! Simple?"

All intellectual content in the fusion/eating problem has gone right past him. Never mind. He exhales. "Go on."

Indifferent to his wretched confusion, his internal typhoon, the woman glides serenely on. "Knowledge used to be power. But as we increase the scale of our activities, we simply must address the limited scope of our understanding, now and possibly forever."

The limited scope of our understanding. He's steadying, regaining equilibrium.

"So we ask questions. Is nature consistent—that is, without true paradox? Is nature complete—is there a cause for every effect? Or, suppose the visible universe, which at present astronomers are confined to studying, doesn't contain enough information to characterize the laws of physics completely?"

As she orders the second glass of wine, she adds: "Or, as Murray once asked a colleague: If you know the wave function of the universe, how come you ain't rich? Well now. You're almost getting off a laugh there, Molloy. Is that because you're rich but don't know the wave function of the universe?"

"You abuse me, dear lady." But it's a smile, almost a grin. He's pleasantly addled, fatigued, and at the same time clearer and lighter than he's felt in years. The beginning of a thaw makes the universe, this or any other, take on new meanings.

"You shouldn't have let me do this second glass."

As he lets her into the Gaelaendewagen, he follows her eyes to a book on the back seat. "Airplane reading." He's grateful the streets are dark, relatively deserted. Though he hasn't had a drop, he might not pass a sobriety test. Beside him she speaks. "*Did* the Irish save civilization?"

"So it seems. Books when nobody else valued books."

"Or was it all inevitable, with or without them? Put it another way. What difference did the Irish make three hundred years after all this book-saving?"

He feels capable of a modest calculation at least. "Let's see, in the century after St. Patrick's death, roughly between the sack of Rome and—the Irish monks have reintroduced the traditions of Christian literacy to the Continent—"

"Okay. Six hundred years later? A thousand years later? Suppose it turns out that the Irish didn't save civilization but actually impeded it? Just what did they save and transmit?"

"It was just airplane reading," he protests mildly. "Coming back from Davos." But her playfulness is contagious, and pleases him immensely. A woman to dance with.

"We got all that bad science from Aristotle," she says. "The mathematics would've been discovered by someone else soon. We got—uhm, the dubious notion of original sin. St. Augustine, right? And the murky notion of the Trinity. Hey, maybe transmitting *The Iliad* and *The Odyssey* kept Herman the Hun from writing the great epic poem that would have defined European civilization differently."

"Herman the Hun had a great poem to write, nothing to stop him."

"Wrong, Molloy, dead wrong. Change is inevitable, but the nature of that change is not. The Greco-Roman gods were depleted; the new Judeo-Christian god wasn't yet ready for prime time. The German tribes had vigorous gods, but probably too many of them, so they split the vote a dozen ways. That, and they lacked one crucial piece of technology."

"The wheel?"

"No, they had the wheel. Try again."

He's grinning, enjoying himself too, something budding that he hardly dares notice lest it capriciously disappear, though once he'd taken it arrogantly for granted. "Horses? They must've had horses. Metal-working? I know they had that."

"A written language, that's what they lacked. Everything we know about the Celts, a.k.a. the Gauls, or their cousins the Germanic tribes, is indirect. Herman the Hun, Gerhard the German, Trog the Teutone, could all have written wonderful poems, changed Western intellectual history maybe, but once the means of transmission breaks down—" She interrupts herself. "Pity the Irish didn't transmit enough of their own indigenous culture—sexually frank, relatively egalitarian. The private confession—personal conscience takes precedence over public opinion or church authority. Too bad we didn't also get Irish attitudes toward diversity, authority, the role of women, and the relative triviality of sexual mores. Excuse me, Molloy, are you Irish? Am I offending you? Yet again?"

He's shaking his head, still smiling, as he pulls the car up near her garden wall. "Trog the Teutone arrived late, but he did arrive. His name was actually Richard Wagner."

She seems to find this droll, and he grins, faces her directly, happily, ready to start along the path she's clearly implied. He lets himself sup on her, beginning at the perimeters, working inward. Picks up her hand. "I'll come in."

Her smile contracts slightly. "It was only a couple of glasses of wine, Molloy. I don't fool around on the first date."

"Hardly a first date. That was me, remember, up with you at four-thirty fucking a.m., as your friend Gabe would say, getting instructions in swarm behavior and freezing my ass off. We've had lunch together too, if I'm not mistaken. Plus, I do believe I just heard that sexual mores are relatively trivial."

She laughs slightly, which relieves him. Slightly. The terms seemed clear; the last thing he'd expected is a negotiation. "Caught. Hoist on my own hot air. Did you ever look up the real meaning of petard? Anyway, I'm an old woman and consecrated to my science."

"Oh, bullshit." He's been teased. Toyed with. Fury swamps him, certainly throttles desire. Freezes him. He tries one last time, but the words come out less than gently. "Does fusing frighten you, dear lady?"

"I've just given you a taste of how scientists work."

He drops her hand. Women and their fucking mixed signals. Is she so monumentally stupid? Scared? No, dear lady, Madame Genius, you don't begin to know what fear is. He's shaking as he touches her cheek, all joy and hope drained from him, uncertain his voice will hold. "This was meant to be recreational, this dinner."

"Scientists never stop working, Molloy. If you're going to connect with the Institute, you ought to know that. It's part of our charm. It *is* our recreation. Thanks for a good dinner. Skiing in Davos, were you?" A polite, inquiring, but dismissive, let's-change-this-silly-subject expression. On Lindy, he'd called it her Manhattanville College look.

Humiliation shrivels him, compacts him without mercy. Other things, too many to sort out, rage, pain, coursing over what's already a battered soul, but above all, humiliation, pressing him down. Is he so out of practice, has he so misunderstood? Across her lap he thrusts open the car door abruptly, his eyes fixed on something beyond the windshield. "No, I wasn't skiing. I was at a meeting. See you on-line."

He's got to her, goddammit, every instinct tells him so, and he's trusted his instincts always. Touched her somewhere deep. Why coyness? She assumes he's used to women yielding immediately and isn't going to be just any woman? Well, God. With immense effort, he masters himself, again grateful for the shadows.

The car door wide open, the cold sharp, pulling him back brutally from the tumultuous edge of chaos to deathly frozen order. She doesn't move. "It's not that you don't stir me, Molloy," she says at last. "I quite like you. But I hardly know you."

Fixed on concealing his rage, his pain, fixed on repairing his vulnerability, he stares at her contemptuously. He'll only remember later on to be grateful for feeling anything at all. Now he says, "That's true."

Predators and Prey

When Maya Sinclair, expressing a cheerful kind of mercy, invited Ernie Holliman, temporary bachelor and worried father, to a quiet dinner in the kitchen of the celebrated picturesque house, he understood that he was to be seduced. He went willingly. He'd waited for it, hoped for it, imagined it in lush if unconvincing detail.

Maya opened her door (to be found on postcards, in travel magazines) and they understood each other at once. She led him straight to her bedroom, overstuffed with the antique furniture that had been brought down the Santa Fe Trail a hundred and fifty years ago. He permitted her to pull him down onto the antique lace counterpane, where she tried to satisfy a longing that could not, in the end, ever be satisfied.

Which didn't stop either of them from trying. Besotted by his suddenly awakened, even raging, genitalia, he could no longer concentrate on his porcelain phrenology heads, and he fretted through the mornings until the afternoons, when he was allowed to visit, at first discreetly, and then indifferent to who might see him, his telltale car parked outside the wooden gates, included regretfully in the snapshots of tourists who would have preferred something of course more picturesque.

In those long afternoons, he buried himself in Maya hourly; he discovered new and different sensations, he permitted her liberties with his body he had never dreamed of with his wife; he took liberties with hers, stimulated by what was first her encouragement, then her goading, always her obvious, flamboyant pleasure. At some point he realized that she was slowly bringing him to feel the pleasures of pain. She introduced silk scarves, ties, clamps, buckles, rings, things that pierced, a sexual armamentarium he'd been ignorant of until now. This pushed him further, and he wondered how far they might possibly go before pain was only pain, and not the exquisitely nuanced pleasure it now seemed.

"I like changing you," Maya said to him once. "I get off on it."

"Changing me?"

"Everybody knows the intense, serious, reserved Ernie. I like to watch you scream your head off." She imitated his cries of pleasure perfectly.

All true, and it humiliated him to be mimicked.

He did not think of his son or his wife while he was with Maya, and when he returned home, spent, with a trepidation that might have been guilt or shame, but wasn't, to find messages from Houston on the answering machine, he felt harried by them, and wished he could ignore them. Instead, he dutifully called back, listened to Nola's grief, and lied. The child she worried over seemed a stranger's child, and he made the same awkward noises of condolence that strangers made. He pretended to rise with his son's triumphs and to be downcast by his setbacks; the numbers jumbled in his head—which ones meant life, which threatened, even condemned his son? He was keeping score in a barely understood game, a distant league.

A nasty virus. He didn't think there were drugs against viruses, but something was being administered nevertheless. The virus disappeared, and he feigned relief. Another child, who'd begun all this the same time as Pete, died. He heard Nola's sobs for a child he'd never laid eyes on, and feigned sadness. A relapse, and Pete's counts were too low to take interferon.

He called Maya after these conversations and asked to come back across town. She sometimes said yes.

If she refused, wouldn't even have phone sex, he lay in his own bed, the bed he shared with Nola, peculiarly chaste now with its white sheets, its handwoven spread, and wondered how she'd feel when she found out about Maya. How *would* she find out? Would he contract some horrible sexual disease, and be forced to confess that way? What if all of them, himself, Nola, Pete, died together of afflictions he refused to picture? Or would Maya leave anonymous messages? Take Nola aside at one of her famous dinner parties, and huskily confess, pretending in her theatrical way to be abject over the betrayal while Nola, selfless mom, was at her sick child's bedside? Make a scene in the gallery?

He imagined Maya recounting their afternoons to her friends, whoever they were (his own friends, his and Nola's); her raucous laugh, which he'd heard often enough the past few weeks, this time directed at him, his ineptitude, his insufficiencies, his failures. She'd mock his inexperience and maladroitness; mimic the sounds he made caught up in passion; describe, in shaming detail, the peculiar shape and meagerness of his parts. He groaned and cursed her; cursed himself for his foolishness; cursed her again for forbidding him to return, find blessed forgetfulness in her bed.

He'd tried to talk to her about his work, but she was quickly bored, and shut him up by fondling him into tumescence, so that the whole thing began again. Once, after a particularly difficult night of imagined diseases, he asked her if she was seeing anybody else.

"Why? You in the mood for threesies?"

He blushed, he faltered; this was not at all what he meant. But what exactly did she have in mind, another man or another woman? His own debauchery, effrontery, shocked him.

"I'm plenty for you," she said decisively, and he was relieved. She was. He forgot why he'd brought the topic up in the first place.

The phone messages were unrelenting. "Where *are* you, for God's sake?" Nola's voice not her own, transformed by frustration, by devastation. I didn't want this, he cried back to the answering machine, his voice echoing through the empty house: this is just what you could expect. Women your age produce faulty offspring. Don't say I didn't warn you.

At least, so he now remembered. He and Nola had been married for twelve years, cozily staring out from their life together like well-garrisoned royalty, a couple who made up their own language, himself the center of her concerns, always first call on her attention, there for him, and him alone. Then she told him that, amazingly, she was pregnant. But she was going through the change, he said: how could that be? That was just it; she was sure she'd no longer needed birth control.

"You won't have it?"

"I think we should." She took his hand and kissed its palm, laid it on her belly. "It's us." "I couldn't *not* have it," she said another time. "I'd never stop thinking about what our child would've been like." Ultimately, "Who'll get everything if not our child? Your awful cousins in Effingham?" Slowly she'd persuaded him to accept this flesh of their flesh, assuring him that the baby would be no hindrance to his work or hers, no hindrance to their life together; the embodiment of their extraordinary closeness. Modern medicine did the rest. From it's us to he's us. He's us and he's healthy. He's us and he's perfect.

The perfect baby was born, but not without tearing up his mother. She was not young, took a long time to heal, and was anyway up almost around the clock tending Pete in the first few months, too tired to do anything else. They hired help, but found the woman intrusive and were grateful when they no longer needed her. Yet something had changed. Ernie wondered if it was just a third person in their world—yes, their creation, but Pete's presence upset an intimate balance that, without thinking very hard about it, Ernie had taken for granted. Baby crises abated, life was relatively normal again, but things were not the same. The ecology had changed, his own niche had altered, and he found it almost impossible to adapt. It was Ernie's private opinion, expressed only once or twice under what he considered extreme provocation, that sex, for instance, was never the same between them again. Nola's pregnancy had flooded her with hormones: she craved him; she was almost like Maya in those few months. Then her craving stopped and did not resume.

Yet he loved Pete. He believed it; that he loved his son. The sweet-smelling skin, the big eyes, the happy little voice; enchanting them by doing all that babies do, doing them for the first time for his own father and mother. His own little boy, bowlegs poking out of a diaper, running flat-footed around the house, discovering everything anew. Love flooded his heart at last: his perfect son growing to perfect boyhood, poised at adolescence, soon young manhood.

A sick son was something else. Ernie was haunted by the idea that they two, old as they were, should not have brought this baby into the world, doomed him from the start with a slip of the genes, a faulty replication, as seed penetrated egg. When he put this to Pete's doctor, the man shook his head. "We don't know enough about the etiology to say any such thing. For what it's worth, the children of young parents contract leukemia too." But Ernie was convinced he'd soon open the paper to see somebody in Los Angeles or Boston had discovered the real cause, and it would be laid directly upon him.

If he hadn't expected to marry anyone like Nola, he'd nevertheless been unhappy with the few girlfriends he'd had before he met her. Every woman he'd been involved with had been unsatisfactory somehow—her teeth, her laugh, her ass, her smell, her focus on the particular when he yearned for the general, the abstract. These imperfections had irritated him beyond all reason. Yet he feared more being alone. He kept each relationship going far too long, preferring to despise a woman's flaws than have nothing at all. All said and done, women for him were no gratification but a source of constant, low-level soreness. Far from perfect himself, as he well knew, he must eventually settle for mediocrity, he must compromise, he called it in his mind. But he rebelled against it ferociously.

He was suffering through yet another affair with another disappointing woman when he saw Nola across a smoky party in Chicago's Hyde Park district. She was exquisite. He approached expecting to be rebuffed, and when she didn't rebuff him, he lied that he'd come alone, and went home with her. He learned that she winked for emphasis, not to flirt. He discovered later that he'd found her that night in a state of exhaustion, a father having just died, a romance having just ended, a protracted dissertation almost done. She was open to him in a way she wouldn't have been a month before, a month later, and he knew enough to be grateful for that. A chance moment had let them fall in love, which is how he—not perfect but a perfectionist—had ended up with a perfect woman.

They married, came to Santa Fe; Nola opened her gallery and Ernie settled down to independent study on his independent income, the result of his father's surgical appliance company being grabbed up during some pharmaceuticals thrash, purchased at almost double what it was worth, the proceeds split among his widowed mother in Phoenix, his sister, and him. Until Pete's diagnosis, he told himself, it had been a flawless life.

Spring 1997

Competition and Cooperation

The world of well-off Santa Fe Anglos is small, and as February pushed into March, making all Santa Fe long for real warmth, an end to the steady wind that blew down from the Sangres, scattering juniper pollen like poison so that it felt as if fire ants had crawled into eyes and nose, Judith inevitably ran into Molloy at gallery openings, parties, benefits. E-mail between them had never resumed: he'd apparently had his fill of complexity. Usually he nodded politely from across the room, sometimes he approached and made awkward small talk, introduced his companion, often women Judith already knew. Twice, but only twice, his companion was Maya, heiress and social entrepreneur. Judith saw the stress between them, Maya too clinging, laughing too easily, and trying too hard: there'd be no third time.

Judith knew she was not entitled to superiority about laughing too easily, trying too hard. She'd resisted trying at all. That their dinner had ended Molloy's calls and e-mail hadn't disturbed her at first, but as time passed, and she saw him with other women, her dismay surprised her. She congratulated herself. He was only a serial fucker after all, and she was glad she'd resisted being part of the series. Yet sometimes she was puzzled, slightly sad, that Molloy wanted something different from who she was. She saw she was not indifferent; a weakness that embarrassed her, so hid it perfectly until such time as the pose was reality.

All Molloy's companions ran to type. They were women of abundant independent means—trust fund stipendiaries, well-heeled widows and divorcees. But not professionals, not women in business. Not artists and writers who kept body and soul together by waitressing or clerking; not New Agers who lived spiritually in desert hideouts with bad plumbing and worse heating. He seemed to seek a combination of polish and pliancy possessed only by women who'd never had to earn their way; he craved a quality of attention that only someone with both money and time on her hands could give. No other gods before me.

It was Maya who informed Judith that Molloy had been married, that there were children back east. What had his wife—or wives—been like? Why hadn't she let the evening take its course? Since her divorce she'd had any number of lovers, though lately she'd grown fastidious, fewer lovers, not counting friendly nights in the nun's bed with Benito. Molloy was attractive and she was sorry her fastidiousness had offended him. But she wasn't sorry about being fastidious.

He was frequently at the offices of New Business, where she consulted once a week, and they waved to each other with the self-conscious friendliness of the undeclared estranged. Then she heard he'd become a principal. "That was quick," she said to Phillips, the CEO. "He's an unbelievable asset," Phillips said warmly. Phillips, whom Molloy would fire within a week.

As acting CEO, would Molloy exact a little revenge, cut off the consulting? She didn't need the money, but she liked dealing with applications to real problems. Business was more daring than academia, willing to try, fail, and move on to something else. To be cut off from New Business would be an intellectual loss. Not to mention a petty insult. To hell with him. All over town, consulting firms were springing up that would welcome her. Georges in Geneva e-mailed her twice a month pleading with her to talk to management teams in Europe.

A journal turned down one of her articles on the basis of a particularly stupid referee's report, and she e-mailed the editor:

> I'm pleased to inform you that the Greenwood and Gunther paper has promptly been accepted by another excellent journal and will receive early

publication as an important contribution to risk management. You should know this only because I believe that you were not well served by this particular referee. Thank you nevertheless for considering our paper.

It was an old game, sticking it to the referee while trying to maintain reasonably cordial relations with the editor for the next paper she might want to publish in his journal. She found herself composing a parallel message to Molloy when the time came that he fired her too.

But she continued to go into New Business on Wednesdays, problems awaited her, checks arrived. Good. If she didn't want to sleep with Molloy, she also didn't want to think the worst of him.

Benito was away at his dig most of the time now, e-mailed her on the progress:

To: jrg@santafe.edu
From: jimenez@sf.arch.edu
March 17, 1997 8:14 p.m.

First, thanks for the loan of the wireless. Only one line inside the ranch house and the kids tie it up. I am sitting comfortably outside my tent while I hear you got snow yesterday.

Found a kiva. Alley-the-Trowel-of-the-Southwest dug it up, a piece of work himself. Diana is down from Colorado and thinks we're on to something big. Me too. I think this is older than we first thought. I may be full of shit.

Would it make you jealous to know a lovely young graduate student has offered to share my sleeping bag? No.

God, I almost forgot. The people who own the land are underwriting the dig. The brother says how much will it cost, the check's in the mail. I was speechless. Money never comes without strings, but so far the strings are me tutoring him in archaeology. It's kind of fun to teach again after all these years. Are you having fun tutoring the tycoon? Has he offered to share your sleeping bag? Don't answer that.

To: jimenez@sf.arch.edu
From: jrg@santafe.edu
March 18, 1997, 4:37 p.m.

Mega-congrats on the new funding! May the strings not bind. Have you told your new student and benefactor about the Artificial Anasazi? That should knock his sox off.

Go with your intuition on the possibilities of the dig. Will it have impact; could it change the world? You've heard this sermon before.

The tycoon fwiw has lost interest in complexity.

I miss you. If you let the graduate student share your sleeping bag, remember to do safe sex. Me, I'm doing the safest there is.

To: jrg@santafe.edu
From: jimenez@sf.arch.edu
March 20, 1997, 6:23 p.m.

Sleeping so bad these nights even the scorpions won't come near. Last night's dream: I'm in an interior in the ancient city, pick up an obsidian mirror, have to wonder who it first reflected. I see wall images, red ochre hunting scenes, wild animals, people gathered for bull-jumping, all this 45 hundred years before the first Egyptian pyramids! The oldest images in the world on human-built structures. In these dreams I'm always searching for something, don't know what. A famous figurine was found in the city—a seated woman so fleshy she sprawls, hands resting on the heads of two male leopards flanking her. Between her thighs the head of a newborn emerges from her womb. It's something. If my mother were alive, she'd know what it all means. I don't.

These spring weeks, she saw Sophie as much as possible, ever aware that time was running out, though Sophie seemed suspended, getting not better, but not worse either. Easy to pretend she'd be suspended this way forever. She was weaker, but she'd surprise Judith by asking to come over, see somebody else's four walls, she'd say. After chamomile tea, serious gossip, Judith would drive her back home. Sophie was no longer interested in the news from her own field, but she liked to hear about Judith's work, and Judith did her best to be entertaining.

Where was Sophie's family? The mother and father were dead, but Sophie had a brother in eastern Colorado; the brother had a family. Judith's own brother—and she in turn—would have been burning up the phone lines to each other, jetting to see, to hug, to cry together. One day she asked.

Sophie was lying on Judith's couch, looking surprisingly well for someone who was dying. As she'd pointed out more than once.

"We don't get along."

"You had a quarrel?"

"With the universe. I got the brains and he got the ranch. He thought he ought to have both, and never got over it, that I got the only brains in the family. Believe me, Jay, when they tell blond jokes, they mean my brother. He's not just dumb, he's mean-dumb. He is *such* an asshole. In high school, my dad sat us down one night and says, kids, I've got enough money to put one of you through college, and since Dave is the boy, it goes to him. Now Dave-the-boy already thought that high school was penal servitude, didn't have the slightest interest in college. For him life's high point was hanging out at the A & W and hoping to get laid on Saturday night by at least one of the town's two pro-am sluts, while I was pulling straight A's and dying to go to vet school. But if it meant that Dave-the-boy would get something that Sophie-the-girl didn't, something she wanted, Dave-the-boy was stoked. So he crawled, hand over hand, pitons, crampons, ropes, ice axe and emergency oxygen, altitude sickness threatening, up the sheer sides of a two-year cow college. Except it took him four, my dad shelling out the whole time. Think less of me if you will, but it gave me intense gratification to watch my brother suffer. Then my dad got sick and that was the end of any money for either of us. It didn't matter. I got a scholarship to Berkeley and got out of the high plains as fast as I could."

Sophie sipped her chamomile tea thoughtfully. Dying, and a reservoir of words must be drained as surely as the doctors drained her lungs. "The only person on this planet meaner and dumber than Dave is his wife Arlie, who is trophy-quality mean and dumb. Somehow among their six kids—six! I ask you, Jay! Who are these people who keep reproducing? This isn't regression to the mean, it's genetic catastrophe. Anyway, six kids and one with a chance of being a worthwhile human being, my nephew Roy, though even he's marginal. By that I mean he got through college thanks to me, and now that I'm sick, I might hope for something besides a get-well card. Oh well. You don't do it because you want something in return. A damn good thing, too. Brother Dave still hangs around the A & W, hoping to get laid by at least one of the town's constant number of two sluts—the personnel has rotated, however. Well, of course: he married dumb Arlie and retired her from the A & W's back parking lot. So basically nothing's changed."

Judith had to laugh. But Sophie's pain also saddened her. "The kid. This Roy. Maybe he doesn't know how seriously ill—"

"He knows. Arlie was already on the phone asking about my will. My will! Uh, like, she and Dave are running a little short right now, and she was wondering if they might have ahead of time what I was going to be leaving them afterwards. Afterwards! *Quelle delicatesse!* Sure you can, because it's zero then, so zero now. She hung up on me. And don't think she got to the point right away; even trophy-quality Arlie knows that common decency suggests, hints, it's better to work up to this with the dying; asking outright the first thing is maybe uncool. So as prelude, I had to listen to endless shit about the greed and wickedness of her own sisters.

"No, no; I blame myself, Jay. Here I am with sand streaming through the hourglass before my very eyes, and I let her spend twenty whole minutes filling my ears with that trash."

Judith refilled their teacups, sweet-smelling chamomile looking slightly urinous. "Your nephew. No matter how much they really care, kids have a hard time dealing with mortality."

"They're not the only ones."

"Where was your mom when your dad was laying down the law about who'd get to go through college?"

Sophie looked away, and Judith saw tears, that the comedy had stopped. "Nowhere, Jay. She let my dad do it. She just sat there all quiet and—let my dad and Dave have their way. For years I didn't forgive her for letting me down that way. Now I've forgiven her. I think. She let me down. She shouldn't have." The effort to keep from crying distorted Sophie's mouth. "This woman could pull calves and foals single-handedly: stick her bare arms up inside an animal and pull out a newborn. Dig postholes and string barbed wire fast as any man. Don't tell me she was too weak to fight for me. God damn to the most stinking circle of hell all the women who won't stick up for their daughters! Guys stick together. We are such a backstabbing, conniving sex, Jay. No wonder we never get anywhere."

She lay back on Judith's couch, exhausted. "Once I read where Queen Elizabeth has lead weights in her skirts to keep them from flying up in a breeze. That's us. We've all got lead weights in our skirts. Anything to keep us from soaring. Why didn't she wear pants? She was *queen*, for God's sake. Nothing to stop her."

"As queen," Judith said slowly, "there was probably more to stop her than we know."

Sophie appraised her shrewdly. "Queen Jay. Will I hear the full story of your life before I die? I'll take it safely to the grave. Lay it out for me, Queen Jay. What hidden parts of the universe pushed on you? I'm pretty clear where you were pushing on the universe. When did that encounter with the divine you were looking for happen? What was it?"

"You know all there is, Soph."

"I know what you tell me, the official story, and I know what I can see, a little bit more. I know as much as anybody, including Ron, though he and I know different things. But none of us knows the full story, do we? Do you, girlfriend?"

"Probably not. I try not to get too personal."

Struggling Uphill

In April Judith went to Tokyo and Singapore, then to London, Madrid and Munich, missionary work, lecturing on the limits to science (sermons to seek converts, with their ritual teas beforehand and dinners afterward). Small signals arrived that members of her group, scattered over three continents but in touch by constant e-mail, might be going astray. For work to go forward, the strays must be rounded back into the fold.

At one of England's redbrick universities, she sat over food punished without mercy by English cooks and coaxed Anthony Blake, an accomplished mathematician but altogether clueless about what mattered, to think harder about what he chose to prove, and more importantly, why. "Ask yourself always. Will it change the world, will it have impact?" she murmured urgently. "This line you've been pursuing, nobody will care. They just won't. You want to do work that stars in the Science Citation Index." Cited by others as crucial to their work.

Tony, deliberately seedy-looking, protested. "I want to prove beautiful theorems, and if nobody ever pays attention to them, it's quite all right. Really." Quite all right to molder here in Lower Downmarket-under-Decline, frittering my life away on the mathematical equivalent of tap-dancing.

The dreadful food grew cold between them (Cool Britannia was attracting young entrepreneurs from all over Europe, especially France, but they weren't eating this rot) while Judith considered tactics. Appeal to his self-interest? His professional pride? His sense of the grand? Tony, we could shoot down once and for all the great Pythagorean maxim, that numbers are not merely symbols, but the essence of all things, that all relationships in the universe can be expressed mathematically. We might prove that wrong, Tony—bring down *Pythagoras* for God's sake!

He studied his fingertips with a concentration that could've cracked Etruscan. Or maybe he was just sulking. Finally she chose, gently pushed his curved and none too clean fingers to the table, itself none too clean, and did not let go. "You, Tony Blake, want to prove beautiful theorems that will stop the bloody world in its tracks. Sperm whales, sulphur bellies, not plankton."

Sulkiness turned to fury. Tony was a vegetarian. He wouldn't even eat Altoids, because they were made from calves' feet, maybe more principled than her U.S. friends who wouldn't eat them for worry of mad-cow disease. Poor Tony. Poor Judith. She'd argued her own reasons, not his, and blundered badly.

At the sadly shabby University of Madrid, she roughed up a duo of perversely obtuse researchers. In a paper they planned to submit to one of the best international journals, they'd hidden startlingly significant results inside drearily obvious ones. "They'll give this to Feydor or one of his people to referee, and you know he'll slash and burn," she said to them irritably. "This *must* see the light, it's so good, but not like this." Rosa de la Cruz, one member of the duo, seemed close to tears; her partner, Alfredo, looked murderous. Not graduate students, bound to do anything their dissertation advisor insisted on, these were professionals, colleagues, at liberty to go away and work on problems that had nothing to do with the grand idea of the limits to scientific knowledge. They could not be coerced. So eager to keep the inquiry moving forward, Judith sometimes forgot this until in her hotel room she fell face down on her bed, weary, frustrated, and finally remembered the fragility of their unspoken agreements with each other, how she could destroy these. Even Captain Ahab knew that when officers and men stood their long night watches, they must have some nearer things to think of than the great white whale.

Nature dares us, she'd say. We're trying to illuminate something that's in no way obvious. Turn metaphysics into science. Lead into gold. Ambitious. Maybe foolishly so. But worth trying.

For what she hadn't bothered burdening Molloy with when he asked about her work was the deepest, hardest question she and her group faced. How to prove, in a formal way, anything about the limits to science?

It wouldn't come by brute force. She was just going to have to be smarter. But the more she was convinced she'd uncovered a deep problem, whose solution would change the way science was done, the very paths scientists pursued, the more she faltered with corrosive doubt that she or her group could pull it off.

If nature as adversary weren't enough, they had human adversaries too. Feydor's fine hand had again emerged. A brilliant and beautiful paper by one of her former students, now in Munich, had been rejected by a major journal as "idiosyncratic, and anyway, inconsequential." Dieter had shown her the anonymous referee's report, one that had brought on a sudden crisis, him wondering aloud if this field was the right thing at all, or anyway, right for him. Judith believed this result reduced all Feydor's and his followers' work to mere special case, a small branch office (lively, well-funded; Feydor knew the ropes) of limits to science as Judith and her group defined them.

Over pizza and beer in a funky little cafe on Schellingstrasse, she worked assiduously, first in English then in German, and finally in a strange hybrid of the two, at bucking Dieter up, reminding him how important what he'd achieved really was, *besonders wunderbar, ein Wissenschaftswunder*; it might take a while to get published, but look how long the Breitbart paper had taken, yes, Breitbart, no kidding, *kein Spass*, now the world calls it one of their group's most significant contributions. Nevelinna Prize material, Dieterle, a Fields Medal for you.

Sunk in Teutonic gloom, he signaled for another beer.

She worked so hard with Dieter because he was the future. The most penetrating of the group's youngsters, certainly more powerful than she'd been at his age, as she was only too glad to tell him, she poured great energy into this, knowing it was only the beginning. Young people must be nurtured who in turn attracted their own students. They must be leveraged into important academic positions, onto editorial boards, pushed forward for prizes, onto committees that were ladders to the Academies. Hard work, carefully planned. Research: just another complex adaptive system. Interaction, aggregation, adaptation. In its social aspects and its core.

Every field sheltered topics no longer intellectually alive, but the people who'd come in when the topic was vital were still in power, writing letters to place their own students into ever scarcer university posts, lobbying to get their like-minded colleagues into the National Academy. No matter how dazzling its promise, any young field was up against this massive inertia, this textbook example of increasing returns, and could perish in front of the frozen fortress walls. Its innovations might be picked up a century later as key to the way the field had subsequently developed, but that was cold comfort to the young who'd been right, but right too soon.

Feydor. He'd once seemed like an ally, or at least, no antagonist. Judith had hardly paid attention to him, oblivious to how much damage someone like that could do. To her sorrow, she'd learned. Feydor became an adversary, and then an enemy. Tenured long ago at a prestigious east coast university, when standards in the field were different, he'd done no significant research for decades. His time and energy were devoted to politics instead. Feydor was powerful. Feydor protected his people, his territory. He'd declared war on Judith and her group—politely but altogether ruthlessly—and would destroy them if he could.

To: jimenez@sf.arch.org
From: jrg@santafe.edu
April 11, 1997

What are you finding?

You cannot believe what I've found. The English group needs major reclamation. Be proud of me, I didn't use any naughty words you've taught me to ream out my Madrid colleagues. Spent most of last night here in Munich with a brilliant kid in a crisis. Lose him, it will hold the work back fifty years.

Usual passive-aggressive message from The Unspeakable One, also responsible for the kid's crisis. Nasty and personal. Why did it take me so long to get it that the grudge is personal? Ancient history between him and my ex? I'm Woman and Unclean? No persuasion, argument, proof will ever be enough to convince him that our stuff's worthwhile. Religious, not scientific war, I lead the infidels and must be laid waste. I always expect the worst; he never fails me.

Tino filed an extension for my taxes or I'd really be up the creek. Back around the 23rd. Will you be in SFe then?

The message from Feydor had been in the form of an anonymous referee's report on a survey paper she'd written, making explicit the large aims of her group. It was such pure Feydor he might as well have signed it.

This is just the sort of vacuous nonsense that emanates from a certain kind of senior scientist. We humor these emanations because, with a lifetime's significant contributions to science, they've earned the right to pontificate. But Greenwood will never be of the stature and is not yet at a point of superannuation (it is to be hoped) to have earned such a right. It would be an intellectual embarrassment for this journal to humor her in an ill-conceived project that seems to have seized and unfortunately further muddled her imagination.

Fuck you too, Feydor. You pygmy.

To: jrg@santafe.edu
From: jimenez@sf.arch.edu
April 12, 1997 3:45 p.m.

What are you finding? I long to tell you not write it.

As for the Unspeakable One, you've given as good as you've gotten. Blocked him from some key committees, kept him out of the National Academy. A drain of energy, true. Cheer up. Great minds are always plagued by midget mediocrities. Science is mortal combat. Win or lose, no second prizes. (This from an impeccable source :-))

I was just in SFe to sign my own tax returns, ta-da, but won't be back up there for a while. The dig is hot. Why don't you come here? I could shoo the luscious young thing out of my sleeping bag for a few nights.

Querida, I want to talk to you about these dreams. You if anyone would understand. I long to smell you.

On her way back from Europe, she stopped in Washington to consult, and was handed a document analyzing lessons Russian soldiers had learned in the small, brutal war in Chechnya in the early nineties. The parallels with Feydor depressed her. The Chechnyans had booby trapped with acute psychological insight—what the Russian soldier would rise to, what would lower his guard.

Feydor had once cunningly suggested a debate, "not to decide which approach is correct, but merely informational." She'd declined, noting politely that science wasn't to be validated by mere rhetoric. But younger colleagues had thought it would be fun, and younger colleagues, without his enormous preparation time, were publicly humiliated. Feydor's booby trap. From defeat they'd learned. She'd kept her mouth shut, for she knew one more thing that the Chechnyans knew, flexible command and control—let the locals figure things out themselves—was more powerful than any edict.

At Dallas-Fort Worth, waiting to switch to the Albuquerque leg, exhaustion swept over her. The war metaphor repelled her; she wished vainly that it hadn't been forced on her. What she ran was the equivalent of a small family business, where she was vice-president for research, vice-president for promotion and sales, vice-president for development. Her radar was ever tuned in search of good applications, not because she particularly wanted to solve problems in finance, or in the petroleum industry, or in medical diagnosis, but because these were the problems that people cared about, and solutions to them would showcase her group's work. New Business was a goldmine for this kind of thing. When she wasn't looking for new applications, she was looking for young recruits, willing to tackle the new problems, so unappealingly difficult for mathematicians used to old ways of thinking. Time and again she forced herself to re-think where she and her people would publish their results, not just in the mathematical journals, but places where new users, possibly new researchers, might be found. She'd learned to tolerate the constant tension between sublime theory and killer apps, pushing her group toward the practical, even as they longed only to pursue mathematical beauty, a longing she understood perfectly. She was not just vice-president, but must also conduct their pep rallies. In rare moments of self-examination, she saw she didn't always know the difference between leadership and imposing her will.

She e-mailed her group as soon as she got home.

> We must solve problems people care about. This is not l'art pour l'art. Information theory had impact because Shannon solved a problem that people really care about. We can change all of science if we do this right. Please, please, bear this in mind as you're planning your research.

The suitcase remained in the middle of the bedroom floor while she checked her e-mail. An update from Benito. Three papers of her own accepted by journals in three different disciplines. The suitcase, full of dirty clothes, rebuked her. She sighed, left it standing, and went to work out her jetlag, her soul's exhaustion, at her health club.

Diminishing Returns

Nola was reviewing slides, but she was thinking about bone marrow biopsies, spinal taps, a glandular biopsy. Positive. Therefore, bad news. How medicine fucked with your language, your head. She knew the numbers by heart. Seventy percent of kids with this made it. Thirty percent of them didn't. It used to be about fifty/fifty. Chalk one up for modern medicine. On the other hand, childhood cancer now occurred in fourteen out of every hundred thousand American kids. Twenty years ago, it was only twelve. So we're only barely ahead of the game, she'd say to anyone who asked.

Focus. Maybe the transplant hadn't worked last time, but have faith in a second round. A vacation this summer? A place Pete could forget for a little while that he was a sick kid? But could be rushed to an emergency room? Maybe next summer if he got through this round. When, not if. Even at his sickest, he was the optimist. "Maybe I've like, hit bottom so things are finally gonna start getting better. Maybe I've like, turned the corner." It was his mother who'd lost heart, who cried in anguish to whatever gods might hear, that this child of her late life, the last gift of her vanishing fertility, a blessing she'd neither looked for nor imagined, was to be ripped from her after all. Don't ask for justice, a Buddhist had counseled her. Ask for mercy.

Steps must be retraced. Pre-transplant treatment, the sealed room for another four to six weeks, chemo and radiation for days one to eight, return of the processed marrow on day ten, then two weeks of waiting until the immunity began to rebuild. If all went well. Convulsions, and the drugs to fight them, shake-and-bake, kidney metabolites out of whack, caused by a brutally high fever. Anti-fungal drugs, specially sterilized food, specially sterilized transfusions, specially sterilized computer, specially sterilized Gameboy. One day Pete had looked at her morosely. "The noise in here is driving me crazy, mom." She hadn't even heard the metallic screech of the ventilators until he mentioned it and he was right, it would drive you crazy. But for him to step outside that room was certain death. The weariness of those weeks, your emotions continually reset to zero, begin again. Sterilized themselves in a sense. You couldn't let down. You had to be brave for your child, brave for his oncologist, who needed encouragement too.

She admitted to herself that while she did not wish her own child dead, she wished for this to be over, finished. She was tapped out of strength and courage.

When Pete had come out of the bubble room the first time and into a regular hospital bed, he hadn't been able to focus his eyes—the result of not looking further than fifteen feet for two months. It happened to submarine sailors, the doctor told him; it would pass, and that, at least, did. The counts held but did not climb. Then slowly, they began to crawl upward. Slowly Pete ate more food and relied on the IVs less. They came home to Santa Fe, where he continued with daily lab tests, transfusions of platelets, which recovered last.

He was not cured but in remission. He did normal things. Until a fever that was not the flu spiked them back into the nightmare full-time. An ambiguous test, followed by yet another painful bone marrow aspiration because other tests were ambiguous; this too was ambiguous, must be repeated. Other worries. Could a marrow donor be found this time? The insurance company had begun to give them serious grief about the second transplant. That she could not think about, she simply could not.

She sighed on behalf of the artist whose slides she couldn't appreciate, put them aside and went home to begin arrangements. From his couch, Pete observed her with sunken eyes. "How's it going, mom?"

"We'll do it again, dude. Destroy Spider Mastermind."

He grunted, talked about his hookup with Alejandro. Boys should be punching each other out, not talking on the telephone, e-mail, she thought. But that was ideal, and this was real. This child knew about experimental drugs meant to kick up the platelets; he understood when stem cells were failing to mature.

"Want some real food? Maybe the last before you have to go back onto astronaut food?" He shook his head. Pete was plainly very sick. "Where's dad?"

"He said he had to go out."

Whose bed, she wondered. She envied Ernie his temporary escape, but it was a slight, condescending envy, the way you envied the serenity of a religious person when you yourself could see no evidence that your corner of the universe was anything but chance, and all you could do was your best. She'd heard Stuart Kauffman lecture once, declaring that we made the world we live in with one another, that we were participants in the story as it unfolds. We aren't victims and we aren't outsiders, he said. We make our world with one another. There's a lot of pain, he'd added; you can go broke in this world we make together; you can go extinct. (He knew about pain; he and Liz had been devastated when their ten-year-old daughter was killed in a hit-and-run.) But here we are on the edge of chaos, because that's where, on average, we all do the best.

Nola was doing her best against accumulating evidence that her best was not enough. She looked down into the abyss of chaos and felt herself swooning toward it. She needed rest, respite, some kind of let-up. Then she looked at Pete, whose fight this was too, by the way, and knew that somehow, she'd find the strength.

Ernie returned late, but she was awake.

"I thought you'd be asleep," he said. "You should be. It'll be long day."

"Do I know her, Ern?"

"Know who?"

"Whoever you see when you haven't got time for us."

He didn't answer. A part of his mind had always known that Nola would discover all this. He also knew that she hadn't got the energy to make a scene about it just now, luckily. When he examined this curious relationship with Maya, it surprised him that he was the unfaithful one, not Nola, who'd been the beauty. He was tasting in his middle age the forbidden fruit inaccessible in his beset young manhood and, as if some balance sheet in life must be satisfied, this tasting, however late, was inevitable and justified. If not, at this moment, entirely opportune. It won't last, he wanted to say. I don't want to grow old with this woman. Instead, he said stiffly: "You're overwrought. Try and get some sleep."

"I'm overwrought," she repeated bitterly. "Ern, I'm about to crack. I know I haven't been everything you need these past few months, but see it from my point of view. I don't know if I can go on, Ern, I really don't. Could you come with us tomorrow?"

He sighed, fighting sleep. "If I don't meet this deadline, Lala, I could lose everything. Nothing I can do that you and Pete can't do by yourselves, in point of fact, better. I'd be in the way more than anything." He pictured Maya's bounteous body, the dinner they were planning tomorrow night when Pete and Nola were safely in Texas, the plans they had for after dinner, which Maya had coarsely teased him with before he left her this evening. Nola was good and beautiful; faithful wife; heroic mom. Perversely, he wanted a whore.

Nola crept into his arms, her head on his chest. Whose deadline couldn't bend for a dying child? "What am I gonna do, Ern?"

"There," he said stupidly. "There. You'll do just fine." As she wept quietly, he slipped off into sleep and left her more desolate than she'd thought it possible to be.

Her own fault. When she married him, she'd known, as a friend suggested icily, he was a mile wide and an inch deep. "Some men, you need to feed their stomachs. This one, you'll always need to feed his ego." Even knowing it was true, she'd broken indignantly with the woman out of loyalty to Ernie. But she needed Ernie then as much as he needed her. Needed him for—what? Sanctuary. The world, its importuning, its attacks, its massive coldness, had been grinding her down.

His protection could be excessive. He resented her friends, insisted on accounts of where and when she spent any time away from him. He still went nonlinear if she wasn't at the gallery to answer his phone call, forgot to turn on her cell phone. "I get so worried about you," he cried. "You don't know how I worry. I was about to call the police. Don't put me through this." "It's three o'clock in the afternoon, Ern. I went to see work at a studio in Galisteo—" But his pleas had moved her. Was it so much to ask, to spare him this pain?

No, she loved him. She could explain each loss of control, each mad moment of fear. He was irrational about being left, abandoned; he was suffering terribly, piteously, from how thwarted in every direction his professional ambitions were. Nobody understood. Worse, they laughed. She above all knew the canonical stories of geniuses unrecognized in their own lifetimes, how they suffered, only to be vindicated years, centuries, later. If she deserted him too? What higher calling did she have? Though her eye was reliable, she was no artist. She certainly wasn't a scientist. She was just—an ordinary person, called to an extraordinary task.

It was torment but she didn't want to stop seeing their acquaintances at the Institute, the Labs, the small start-ups around town. Their success—conventional, the result of obediently playing by the rules—was an awl driven daily into Ernie's already bleeding eyes and ears. He loved them. Envied and hated them.

Nola considered each of them, wondering to whom she could reach out on her own. What would she have said? My husband doesn't like me to make phone calls. My husband goes berserk about time I spend elsewhere that I could be spending with him. Goes off the deep end if he can't find me. My cell phone's alive at all times, though his isn't. My husband resents his own child as an intruder. She and Ernie had become a team and the world loved them as a team. If she broke away, who'd pay attention to her? Single women were pariahs, except to other single women. Who'd even find it interesting to be her friend, never mind shield her from the way the world has of grinding you down without mercy? Who in the world did she matter the slightest to, except her child? She blamed herself. So weak and timid. She'd made her bed. She kept silent. To protect him. To protect herself. Kept to herself the shame that she'd failed to foresee so much. No, worse, that she'd foreseen it and went ahead anyway.

At least he hadn't said that Pete was the child *she'd* wanted, *she'd* insisted on bearing, so finally *her* problem. Not in so many words. But that's what he was thinking. Conceivably he actually hoped—no, she wouldn't think that about him. But the accusation persisted. He did not want his son to live. A delusion that with Pete gone, life would return to what it had once been, a period already

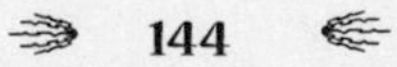

over-rosy in his nostalgia. For a year after Pete's birth, he'd lost any sexual interest in her; she'd had to coax him back to an erotic connection. Wasn't sure why she'd bothered. It wasn't like sex was in any way gratifying for her these days.

Life couldn't ever be the same again, she assured him snoring lightly beside her. Pete had been born. Pete had changed her life irreversibly. Pete was still here, damn it all, and she'd do everything in her power to make sure he lived. To Pete, she mattered. In her heart, she raged at Ernie murderously, but beside him in their bed she lay deathly still, embracing her rage like a lover, screaming mutely, for she feared to wake her son in what might be his last night ever in his own bed

Modest Compromise Solutions

The late twentieth-century health club might be compared to an early twentieth-century factory, slides and flywheels of rowing machines grumbling under the shriek of treadmill belts, the asynchronous rhythms of stair climbers (in Victorian jails, a much-feared punishment), the occasional thwap of weights ending a freefall, iron out of control.

Eyes shut as she works, Judith hears with half an ear the regulars, the Buffmeister, Prince Climax (was it good for you, hon?), a couple of retired CEO's shouting at each other from their stationary bikes. It keeps her from first hearing someone who leans over her bench and repeats himself louder. "Pretty good for an old woman consecrated to her science."

Molloy stands over her, eyeing the heft of her weights. Which she lets down gently. "I do what I can, Molloy. How's it going?"

"Great. Come and have some juice when you're done." So whatever offense he'd taken has dissipated. She's surprised at how buoyed she is.

He's on the terrace, looking over the golf course, across the Upper Rio Grande basin to the Jemez Mountains, indigo in the distance. It's the first pleasantly warm weather, and golfers can be seen, though most flowers are still timid. They sit in silence. She wants to speak, connect with this strange taciturn man, recapture the easy fun they once had.

"Here comes this afternoon's storm." The weather. Brilliant. "The Pueblos talk about those clouds as blossoming flowers."

Black sunglasses acknowledge her impersonally. Then Molloy speaks, but not about metaphor. "Some issues I don't quite understand. Are we still on for the tutorial?"

"Ah, Molloy. So goal-driven. Fire away." Her cheer, her buoyancy, deflate. No poetry in money. An image comes unbidden, unkind, the Incas smelting gold to liquid, and pouring it down the throat of one of the conquistadors to satisfy his thirst for gold.

"I'll say first that I'm awed by the amount of European history a couple of glasses of wine pulls out of you. The advantages, I suppose, of a first-class education."

Is he mocking her? Then she catches on. "I faked it. I'd just read that book on a plane too. But that's how we work. Question the obvious, especially the given. Sacking the library at Alexandria is always thought to be one of the great planetary acts of vandalism. But suppose we unearthed the back-up tapes, and it all turned out to be trash? Suppose that much-lamented sacking was a great and cleansing intellectual gift to the world, erasing the dead and heavy hand of the past?"

He shakes his head, smiling. "Suppose."

"You should see me at work sometime on why the Diaspora saved the Jews from being just another no-name Middle East tribe."

"And the Holocaust?"

"No, Molloy," she says gravely. "There's nothing to be said on behalf of the Holocaust." Oh, Germany. All our human sins, commission, omission, writ large.

"No great karmic meaning? Or is death meaningless?"

Something personal, his own death, maybe? Rich men have strewn the world with monuments to immortality, most of them ruins now. But death. Can't we pick up with the usual? Get much skiing in before the season ended? Been away? Business or pleasure? Been there; haven't; don't the airlines suck these days? No, he probably has his own Gulfstream.

Is the ordinary so impossible with this man?

"Heresy here in the capital of the New Age, but yeah. Death has no particular meaning. A life does. Not a death." He's impassive. She tries again. "Death is inevitable; premature death happens more or less randomly. If you need to learn life's lessons, go get a book. My best friend here is dying. We hoped she'd get into an experimental program in Denver, high-dose chemo then a bone-marrow transplant, but chemo had already damaged her kidneys so much it kept her out of the program. All a holding action now. Anyway, I learn something profound from that woman every time I see her. But is that what it's for? Did six million people die for our enlightenment? Their own?"

"Who says that?"

"New Age types all over this town. Same folks who say you brought your cancer on yourself. It makes my flesh crawl. What can I tell you about complexity?"

"I'm sorry about your friend. Death is rough. Death is hard." These terse platitudes come with such conviction that she understands she's meant to hear them afresh.

Her voice changes on her uncontrollably. "I'll miss that woman so. We've known each other from way back. By luck, we both turned up in Santa Fe. People die, and they take a part of your history with them. A piece of your heart. She remembers girls say yes to guys who say no." The *sumi* brush eyebrows rise above the sunglasses. "Before your time. Draft resistance at Berkeley. When fucking was a political statement." Judith gazes toward the distant mountains, hoping her own sunglasses conceal the betraying tears. I grieve, can't weep—except at the most inconvenient times.

He doesn't reach to comfort her, even a hand, absorbed by something else. "I'm mystified by death. Not the biology of it. The way—the way it ends things. Banal, as your friend Gabe would say." A brief, unamused smile. "So you grieve. For a good life gone. And almost as much for a wasted life. A close friend died horribly. My wife died. If there was meaning in either death, it escapes me. That's part of the reason I'm in Santa Fe."

"I didn't know that. I'm sorry." These are the first personal things he's disclosed to her, and his obvious discomfort says they might be the last too. Does he grieve good lives or wasted ones? Did, so many weeks ago, the confession that he was on the edge of chaos somehow refer to this? A place to learn, the edge of chaos.

He pushes his finger around the wet ring the glass has left: his turn to gaze safely out onto the golf course. Looks back with a flash smile that isn't a smile at all but a way of controlling face muscles again. She's glad to be left alone with her own grief. Yet one of the lessons Sophie has taught her is the futility, the waste, of evasion. With effort she focuses. "Remaining in New York was painful?"

He shakes his head. "I'll be getting back from time to time. I still keep my place there. My season ticket for the Knicks. Hey, on the floor courtside. They're hard to get."

"Are you grieving good lives or wasted ones?"

He doesn't answer. She's sorry she asked. He owes her no penetration into his secrets. Finally, she acquiesces to the silence. "The tutorial?"

"Right," he says slowly, "the tutorial." Fingers playing with absent worry beads, then to his face, whose tender midday crop seems to comfort him. "Increasing returns."

She's relieved. "Don't ask me. Ask Brian."

"He's elusive."

"All right. In a nutshell, them that has, gits. Who's ahead? Because who's already ahead will probably get further ahead, and who's behind will fall further behind, winner take all. Winner takes most. The best-seller list, a title gets on, tends to persist there, while other books, at least as worthy, maybe even worthier, never have a chance. Movies, popular songs, same thing. Nola's gallery. What's a town the size of Santa Fe doing as one of the largest art markets in the country? Not tops—not New York or L.A., but way out of proportion to its population. First comes history—artists love to come here because it's beautiful, and in the early days, cheap, socially free-and-easy; the blending of the cultures; then luck—the railroad hires a canny Brit promoter named Fred Harvey, who sells train tickets to the southwest by promoting Indian art—and the network grows, perpetuates itself, establishes an infrastructure. Museums here even before formal statehood. Anthropologists do their bit. Art sales become an important part of Santa Fe's economy, so the various levels of government move in to support it. In prospect unpredictable, but success begets further success. Increasing returns."

Why do we rush to escape into all this? But the approach to intimacy, tentative and unaccustomed, has troubled her; the retreat to safety is a relief.

She does not want to be vulnerable to this man. He seems just as glad to back off too.

The sun is brilliant. He gets up, moves the umbrella to shade them, all competence. "Then what?"

"Like this umbrella, the paradigm shifts, and we start all over again. It's about biology. Populations crash just like they grow, so get ready to jump to the next opportunity. Plenty of them for the having. The old, the new economies differ, the way you manage them, the nature of competition. What works in one doesn't work in the other. The new economy is for the gutsy—a casino, not a poker game. But you knew that. It's what you're doing at New Business. Why didn't you fire me while you were spring cleaning?"

"I ran the numbers. You're still a profit center, Dr. Greenwood."

"When I'm not?"

"Learn. Adapt. Take your chances like the rest of us." He's completely opaque behind his sunglasses.

"What will you do with New Business in the long run?"

"In the long run we're all dead. Meanwhile I'm looking around to reposition the company. It's very good at what it does, hot stuff now, this dragging old economy firms into the new economy by teaching them how complexity applies to business. But we get stuck there, we'll die. As Gabe saw, I'm into creative destruction. Even if you weren't a profit center, I'd like your smarts around to help unstick things."

"I heard you came here to retire."

"Trumpets and cannons still make the old war horse twitch. Good for another battle or two."

"Always a pleasure doing business with you, Molloy."

As she gets up, Molloy takes her hand, both pleasant and disturbing. "Why do you do this?"

He doesn't let go. Since she can't see his eyes she looks down on his hand, its back rich with hair, Esau's hand. The correct answer is I don't know. She improvises. "The virtuous circle. Give knowledge away so that everyone's success is shared, leveraged by everyone else. In other words I assume something's in it for me, though I don't know what yet. Are you joining the Institute's board?

The reason for this tutorial in the first place?"

"We're still talking," he says at last. "Other things—" He squeezes her hand gently then releases it. "I'm having a few people over for dinner at my new house. Did you know I'd bought a house? Thursday at eight? I'll e-mail you directions."

Stable and Unstable Attractors

Molloy has indeed bought himself a house, or more correctly, a compound. It's not, as Judith secretly feared, some vulgar leviathan stranded on a ridge top, grandfathered in under zoning laws that now protect what's left of the mountains. It isn't even out on Tano Road with the movie people. It's just off the Alameda, down the other fork from the one she takes to Benito's. Molloy has become an unexpected addition to the network of people she can reach on foot.

This early Santa Fe compound is still a monument to money. Somebody—not Molloy—has lovingly restored it, garden walls and house real adobe, which means he must reface every spring, or the mud will melt back into the earth. Did anyone warn him? The interiors are hand-plastered and whitewashed in the old style. How were workers found to do that? It's a dying art, something only the very rich and the very poor can afford.

She stands in the entry hall letting the impressions sink in, refusing her shawl to the maid. A rich man's house, but in its austerity, not its opulence. Above her, the *latillas*, cedar strips, are herringboned beautifully in place above the *vigas*, the pine log roof beams. Spanish terms, but the style was borrowed from the pre-Puebloan people. She approaches her host, he smiles in mid-sentence and continues. "A tribe somewhere in Asia Minor. Travelers said their temples surpassed anything in the world for elegance and grace. Unfortunately, they were built of mud, so eventually the walls melted away. All we have left is the legend."

So he's been warned. He's unusually winning, almost courtly this evening, telling the history of the site, how the land once reached the river (he's always lived on rivers), how, though it's only a ten minute walk to the plaza, this was originally an isolated farm, walled against the Comanches. He's making an effort to conceal his pride in his new house, the time he's spent in the city archives looking things up. From the *portal*, he points out the former stables (he trades there now), the sheep and pigpens, the poultry house and corn cribs, transformed into a sequence of spare, refined rooms. If the wind's right, he can hear church bells from Cristo Rey *and* from the Cathedral. He likes that; he's used to church bells. Room after simple room furnished with nothing much, except what makes Judith think Molloy might be forgiven everything. He has exquisite paintings.

Chosen with discrimination, Molloy's Anselm Kiefers force a double-take: those quintessential dead-of-winter German fields sitting up here in the clarity of the Sangre de Cristos alongside an encrusted canvas from the painter's Osiris series; Diebenkorns that demand you re-see the sky above, the earth below. He has Stellas and Tanseys and Johnses. Even a Twombly or two. The tumbled brick-and-sand floors are bare except for the famous Navajo rugs bought at auction, the kind other people put on walls. Maybe there's more to him than meets the eye. She remembers his plea to be taught science, move into the future. Or is all this—science too—nothing but rich-guy trophies? She watches him, wonders.

It's a warm evening, and the curtainless french doors are thrown open to the *portal*. He's seated Judith next to him, and while he's scrupulously attentive to his other guests, he turns to her, speaking intimately. Incongruously. "Tell me about traffic flow as phase transitions."

It stops her. He seems perfectly serious. She murmurs back flirtatiously. "I love it when you speak jargon to me. Jargon. Derived from the Old French for bird twitter."

He seems almost hurt. "Isn't that the right term?"

So maybe this isn't some adolescent revenge for that night outside her garden wall. Then what? No ordinary needs? Show off the new house, explain the animating desire behind the collection? She pats his forearm reassuringly. "I don't know much. Los Alamos has a big project going. I saw some things in

Germany last month. Saw it in real life in Seattle while I was visiting Microsoft, Bill Labs."

"Phase transitions—water to ice kind of thing? Fly or float, like at El Bosque? In complexity, everything is like everything?" He leans forward, working at making connections.

"Not exactly." She looks around, recognizes the catering staff—she's used them herself—then turns back to him, puts her wine glass down. "Molloy, don't you ever give it a rest?"

"Think of it as adding more virtue to the circle." A smile that barely hides a touching earnestness. Freshly shaved for the party, he's nicked himself.

"Did you get the impression I have nothing else to talk about?" Limits to Molloy? She inclines her head, answers his smile. "As you've pointed out, I have strong opinions about art. I have political views. Not entirely original—derived from Oakeshott—but sound, and hardly what you'd call received wisdom. I read competently in four languages, English, French, German, and Spanish, and can muddle through Russian detective stories if they aren't too demanding. I've traveled on every continent except Antarctica, and I cook, garden, ride, sail, ski—not in your league, Molloy, but I ski—and play the piano passably, none of these brilliantly. It's come to my attention that neutron transport and photon transport are exactly the same problem, so it doesn't surprise me to find that work done at Los Alamos can conveniently be adapted into computer graphics. I'm wide and not deep, a fox not a hedgehog, I learn easily, quickly, just like the Institute's Artificial Stock Market. Surely Molloy, surely, among all these topics we can find some subject of mutual interest besides complexity?"

He allows himself a grin. *"Wer um die Gottin freit, suche in ihr nicht das Weib."*

He might have stabbed her. "Schiller. I thought there was no poetry in money." He'd go to Düsseldorf dealers for some of these; he's said to have had a hand in planning for the euro. Something of the German *Geschäftsmann* about Molloy; he must've fit in just fine with those trim, solemn businessmen she's seen around the Frankfurter Börse, their Italian trousers blousing slightly beneath loden coats that flared like opera capes, trailed by clouds of pungent aftershave. Still, Schiller. She queries him silently.

"I owe that to dear old Father Joachim at St. Joseph's: *When you shpeak*

Cherman, Molloy, the man in front of you should vipe off his neck, ja?" His eyebrows rise eloquently, and she can see him in a meeting of financiers, determined to push through the impossible, though with as much courtesy as possible. "Are we on the same page? *Who'd woo the goddess doesn't seek just the woman in her."*

She flushes. She's miscalibrated him, but isn't sure how. The money's oppressive, certainly. Money, that curious mass consensual delusion. In the brief history of the human race, it was doubtless a great social step forward to substitute money for goods, another to substitute it for violence—pay your Dane geld and be spared; pay off the man you'd offended and put an end to his family's war upon you and yours, generation after generation. Money as well-being, a moral good: I *owe* you a favor, you *profit* from the experience, get *credit* for it, reciprocation, retribution, restitution, karma, all the terms of moral bookkeeping, resting in metaphors of wealth. Commonwealth. But when money becomes its own end, Incarnate, abstract desire? Alberich, that repellent gnome, forswearing love for gold; Valhalla as Wall Street. Money satisfies needs. What does Molloy need? He's speaking to the woman on his other side, a European polish verging on the slick. Wooing the goddess in her too? A very cosmopolitan serial fucker.

His attention returns to Judith, and she gazes over his shoulder at the paintings. "Have you spent much time in Germany?"

"Off and on," he answers politely.

"*Und ich auch*, me too." This explains Molloy's small gestures, familiar but not American, the way he purses his lips in thought, the way he rubs his chin. He's absorbed and carried them back, like an accent. So—more time abroad than just off and on. "I go back, bring my slang up to date. Although these days, German slang is mostly English." Although these days her friends, given their ages, are still speaking twenty-year-old slang.

She excuses herself to find the powder room, but along the bare hall, opens the wrong door. An automatic light reveals a rack of polished hunting rifles, dark, upright and adamantine. Her libido rush is so transparent, so primitive, that she can only laugh.

Back at the table, she turns her mind to the paintings. Art in the eighties had been perfervid, more about money than anything. Yet few of his paintings are by the glitzy stars of that era. She recognizes some young Germans.

Americans too, cerebral ones. "Your art—" she begins. Is deeply intellectual. Sometimes lacks sensuousness. But she doesn't say that. *Your art* lingers unfinished between them.

As the guests get up from the table to move to the living room for coffee, Judith stops in front of a Tansey.

"Do you like that?"

"Very witty. Very witty indeed."

"Another reason why I'm here. The answer to a question you asked so long ago, Judith—why are you here? If I'd said because of a painting—" He reaches over and brushes her hair out of her eyes, an intimate gesture; studies her face, openly appraises the gray silk she's wearing, the massive silver jewelry. "The Institute's work has been an influence on Mark. This one's called *Competition and Cooperation*. I beat out the Walker for it."

"Is that right?" Did you get your heart's desire? And what is that, really?

Molloy is fixed on her. "Over there—" he points to a colorful canvas, "—the work of a painter who, you might say, invented a theory of complex adaptive systems all by himself in his studio. The painting's actually done by computer. The artist did the program, and it's nothing less than a complex adaptive system. Though I'm quite sure Harold didn't know that term when he started. He just did what he thought was right. What he had to do."

She withdraws from those eyes, examines the painting. "Luscious colors. Like, oh, Kandinsky in nineteen ten, nineteen twelve. I didn't know you were such a serious collector, Molloy."

"As you once famously said, you hardly know me. I think that little speech you just gave me now was to say I hardly know you." He releases his gaze, turns back to the painting. "Kandinsky, when he was with Gabriele Münter. Could be." Still looking at the painting: "Stay on when these folks go. We'll talk about art for a change." A challenge as much as an invitation.

Judith feels his heat, palpable. Feels her own in response. Sexual desire, so immediate and liminal, and therefore different from the abstract desire for money. At least for her. For him?

Maya's suddenly beside them. "More art talk?"

"You're psychic, Maya. I was just saying to Judith that she ought to stay on after you folks go so we can exchange views on art."

Maya isn't fast enough to control her face; stalks off.

"Christ, that was cruel, Molloy." Is that what it's like when you're fucked by a shower of gold?

It's as if he's read her mind. No, he replies silently, I was always like that. Then aloud: "You've just learned something else about me." The same anger he'd once shown in the dark car flares; with effort, he masters himself, thug, then desperado, fighting for dominance. "You think I'm a schoolboy. Maybe so. I haven't done anything like this for a long time; I'm more than somewhat out of practice. If there's a grown-up way to do it, I haven't learned it yet. *Tschüss.*" He moves off to talk to his other guests

Adaptive Equilibrium Dynamics

He's got a straightforward case of the blues. These days he can tell the difference between that and big-time depression. It's a luxury, the blues without too much worry about a slide into something more serious. He's flat out on the couch, listening to Garcia the album (to indulge) and trying to remember the opening lines of Caesar's Gallic Wars in Latin (to snap himself out of it).

Gallia est omnis divisa in partes tres. Everybody remembers that. After all these years, no more will come to him. Okay, one part belongs to the Belgae, another to the Aquitani, the third to a people called in their own tongue Celtae, in the Latin, Galli. His own forebears, presumably. The Belgae are the most courageous because they're nearest to the Germans, who dwell beyond the Rhine, with whom they continually war. Then author Julius Caesar digresses: braver still are the Helvetii, themselves Gauls, Celts, because they struggle in almost daily fights with the Germans. It had impressed him deeply that before the Helvetii went to attack the Germans, they burned their own homes and stockades, burned all food except what they could carry, so that by removing any hope of returning home, they might not shirk from the worst perils.

Still the Latin won't come, though pieces of Ovid skip through his mind, something about chaos turning to order, thanks to passion.

Instead of making war, this Celt went off to do business with the Germans. Got along with them just fine, and sometimes he thinks he could always go back.

Father Yokkie at the old priest's home, his eczema a red, flaking curse across his face. "Can't something be done for him?" Molloy had asked the nursing sister, a sister still in a habit, too old to change, nearly as old as Yokkie himself. She shook her head. "Not now, not now." Meaning the condition was intractable? The old man was?

Whom he'd sat beside in the old man's austere cell, a crucifix on the wall, a table next to the bed, the chair a torment to the flesh. As intended. Yokkie had remembered him, wasn't particularly happy to see him. The conversation labored on, part in English, part in German. Molloy was now sensitive enough to peg Father Yokkie's accent, *echt Berliner*.

"Are you a faithful Christian?" the old priest had growled, as if they were about to go through the Baltimore catechism. Molloy had been amused by how time slipped away; how he almost but not quite resumed being that ever-horny kid in Father Yokkie's tenth-grade Latin and German classes, the mortification of standing up to recite a translation, convinced he was angled out like a flag-pole. Which he was. Those were the days. He did not lie to the old man now. "Not really. No."

To his surprise Yokkie smiled with satisfaction. "Married?"

"I was."

"Divorced, then?"

"No, widowed."

"You're young to bury a wife."

"Yes."

"Children?"

"Two, a boy and a girl."

Then silence, the old man scratching at his arms, where the eczema was at least covered by striped pajama sleeves. Molloy had leaned forward to him, discharging a debt, and said softly, "I wanted you to know how your classes changed my life. How grateful I am to you now, if I didn't know it at the time."

The old man didn't smile. In acknowledgment or anything else.

"I used to work in Germany. I still have interests there. It's really thanks to you."

"Where? What city?"

"Frankfurt."

"*Natürlich*," said the old man with contempt.

He'd been all piss and vinegar in those days; unstoppable, his Mackie Messer phase. When his boss flew in from New York to oversee a deal that Molloy had worked on for months, fitting each piece into place as painstakingly as if he were tesselating a mosaic, the man showed up for the crucial meeting twenty minutes late. With the Germans, you might as well not show up at all. Molloy had let himself lose his temper: "This isn't fucking Mexico City." But of course it was his own fault for not telling the man about Germans and punctuality. Though nobody ever needed to tell him. His American firm didn't have a chance to whack him; he had the creds, street and paper; quit and went to work for a German firm instead.

"Is there anything I can do for you? Would you be more comfortable somewhere else?"

Elastic spittle tented across the corners of Father Yokkie's mouth as he tried to speak. His mouth had shrunk and his false teeth, oversize now, clicked independently. "They came to ask about you as a candidate for the seminary, did you know that? Straight A's in Latin and German, this is a boy for the vocation. I near busted a gut laughing. Jackie Molloy? He wants exactly two things out of life, *pudenda et pecunia*. He wants them so bad he'll near kill himself to get them, and kill anybody gets in his way." With effort the priest leaned over and fingered the fabric of Molloy's vicuña topcoat, folded over his arm, left a ghostly trace of flakes on the sleeve. "So you got the *pecunia*. In Frankfurt." He might just as well have said in hell. "And you're probably getting the *pudenda*, widower or not."

"Is that how it looked?"

The priest snorted derisively.

Sadness, disappointment, a deep pain, had suffused Molloy. The man he'd thought so wise, penetrating, the one human being on earth he'd imagined had really understood him, could appreciate the distance between what he'd begun as and what he'd become, could not after all; hadn't seen through the immediate needs to the great gnawing hunger in a boy's soul. We never appear as we really are. Or maybe that's how he really was then.

Seminary. Shooting hoops in the schoolyard with Tony Morabito and Bobby Innocenti, the delicious satisfaction of a ball swishing into the basket just so, clear of the rim, and Tony says out of the blue: Jag-off, could you ever be a priest? Strangely enough, it's crossed Molloy's mind, since he doesn't know anybody else who makes a living reading books. He recovers the ball, dribbles it back to the penalty line, shoots again, watches with satisfaction. *Chooch*, he says to Tony, I love pussy too much. At that time he has sunk his cock into exactly two pussies, because he doesn't count dry-humping, blowjobs, hand jobs, or five-fingered-mary, but he knows the truth of what he says.

He dropped his voice: "Is there something I can do for you? Would you like to be somewhere else?" He had in mind anything the old man wanted, from a drive in the country to a new nursing home.

Father Yokkie told him where he'd rather be, another time, another place, a life to live over again, none of which Molloy could help him with in the slightest. A great wave of pity overwhelmed him, mainly for the old priest, but also for himself, and he took the old man's crusty hand and held it gently enough so that the old man could withdraw it, but he didn't. After a while, maybe because Molloy would sing to his kids as they were going to sleep, maybe something else, he sang softly to the old man, from *Die Dreigroschenoper*, a sad song about the world being poor and man being bad. Weill had intended it to be sung sardonically, a cheerful Berlin bite, but Molloy sang it straight and sad. The old man's eyes got watery, and he mouthed the words too. Molloy, knowing what he now knew, had a flash of Yokkie, then Joachim, as a young Berlin bon vivant, even a *Lebensmann*—a rake—having this song by heart, never once dreaming he'd end up like this.

What might have been. The conditional pluperfect. More perfect than perfect. A futile path to wander down. Molloy shifts on the couch, the music soothing, letting him wallow in Jerry's barely passable voice. Missing in action now. Once in a European park—where? Place des Vosges?—he'd watched lovely French mothers looking after their well-behaved French children (while he looked after his less-than-well-behaved American children) and wondered how things might have been otherwise, a *maman*, a *mutti*, a mom who promised you that all would turn out fine in the end, and here, as token of that promise, was a warm hug, a soft and steady hand cradling a sobbing head. Not him, not his kids. Moms missing in action.

He was thirteen or fourteen, eating a bowl of cereal after school in the kitchen, when his aunt Charlotte told him that his mother had taken sick just after he was born, never got over it. They call it the post-partum depression now, she'd said, but we didn't know what to do about it, that anything *could* be done. Your dad just. She shrugged. Ran away with the circus, I guess. It's a shame, he'd of been real proud of you. You've got the look of him. That's not easy for your mom, seeing him in your face every day. Always reminding what might've been, you know? He was a good-looking guy, Jackie, black Irish like you. For a while she wanted to tell you he'd died, but I said no, what if he shows up on the doorstep sometime? Jackie, this is your dead father, alive and kicking after all. Whoops. Anyway, why should he get away with ducking out from his duty as a man? His son should know. Your uncle Jack and I did the best we know how, but it's not the same, I know it.

A plea. He shook his head, humiliated. Ashamed of his black Irish father, his phantom mother, always resting in her darkened room, God's own sunlight too much for her, though God didn't exactly send sunlight by the acre-foot to the Monongahela Valley. He chewed his cereal ceremoniously. Finally understood what was expected of him, pushed out from the table and got up. You've been super, he said; put his arms around aunt Char, kissed her. Didn't say how a hollow in his soul was never filled, because you had to know it could be otherwise to complain.

It was much later, the months with Ross, when he saw what role he himself had played for the childless Char and Jack, the subtle conflicts that might have inspired his mother to name him for her brother, instead of for his father, or his grandfather, or nobody at all. His few fantasies of his father—meeting him by accident, getting an unexpected phone call—withered and died early.

Then what? Gets himself the hell out of the Mon Valley and all it stands for, starts a new life in a new country, and ten or so years later? Repeats the pattern.

The music takes him somewhere else. On a warm summer's night he's lying flat on his back in the Sheep Meadow, smoking a joint, staring up at the stars. You need a dip in the ground so when the police shine their lights over the meadow they can't see you. A woman beside him, he can't remember who. By then he's Jack Molloy, up and coming in every sense. He wonders if kids still do that, get high on the Sheep Meadow under the noses of the cops.

Jackie Molloy, known among the priests at St. Joseph's for wanting pudenda and pecunia so bad he'd near kill himself to get them, and kill anybody who got in his way. So focused, colleagues would say with admiration. Mackie Messer, Jürgen teased, and gave him the Lotte Lenya record. *Erste kommt das Fressen.* Which he'd later replaced with a CD and would replace again when the next big thing came along. So goddamned, stupidly obsessive that by the time he was simply Molloy, he could leave a man on a mountainside to die. Who, luckily, only got frostbite and lost a few toes.

Lindy was less fortunate.

Don't go there.

Christ, that was cruel, Molloy. The woman's face a mixture of disappointment, hurt, and yes, disgust. The lady giveth and the lady taketh away. With her Punxatawny Phil first poked his head up after a long, bleak winter. Affliction, Ross said, can mature and ripen you. Even Mackie Messer apologized to everybody as he was about to be hanged. The months with Ross. Very useful for sorting things out.

When he'd started reading history, he recognized something of himself in the Ottoman sultans. He wanted the affinity to be Suleiman I, twenty-six when he ascended the throne, "a statesman who combined vision with practical talents, a man of action who was also a man of culture and grace, worthy of the Renaissance into which he had been born," wrote Lord Kinross. Suleiman the Magnificent, Suleiman the Lawgiver, Suleiman who brought the Ottoman Empire to its zenith, whose mosque in Istanbul had awed Molloy. But there was also Mehmed III, Suleiman's grandson, who, upon his accession—about the time the Spaniards were first settling Santa Fe—instructed his mute slaves to strangle his nineteen half-brothers, thereby eliminating questions about succession. Nineteen half-brothers, plus six of their pregnant favorites, plus, for good measure, his own son.

Okay, conjugate the irregular verb to be. *Sum*, I am, *es*, thou art, *est*, he, she or it is (though Father Yokkie had made them say she, he or it, so they wouldn't slur the she and it into shit) *sumus*, we are, and then—and then—*sumus, estis, sunt.* A little rusty there, Jacko, in the game of being. Why is *to be* always irregular? A deep linguistic commentary on life and being in the Indo-European worldview. Try the future perfect, where the future is always perfect: *fuero,* I will have been, *fueris,* thou will, thou wilt? have been, *fuerrit,* he, she or it will have been, *fuerimus, fueritis, fuerint.* A loopy daydream of cracking a great code, like some past amateurs, whatsisname, Sir William Jones, the magistrate in India, teaching himself Sanskrit at night and discovering enough similarities between it and other European languages that he can announce to the Asiatic Society in Calcutta: human languages have a primary source and let us call it Indo-European; the architect Michael Ventris cracking Minoan Linear B, which had baffled generations of experts. Daydreams. He could get back into all this, given a chance. Funny that the woman plays around with language too.

Or maybe the great study waiting to be done of ideas that were transported in the cargoes of merchants along the prehistoric trade routes, how they changed civilizations. Marriages, alliances, and raiding expeditions did their share, but trade had dominated, dispersing goods, metal artifacts, especially jewelry and weapons, and above all, ideas, over vast distances in the Bronze Age. By 5000 BCE, great trade routes from southeastern to northwestern Europe: Hungarian metalwork in Danish bogs, the Carthaginians had traded salt across the Sahara for Black Africa's gold.

Yes, the merchants. Not the scholars. Not the aristocracy. Not even the soldiers. The much-despised traders, freighting ideas along the Silk Route, the Spice Route, the pilgrim routes, along a hundred other nameless routes on every continent, and then across the seas; ideas to undermine, to revolutionize, to enlighten, packed inside their bales and saddlebags, sloshing in their sealed amphorae. He dreams first of a book, then, after a provocative conversation with the Yale economist Martin Shubik, who visits the Institute regularly, thinks yes, okay. Why not? A major museum devoted to all this, money, basic economics, financial institutions, trade in all its aspects, particularly as it transports ideas. He has the ways and means. And what else does he have but time?

He loves pictures, but has never wanted to make them himself, not with paint or pencil, not with camera. He makes money instead, which he doesn't particularly love for itself, but the process is big fun and what it gets you is very pleasant. Today the Dow closed up at 8783.14, the NASDAQ closed up at 1823.57, the DAX closed up at 4841.72, the Footsie One Hundred up at 5622.90, the Hang Seng up at 10,508.25; the long bond yield was 5.32; and if we can't remember Latin, at least we're not having an Elder Moment. His trades are market-neutral, so he wins up or down. Today he bet on the ECU, the D-Mark, the Swiss franc, and went nuts with the Turkish lira, but came out fine in the end. He's begun closing his positions each day, but since he trades across many time zones, what's a day, exactly? He believes in the euro and his money is where his mouth is (but hedged: positions that will make money whether German and Italian bond yields converge, or volatility surfaces diverge, a crash-tested strategy). He still sits on a dozen important boards in Europe and the U.S, anonymous holding companies chartered in Luxembourg, or Delaware, or wherever things are relaxed without being shady—he's never gone in for offshore scams. He's connected with, okay taken over, a little consulting firm here called New Business, to force him out of the house a few days a week, or he really would be off down the slippery slope again. The firm badly needed restructuring, reformation, but he didn't come to Santa Fe for that. Still, waste and shortsightedness offend him.

Yo, Jacko, whatcha gonna do with it all, hey? All your money, all your life? Kids provided for, you too. Plenty left over. People he knows have made second careers out of spending what they earned in their first careers. A foundation, pet causes well funded, giving you back your own money in commemorative dinners well ventilated by the drafts of sucking-up speeches. Do it, Molloy, they say. A few million for starving artists, another few tens of millions for, oh, an artists' colony and its endowment, the new Guggenheims, the new MacArthurs, whatever.

In that elegant and subtle dance called being on the board, several museums, performing arts boards, and two universities in New York City have already approached him. To such invitations you do not say no. Either you say yes, or you say perhaps. He's said yes to the most desirable museum, and to all the others, perhaps.

Meanwhile: commission works of art, Molloy; be the new Lorenzo the Magnificent. Underwrite a new production of an opera, a new play. He's come close, written some checks quietly to experimental theater groups, where, clad in black sweater and jeans, he slips up and down stairways—these places are always in Manhattan's lofts and basements, its far West Side warehouses—and is thrilled or dismayed by the audacious ingenuity of playwrights, actors, directors, scene designers. It amuses him to find his way to places like Brooklyn's Red Hook, go under the Gowanus Expressway on foot, threading among the empty warehouses until he finds the one that some artist has converted to a studio and dwelling, see the art, sometimes good, sometimes not. But a full-time job?

Friends have gone into the government, giving back righteously. But a public life of any kind repels him more than ever; being at the beck-and-call of elected yahoos is even worse. Against his better judgment he allowed himself to be lured out momentarily onto the gasbag circuit, a pundit on the basis of his fortune alone. Though he's actually pretty good at it—all those years of presentations and persuasions—he can't see making a new career of that either.

He knows people who do nothing but cruise around the oceans of the world, which seems the stupidest, most mindless choice of all.

Jacko, if you ain't who you were—Jackie Molloy, or even Jack; no longer Mackie Messer, or even Wall Street's starchy J. B. Molloy (& Co.); no longer the Chief White Eunuch, master of other people's revels—then who the hell are you?

And why are you here?

Chaos is a Continuing Struggle Between Stretching and Folding

Sophie had become a kind of seer. Death's imminence seemed to strip away the false, the foolish, illusion from reality. She still took an interest in the lives of her friends, even permitted herself to offer advice. Like her speech, it addressed essentials. Judith watched carefully, knowing that when this faded, Sophie would have passed over another boundary.

In this long twilight, a question once answered carelessly now demanded a thoughtful response. Terms had changed, no time to spare. So when Sophie, lying on her patio chaise, bundled in a blanket against what was, in reality, a sweet June breeze, asked how dinner was at the rich guy's, Judith thought about the answer.

"We both made fools of ourselves. We don't know how to talk to each other. His idea of coming on—I think it's coming on—is, tell me about complexity. Really. We're into the second course, and here's this character whispering phase transitions."

"My God, what's his foreplay like? Sounds like your kind of guy, sweetie. Got your number. To five significant digits." The chemo, the disease, had straitened Sophie's voice, aged it, pitched it higher; she sounded like somebody's impertinent granny.

"Not JAWS, I'll say that for him. One minute it's Ito calculus, the meaning of death, or direct quotes in the German from Schiller; the next he's gutted Maya and left her for dead. God knows she richly deserves it, but you'd hate to put yourself in a place where it might be you."

"He's either very, very clever, or—" Sophie broke off, lost in thought or because her strength had failed her. "Or, he's overwhelmed by you, bowled over, blown away, and doesn't know what to talk to you about except the big issues. Take the full frontal approach: hey, rich guy, how about a roll in the hay?"

Judith smiled. "Why not? He hit on me early on, but it felt—oh, you know. He was scoring. Double-parking. Like I should be worried about that at my age. Meanwhile, he's fucked everything on two legs in Santa Fe *except* me. A very serious collector."

"And you don't want to be a mere item in the collection. Right. Standards to maintain." Then, not mocking. "I wonder if you're reading him right."

"The serious collector and I have a conversation, and it's me answering questions—good ones, but his, not mine. He replies probably less than half the time; very big on the enigmatic smile. I thought at first maybe the guy's a bit dim. But when he talks, he's no dummy. Gabe once observed that Molloy never lets go and laughs. Fundamentally a sad guy."

"Maybe he's dumbstruck with admiration."

"Maybe you should change your meds. Or maybe I've forgotten how preposterously young a younger guy can be."

"What's the gap?" Sophie inquired with interest.

"People-years, around a decade. But since we all know a woman's age is measured in dog-years, it feels wider." Sophie snorted, but Judith was pursuing something else. "When my father got sick, we had this home help called Martha who made him the center of her life. As far as we were concerned, Alzheimer's was like some alien who'd taken over his body. But she adored him, told us how deeply she'd come to know and respect him. She wasn't just trying to make us, the family, feel good; she really did think she knew him in a way we didn't. At the time, I figured some kind of massive projection going on, or this is how the human heart gets through five years of literal shitwork—"

"Jay, cut me some slack. I'll be somebody's shitwork soon enough."

Judith leaned over and kissed her friend's forehead. "I'm sorry, Soph. That was so dumb." She held Sophie's hand, this once almost silent woman, with such immense will, such an unshakable sense of doing right, who'd chained herself to the White House fence in protest against the Vietnam War—and then ended up at Los Alamos National Laboratories. Not really a contradiction, but Judith guessed she was one of the few who understood that. Words for a memorial service. What she wouldn't say was how, at some point, the fight had gone out of Sophie. Rage against the machine had dissipated, maybe to be replaced by some other kind, more obscure. Hazards of atomic waste disposal, the lack of diversity at the top levels of the Labs—on these, Sophie had shrugged, kept silent. Forget talking about Sophie's days as a biker chick too, this a few years before the war protests, when Sophie wrapped her legs around any hog willing to let her ride; when she got pregnant and aborted, before it was legal.

"Back to Martha," Sophie said patiently.

"Did she really see something in my dad that was invisible to us, because we'd known him at his wonderful, rational, witty peak and when he descended from that peak, we discounted everything? Or was my dad for Martha something she imagined? We make our world, Soph. At the last, I was in the hospital with them, and Martha was yelling at my father, all but shaking him, slapping his face, *wake up, Cookie; you've got to try, Cookie!* Cookie! Nobody ever called my father Cookie—and I'm thinking, hey, if that were me, I'd want to go gentle into that good night, nobody screaming in my face, but it isn't me, so what do I know? Soph, how did I get to Martha?"

"How we're sometimes blind. Dinner at the rich guy's."

"The serious collector's. Molloy. His name is Molloy."

"First name or last?"

"Don't know. That's all he's ever called." She got to the point. "Yeah, he's under my skin. Is he entitled to be there, or is this some kind of post-menopausal ditziness? I think—I think he scares me, and my fright comes out sounding like malice."

"What's scary? Not high-octane sex. Not you."

Judith nodded slowly. "I'd do him in Planck time, just like every other woman in Santa Fe, except—" The word lingered, and she turned to look out the window, where the shadows had deepened. "Except I really don't know."

"Limits to knowledge," Sophie laughed and then began to cough, deaf to Judith's affectionate reply: Bitch. It's limits to *science*. Coughing ended, Sophie heaved a breath. "Jesus, Jay, you are so smart about things that don't matter and so dirt-dumb about what does. My deathbed blessing: *carpe diem*."

"Soph, is this what it's come to? We're back talking guys again after thirty years of talking substance? Devolution, I'd call it. Anyway, I really don't know a damn thing about the serious collector, who, by the way, I first saw all buff in starched shirt, rich tie and well-cut suit. And oh my God, so—uhm, stiff. Laugh, Soph, laugh. I make the leetle joke. Molloy is a wonderful inkblot you can project anything you want on to. He's very rich. That's maybe our one real data point. What the hell does that mean? Rich, rich, as if money is some attribute of the gods. It's not. It stands for, but it's nothing itself, and what it stands for with regard to him I haven't a clue. He doesn't act rich—no gaudy toys, no big household staff. The house is—very nice, but mercifully monkish. Okay, a drop-dead collection of paintings, but that's it. His wife died. Is he grieving, or glad she died before she could escape with her part of the domestic treasure? He mentioned a close friend who died—death puzzles him he says. Okay, it puzzles us all. I have no idea whether he's the worst kind of right-wing nut, or—or getting ready to distribute all that treasure in a wise and useful way, and I should write up a grant proposal toot sweet. Oh hell, what if he doesn't even know who the Dead were, and loves gangsta rap? New Age slop?"

Sophie objected, her voice weaker. "We weren't talking guys thirty years ago, we were planning protests. Taking prelims. Coding in assembly language." She was lost in memory. "Remember what you said: ignore your fears, get over your timidity. Take more chances. For starters." She'd exhausted herself, and snuggled into the chaise cushion, the blanket pulled to her chin.

They were not in the same realm. Sophie had already crossed over one border, left Judith in the land of the living, where strategies must be thought of, consequences reckoned with, coherent images upheld, at least in your own mind. Sophie made a great effort and was still nearly inaudible. "Not just any old *carpe*, any old *diem*. Never defect first. Reward good behavior by cooperating the next time. Punish uncooperative behavior. Be clear enough so he can figure it out."

Judith slapped her forehead. "Oh my God. Applications of game theory to sportfucking. One last paper there, Soph?" Tears could come after all. She wasn't ready to let Sophie go. She leaned forward, straining to hear Sophie's failing voice.

"Benito is sportfucking. Friendly joy. Lucky you. We should all . . . I've envied you Benito, you know that, but I never thought he was enough for you. This Molloy guy, this serious collector, this callow youth who, for all we know, sits home blasting Nine Inch Nails day and night." She stopped, past exhaustion. "You I can read, sweetie. It's more than sportfucking—it could be—and that's what scares you, hey? An encounter with the divine. After all this time. Courage, sweetie, courage."

"Soph, you haven't seen this guy. One look, you'd get it. He's mega-high-maintenance. The women he chooses. Beware the guy who admires what you've accomplished so much he admires you into a professional train wreck."

Sophie lifted an eyebrow. "I never met the problem myself."

"It's never occurred to you why women in science freak everyone out? Crash the men's locker room, bad enough, but our unforgivable sin is—*we will not serve.* We don't exhibit ourselves like artists or athletes, don't cure like doctors, defend the downtrodden like lawyers. We do It for ourselves alone. For a woman, anything further off the grid? Outside the schema? The first and most famous to say I will not serve? Lucifer, Soph, the fallen angel. *Non serviam. Better to reign in hell than serve in heaven.*"

Sophie stirred. "Something to think about, girlfriend. Wanting to be a vet was okay. But molecular biology . . ."

"You're welcome. Look, this guy's finally a trophy hunter. Not the usual trophy, but it's still a trophy. Heaven? Maybe. But not now, not ever, I will not serve. Nobody's trophy. Hoping to bag a few myself." Judith dropped her friend's hand, jumped up, walked restlessly around the patio. "Look what I'm trying to do, Soph. Spent my life aiming to be a—a master builder. I accept that the project will last beyond my lifetime; the structure could collapse into rubble anytime. A chance worth taking. It's the greatest adventure I could hope for. No false modesty here, this work *is* a damn cathedral. Find, prove, impossibility results in science. *The forever unknowable.* Nail that, and the whole map of science changes completely, is fabulously enriched. My God, it's a problem to sink your fangs into, win or lose." She was talking to herself. In ways she wasn't ready to admit, *for* herself. She spun back to Sophie. "How many points from history for succumbing to a grand passion? No ma'am, if anyone's going to gamble with my career at this stage of the game, it's me, thanks. There's so much left to do."

Sophie watched this ardent outburst with interest, but had no energy to reply. In her realm, she could take a larger, longer view; indeed, spent her quiet days in bed meditating on her life in a detail that would have astonished her a few months earlier, not only teasing out the patterns, but forming a grand synthesis, a story, an epic poem for herself. Of herself. Who she was, what she'd done, what her life meant, even if she found no meaning in her death. This *non serviam* business—Sophie wanted to be alone to think about it. Quotidian life seemed spectral to her now, beside the point, and she wished release from it. She observed Queen Judith wearily, who'd surely end up reigning in hell.

Summer 1997

Pairwise Interactions

The summer rituals moved forward. Priests blessed the *acequias* and fields beneath vivid blue skies, skies that were festooned with the first puffy white clouds of the summer to scud up from the Gulf of Mexico. In the pueblos prayers, dances, songs and drumming honored the corn (and not pickup trucks or burgers, as one sardonic tribal elder suggested); new art was previewed at the Eight Northern Pueblos show; the chamber music festival and opera opened. In mid-July, Benito came back from his dig to roam Spanish Market with Judith, for him an enterprise less about art than talk. If he wasn't related to every second artist or craftsman, then he'd gone to school with them, had lived in the same parish, or met them dancing to Father Frank's band down at Club Alegría on Agua Fría. He greeted them all, men and women, with a friendly *abrazo*.

New Mexican Spanish was a stately music, part 16th and 17th century Castilian, brought by the first Spanish settlers and preserved, though with some odd local mutations; part 20th-century Spanglish (*sí, mi güisa*, yes, my sweetheart; *bueno bye*); some Náhuatl from the Aztecs; adaptations from the Rio Grande Indian tongues; even 19th century Mexican-Spanish. It was a dialect unto itself, always elaborately courteous. Though her ear was better tuned to modern Latin-American Spanish, Judith could follow the gist. Benito, raised in northern New Mexico, spoke it fluently, though he could also speak what he called "true Spanish" and English perfectly. For that matter, he was conversant in the living Tewa languages, and could also speak enough Navajo and Hopi to put the old-timers at ease. That came, he said, with the territory.

They lay side by side in the nun's bed, comforted by each other's nearness. "Your dreams?" she asked.

"Why don't I dream my own cities, my own symbols?"

She laughed. "Which are?"

"Yeah. Which are." Through his veins ran blood he couldn't assay. The conquistadors were Spanish, a gloriously mongrel group to begin with—Arab, Berber, Celt, Basque, more. A disproportionate number of those *bravos* riding north in chain mail were *conversos*, Spanish Jews and their descendants, apparently converted, though the *converso* tradition in northern New Mexico persisted: ranchers who kept their hats on during a Friday night candlelight dinner, avoided pork, went to mass on Sundays. The old *norteño* musicians still sang in Ladino, and northern Mexico had one of the world's greatest concentrations of that Mediterranean Jews' affliction, Tay-Sachs disease.

But he'd been digging pueblos all his working days; shouldn't the city he dreamed be one of those? Shouldn't its mysteries be the mysteries he spent his working days trying to solve?

You don't get to choose what you dream, his mother Luz had said once, any more than you get to choose who you fall in love with.

By Indian Market in mid-August, he was back at his dig, and Judith went alone. Nowadays, she acquired pots and rugs from artists directly, but Indian Market was too much fun to resist. Downtown hotels had all been booked for months; visitors overflowed to every dinky motel on Cerrillos Road.

As artists were setting up their wares in the chilly dawn, the booths spilling out from the plaza along the side streets, she wandered happily among them. With the sun still behind Atalaya Mountain, the midday heat was a distant promise; the afternoon thunderstorms seemed even more unlikely. She waved to the Ortiz family, Cóchiti Indians, setting up their booth of droll figurines; had a kiss on both cheeks from a Nambé potter of national distinction who floated gracefully between his own spiritual world and the world of high art ("You haven't forgotten I want an *olla*, Lonnie?"); had a friendly dispute with the Romero brothers, potter and painter each, also Cóchiti, who denounced everything in the market as tourist trinkets; and was finished in time to meet Gabe and Ron at Cafe Pasqual for breakfast at 8:00 a.m.

They rode off huevos rancheros with their annual Indian Market bike ride, then home to Casa Rongabe. There she stood, crane-legged on the balcony, exhilarated and pleasantly sleepy, hand pulling at the raised foot, stretching quads and hamstrings after a glorious ride down the Aspen Vista Trail.

She was fond of this house too, also a short walk from her own house, just off Camino San Acacio in the old barrio. It sat on the low shoulders of Talaya Hill, the front rooms and balcony giving out over the barrio rooftops to the northern Sangres, even to Colorado on a clear day. Much like their bookshop, the house was warm and light, full of oddments brought back from Morocco, from exotic Malibu. Gabe had become an avid gardener, and coaxed flowers out of the hopeless high desert soil nearly year round.

People would soon be gathering here, by foot, bike, car, for the annual Indian Market barbecue Ron and Gabe always threw, a midyear complement to their Christmas Eve party. In this quiet moment beforehand, Gabe was fussing in the kitchen, Ron was fixing drinks. Judith stayed out on the balcony watching the eastern clouds from the Sangres strain toward the western clouds from the Jemez, wondered idly which would reach Santa Fe first.

She was conscious today of how she loved these men. Shared history yes (with Ron, anyway) but she loved them because they were lovable. They welcomed her love, returned it as nobody ever had, not even her brother. Certainly not her parents, real 1950s Episcopalians, the frozen chosen coined for them, mom struggling into her armored girdle and stockings, never pantyhose, to this day.

Ron and Gabe had given each other the great gift of opening up latencies. Ron, hollow-chested and pallid in his adolescence, nicknamed variously *der Pilz*, the mushroom, *der Spargel*, after the white asparagus he resembled, above all, *Count Dracula*, fleeing from the sunshine like—well, Count Dracula, pimply, bookish, had found his physicality with Gabe. Though it must've begun sexually, Gabe had transformed Ron from the worst kind of effeteness to a middle-aged athlete, biking and skiing where she often joined them, hikes to places that Judith's knees forbade. Gabe had enrolled in Ron U., where his natural intelligence had been lovingly cultivated.

Gabe brought out chips and salsa. "So how's Molloy the mogul, Molloy-polloi, Molloy-Muh-Boy, Molloyin King?"

"Haven't seen him for a while, not counting over the conference table at New Business." Seldom and briefly there.

"No? We invited him today, but he's out of town. Maybe off bashing the baht? Wringing the neck of the ringgit? Repudiating the rupiah?"

Ron joined them with lemonades. "Wiping up the won? Yanking the yen around? Punishing the Philippine peso? Dinging the dong? Hey, I like that one."

"Molloy trades currencies? I didn't know that," Judith said lazily.

"Just what does trading currencies consist of?" Gabe asked.

"You're hoping the exchange rates between what you're selling and what you're buying will widen or narrow to your advantage. No different from selling apples and buying oranges in the belief that oranges will be a better investment. Yeah, Molloy trades currencies," Ron said. "In mega-sums. Interbank trading, which game I understand—not from him—takes a twenty-five mill line of credit just to play. This, however, is pocket change for Molloy, if I reckon right."

"Ron, please."

"One of my New York backers does this kind of thing. Makes, depending on the leverage, between sixty and four hundred and twenty-five million a year."

"Serious money," Judith conceded. "But Ronnie. Between sixty and four hundred and twenty-five? Those are big error bars."

"On that scale, who cares? Hold it, Molloy, if we're not into triple-digit millions per annum here, consider yourself failed. Of course my friend in New York is a quant, and Molloy does it by gut instinct. Whether that means he makes more or less, I couldn't say. Molloy keeps open lines to his brokers and trades anonymously so he doesn't distort the market. The big company, the hedge fund, that still has his name he sold, but started another little one for recreation, my micro-firm he calls it. In addition to New Business, which I hear he's also bought. We talked about trading that weekend at El Bosque. Talked about it off and on since. You still do big-time currency trading by phone—it's all personal psychology, these guys all know each other's quirks, weaknesses, and strengths. He invited me to his trading pit at Camp Rheingold—the house—once."

"Ronnie, that's not his word?" She answered his wicked smile. "*Du bist sehr frech.*"

"You been there? No? Fun to see how the big boys play: clocks across the wall, times from Hong Kong to Frankfurt—I'm thinking, a smart guy like you can't calculate what time it is where you want to trade? Then realize he's not putting one extra cycle anyplace he doesn't have to. A bunch of screens, a dedicated real-time quote machine, a regular desktop, and CNBC with the tape running. Maybe Bloomberg there too, I don't remember now. I stopped counting the phone lines.

"Then the music." Ron is laughing. "The day I'm there, it's the Franck Sonata in A playing, because he says that's what the charts say; today's a Franck day. Yesterday it was Stockhausen. All last week it was Messiaen. The whole damn week. Random noise? I say. No, he says, patterns, neither apparent nor comforting. Is this like a soundtrack? Well, *that* gets me withering scorn. No, he says, the markets have patterns, and I pick music that matches those patterns to help me focus. So I think of my buddy Stevie, a vice-president at MTV, his office fifty stories above West 45th Street, also two screens going, CNN and MTV, but the sound system is doing Debussy. I also think, it certainly beats betting the numbers you dreamed last night, or your uncle's social security number. A trillion dollars a day gets traded in currencies on this planet, and our boy does a significant share of that, with the help of two or three assistants in Manhattan. One of whom, oh irony of ironies—" he reached for chips, gave a thumbs-up to Gabe when he tasted the salsa, "started out as a superbly-trained Soviet mathematician. Totally unemployable in Moscow and making a fortune here. 'Volodya,' I hear Molloy say on the phone very gently, 'we don't curse at the market-makers in my company. At least not in English.'" Judith laughed. Ron had Molloy's inflections flawlessly. "'You want to deep-fry, salt, and serve up for snacks his tender parts? You want to rip him a new asshole? You must tell him only in Russian, okay? And if he understands Russian, if he's one of your compatriots, you'll have to change to Lithuanian. We're gentlemen in my company. Yeah, Volodya, I know; I know; I've used German when I had to. This is how it is, Volodya.'" Ron grinned. "I hear he even does business with the Fuggers—like it's the Renaissance, monopoly on the salt trade, the mines, loans to the crowned heads, even crowning those heads. All that."

Judith tried the salsa herself. "The Fuggers? They're still in business? How did they write down all that bad debt from the Holy Roman Empire, the Spanish throne? Molloy owns New Mexico?"

"Ted Turner owns New Mexico," Gabe said.

"The Hapsburgs damn near sank them," said Ron somberly, "but sank themselves instead. What's the take-home lesson, that the Fuggers are still in business and their clients aren't? Okay, okay, the Spanish throne; but really. Can that count?"

Nonsynchronous Trading

The talk that first afternoon Ron spent at Molloy's had come round from trading, as Ron knew it would, to Judith. As Ron knew he'd been summoned for.

"You're old friends," Molloy says casually.

"Known each other since high school." They're sitting on Molloy's *portal*, overlooking the early summer green cottonwoods edging the Santa Fe River, a bit of the cotton still flurrying in the breeze; the city and the indigo of the Jemez range beyond. They sip Molloy's excellent single malt. Ron observes Molloy, deciding how he'll describe it to Gabe over dinner tonight: Molloy trying so hard to be casual and so *not* casual in every muscle. I intended, he'll tell Gabe, to control this conversation. If Molloy has an agenda, me too. So I say, "You might wonder how people like Judith and I are friends."

Noncommittal, Molloy watches him.

"Not many people know this story. Gabe, of course. *Dissolve, flashback*. We were both in the American high school in Munich, but parallel universes. We called her Queen Judith. Not princess, mind you, but Queen—you might smile, you might smile—an extraordinary creature, the goddess all the boys want to have and all the girls want to be. You can't imagine how beautiful, how heart-stoppingly ravishing Queen Judith was in her radiant youth."

"Oh, maybe I can." *Ronnie G.'s POV*: Molloy's smile says it's a topic he's given some thought to.

Angle on Ronnie G. and Molloy. Ronnie: "Studying Wordsworth then, *She walks in beauty like the night.* You get the idea. Then as now, beautifully groomed, mucho indulged by her parents, but that's another story for another time. Oddly, that's not how she looks back. But we never really see ourselves as others—" He trails off, annoyed with himself, goes back to his story, Molloy attentive, giving it all away despite the self-control. Maybe because of it. "She was in my English class, so I also knew this celestial creature had an extraordinary mind. Not just the good girl who has her homework done every morning, neatness counts. An incisive intellect. She was very funny about Lady Macbeth—well, neither here nor there. The looks threw you off. You thought, she's got all that; how come she gets to have a mind too? Where's the justice? So if I knew she wasn't just your basic cupcake, there's no way someone like me, zits, braces, as repellent as la divine Judith's beautiful, will ever get close enough to know more. That's the way it was.

"Add to this my somewhat confused sexuality. This is the early sixties, so basically the extended fifties. In addition, we're maybe ten years behind stateside on the topic of sexual orientation. All I know is I can't be queer, a fag, a *homo*, as we used to say in those days, because I'm head over heels in love with, I worship, Judith Greenwood, right?"

Molloy looks out in the distance, smiles slightly in acknowledgment.

"You know Munich a little, the Englischer Garten? Summers we'd go swimming in the Eisbach. If I was there to scope out the older German guys who swam nude, I didn't really know it. I was there with my classmates, Americans; we swam in swimsuits, believe me. And *Königin* Judith was down the brook a little ways, also in her demure little swimsuit, laughing with her girlfriends, all golden hair and honey tan, the center of it all, and us pitiful losers lying on the grass under the chestnut trees feeling sorry for ourselves.

"So one summer night, dark comes late that time of the year, that part of the world, it's finally time to go home. I'm biking down toward Prinzregentenstrasse—my family lived in Lehel. In a dark part of the woods, I go over my handlebars. First I think a flat. But I start to get up, and I'm hit from behind, right between the shoulder blades. Suddenly I know a stick went through my spokes, this is deliberate. Then the beating. The words. Not yelling at me: it's more like a whisper, somebody's working real hard and words are an extra effort. Faggot. Queer. Faggot. In short, I'm being queer-bashed and I don't even know I'm queer! I don't see them, they're American. Some voices I know, not others. Later I think maybe some American soldiers. It hurts like hell, I'm probably screaming bloody murder, but mostly I'm just psychologically stunned. *Why me?* It crosses my mind I'll die; these guys aren't letting up.

"Then a voice I absolutely recognize, Judith's. She's just happened to come behind me on her bike and she's like a banshee, screaming at these guys, calling them by name, telling them to get the fuck—get the *fuck*—the queen doesn't use such language!—away from me. They do. They scatter. She's there. She's crying; I don't know why, but she's crying. She takes me in her arms, and tells me everything's going to be okay. Helps me up, walks me and my bike home, tells my parents I went over a rock in the path or something, and she just happened to come along.

"I didn't go back to school for a few days—I was a mess. Judith came by with homework, checked to see how I was getting along. That's when we discovered that we were neither quite what we seemed.

"I think once back to school, she'll ignore me. I mean—me. Really. But that's not how it was. I was her pal. Her pet. A court favorite, okay? She'd put her arm around my waist in public. Not exactly I'm a student leader overnight, but something happened. Invitations to parties, to join people doing this, that, the kind of thing high school kids kill for. Impossible to tell you what this did for me. For my subsequent sense of myself. For my subsequent safety.

"I remember high school," Molloy says at last. "That took moral courage, what she did."

"Judith saved my life. That one could've been fatal. The next one would've been, and there'd have been a next one. She re-made my life in some sense. But—" he stares at Molloy's impassive face. "Be careful. Maybe I wouldn't call it moral courage, exactly. Yeah, sure, in some ways. But also Queen Judith having her way—by God she's going to show these assholes what they need to be shown. Impose her will. That sounds ungenerous. No. I mean that Judith is very complicated. Never underestimate that. Sometimes she just barrels right on through, completely oblivious to you, then hello? you aren't with me? That's dumb; we could've avoided this whole thing if you'd done it my way in the first place. Queen Judith."

"She wasn't what she seemed?"

"Then? All-American girl." Find out the rest for yourself.

A long silence. Molloy breaks it. "Did you know her husband?"

"Oh God, Jonathan. I met him a couple of times. A real—I don't know, I'm not the one to ask. A putz. Figure that one out; I wouldn't swear I've got it right yet. Jonathan was—very brilliant. If they gave Nobels in mathematics, which they don't, Jonathan Sichel would've been a Nobel laureate, okay? He won all the, whatever prizes and medals mathematicians give each other. Strange old guy, a senior member of her department when she went there as young assistant professor. A certain academic type—totally self-absorbed, and almost—desiccated. No juice in him. I couldn't figure out what the hell they were doing with each other."

"What were they doing with each other?" *Close-up of Molloy the stiff, still trying so hard to be casual. I swear, I live my life just so I'll have stories to keep you entertained over dinner, Gabes. Frame by frame.*

"He rang her bells, what can I tell you? Some of them. Not others. It was like, I began to think later, the pattern of Judith and Ron. Judith was drawn to me because I kept her amused without making any other demands, didn't, still don't, probe unduly. Be clear. The lady's passionate. Deeply passionate. The marriage more or less broke up, I take it, because she couldn't keep her hands off studmuffins. But there was always this—" Ron's hands parted "—dissociation, I guess is the technical term, between her intellectual and physical passions. Nobody, so far as I know, has ever touched the lady's emotional passions. Murky. Maybe I don't do her justice. I don't pretend to know the strange ways of you hets. Most guys find all that intensity wearing. She started up with Benito, I thought good, a smart guy, all carnal instincts intact, but laid-back enough to take her highflying in stride."

"Her boyfriend?"

"Yes. No. Sort of." Molloy shoots him a quizzical look, yes or no? "Is this important to you?" Molloy is silent. "I've said more than enough. Nothing like a late afternoon scotch to loosen the tongue. So I'll say one more thing. If you're asking whether Judith is available, I'd say possibly. Possibly. Judith doesn't confide in me. In anybody, for that matter, not even her friend Sophie, though Sophie gets more of the day-to-day stuff than I do. If Judith wanted Benito to have and to hold till death did them part, believe me, Queen Judith would have Benito like *that*. She's a willful woman. Since there's nothing legal between them, I assume that's the way she wants it. She still has a roving eye, so that may account for the informality of the arrangement. This from Sophie, who isn't entirely reliable, having her own issues with Queen Judith. My God. At our age, Judith's and mine, this stuff is supposed to be over and done with."

Molloy nods slowly, solemnly, then allows himself a smile. "In risk arbitrage, we always asked ourselves, why is this game available to be played?" A long silence. "And Sophie's issues?"

"Judith's going to change the way science is done, she announces to one and all. Upend what we mean by reality. Oh, it's truly rich, think about it, Molloy. The most imperious woman in science is going to impose humility on science. Thing is, she's got the chops. If it can be done she'll do it. Neither Sophie's ambition nor abilities aspire to that level. It causes problems, I think. Jay's oblivious. Just as well."

He doesn't add the other issue, only speculation on his part. Glass to his forehead to cool off, he scrutinizes Molloy. "Judith's one of those rare women—rare enough these days—who genuinely likes men. Not just a sexual thing, though it's that. She gets off on male energy, straight, gay, it doesn't matter. Makes her a good friend. If you're lucky, she'll at least be your friend, Molloy." He waits, watching the man across from him, trying again to phrase for Gabe the expressions on Molloy's face: *like some special fx, he'll say, the helmet beginning to melt, to morph, to give way to something human and vulnerable—pain, fear, longing, who knows.*

"You get to talk, Molloy. It's what's called a conversation."

Molloy shy, maybe distressed, opens his mouth, closes it again, shrugs, begins a sentence and can't finish, stares off across the Rio Grande basin. "Bear with me. I've had a lot of practice keeping my mouth shut. Less practice opening it, at least when it comes to." Another full stop. His head turns this way and that, like a coin's rolled onto the floor, he needs to wring out a crick in his neck. From deep in his throat little noises, between a gasp and a sigh. *Gabe will be told.*

It verges on the absurd. A man this frozen in pursuit of Queen Judith?

Too hopeless. Nevertheless: "I hope it's clear to you that my loyalty to Judith is mighty deep, mighty wide. She's more than family to me." Quite capable of killing somebody who gives her the slightest grief. Old enough to take care of herself, okay, willful when she wants to be, but to me Queen Judith, golden girl forever.

Molloy fingers his cheek, rubbing his own shadowy bristle. Nods again, very slowly, very deliberately. "*Alles klar*."

"Now you. Nobody knows much about you."

Molloy makes a self-deprecating gesture. "Well."

Ron is ready. "The American west has a long and honored tradition of tall dark strangers who ride into town wanting to forget their pasts, start anew. No reason to deny you that opportunity, Molloy. But Judge Roy Bean, appointed judge by himself alone, the only law west of the Pecos at the time, once said this. *[Ronnie G. snaps his nonexistent suspenders and assumes a Hollywood cowboy twang.]* Most of the men I sentence to be hanged are guilty as charged. *[A rich lunger in the general direction of the spittoon.]* Even if not, they're certainly guilty of something, since no one would've fled here except to escape hanging."

Molloy smiles. "No hanging offenses in my past, Ron. Gross negligence from time to time, I guess. That's all." He rattles the ice in his glass, which, Ron sees, is all but untouched. "And Queen Judith. Does she know you protect and defend her?"

"She'd hoot. She'd think it was goddamned impertinent. But there it is. Tell me about your time in Germany."

Molloy shifts in discomfort, more than unaccustomed, obviously downright averse, to self-disclosure. But smart enough, Gabe will hear, to understand that he's in a transaction, now owes something. He probably also wants an ally. Too bad. The most counter-productive thing to be done with Judith is to put in a good word for Molloy. For anybody.

Contrary to his clear inclinations, Molloy submits.

He spent, he says, twenty or more years shuttling between New York and Frankfurt, eventually in at the first stages of planning European Union financial consolidations. He'd had to be careful, consciously trying to blend in, to offer only advice, not to be a pushy American; to persuade others that his vision, one

continent, one currency, was actually theirs. He'd helped establish what would eventually be the European Central Bank and the euro (the "oyuh-ro," Molloy says, giving it the German pronunciation). He'd even lived in Frankfurt for a while ("always a pleasure to live in a country where people still entertain themselves by talking to each other") but he alludes to family difficulties and says no more.

Ron can't let this go. "You had family there?"

"For a few years. The usual ex-pat story. My wife just never acculturated. She went back to New York. She was already sick by then. Her mother—and a nanny—took care of the kids when she got very bad. Then when she had—when things got acute, I brought the kids back to a German boarding school so at least they'd have me close by. Until they went to college. Here in the U.S."

"And your wife?"

Molloy turns to him. *Extreme close-up, a face without grief, relief, certainly not joy.* "She died, Ron. Eventually she died."

At last weariness had set in, the transatlantic commutes, the endless hotels and restaurant meals, the Sunday afternoons in provincial cities with nothing but sleep and books to pass the time. He'd reestablished himself in New York, and then let go of that too. He'd withdrawn, was watching the birth struggle of the euro with interest, no longer passion. He'd chosen Santa Fe largely because it was so remote. Or maybe because it was the last piece of Europe intact in the United States. Or. He shrugs. He got back pretty often, a few boards, private banks, holding companies, in Frankfurt, Luxembourg, Brussels, New York.

"There's something I'm missing, pal. What to call it? The you in this equation, okay?"

"Oh well," Molloy says diffidently. "Either I'm some kind of woolly mammoth defrosting from my own personal ice age, or it's a dead-cat bounce."

"A what?"

"A trader's term. A stock drops by half, it's there to stay, but it does one last little jump, a couple of points, let's say. Nobody's fooled. It's still a dead cat."

"And you are which?"

"Good question." *Freeze frame.*

Deep Nonlinearities

A producer knows the pathways of money as well as any financier (his friend the New York quant had backed more than a few of his productions), and after the visit to Molloy, Ron made some phone calls. He began with New York, and was directed straight to Frankfurt's *Bundesbank*, where he heard the news from two separate sources. Molloy had, if anything, been excessively modest. In an era of inflated self-representation, Ron was pleased to give him credit for that, and also reassured on Judith's behalf. He didn't discount the fear he'd first seen in Molloy at El Bosque, but after his talk with Molloy wondered if he should have given it a different name.

Was it possible that Molloy was, in a sweetly old-fashioned way, not so much afraid as in awe of Judith? It seemed ludicrous, given the intimacy Molloy seemed to have with heads of banks, international financiers, economic ministers whose faces regularly appeared on TV, whose names were familiar from the paper. ("Mackie Messer?" a German voice said. "That brings back memories, *ah ja*. How's he doing?" And later in the conversation purred, "I am sure that he has been approached for posts at the cabinet level in your government.") Anything was possible. Ron's sources, American and German, conceded that Molloy was, well, somewhat eccentric. For a man in money.

"Find out what happened to him personally," Gabe said when he heard the story.

"Bankers and investors don't have personal lives," Ron replied. "At least not to each other." There he'd drawn a blank. People seemed aware that something had happened, but not what.

"Every man has a secret life," Gabe persisted. "You look at the outside, turn it around, and you can almost figure it out."

"A hard-assed financier on the outside, but secretly into lace lingerie, sexual apparatus, booze and dope, or what?"

"You toy with me, don Ron," Gabe said with mock disgust.

In the end it didn't matter. Nothing between Judith and Molloy after all. She hadn't even troubled to find out anything about the man, sat on the deck this Indian Market day, imperturbable, concealing no secret fascination so far as he could tell.

"Currencies aren't all he does, I'm sure," Ron said aloud. "The new micro-firm specializes in derivatives, though he makes it sound purely recreational. I gather he does commodities futures, too. Equities, of course. Ours and theirs. We exchange red-hot tips by e-mail. Exchange as in I ask and he tells, or out of the blue e-mail will come, pay attention to this. I've made a nice little bundle this summer thanks to our friend Molloy. For a while he headed the risk arbitrage desk at a big German house. Remarkable, an American doing that. Currencies. I wouldn't have the nerves, the stamina for it. Very entertaining for him these last few weeks, Asian currencies tanking. Currencies?"

She responded quickly. "Too easy. From the Latin, *currere*, to run. From the same root, courier, concur, incur, occur, corridor, discourse, and, of course—"

"Corsair and intercourse. I thought by now you two would be an item. Not so? Too bad. He was good for you, in my humble. Speaks excellent German. Only traveler's French because quote, in France there's never been any action to speak of in my field, unquote."

Gabe added: "A trifle gauche, but you could've fixed that, hon."

"And most of the gaucherie had to do with you anyway," Ron said.

"Lord, yes," Gabe agreed. "Schoolboy crushes are so cute, but they do unman a man. He's really an old smoothie when he's not smitten."

"Guys, please." It was unlike her friends to gang up on her.

"Are you blushing, fair Judith? We have a stake in all this, since El Bosque. How come it didn't take? Did you at least get him to eyeball your portfolio?"

"What are we talking here?" she protested mildly. "Molloy is smart and he's rich. Period. Well, my life is full of smart people, and knock on wood, I've got all the money I need. In the brief time I tutored Molloy, I never figured out whether he had money—wealth as a fact—or money had him—wealth as an attribute. Neither one's compelling." She stopped. "Extremes are always interesting because they're extremes. The most boring guy on the planet is, in a paradoxical way, interesting merely by virtue of being the *most* boring. But this guy isn't—that extreme in any sense."

"I disagree," Ron said mildly. "He's an extreme. Though extremely what would be interesting to find out. Anyway, fair Judith, this isn't a novel by Trollope; the expected pairings aren't impeded by capital, or lack thereof, on any side. You can choose a lover for entertainment value alone. Doesn't he divert you?"

"The expected pairings?" A dismissive shrug. The wind blew her hair around her sly smile, a wind so dry that elsewhere, it would be a *föhn*, a *mistral*, a sirrocco, but here, was only the wind. "I got it wrong from the beginning. Just another corporate idiot, I thought, who finds the Institute so attractive that he wants to remake it. Not his game. But what is? Not, to his credit, JAWS." After a moment. "A former poor boy, that much you can see."

Gabe was interested. "For my continuing education, how can you tell Molloy-polloi is a former poor boy?"

Judith was licking her fingertips, had enjoyed the salsa. "He dresses too well, for one thing. Never a crease out of line, never a pill on a sweater, a fraying, straying thread. Born rich, you don't even notice that stuff, just wear it till it wears out."

"The black? Black cashmere, black cotton, black—"

"I'm sure I've seen him in charcoal gray on festive occasions. Pinstripes, anyway. That's just your basic New York tic. Never mind what we're perpetually grieving, us New Yorkers. Maybe someone told him it sets off his black curls."

"Black," Ron said, "was symbolic of fertility among the Old Europeans, before the Indo-Europeans came rolling in."

"Molloy as fertility symbol? It's a concept. Ron, have you ever thought of going on a quiz show?"

Ron persisted. "Or, as dear old Oscar Wilde once said, with an evening coat and a white tie, even a stockbroker can gain a reputation for being civilized. Maybe casual Fridays drove him out."

Gabe nodded thoughtfully, taking this in. Then turned to Ron: "Were you right the first time, don Ron? What Judith's really ready for is a woman. We have her full attention now. Don Ron's little theory is you're probably moving into a place where what appeals most is a same-sex relationship. Dozens of candidates for Ms. Right, whenever you're ready. Some of them coming today, in fact."

"I don't think so," Judith said with amusement.

Gabe jumped up, put his hands on her shoulders, and said with mock sternness: "What caused your heterosexuality? When and how did you first decide you were het? Is it possible it's just a phase you'll grow out of? Does it stem from a neurotic fear of people of the same sex? Maybe you just need a positive gay experience. Hets have histories of failures in gay relationships. Did you turn to heterosexuality out of fear of rejection?"

She was laughing hard, Gabe pressed on. "If you've never slept with a person of the same sex, how do you know you wouldn't prefer that? By the way, your orientation doesn't offend me as long as you leave me alone, but why do so many hets try to seduce others into that orientation? Most child molesters are heterosexual. Do you consider it safe to expose your children to hets?"

"Migod."

Gabe let up on her shoulders. "It's not original. I downloaded it from the Web."

"Men and women are so different," Ron mused. "A gay male knows he's gay from the moment he can lift his head in the crib. Well, sometimes a period of denial. But the number of women I know who did the complete het thing—husband, kids, home in the suburbs—then one day, up and ran off with some wonderful woman. The great overlooked social phenomenon of the decade."

"We think it might be wired in—you know, reproduction stops and something else kicks in." Gabe was pouring them more lemonade to quench the unquenchable Santa Fe thirst. "Or, it could just as well be social. Men of a certain age are more trouble than they're worth. But hey, somebody's gotta hug you in the still of the night."

"You thought—?"

"We gave you credit for that kind of discernment, yes," Ron said evenly. "But when Molloy showed up with us at El Bosque, I revised my theory. I'm the last one in the world to deny the power of hormones."

Gabe started up again. "Why must hets be so blatant, making a public spectacle of themselves? Can't you just be what you are and keep it quiet? Let us not even get into unhealthy, narrow, stereotyped sex roles that hets lock themselves into. And divorce—society supports het marriage totally, and the divorce rate continues to spiral. Does that tell you something?"

Ron cuffed Gabe's upper arm to shut him up.

"It hasn't happened. It won't happen. Molloy, I mean."

"Too bad. How come? Hey, I'm an old pal. You can tell Uncle Ron. The magnificent Molloy wilts in the sack?"

"For God's sake, Ron. I have no idea what the magnificent Molloy is like in the sack. It never went there. It never will."

"I'm shocked, do you hear me, shocked. Why not?"

She turned to face him. "I could tell you I didn't want that, and it's even true. Partly. The opportunities would come along, never just right. Somehow we vexed each other. Finally the opportunities stopped. That's all."

Under his Ecuadoran sombrero, Ron looked thoughtful. "Didn't even pick the cooties out of each other's fur? Pity. Prisoner's Dilemma. But you could've played to win. Tit for tat always comes out on top." After a moment, he said: "Back to the first theory, then. Let us fix you up with someone special, hey?"

She shook her head gently. "I'm an old lady and consecrated to my science."

"I bet you even believe that," Gabe hooted. "A disproportionate number of criminals, welfare recipients and other irresponsibles are hets—why would somebody hire a het in a responsible job? Speaking of irresponsibles, there's Maya's car. What does it signify, I wonder, what is *l'explication du texte*, that she's always the first to arrive? Maya. Do you think her parents *knew*?"

"One has to invite her," Ron said with exasperation. "I wouldn't hurt her feelings for the world, but my God that woman suffers from—well, halitosis among other problems."

"Don Ron. Such careless syntax. So uncharacteristic. We're the ones who suffer, not her."

Deforming Landscapes

Following Maya came others, bearing cheeses, breads, salads and desserts, bestowing hugs and kisses, cries of greeting. Judith thought of the birds at El Bosque.

"I have news for you." Maya pulled Judith into a corner of the garden, beside one of Gabe's lovingly tended apple trees, whose knobby but promising fruit gratefully absorbed the heat from the garden wall. She was both confiding and triumphant. "Molloy's in love."

The absent Molloy was besetting her this afternoon. Molloy, Molloy. Who invited this sorrowful dark man to cast shadows into her life?

"Not what you'd expect," Maya went on. "Not, as you'd put it, one of the pliant wealthy. Her name is Inéz Gallegos, and she's only half his age, surprise, surprise. We never had a chance, Jude."

Judith smiled blandly. Don't call me Jude.

"Did you ever sleep with him?"

Gabe's tree stirred in the afternoon wind, its leaves whispering useless replies. A child squealed; somebody had started to play a guitar. "No. Did I miss something?"

"Yeah, I'd say you missed something. Well, too late now." Maya yearned for company, sympathy, acknowledgment that they lived in a world that was cruel to women like them, of a certain age. She stood before Judith insisting on a cruder, blunter version of thoughts Judith barely allowed herself, dismay as her flesh came to feel like someone else's loose-fitting clothes. This slow sepa-

ration, body from soul, could be denied at an intellectual level: the mind-body division had long ago lost scientific respectability. Yet as Sophie once said about the sense of belonging to oneself, mind-body was a persuasive delusion. Possibly even useful.

At the height of her vigor, her thirties, her forties, Judith had felt, when she stopped to think about it, utterly seamless. Sometimes she had stopped to think, been grateful, because seamlessness had been so long coming. She'd been an awkward child, a spindly adolescent (about as far from Ron's voluptuous Venus as possible) used to dissembling about her multiple, her secret selves, the essentials. Only in her mid-twenties did fusion begin. But mainly she had not thought about it.

Now not only did signs of age press upon her, but she had Sophie to remind her that some women didn't get to age at all.

A recursive species of shame pecked at her, shame for aging, shame that she succumbed to such shame. Yes, this time and place despised the appearance of age in women, made of them a scapegoat for the ineluctable fact of mortality, but she'd put her bets on her brains, not her looks. Age, when it came, she'd thought, would cause her no special pain. And age had never seemed entirely real. Even now she could see an old lady struggling along on a walker, and think, not me, ever.

She'd been chastened. Biases had seeped into her bones after all; some part of her keened for her youth. It flickered spasmodically, the throat in the rearview mirror, her shifted image frozen in a snapshot, the bathroom scales unaltered but clothes that no longer looked right. Now, with mortifying clarity she saw that all the imagined reasons for resisting Molloy might hold, but a further truth went unsaid. It rested there, as vividly ugly as a toad on her palm.

She'd withheld herself from Molloy out of shame. Itself nothing to be proud of. An act of penance to confess this to Sophie, though she knew what Sophie would reply. Well, too late now. She was ashamed, yes; but also relieved, immensely relieved, that she'd kept her distance from Molloy, spared herself yet more tumult.

And yet, and yet. Even bigger, deeper stakes here eluded her. Or she couldn't face.

Maya stood before her, a raw and injured rebuke to her complacency, her confidence that she'd be an exception. Maya bore that oldest of tales, the older man, the younger woman, a tale Judith had once had a part in herself. Maya, raw, injured, waited impatiently for a response.

"Not even Molloy deserves to be turned into pulp fiction, Maya." Dark Molloy. Destructive Molloy.

Released, Maya rushed on. "Don't you have some friend in San Francisco who used to be a plaster-caster?"

"Cynthia? She's retired."

Maya leaned toward Judith's ear confidentially. "You get Miss-Cynthia-from-San-Francisco out of retirement and down here and get this one, hon. Worth a special trip, as the Green Guide says." Maya, so Wife-of-Bath that Judith had to laugh. But she wouldn't forget that now-useless datum, either. "Anyway, Inéz Gallegos, and she runs a shelter for battered women out on the roughest stretch of Agua Fría." The old El Camino Real, where conquistadors, priests, dusty mule caravans had come and gone for centuries.

"Did he say how they met?"

"I didn't hear this from him, Jude. Migod, really. Karen Christiansen told me." Karen, one of the pliant wealthy to be seen with Molloy from time to time. Maya moved her hand through her hair brusquely, a leftover gesture from adolescence when she must have been captain of the field hockey team. "The shelter gets funds from one of Molloy's boards, and he took it into his head to do a little first-hand observation. He met Inéz there, the rest is history."

"So we'll all meet her one of these days." Something deep within mocked her.

"She's supposed to be very beautiful, but you know—age, IQ and bra size all within ten points of each other."

"No," Judith said. "If Molloy's really in love, she has brains." Relief and regret tangoed riotously through her heart.

Maya waved theatrically to a couple across the patio. "Benito Jiménez. Now you *are* sleeping with him, right? For the record?"

"There's no record, Maya."

"I worry about you, Jude. A healthy woman like you."

"Please don't. I carry a lipstick-size vibrator in my purse in case of emergency."

She soon sees them at a Canyon Road gallery opening. Molloy, almost fatuous with pride and self-satisfaction, escorts Inéz over to meet her. Not so sorrowful now.

Her combined Spanish and Indian blood have blessed Inéz with cheekbones that evoke a champagne flute; her long black hair, as straight as Molloy's is coiled, seems to glow from some interior radiance, though her reserve makes Molloy, himself a guarded man, frisky by comparison. She's quiet, self-effacing, while Molloy and Judith talk aimlessly, Judith looking her over, struck by the odd notion that if Inéz's hair glows, Molloy's sable hair seems to absorb light, absorb everything near it.

At New Business, another surprise. He insists, now that he's a principal, on giving the opening overview to each group of fresh clients. An impediment has suddenly been removed; what's been dammed flows. He leads discussions persuasively, flipping through the PowerPoint slides at such a no-nonsense pace that she wonders if the clients can assimilate this: business in the information age, the learning organization versus the old-fashioned fabricative organization; nonlinear feedback among business variables; creative interference; the focus on holistic goals.

They don't look bewildered but stimulated. Which he'd expected, he says later to the staff in a post-mortem. That complexity arises spontaneously from simplicity, and that the properties of the whole emerge from the actions of the parts, is in business a natural point of view. They already understand that markets are the sum of individual customer decisions (call this agent-based modeling if you want to get technical, but business people don't); that organizations are social systems with properties that alter, depending on how people relate; that innovation can't be planned or controlled, only encouraged or discouraged. Finally, exposure to the environment, in this case the market, is the only true measure of fitness.

He doesn't charm the clients in conventional ways, little jokes and asides, but wins them with substance, with authority, and with the most focused, laserlike attention to each one she's ever seen. It's a luxury they might not even know they crave, but in an age of insultingly brief attention spans, it takes them by surprise, and they surrender. This, then, is the Molloy who once captivated the grayest, most cynical heads in Europe, captivated, persuaded, and built himself a fortune.

In these shadowed conference rooms, she takes Molloy's measure, which at least along these dimensions, is superb. He knows what to say and how, in terms that even the most stubborn industrial-age holdout can understand; speaks simply and directly of the inextricable ties between technology and complexity, the new metaphors derived from biology, the ecology of ideas, their natural history, their practical consequences. In a rich basso, a public voice she's never really heard before, he shows them the business continuum—risk, uncertainty, complexity—and crisply defines the differences among them, his red laser pointer pricking over the screen. Business decisions that depend on choices made by other agents, by nature, by both; perpetual novelty, decentralized interactions, continual adaptation, no global control.

Occasionally he'll glance at her over the heads of these lean and earnest initiates who are hoping New Business can drag their firms from the Old Economy into the New. *Did I get that right?* Why not? She's coached him through this from the beginning, though now his talk is what he's figured out for himself, leaped ahead with, invented, boiled down to simple rules that will mean something to his fellow business executives. The conference room seems some oracular cave, her own thoughts on exhibit, but altered, amplified, elaborated upon, extended; above all, simplified. Though some of her colleagues balk at their work reduced to slogans, she respects it. After a few sessions she can plot the course of these introductory talks, the collective skepticism giving way to neutrality, then to enthusiastic conviction. They love him and his truths.

"The new reality of the information age," he says one afternoon. "We're intellectuals in spite of ourselves, examining our ideas rigorously, letting go of what's no longer useful. Consider the former Soviet Union and Eastern Europe—but it's true here too." He pauses for effect, his listeners shifting uncomfortably: the Soviets lost and we won; this means what?

"As we like to say here at New Business, organizations—not just the individuals inside them—must learn continuous innovation. Complexity, technology and biology point the way; offer models for meeting the challenge. We must be adaptive enterprises, recombinant, ready to entertain the unthinkable. Note, for example, ideas of cooperation and competition. Not contradictory but two sides of the same coin, as my colleague down the table, Madame Genius, would say." The brief smile that isn't a smile, flashing in the dusky half-light.

Judith starts. Attending at several levels, she's received another message, unequivocal. Objects silently. Don't for a moment think I resisted you because I'm incapable of innovation. That I can no longer learn. All the things it was, it wasn't that.

An initiate raises questions more challenging than curious. "Okay, business competition. But business cooperation? How are you saying a business ought to look these days?"

Molloy regards the challenger so benevolently that the man imagines he's swiftly penetrated to the intellectual core of things, but Judith is learning to read Molloy better, and can see that fundamentally he scorns the question, the challenge. "There's no fixed way of doing this," Molloy replies mildly. "Organization isn't structure, it's process. Multiple adaptive agents playing off each other." From his laptop the slides shunt backward to adaptive agents, letting the initiates re-digest the chart. "Each agent doesn't just *react* to others, but itself has needs, wants, expresses them, maybe successfully, maybe not. Each agent forms and expresses *ideas*. As agents, we must listen attentively to our fellow agents; hear their needs, even if we can't fulfill them. We used to say listen to your customer, now we're saying listen to your competitor too. Listen to everybody on your team, in your firm and outside it. Find ways to cooperate to your mutual benefit."

I listened to your needs, your wants these past months, couldn't meet them, didn't wish to, but you never even heard mine. What if you had? Where then? Idle to speculate. Adapt instead to the new environment.

"Optimal-sized groups," Molloy's saying. "For humans it may be about a hundred and fifty. Apparently the human brain can't sustain more than this number of significant relationships at one time. Why is this bio-limit important? Because adaptability—the group's ability to learn and change—depends crucially on the number of linkages among agents. If the organization's subunits are too small, the organization falls apart; too big, it freezes in the face of new circumstances.

"Our primate cousins nourish these links by social grooming—picking the cooties out of each other's fur, I've heard it called—" he doesn't even glance at her. "But human interactions are so complex that we express our social grooming in words. We talk to each other. Each agent constantly learns in each interaction—learns what 'works' for itself, what not. Magically—" he corrects himself, "no, not magically, but in ways we can't explain yet, can only see—something emerges that's on average the best outcome for everyone."

You're conflating hypotheses with facts, but so what. What didn't you put into words? What didn't I?

"Organize for innovation, you organize for learning," Molloy goes on, "an opportunity to reformulate ideas. One test. Do they improve the organization, the reasons why it exists at all?"

We're clear on which ideas of yours I was trying to reformulate, just as you asked. Which of mine were you hoping to change? Why? No answers, further questions beside the point, though she's troubled. Has she been the impermeable one?

Outside the window, the purple sage is in full and feathery bloom; in the distance fields of brilliant yellow wildflowers, black-eyed susans, miniature sunflowers, daisies no bigger than alpine plants, sway in the afternoon breeze. The flowers are at their abundant peak; crying out to the departing birds and bees, *take me! take me!* Why didn't you cry out, seduce, in high summer, she wonders, when the birds weren't preoccupied with leaving? Wouldn't it have been easier then? Nature isn't efficient, Sophie often scoffs. Nature gets the job done, is all. Most of the time.

Nearby in the sun, a gardener spades earth, stops, fetches sacks of topsoil and fertilizer, spreads again, preparing for next year. The agricultural age right alongside the industrialists, so eager to learn, move themselves and their businesses into the information age. Three parallel tracks of history. The gardener pauses, pulls off his hat, wipes his forehead. Muscles flexing under his tee shirt, what would he make of all this reformulation of ideas? Tonight, his feet up, his back aching, a cold Corona in his hand, could

he even imagine that what they do in this room is work?

"Eliminate linear, formula, authorized thinking. We learn because we must," Molloy says crisply. Linear, formula, authorized thinking. How much of that has shaped her behavior with him, even if she evades it in every other part of her life? Finished, he appeals to her almost innocently. Did I do okay? The innocence, the desire to please, wrenches her. She's too hard on him. She forgives him for disturbing her, answers with a slight smile: not bad at all.

Linking and Leveraging

Molloy announces that dinner will be at his own house for he's sure, he says soothingly, that everyone will appreciate a social occasion after such a long day. For a moment he sees Madame Genius balk, then reconcile herself to showing; she's expected, getting paid for it. He happens to open the door himself to her, finds her in a simple black dress, but this to set off the iridescent woven shawl, edged with real peacock feathers, a fire opal at her throat the size of a fist. Dinners are theater, she's saying, and she'll do her share. Before he swings the door open completely he murmurs, "So nice to see you in your just-plain-folks get-up."

With the clients, he's mixed in some of the Santa Fe regulars, including Nola and Ernie. He's coming to like Nola, and Ernie's part of the package. And he himself needs something besides business to talk about. He introduces Nola to the out-of-towners as someone with an important gallery. True enough; maybe generating some business when she could use it most—as distraction, not income.

As his hostess, Inéz too has gone in for theater, in a ruby-colored velvet broomstick skirt, a blouse to match, Indian silver, setting off her dark looks elegantly, very Santa Fe. She's so beautiful in her freshness, her symmetry, her reserve, that he sees people drawn to look at her whether she opens her mouth or not. Aside from minimum courtesies, her quiet persists, though no signs of being uneasy in her silence. Rather, she observes the guests, his friends and clients, with a patient, friendly curiosity, as if she's never quite encountered their like before; waiting and watching long enough, she might understand their odd Anglo ways.

He'd prefer—but forget that; she's what she is, and her silence doesn't matter, since his own mouth motors on unstoppably. He's repeating now how clearly people saw the necessity to change in Eastern Europe and the former Soviet Union, and how much other businesses need to be aware.

It's Judith who asks: "Were you involved with Treuhand?"

He explains to the table. "That agency took on the problem of privatizing businesses in eastern Germany when the two Germanies were reunited." To her: "Yes. Only as a consultant, of course. I'm not a German national. An enlightening experience, all in all." He stares into his nearly untouched wine glass, keeps his smile enigmatic. "Politics more Byzantine than anything I ever saw in Istanbul." He's discreet enough not to specify.

"Perhaps people here would find it valuable to know the difference between the firms that failed and those that succeeded." She's very well behaved tonight, he thinks with amusement. The perfect colleague. And for once not looking at him like he's dogshit on her shoe.

He reflects, remembers, pulls it all together, and abstracts the lesson. "Three good men," he says at last. "You always needed three. One couldn't do it. In their late thirties, early forties—the old guys who'd come up managing under Communism couldn't adapt. But the new ones, taking on management for the first time, they were the ones. You needed a leader, and you needed two guys who shared his vision and could follow him. Then—anything's possible." He sees an old factory in eastern Germany, the wooden floors ground down to splinters, and when the manager invites them to lunch, he has to reach into the bottom drawer of his battered pre-war desk to provide mess kits for them all. In the people's glorious paradise, the people have lifted every knife, fork and plate from their factory canteen. A miracle they produced anything at all, never mind the optical products they were still known for worldwide.

"You invest in Eastern Europe?" someone asks.

"Aggressively."

"Had much luck?"

He smiles. "Win some, lose some. My involvement with privatization in eastern Germany was quasi-official, so conflict of interest kept me from investing there personally. The surest bet. Hungary and Poland have been my best performers, though problems persist." A summer lunch on the terrace at the Gellert; hospitable visits to villas in the outskirts of Budapest and Warsaw, beautiful old Art Nouveau places that had somehow survived sixty years of depression, war, and Communist neglect, but that were slowly being reclaimed as architectural treasures. "Russia remains to be seen. German colleagues are heavily exposed in Russia, but I chose not to. I'd like Russia to do well if only because I have significant interests in Turkey." He sees his listeners imagining tea boys with their little tin trays running through the Grand Bazaar when in fact business in Turkey is done in the same dreary, shabby high-rises as everywhere else in the world. But let it go. He's done business in the bazaars too, taken tea, but business of a different sort. "The Czech Republic should've been much better. So many smart people; so many foolish decisions. Lacking a masochistic streak, I didn't go near Bulgaria or Rumania. I keep an eye on them, though. The fundamentals might improve."

"And the euro?"

"Ah," he says softly. "Close to my heart. This Asian currency crisis. Some European firms have taken a twenty percent hit; they're that sensitive to currency fluctuations. The euro might give the dollar problems that way. The Chinese Central Bank, for example, holds about sixty percent of its reserves in dollars. It's already said it'll diversify into euros when the time comes. If they move down to, say, forty percent, they'll need to sell twenty-eight billion in dollars. Other central banks might follow suit." He leaves it to the people around the table, every one whose wealth is counted in dollars, to imagine the effects of twenty-eight billion dollars suddenly for sale on the world currency markets. He looks unperturbed, permits them to infer he's already prudently stashed money in—what? D-Marks? Soon-to-be euros? Swiss francs? The mattress?

It's finally back in full force, his sense of well-being, his focus; he can almost taste it on his tongue, feel it strengthening the farthest parts of his limbs, and he says a little prayer of thanksgiving. In trading it never deserted him (which is why, Ross had led him to guess, he kept on trading so obsessively, a kind of meditation, a centering for him when the rest of his life was a shambles). Now he presides over his table with confidence, commands attention effortlessly, the unchallenged alpha. Yes, his own territory, intellectual as well as real estate, but due credit, it's Inéz too. A bellyful this spring and summer of women who faked—what? Deference, submission. He doesn't want that, he wants—not submission, not even gratitude. Appreciation, maybe? As in art appreciation—a delight in finding the hidden, the unexpected connections, the small and subtle patterns, from which the whole emerges. Recognition of technique, mastery, innovation, problems set and problems solved. An understanding of context, history, public and private. The acknowledgment—emphasis on knowledge in its deepest sense—that Jack Molloy has accomplished something out of the ordinary. *Goddamned bravura.*

He understands he'll never get all this from Inéz. She knows nothing about his professional life except that he must, in some sense incalculable to her, be rich enough to have his own house, sit on a board that supports her shelter. For Inéz tens of thousands are equivalent to trillions, and how he'd got it is uninteresting. Ideas don't move her. She's incurious about Treuhand, the sciences of complexity, art beyond the pretty, and always will be. To that extent, a typical dolly. But money doesn't move her either: she's passionately committed to a cause. That raises her above dollyhood. Her passion for her cause is delightful, and he's yielded to a sexual fever he hasn't felt for a very long time.

She's released something in him that makes him feel, act, more human. He lets himself entertain his guests, first a tale of misunderstandings. "Her husband is in African currencies, she says confidentially, it's going to be very, very big. African currencies? I think. There's a rock I never thought of turning over. So I press a little. Kenyan shillings? The Senegal franc? Moroccan dirhams? Oh no, she says, it's the pre-colonial money—it's very beautiful. Works of art. He's an expert in African art. I have to say, when I saw this stuff she was quite right."

They laugh more than he deserves, which encourages him to recount his experiences at an anti-terrorist course, held at a fine estate outside Augsburg. "First and always, remain calm. Remain calm? If you don't know that, you don't belong in risk arbitrage." Moderate eye contact with the kidnappers, you're human but not threatening; crossfire, mortar attacks, grenades, working the margins. For him, a natural. He also remembers, but doesn't mention at the dinner table, *kravmaga*, savage Israeli combat techniques, a throw that ends with you biting the flesh of your assailant's throat. "You taste flesh, be sure your teeth connect," Zvi had said laconically.

On to a tale of hunting wild boar, the dogs fit to jump out of their skins, the animal flushed from the underbrush, snorting, charging: he tells it with studied understatement. "I nearly didn't fire. The creature seemed so small; it flashed on me I hadn't allowed for poetic license, what I'd seen in paintings was exaggerated. Then the big one arrived." The *sumi* brush eyebrows rise eloquently. "Some people in Germany won't do business with you unless you can keep your cool with a few hundred kilos of crazed wild boar hurtling at you. As a test, it has some merit."

Everyone laughs except Inéz, disapproval evident. The dolly factor, primmer-than-thou. Not for the first time he tells himself this will be fucking hard work. The brows rise again, this time ironically. "My dear, neither of us are vegetarians, and it's certainly more interesting than golf." Yes, he answers someone, you can still hunt wild boar in Germany; this had been on a private reserve.

Surfing on his own self-confidence, he's aware of Judith pricking him somehow, alpha to alpha. Please don't introduce me as doctor, she'd said quietly to him at the beginning of the evening. It's important, he'd said, overruling her. He didn't say important to whom. Questions seem to rise to her lips, but she swallows them. This version of Molloy intrigues her, he can see that; maybe she regrets lost opportunities. "Treuhand," he hears her say to the man next to her, "I'd no idea any foreigners were permitted near that."

Not just any foreigners, Madame Genius. But then without being told, she'd known what Treuhand was.

A subtle shift has taken place between them and he wonders why. The dolly factor? If so, he'd have applied it long ago. He hopes not. He wants to think better of her. No, she's seen him often enough with other women this spring and it didn't do a thing. Himself the deficiency, tongue-tied and loutish at crucial moments, anything but bravura? But that doesn't appeal either. This archaeologist? Maybe no more than bad timing. Maybe only the flap of a butterfly's wing somewhere along the way, changing everything.

A silence, and somebody sighs. Opposite him, a small and hopeful smile animates Inéz's face for the first time. He sees and ignores a problem he doesn't want to see.

He checks the progress of dinner up and down the table, people beginning the cheese course, then offers Inéz a sly intimate smile that says wait, it will be over soon. Sees that Judith's seen, and grasped it all. Across the debris of dinner, Judith's complicated face. The smile meant to placate Inéz has relegated everyone else to encumbrance, impediment to private events. Judith is affronted and doesn't disguise it. So Inéz doesn't have the patience for talk. Maybe not even the brains. This new relationship begins and ends in bed. If that's good enough for him, he wouldn't have been happy with her, whatever his fantasies. She gazes at Inéz, back at him. Then away, the fire opal flashing. Christ, he can't win for losing with this woman.

Perpetual Novelty

The dolly factor. The gruesome dinners he's sat through when his colleagues insisted on bringing their dollies, frozen desserts of faces, stupefied with boredom. As soon as he'd begun to understand art, a blank face could no longer be beautiful to him. Fucking a frozen dessert, you might as well fuck a *crème brulée*. It took the edge right off and was a lot less trouble. Given European notions of courtesy, dinner conversations in the presence of dollies had to fork: talk was mindless, to suit them; or it ignored them entirely, okay, because they were only dollies. Both routes distressed him. The next morning, God! He'd see them at hotel breakfasts, the guy reading his newspaper in the dolly's face, babbling into his cell phone; her sullenly staring off into space, or feeding the birds on the terrace. He'd sworn he wouldn't have it. And wryly recalled that these contrarian opinions had been formed as his own libido had exited stage left. He hadn't always been so fussy.

Inéz moves fluidly, skirt swaying around her ankles like a flamenco dancer's, and closes the french doors as Molloy talks. People listen to him, watch her. Back at the table, she fails to conceal a yawn.

The other guests do their duty and take up the discussion with proper liveliness. Market share. Market value. Recouping R and D. Pick partners carefully, not so big they'll swallow you nor so small they'll add nothing to the alliance.

With a discretion he admires (one professional to another) Judith has been assessing his new partner Inéz, who's so distant from the conversation she seems dazed. Madame Genius's thoughts are all too clear. Inéz so beautiful, so dumb, so much the precisely expected, obvious thing. Just like his four trophy wives? No, Madame G., dear lady, Jacko's one and only wife was not like that.

An elegant European woman he'd admired—happily married, alas, so not for him—had once remarked about May-December couplings that if men envied each other, women only laughed. Who did they think they were fooling with these transactions? A man who had to purchase it, who couldn't cope with an equal. Contemptible, really. Transparent as a comb-over, Magda had added wickedly. An acquaintance managed to lose a headline-grabbing fortune in a badly run hedge fund, and suffered not only that humiliation, but the trophy bride-to-be ostentatiously called the whole thing off. Just in case you entertained the idea that love had anything to do with it, bozo. The older ex-wife, who'd hammered a good settlement earlier on, was the only one left sitting pretty. He could see Magda closing her eyes, a knowing smile on her perfectly shaped face.

For years he's sat at tables with colleagues and adversaries, earning his money because his antennae are so finely tuned to shifts, from hairline fractures to the seismic. Now he senses something at this table has again shifted. Judith is feeling herself unwillingly, reluctantly, placed in opposition to Inéz. Well, that's something. He gives the small shift a maliciously calculated shove.

"Psychological positioning is also important," he says soberly. "Under increasing returns, rivals will back off from you not only if you've locked in the market, but if they believe you probably *will* lock it in. That's why you read all that stuff in the business pages—the announcements, the rumors, the possible future partnerships, the vaporware. This is the primate colony, displaying in the hopes of discouraging competitors."

He pauses, and Judith glares at him in what he alone can see is fury. *Between us, it was more complicated than that.* Ah, a friction point. But the momentary satisfaction dissolves. Madame Genius, Queen Judith, hovers so elusively out of reach, would mock, if she knew, what formal credentials he has to his name, is also unimpressed by money, regardless of what it stands for—well, to hell with her. No, Jacko, suppress the croak of ego, fatal to any successful outcome. Protect from short-term loss with a long-term horizon. Never forget the long run. In which we are all dead.

"Dr. Greenwood—" a voice begins.

"Judith," she corrects. "I'm sure Molloy joins me in urging you all please to bear in mind that the sciences of complexity are barely ten years old. We don't have all the answers to all problems. This afternoon we heard a lot about the virtues of adaptation but we really don't know in any scientific way what's required for a system to be adaptive, even if we think we know adaptation when we see it. The number of variables rises, complexity increases, and human understanding decreases. Many of our ideas are barely risen, let alone ready for the oven. New Business is not hawking snake oil."

Thrust and touché, Madame G. He's been publicly swatted, and the silence is unpleasant.

Nola the art dealer turns to Inéz and says as pleasantly as if nothing has transpired, "Molloy says that as well as your work at the women's shelter, you're an artist."

Inéz's reserve and dignity suddenly desert her. She appeals to Molloy for help, but he's feeling peculiarly ungenerous, pissed, edgy, offers nothing.

"What do you do?" Nola asks gently. Winks. The silence grows too long, and Molloy toys with intervening. To say what?

At last Inéz replies. "The desert. I do the desert." She has, when they finally hear it, a girl's voice, odd at the dinner table, pretty to a man's ears in bed.

Nola hasn't intended a challenge, Molloy guesses. She's much too kind. A question anyone might ask an artist. Some can articulate their preoccupations, some can't; you can never judge how profound the work is by how profound the answer. But the question's always worth asking. "I should have made myself clearer," Nola's saying gently. "Do you paint? Sculpt?" She waits, winks encouragingly.

"I do—collages."

"Ah. And where can we see your work?"

"Nowhere, really." Inéz seems to mean no gallery represents her. Or that the art is virtual, something she's getting around to doing. The artist wannabe is legion, especially in Santa Fe, and nobody will hold it against her, but he knows it makes her liaison with him, the serious collector, all the odder. "The shelter is a more than full-time job. So I don't always have time—" The girl's voice stops inside the woman's throat.

Nola rescues matters herself. "Your work at the shelter?"

Inéz suddenly rises to the challenge. "My work at the shelter is life-affirming. I've been close to death more than once." She pauses significantly, in case anyone has missed that it's her own death she means. "Somehow—somehow I got back. Hands and knees, I crawled back. These women suffer so much; they should have a chance to get back too, to see that—it can be done. I'm their role model. I touch their lives, I cut right through all the bullshit they live with day after day, I see inside their skin all the way to their soul. Women experiencing pain and joy on that *real* level, they love me for my truths and my love and my intensity. On their feet, away once and for all from this guy who's been coming home waving an open razor, a Saturday night special, maybe one day they'll say, there was this woman who ran the shelter... They couldn't stand that intensity, love, truth all the time. Not many people can. But that's who I am and how I work, take it or leave it."

Though Inéz's declaration has been fervent, though breath has been sucked in and expelled around the table, eyes have fallen in embarrassment. He wills himself to maintain his composure. Bet the company every day, self-control's crucial. Judith sits back, her eyes on some middle distance over Inéz's head, not quite concealing her disbelief, her mirth, her fucking superiority. Her eyes meet his in reappraisal. The opal flashes. The peacock eyes on her shawl wink. The dogshit look. Thus things shift again.

"So the art," Inéz concludes, Inéz who will suddenly not shut up, "is just my way of keeping from burning out altogether. The needs at the shelter are so great, keep me so busy, I just don't get to do art so much."

Molloy remains impassive. Then turns to Nola. "How's Pete doing?"

Nola is pained. If Molloy has strategically changed the subject, it's to her own obsession. "All right, I guess. As well as can be expected." For the strangers at the table: "My son, our son, has leukemia."

They murmur the expected combination of genuine sympathy, slight embarrassment, all implected with *Schadenfreude* that it's not themselves worrying over a beloved child's mortality. They also look as if they hadn't bargained for all this over coffee.

"We had a bone marrow transplant. We'd hoped to avoid it." The inclusive we moves Molloy deeply. Ernie. Is he part of that we any more, sitting back, so detached he hasn't even made the effort strangers make? Molloy knows very well, oh so very well, that people respond to grief in different, even incomprehensible ways. Ernie's detachment might be his self-protection from the unthinkable, the unbearable. Yet the weight on Nola. Nola deserves better. So does Pete. "It didn't succeed. We had to go back and do it again, this time from a bone marrow donor. I've had to close the gallery temporarily."

"Is it help you need?" someone asks. "We could pitch in."

Nola appears politely grateful for that but shakes her head. "No. No. That's not it. Your kid's leukemia is a full-time job. And then some. Hard to think sensibly about art under the circumstances." A wink. We are co-conspirators. I mean it.

Molloy says tenderly, "You call on us. We can help. You're not alone, Nola. Don't ever think for a moment that you are."

Nola manages a smile that might pass as gratitude, but which tells them that she is indeed alone, and there's no remedy for that. She's right. He's been there.

Bounded Instability

Dinner had been, well, informative. Whatever had once tied Molloy's tongue was gone for good: an unintended consequence, Judith noted, of falling in love. Or at least of sex, one of the great complex adaptive systems. Interaction, aggregation, adaptation. She ought to use it as an example next time she had to teach.

You two, both complex adaptive systems in your own right, a lifetime of expectations, memories, experience, genetic expression, gaze at each other long enough to let pheromones exchange greetings. A hand touches a hand. Accident or on purpose? Ambiguous. No response. One backs off. End of story. Or instead, passivity appears to be an invitation to move the system from one phase to the next. Unambiguous now, a hand grasped. A responding squeeze; on to the next phase. The chorus of chemical messages has already begun, sub-systems singing back and forth to sub-systems, arousal, excitement, bonding, so far below consciousness you don't know they're there except—your face in a stranger's hands, warmth on your cheeks, a fugue of sweet cherishing, protectiveness, a descant of possessiveness, has all undone your equilibrium. You kiss. A stranger's intimate human scent serenades receptors you don't even know you have, and your own chorus is doing its part. Experience (not to mention what's wired in) promises better phases to come, and the two systems improvise with each other, adapting to move from phase to phase, a glance, a gesture, a hand guided here, a tongue there, a little laugh, the obvious pleasure of the other, all looping back, encouraging. Getting from phase to phase is half the fun. You together

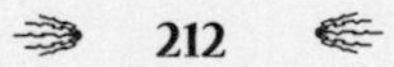

change the world, produce novelties of exquisite degree.

Your internal chorus sings not only to the stranger, but also to you. No, not this guy, he's nothing but trouble: it brutally, self-protectively, overrides treacherous promise. Short-term pleasure, maybe; long-term grief for sure. An end before it can begin.

One of these was Benito. One of these Molloy.

Well, not for classroom use: somebody would sue you for sexual harassment. Not for individual tutoring: you'd be misunderstood.

Though she didn't get how come Inéz, given other women available, she found she could now relax with Molloy. He seemed less mysterious, hardly dangerous. He was straightforward, his words stripped of hidden meanings. They sometimes had a quick dinner together after work, even saw a movie if Inéz was working late at the shelter. Judith gathered Inéz had moved in with him, but he never included her in these impromptu occasions.

One evening Judith saw him alone at a production of Gounod's *Faust* at the Santa Fe Opera. It was late in the season, the last year the theater would be open to the skies, the stars above, the dramatic show of midsummer thunder and lightning behind the production that competed with, and sometimes dominated, what was onstage. Tonight a moon hung in the starry southern sky more theatrical than anything onstage. He sat not far in front of her, a score in his lap, a pen-sized flashlight to follow it. If, as Sophie speculated, he sometimes sat all alone blasting Nine Inch Nails at midnight, he also liked opera. At the intermission she followed him.

"Do you like it?"

He smiled, shook his head. "I like German opera. I like French opera. But not together in the same work. Faust as erotic adventure. Trust the French to trivialize."

"Don't waffle, Molloy, speak up and tell us exactly how you feel. Inéz not here?"

"We have different tastes. She thinks opera's silly. Tonight I'd agree. You?"

"Not the best thing I've ever seen. Pretty melodies, though. If I'm bored I look at the mountains. Did you see *The Magic Flute* last week? You missed something. The Queen of the Night seemed a little unsteady in the first act, but in the second she came back like dynamite. I called a friend on the staff to find out what happened. Turns out there were two queens. The first one got sick; they called a sub before intermission, but she said no, she was hosting a dinner party and was on her third margarita. This is an emergency, they said. So down she came, squeezed into the costume, slathered on the make-up, went out and sang her heart out. Of course with three margaritas, *I* could sing Queen of the Night."

"I'm sure you could. So accomplished, the lady is." Not said unkindly, but she picked up a mocking edge. Couldn't resist parrying.

"You aren't charmed by a Marguerite who covets only jewels and gold?" Though his face barely changed, she saw she'd wounded him. Regretted it. How could she ever have seen that face as thuggish, a desperado? Sad, deeply sad, as Gabe had been first to say. "I'm sorry, Molloy. That was uncalled for."

He didn't answer immediately. "It would always have been like that, wouldn't it? No poetry in money, said the lady. Well, you're wrong. You're quite wrong, Judith." The face closed, hardened. With a brusque asperity, he rolled up the score he held, drummed a tight tattoo against his open hand. "By now I've now seen you quite a bit. A clear-eyed, sweet-natured woman, not given to the easy wisecrack. Yet something about money—my money—just sets you off. Is it the money, or the fact that I got it all winning cockfights? Ever seen a cockfight? Every guy on his haunches, his cock between his thighs, and he's stroking hard to get it up as the biggest, fastest—"

"Such finesse. Such subtlety. Bloody takes your breath away."

"Why mince words? It's a fact about me, Judith. Some people even regard it as an accomplishment. You don't. Your choice. Maybe making money isn't up there in the stratosphere of discovering the secrets of the universe, the limits to scientific knowledge, but it ain't—"

"Now who's got the easy wisecracks, Molloy? Next comes the sanctimonious little sermon about how you really want people to appreciate you for yourself and not your fortune. Sure, but you don't make any secret of that cash, just in case. The old silverback and his broadside display. Jesus, why are we having this conversation?"

They eyed each other, a silence of unexpected pain, of shadows looming longer and more treacherous than their source. He looked away at last toward the mountains, nearly invisible now in the dark. The score unrolled, fluttered to the floor.

She said softly, "I'm sorry. I'm sorry in every way possible." Anything to make things normal, to back off from those menacing shadows. She continued to his averted head. "Ron told me you were fluent in German." Repeated it in German.

He turned back, but his eyes were still focused on the distance, dismissing her. In German he answered politely; he was indeed fluent. "It was the best of times, in some ways the worst. A closed chapter. I never feel more American than when I'm in Germany. Though I did love it there." He paused, lost in thought, then glanced down at the score at his feet, bent to pick it up. "*Faust* doesn't speak to me the way it speaks to Germans. Part of being an American, maybe. All these women immolating themselves to redeem some man. Bizarre." He spoke a foreigner's, a radio announcer's German, the German of the canned announcements on the tram; bleached of any local dialect or accent. Her broad Bavarian accent must seem comical to him.

She tried again. "Did you really hunt wild boar?" She would not be the first to use *du*, the intimate, the familiar, not after all this.

"Naturally. Often. Did you think I was making that up?" He was struggling to continue courteously despite everything. "It's about slaying the totem animal. If wild bear still roamed Germany they'd have put me up against a wild bear instead. Can't entrust the family fortune to the fainthearted. Anyway, wild-boar hunting in the Schwarzwald isn't so very different from deer hunting in the Alleghenies." An odd gesture with his hand, then, acknowledging that the discrepancy was in fact vast, the comparison too silly. "I preferred my host's hunting lodge to my uncle's camper, let me put it that way."

The gun closet. That rush of libido. She'd hardly known him then.

The orchestra had returned to the pit and the languid squabble of re-tuning had begun. It brought him back from wherever he'd been, and he switched to English. "So many lessons—from Germany."

She understood. Some periods of her life she could not speak about honestly; couldn't lie about either. She said in English: "A lot of Americans still have hard feelings because of the war—the Holocaust—so I don't often tell people I've spent so much time there. That I loved it, still love it. Love the language. A secret guilty pleasure. Nice to find a kindred spirit."

"*Ah ja.*" It issued, as it did from all male German throats, like a small, domestic growl. "I hadn't known that about you at first." Then almost as compensation for his unwillingness to disclose any more about his time in Germany, a kind of token that he'd forgiven her blunder, perhaps forgiven himself for his own thin skin, a signal that they could meet next time and not have to take all this up again, that he too preferred tranquility to dispute, he offered her the fact that he'd heard of her before he ever arrived in Santa Fe—an article on her in *Risk* magazine, or someplace. "You're always surprised, and pleased, about where your work can be applied," she said. The lights were flickering to signal the end of the intermission, urge them back to their seats.

"I'm cutting my losses. Want a ride?"

She'd have liked to go with him, not because she wasn't enjoying the opera, but her curiosity remained fresh. She wanted to make amends. She had practical questions too: what should she do with her portfolio? What was he doing himself about Y2K, and what did he advise? But not tonight. "I'm here with friends," she said in explanation, apology, refusal.

He shrugged. "*Tschüss.*"

She went back to her seat, to Gounod, and might just as well have left with him for all she could pay attention.

Complex Foresight Horizons

They've eased into being colleagues, into a kind of friendship. He lets himself hope it's friendship, that what Ron called male energy accounts for the new warmth he picks up these days from Madame Genius. Maybe nothing to do with him. Maybe she just gets off playing this game, deep-diving into some firm's business, laying out its problems as people in the firm see them, turning it all inside out, upside down, discovering that the real problems are occluded by a flawed point of view.

She once told him that her talent was for asking the right questions, even if she couldn't supply answers, and he sees it often at New Business, the query that penetrates to a problem's core, blowing away all peripheral issues. Having with one acute question rearranged everyone's mental furniture, everyone's metaphors, everyone's point of view, Madame Genius shrugs with a sweet smile he finds more endearing than he'd wish, and clams up.

Friendship comes tentatively during dinners grabbed on the run, movies (which come and go quickly in Santa Fe; he has to get used to that). Though Judith seems to love all movies, she hates the sentimentality that saturates the Hollywood product, detects it ruthlessly under its most baroque disguises, pulls it into daylight, and denounces it. He'd have considered that unfeminine once, but thinks now he values it. He shuts up about his own capacity for sentimentality, how cheesy music can nearly make him cry even when he knows he's being manipulated. Of all the subjects their talk ranges across, he hesitates only to bring up painting, afraid she might like what he despises, which would pain him in a way he won't think about. This is the only sign to him that the door in his heart slammed shut so many times isn't yet completely sealed. Too bad.

One night, when they've spent the entire day trying to educate a hopeless client, they duck out from the official dinner in frustration and end up eating green chili stew on Cerrillos Road, wedged in between the fast-food outlets and tire shops. He's tired, frustrated by the day's failure. "People need to understand the feedbacks in their markets. They need to understand the ecologies they're in. Do they have the resources to play—the best of technology, timing, deep pockets, strategic pricing, a willingness to sacrifice current profits for future advantage? It isn't just dollars: it's resolution, courage, will. The ability to sense when to hold and when to fold."

"Poker, Molloy," Judith says lightly. "Wrong game."

No, he thinks, not poker but *vent'uno*, played after school behind the barbershop so many years ago, with old Italian guys, Calabrian accents thick as sauce, embryonic Mackie Messer learning to keep both his face and his bets straight.

Madame Genius is still teaching him too. He asks her why.

"I don't do it often. If I did, I'd have to charge you a personal consulting fee as well as charging New Business."

He spoons the chartreuse chile around in his bowl, hardly touching it, though he's getting to be a real New Mexican: this is his third meal today with chile. "Oh? What's the going rate?"

She grins. "More than even you can afford, Molloy. But then I have to ask, why are you doing this? We'll assume you don't need the money."

"Oh, the money." The fucking money. Not that again, please. "Money's just keeping score. Discipline. If I want this stuff to sink in, if I really want to know it, then I need a fast feedback that tells me I know it. For that, money works just fine."

True but evasive. He knows very well why he's doing it. Jack Molloy is being superseded. It doesn't frighten him, but it saddens him. History will win and he'll lose. Learning all this delays his obsolescence.

He's not a quant, as Wall Street might define it, and never has been. He's always placed his bets based on his intuition, which in fact means an unconscious harvest of facts, trends, movements, history, and external influences, an unexamined, a subliminal perception of patterns, all processed instantaneously, to guide action. Though he's seen quant models fail again and again, underlying assumptions prove false, at best incomplete, he admires the idea of quantification, the people involved; Doyne Farmer in downtown Santa Fe at Prediction Company; David Shaw in Manhattan; both of them Ph.D.s, and their teams the same. He admires anyone who can get through, never mind comprehend, Merton's classic book. For all this too, he admires Madame Genius.

He's concluded that he's the quants' old-fashioned predecessor, the barber-surgeon before physicians and antibiotics. If he's had more luck so far in calling the turns (that isn't clear; an important part of the game is to be coy) history suggests that theirs will be the victory in the end.

Even the spectacular crash of a colleague's hedge fund—holding, it was said, contracts in billions, perhaps trillions, of dollars it couldn't meet—hasn't soured his faith in this new generation. Nothing wrong with rocket science, computerized trading programs. These particular people made a very human error. They bet borrowed money in the belief that things would normalize before the money ran out. They failed to think through the worst-case possibilities. Gambler's ruin. It happened to ordinary guys in poker games, at roulette wheels. It happened to guys with Nobel Prizes.

He'd seen this colleague at a professional dinner not long afterward, there to receive a prize announced just before the Hindenberg-scale crash and burn, and, as Molloy knew (a member of the awards committee, a past prize-winner himself) it was a prize nearly rescinded. He himself had argued strongly against withdrawing the prize in the wake of the debacle. It seemed small and squalid to him, plus making them all look like the sharks everyone believed financiers were.

After all, what was the prize for? he asked his fellow committee members. For ideas. The ideas weren't wrong, just needed refinement. Perhaps badly timed. Bridges sometimes collapse. Buildings sometimes topple over. Rockets fall untimely from the sky. Do you throw out all of physics, everything known about construction techniques, about propulsion and gravity, when this happens? Or do you acknowledge the fact of outlier events, pick yourself up and learn from what happened?

Because he was well known as an intuitive, not a quantitative trader, and because that seemed to imply his own disinterest, he got his way.

Worst of all, the debacle could've befallen anyone on the committee; in their hearts, they all knew it. Though he put it forward more diplomatically, he despised the confusion between self-righteousness and luck. He'd seen almost every one of these men standing in trading rooms, transfixed by a screen, and as investments were mauled by a sudden turn, desperately, unconsciously, primitively, reaching in misery to touch their balls for reassurance. He'd met nearly every one of them in the men's room, not all of them making it in time. Scared shitless wasn't just a pungent figure of speech. Who were they to pile on? Leave that to the editorial writers, whose stake began and ended with babble.

It had nearly happened to him and he never forgot the terror, how it humbled him. Catastrophe had rolled toward him like a colossal vehicle, its wheel rims quarreling loudly with the uneven ground, its axles howling under the weight, while over the clatter of those quarreling wheels, howling axles, he could hear disorderly, arrhythmic trumpets bugling, drums pounding, steam whistles blowing, an unearthly racket, assaulting his ears with impending doom. The vehicle called Catastrophe ground flesh and bone beneath it as it rolled inexorably, indifferently forward. He had composed himself, prepared to be crushed, and the vehicle had stopped. Lurched into reverse. Rolled slowly away. He had been merely lucky.

He also knows that some disagree. They argue that the dirty knowledge someone like Molloy has accumulated so superbly, called experience—those days in the trading pits watching the tape obsessively, learning the lore of the market; those deals put together from one end of the planet to the other; that willingness to trust your gut, to try again and again in the face of imminent failure and, when failure shattered you, to get up and try yet again; that willingness to yank things out of play when the rest of the world was confident the returns could only increase. All that will never be modeled quantitatively. It will need an altogether different kind of simulation to capture what he knows and how he knows it, and in this he approaches Judith's hypothetical border between the known and the unknowable. But if he agrees in general, he cannot, will not, dare not, examine his own work that way. I'm painting, he says to himself; they're photography. Neither better nor worse, just different. Except photography changed painting. And then the world moved on.

He believes he's yet capable of learning. He'd taken a house on Lake Zürich one summer, hired a bright young graduate student from Einstein's old school, the Swiss Federal Technical Institute, to tutor him, while the student's girlfriend looked after Molloy's children. Though he'd more or less grasped what he was being taught—continuous-time stochastic processes, mathematically more complex than discrete-time, including stochastic dynamic programming and Ito calculus—though he took pleasure in mastering it, he found the mathematics more muddying than clarifying for any real-life action. In short, he'll say, the general problem of investing cannot, at the moment, be mathematically modeled or solved.

One day yes, he believes. No grand unified theory of the market, no single model that captures everything, of that he's confident; for if so, that would be the end of the market. But a host of models for different aspects of the market will emerge, be refined, and they'll beat anything an individual can do, hands down. He sometimes wonders if, given a different education, he might have done some of that modeling himself. But that's idle. He regrets, is humiliated by, his dismal formal education, and has an almost superstitious awe of people like Farmer and Shaw, and Judith, with all the credentials and certificates.

A further hypothesis was once presented to him. What Molloy calls intuition, this man had called informed. Informed had nothing to do with anything but the seat you occupied, the information that flowed past you as a consequence of sitting in that seat. This man, himself a certified quant, a Ph.D. in theoretical physics from one of the best physics departments in the country, had made billions sitting in a seat at one of the privileged bulge-bracket firms, and when he'd left to start his own firm, thought surely the leviathan firm would notice. In fact, it had an even better year following, with traders who weren't necessarily as bright. History made sure that people occupying seats in that venerable bulge-bracket firm, handling five or ten percent of all such transactions in the world (not much maybe, but a dominant fraction) knew where global money was going, the products it chased. They knew it earlier and acted on it sooner. So factor that into his own success, Molloy thinks. He's sat in good seats for a long time.

Who knows? He's bone-tired, acutely aware that he's fighting a losing battle, scaling the north face of the Eiger with rudimentary equipment, hemp ropes and nailed leather boots, when high-tech apparatus is coming. Does it matter? He trades now out of habit, not need. (Need? These days the deals arrive impeccably burnished, everything from sober German jumbo bond instruments to Latin American real estate trusts, seeking only his imprimatur, a gesture from associates who'll gladly return 25%, 45% on his investment for the cachet of his name.) Trading is a kind of crossword puzzle, a recreation; after all these years he can do it in his sleep and nearly does; and so what if the ruble or the yen falls into a black hole?

Ego aside (as if) he knows it's past time to do something different with his life. That's another reason why he's in Santa Fe. He's become so very good at the money, so accustomed to success, that he sometimes worries he lacks the courage to try something completely new, to risk failure. Ski without falling down, and you're not skiing hard enough. He thinks for one fleeting moment to confess all this to the woman across from him, relieve himself just once of these doubts and fears. But he fears her too, her impermeability, her supreme self-confidence. If he confesses to her, her scorn. She can sting him like no other.

She's been watching him with concern. "May I say you look totally fried tonight, pal."

"Was I zoning? Forty hours and counting since I saw my bed." He'd let himself get caught in a series of trades instead of closing the positions, couldn't let go. "You wouldn't have picked up on it twenty years ago. Ten." So. Overtaken by time too. Which is running out.

"Maybe we'd better call it a night. But one more thing. You were very kind, very comforting to Nola a few weeks ago at your dinner party. I appreciated it."

"Oh Christ, that shithead she's married to. Is he Pete's father? He needs a heart transplant himself. What an asshole. Why would a lovely woman like that?"

"The great mystery of couples. You're always amazed at the people who pick each other out. She's still beautiful, I think, but once—well, guys walked into lampposts, and she all but said that she just got tired of being hit on, the marriage was a kind of refuge. But to stick it out—it's got to be more than that."

He glances at her warily, wondering if she's implying something about her own marriage. Madame Genius will talk your ear off about history or mathematics, but goes mute when things get personal. "He should get over it. The boy needs him. His wife needs him. Failing to be where you're needed and when is about the biggest human failure there is."

"One of several," she says.

"What compares?"

"Failing to rise to opportunities, to be equal to challenges. Failing to welcome the new because the old is so—convenient."

He doesn't believe in mind reading, though this woman and he seem to have read one another's minds from time to time. Call it coincidence. For she's misread him often enough too: in a dark car, when what he proffered was fresh and fragile, almost evanescent, and not, as she seemed to think, predatory. Reality check: he might sometimes have misread her. We reserve infallibility for the pope, Jacko.

"I've seen the New Business website," he says brusquely. "Shit, I wrote that copy." Signals for the check, and kisses her good-bye perfunctorily on the cheek. Humiliation has overtaken him. Christ, let that door seal itself once and for all.

Heterogeneous Expectations

Judith let herself in through Sophie's gate, pushed through the front door. She carried vegetables and meat to make broth; yogurt and eggs; the few items Sophie could once more eat, and was loaded down with mail: utility bills that thrust their persistent ordinariness into a life that was no longer ordinary; a note or two from the few friends who didn't use e-mail. But her main burden was catalogs of things Sophie would never want, had surely never wanted—glossy pictures of objects photographed to call out "buy me," futile in this household. Catalogs were a special burden, because if Sophie sometimes had the energy to walk out to the mailbox, she could carry in only envelopes—catalogs had to wait until Ellie, her home help, or Judith, could bring them in to go directly into recycling.

Judith's mind was elsewhere. For days she'd been stewing over a problem whose solution required proving a theorem to show that no method, regardless of any improvements in computing, could ever be found that would solve this particular class of problems in less time—the very definition of lower bounds. A set of problems to solve for its own significance, but, she thought with caustic candor, important to solve for other reasons. She'd begun to fear, not for the first time, that she'd finally run out of ideas.

The fear of anyone who walked on the edge. She'd told herself she wouldn't hang on longer than she should, be the old athlete limping on to the field, the dancer whose ankles trembled, the poet singing the same old song. But a year, two years, she'd been running on nothing but momentum. One year, all right, it happened. But if it wasn't just one year? Not just two? The top of the S-curve, and nowhere to go but down?

"These are going straight into the trash unless you want to browse." No answer. She dumped her burdens carelessly on the kitchen counter and entered Sophie's room. "How's it going?"

Sophie lay on her daybed, her face truculent beneath her new hair. "Could you not at least knock?"

"Knock? I had my hands full, Soph. When was the last time we knocked on each other's door?"

"Judith, you really are a thick bitch. I always knock on your door, wouldn't want to catch you with your pants down. I can understand you don't worry about that here, but start."

"Worrying? Knocking?" Judith stood over her, genuinely puzzled, dropped to the bedside and took Sophie's hand. "Hey, what's eating you, girlfriend?"

Sophie spoke with more strength and vigor than in weeks. "You can't figure it out, I'll spell it out loud and clear. God knows my world has shrunk to this house, this room but. It. Is. Still. My. World." Words cleavered from one another, meant to be sharp enough to hurt. "This side of my threshold, this little patch of earth, may be the only place I have any power left; what I say goes, it's still mine. So far. Not yet in the hands of people who'll take over everything for me. Act like you get that, even if you don't."

"Sophie—I only meant to help."

"You and every other busybody in this town. I am fed up to here with being the patient, believe me. How are you? Fine, I say. Dying, of course, but hey, otherwise fine. Can we move on? I am fed up to here with all the people who come pressing in saying, in so many words, what? Still kicking, Soph? This is a stone drag, Sophie; you're outliving our sympathies. Outliving our expectations. Get on with it, woman. Oh, did you read the paper I sent? No? What the hell do you do all day? What I do all day is, I try to cope. The chemo's mashed my brain, no question. I can read a trashy magazine, that's about it, so take your fucking paper and shove it."

"Who sent you a paper to read?"

No answer. A paper wasn't the problem, thick bitch. Sophie had only seemed reconciled to dying. The serenity hadn't been a pose exactly but neither had Judith known how brittle it all was. Suddenly, belatedly, Sophie was in a rage with the living who'd die too, but not now, not soon. "Oh, Aya Sofia," Judith said softly.

Sophie looked up sharply. "Must everything you say remind me of how damn wasted my damn life has been? How glorious yours? You've seen Aya Sofia. I haven't. Must you rub it in?"

"We've always called you that, Soph. Gabe wouldn't offend you for the world." Gabe and his affectionate nonsense, calling her Jay-bait last time she saw him. "Not a waste, girlfriend. You don't need me to remind you your stuff's been fundamental to—"

Sophie interrupted her disdainfully. "I am one fucking grub on the shitpile of biology, and this I recognize. My so-called research is already being overtaken. Already! What took me years, long, back-breaking, grueling, never-to-return years of my already downsized, abbreviated, abridged and soon-to-be terminated life, working with first-generation instruments, can now be done in minutes by a new machine. A microchip. No human interference. A lab assistant to push a button. I lie here in this bed and I think, what if I'd known that then? What if I'd known I was going to buy the ranch, kick the bucket, cash in my chips, take a permanent powder, fucking *die* at fifty-four, and the work I thought was so important would, by that time, be automated so that anybody with a community college degree could do it faster, better, cheaper? Would I have broken my butt over it?"

Shadowy paths. "Would you?"

Sophie glared. "You expect me to say yes. You expect me to say, hey, the step had to be taken, I'm the one who took it; credit for getting there first; anyway, I loved every moment even if it's obsolete now. The real answer is hell no. I'd have—Jay, I've got the world's most wonderful retirement package. Savings and investments up to here. Prudence my middle name. Vacations never cost beans; I put a nephew through college without even noticing. The little bastard didn't notice either, but let's not—" She stopped, out of breath. "I saw a designer dress that time we went to New York—I can still see it, black, off one shoulder. I thought how pretty it was, I should buy it for myself, blindingly expensive. Didn't because there wasn't anyplace I'd ever go to wear it. Didn't have your life, Jay." She had stopped again, her breath raising her chest, the bedcover, alarmingly. "I thought, one day I'll have it, that life. Not this year, next, but time will come I'll have it. I'll go all the places Judith's been, and I'll—" She began to cry.

Judith was appalled. She'd never seen Sophie in such raw need, not when she'd announced her diagnosis, not when the chemo had flattened her again and again. She bent down, took Sophie's hand, whispered. "You've idealized it, Soph. It isn't just glam designer dresses and the Orient Express."

"No? What, then?"

Time running out, the obligation to speak honestly. "It's being afraid . . . that someone'll call your bluff. Somebody discovers how little you really know, how much you've been faking it." That Feydor, damn his eyes, will win. "You're just another old ghost hanging around who never got beyond some simple, fixed ideas that once seemed brilliant, but weren't. People can hardly hide their yawns. You go from being a living legend to someone whose name means zilch to anybody under forty. The people who matter, Soph, people who'll lead the field." She sat back murmuring almost to herself. "The work you cherish most wasn't ahead of its time, you're still waiting for people to pick up on it. You were—irrelevant then, irrelevant now. Nobody cared, ever will. Not important work, this cherished effort, how could you have suckered yourself into thinking so? I might finally have become a real scientist too late. I've given myself a few pleasures in the way of travel and other little toys, boys, because I was afraid that's all I'd get out of all this."

Sophie pulled herself up from the bed screaming, her face colored hotly, dangerously, her hands fisting. "You don't get it! You just don't get it! That *is* all you get out of all this. If you don't get that you get nothing! I fucking hate it that you did it right for all the wrong reasons. And I did it wrong for all the right reasons. Get out of here. Just get out of my sight! I mean it! I'll call the police if you don't get out!"

Judith backed out, swamped by the poison. Secrets of her soul, words she'd said to no one, Sophie scorned, belittled.

The resident automaton in Judith's nerves and muscles got her safely home along the familiar dirt road, and she sank onto the bedroom chaise longue in a kind of suspension. The wind had changed; a storm chilled the house instead of cooling it off, the sumac was already bright red. As twilight fell over the Sangres, she also darkened, swollen with a numb misery that blackened to fury, then dissolved, something else. Sophie was dying but not yet dead, and had no license to wound like that. Her words played back again and again derisively in Judith's head: *right for all the wrong reasons*. Molloy at the opera, slightly mocking: *So accomplished, the lady is*.

Late, late; altogether dark, moon gone, stars hidden, she admitted it was unequal: she was not dying, Sophie was. Maybe Sophie already regretted her tantrum—a trifling word for the expression a lifetime's bitter jealousy, festering inside what had seemed a sweet, good friendship, jealousy Judith had stupidly, willfully blinded herself to.

Yet she owed it to that friendship, not quite dead yet either, to try again.

Sophie did not answer her phone, and though Judith left a message the first time, she left none when she tried later, still got the machine. Not e-mail. She ached, a soreness she could not salve, rupture that was unendurable, forced into reassessment of their friendship that made her ill. A fool. The right thing for all the wrong reasons. Aya Sofia, Aya Sofia, maybe so.

Friendship disappearing now, sooner rather than later. It had never been easy. Nearly all the people close to her she'd known for many years. Making new friends flummoxed her. If she'd known how, it must be time-consuming, false starts until friendship took root. Time one thing she didn't have. Admire Molloy, picking up from New York, Europe, arriving in a new town to start all over. How? Maybe he didn't need friends. She hadn't thought she did—hadn't given it thought at all—until friendship was suddenly denied.

She crawled under her comforter, tormented by what she hadn't added to her confession. That she feared she'd look back, see she'd passed great but difficult opportunities because smaller ones seemed so easy, glitter instead of gold. When she'd become a real scientist—when she genuinely didn't care what others thought—that great surge of once-in-a-lifetime brainpower had almost passed.

That she feared she'd look back, see that the very transformation she'd come to Santa Fe to seek, whatever it was, had passed her by after all, for she'd been oblivious. Or had seen it, but lacked the courage to embrace it.

That she wondered every day who would be her own Judith when the time came.

Ellie the home help answered the next day at Sophie's, told her sadly that Sophie didn't wish to speak to her. Ever. "It gets like this sometimes when they're dying," Ellie whispered. "You shouldn't take it personally."

"How else should I take it?" she said later to Ron.

He didn't immediately reply. He'd seen many friends through this, a gay man in the age of a devastating disease that had afflicted the gay world disproportionately. He knew it was very personal indeed. "It's not like the movies," he said finally. "She may not ever want to see you. Sometimes they don't. Don't look for a deathbed reconciliation. It could happen, but don't look for it. How you doing yourself?"

"Aching, just aching. Feeling so—misjudged. Love her, thought she loved me. I've offended her, she should've told me so in plain English a long time ago."

"Would it have changed things? Changed you?"

"I don't know. We could've talked."

"Would it have helped? Sophie is—something of an oddment." No explicit reason, he and Sophie had hated each other on sight, and endured each other's company civilly only because they both loved Judith—Sophie in ways she herself didn't understand, which, in Ron's opinion, was a big part of Sophie's problem. Fool yourself, pay the price. "No use whining about it, Jay. Take what you can from it and get on with your life."

"Oh, sweetie." Gabe put his arms comfortingly around her. "Oh, sweetie. You go ahead and have yourself a good cry. Ignore Mr. Tough-Love there. What the hell does he know?"

Crawling Around the Landscape

To: jimenez@sf.arch.edu
From: jrg@santafe.edu
August 25, 1997, 6:33 p.m.

Darling man, are you ever coming home? I'm having a dinner party. I need you here.

To: jrg@santafe.edu
From: jimenez@sf.arch.edu
August 25, 1997, 9:49 p.m.

Say when, I'll be there. So much to tell you. Ask you. One part the ancient city, one part this city I'm digging up. Driving me crazy. I'd have come up to be with you soon anyway. You need me? I miss you. Love, B.

Inéz surveyed Judith's living room critically. "You've probably seen all this, Molloy." Girlishness gone, the voice verged on accusatory.

"Once, yes." If he seldom mentioned Inéz at business, she was always with him at openings, parties, dinners. Judith had observed the change, how she no longer hid shyly behind Molloy, but entered a room on his arm taller, more self-possessed. Another unintended consequence of falling in love.

Even as Inéz had unlocked his tongue, Molloy was in turn undoing her reticence, teaching her perhaps that fine and underrated Manhattan skill of speaking divertingly about anything whatsoever—your job, the rascals in politics, the meaning of life, finds to be had in the alleyways of history. Molloy hadn't seemed to possess it, but as Judith now knew, disposed to, he could talk very well.

Long past time to get to know Inéz, Judith thought, or Inéz and Molloy together, the new thing they'd made of each other, co-evolving these months. Inéz's outburst at the New Business dinner party, grotesque then, might have been no more than stress, an urge to bring Molloy's clients, his friends, down a notch. Surely long past time to move into the next stage of her own life, wise woman, crone, whatever the phrase was these days. Crone, cognate to *Krone*, crown? the summit of your life? She looked it up. From the Middle Dutch, *croonie*, old ewe; from Old North French *caronie*, carrion. Dead meat. Oh wait, the perpetual girl within cried, not yet. The adult took no notice. Inéz—and Molloy—were possibly the occasion for this tardy recognition of the facts, thrown up by the universe for her to learn from, or stupidly go on deceiving herself. The old ewe would meet the lamb properly.

She'd considered other guests, finally settled on Betty and Carter McMahon: Betty, a fundraiser for one of the Indian museums in town, Carter, an Anglo lawyer who was working for the Navajo nation. Betty might peel a few dollars from Molloy. But in the spirit of spinning a web to support herself, she invited Ron and Gabe, and of course, Benito, the archaeologist who could pass as an artist if necessary. Or was it the other way around?

Not Sophie, who could not sit up at dinner parties any more. Who would not have come here even if she could.

Inéz moved slowly around Judith's large central room; stopped at the pots, just as Molloy once had. "What's this?"

"Chinese," Molloy said quickly. "Very old. Where did you come by it, Judith?"

"It was left to me by—a serious collector. He knew I loved it. Everything else went to the Met." Suave, while the images in her mind chilled her. Jonathan, his collection of elaborate Javanese bronze Buddhas, every surface incised, curved, repeating in on itself; his soft, shrewd and heavily accented voice: "I picked them up for a song. Nobody else was interested in such things." His deeply shadowed Riverside Drive apartment, where he joked, squinted, blew the dust carelessly off a small Buddha and shined it with his thumb. "Too baroque. Too elaborate. Out of style." But Jonathan had grown up in *Mitteleuropaishe* overstatement, old aunties' antimacassared parlors and glutted grandparents' flats: the Buddhas pleased him.

"A mathematician. A mentor."

At his bedside in the nursing home in upper Manhattan, him tethered to a ventilator and dialysis machine, gasping as life ebbed from him, his consciousness elsewhere, and the meter running at nearly a thousand dollars a day. He'd have been scandalized. She'd taken his hand, called his name softly. No response. So she'd wished him a merciful delivery, which could only be merciful if swift. "I once asked him which was harder, mathematics or collecting. I thought he'd say mathematics, that the collecting was just for fun. No. He said they were both hard, they both called on the deepest part of your intelligence to do them right."

"I'd agree." Molloy looked better than when she'd seen him last, though still weary, not up to the picture of him smiling at her from the snow, face animated by an appealing sense of fun, even mischief in that smile—so uncomplicated, so unvexed then. But much time had passed. For them all.

Others arrived, the talk was polite ritual. Ron and Molloy stepped aside. They murmured in German, Molloy facing her direction and saying something like, I respect that, but you knew I'd hear. Ron grinned, somehow found out. Gabe joined them, said something friendly. Molloy nodded and switched to English. "I grew up inland. Always wanted to do that. Probably all that Brian Wilson when I was a kid." "Anytime, dude, anytime. Just say when. You ski; you'll rip."

Inéz had resumed her tour, though Judith sensed that she herself was being studied as carefully as her modest collection. Inéz stopped before a dreamlike image of an African in blue robes, an Asian monk in crimson, hurrying barefoot along a desert road, bearing between them a cloth of some kind, filled with human heads. Above, thunderclouds loomed on the horizon, releasing tresses of rain that evaporated before they reached the ground, a band of cobalt in the distance. A New Mexico summer sky.

Inez studied the painting. "Molloy admires you very much. The work you do is very important, he says." Her physical beauty was glorious, flawless, delicate bones, glowing skin, enormous brown eyes, lush hair. Judith stared shamelessly, awed by its power.

"I've been lucky. I have work that matters to me. If it matters to the rest of the world, that's just icing on the cake, isn't it?" Fake even in her own ears, though she meant it: she'd been lucky, she did do work (and not inconsequentially, was well-paid for it) that mattered to her, got her out of bed every morning with joy in her heart, had for decades. Whatever else it got her.

"What I do matters too," Inéz said slowly, "and not just to me. We're not talking icing on the cake—" contemptuously, and Judith was mortified, knew she deserved it "—we're talking women's lives. Lives of their children." Inéz turned to face Judith, appraised her, clearly found her morally wanting. And enjoyed just a little too much, Judith thought, her own superiority. I have lived, Inéz was saying silently, and nearly died—several times. No man has ever threatened you with knife or gun, bottle, fist, the back of his hand. You are soft, privileged, and don't know shit. "But as Molloy says, I only rescue one woman at a time. Sometimes only for the moment. They go back to the—situation. Or get into another inappropriate relationship. No *ideas* in rescuing battered women, he says." In Inéz's mouth, mere ideas too were contemptible. He can be such a bastard, she didn't say. "No ideas. Just billions of women on the planet."

"Luckily, not all of us need to be rescued." The iron rules of hospitality stopped Judith, and she silenced such thoughts as she'd had on the subject, that a woman once beaten, even threatened, had a screw loose to stay with a monster; that any sentient female in the last part of the twentieth century should know by the time she was eight that she could not dumbly rely on a man for her bed and board, and be prepared; that she was obliged to assess the man she'd have babies with before she had them; that since 1972 no woman in this country, at least, was compelled to bear a child she'd conceived; and please spare me the cant about low self-esteem, the culture of *machismo*, victimhood and all the rest. But as her colleague Alan liked to point out, intelligence was nine-tenths point of view.

She was determined to be courteous. "One at a time seems to me just fine, admirable." Give Inéz credit, it was hard enough getting a woman and her kids out from under some guy's thumb, never mind the triage needed to distinguish among the women who'd go right back regardless; the women who were drama-queening; and the women who could actually use a hand. Did Molloy expect Inéz to have *ideas* about this?

Judith added smoothly: "Of course ideas are here. The Rights of Man. *Liberté, la propriété, la surété, et la résistance a l'oppréssion*. You can read it in one of the first articles." Why had it popped out in pretentious French? "It knocked people's socks off at the time. Extending the rights of man to women—that's a radical idea in many parts of the world today. If it ever takes hold in a big way, the whole planet will be different."

Inéz shrugged, not so much indifferent to ideas as impatient, she implied, with thinking—endless talking—and not doing. Her passion was here and now, the succor of those in desperate need. It wouldn't have entered her mind, Judith thought, how much Inéz herself needed the needy.

Inéz now saw the sculptured skeleton sitting in the dining room corner. "*Dios mio!*" She crossed herself and turned away from it. "How do you live with that?"

"Very easily. I love her," Judith said. Inéz? On speaking terms with death?

Molloy, Ron and Gabe had followed them. "Ah, the local figure," said Molloy. "Who is she, again?"

Judith ran her fingers lightly along the sculpted spine. "*Doña* Sebastiana, the New Mexican symbol of death. This *carreta*, this cart she sits in, is drawn by the souls of the dead—or those who will be dead—while she aims her bow and arrow at us. She lures us with her smile. She'll eventually get us, but she wants it to be sooner, not later. Seductive, no?"

Molloy murmured, "The divine assassin."

"The Penitentes—has Inéz told you about our homegrown religious brotherhood here in northern New Mexico?"

"No," Inéz said sharply.

Judith saw Ron register this. "A pity," he said mildly. "It's one of New Mexico's most interesting traditions."

Benito let himself in through the back door, kissed Judith warmly, gave a New Mexico *abrazo* to Ron and Gabe in turn. He held up a bottle of wine. "Your favorite, *querida*. Hello, everybody, I'm Benito." Conquistador-erect, an aristocratic ease, self-possessed and proprietary too about his familiarity with this household, the public use of the endearment.

"I was just explaining *la doña* and the Penitentes." Judith slipped her arm around that slender conquistador's waist. "Now that we have a native son here—"

Benito grinned. "Go ahead, *querida*. I'm here to correct only when you stray into error." He entered the kitchen where everyone could see that he knew exactly where the corkscrew was; had the ease to stick a finger in a sauce and taste it, signaled approval. Judith smiled after him.

"The Penitentes keep a figure of *la doña* in each of their *moradas*, their meeting places. During Holy Week they pull her cart through the village streets, a reminder that death must eventually come for all. But the rest of the year, the Penitentes have no fear of her. They offer her daily respect, and if they dare ask anything, it's only that death be easy and none too soon. Me too."

Inéz seemed agitated. "Death isn't my idea of art."

Ron and Gabe exchanged glances.

"When I first saw her in a gallery, she shocked me, I grant you. But obsessed me too. I came back again and again. Look at those beautiful long hands and feet, that sinuous spine—a single piece of aspen. That grinning skull. Untraditional, this one, not a bow and arrow, but proffers a red rose. She also seems young not old—hair lush and black like yours, Inéz, instead of the stringy gray you see on most *doña* Sebastianas. If you're going to seduce your victim, better be seductive, right? You could say I accepted the rose *la doña* offered, brought her home and settled her here. It's still a bit odd to eat dinner under her gaze.

"My family used to take their summer holidays in the Austrian Alps, and my father's favorite table at our hotel was in a corner, *ein Tisch in die Ecke, bitte*, where a freshly crucified Jesus was nailed up and bled all over. Painted wood, I rush to say. Not a local martyr. You'd think a kid exposed to that every summer would be a vegetarian, but not me, I was fascinated."

"And you should see what Benito has on *his* living room wall," Gabe said mischievously. "Saint somebody or other about to have a double mastectomy."

"Agatha," Benito supplied. "One of our very finest."

Molloy was carelessly hiding a smile, but Inéz made her horror theatrically obvious, exhibiting a kind of delicacy she seemed to think expected of the truly sensitive. In art she loves cute little pooty-tats, and weeps buckets over strays, Ron said to Gabe later.

Judith missed all this, was gazing at *la doña*, remembering the first time Sophie had come for dinner after the diagnosis. She'd smiled sadly, asked aloud that death be easy and not too soon. "Of all the art I have, she alone demands serious attention every time I come home. We live together so intimately, *la doña* and I, that I'm surprised when she makes newcomers uneasy."

Gabe grinned. "Didn't somebody wonder if this was a shrine to the Grateful Dead?"

"Inéz," Judith continued, "if she bothers you, I can wheel her out. No trouble." Maybe Inéz had been raised Navajo, with their great aversion to the dead.

"It's all right." Inéz took a drink from Benito. "But you're not an Hispaña, so I wonder why you collect Hispanic art." As in, it was second-rate? Or as an Anglo, Judith had no right to cherish it?

"I suppose I think of it as human art," Judith said. "Which category I also belong to."

"No wine, my friend?" Benito asked cordially.

Molloy shook his head. "I may be trading later. Where did you grow up that you ate dinner under bloody crucifixions?"

"Munich," Ron answered for her. "Judith's father was at Radio Free Europe; mine was helping to jump-start the German film industry. Judith and I lost touch when we came home to college. Then by accident, found each other here."

You knew that, Judith told him silently with more puzzlement than pain.

"There are no accidents," Gabe said portentously, wickedly mimicking the

New Agers who hung around Downtown Subscription drinking black coffee and reading the magazines for free.

"*München*. It must have been hard early on—after the war," Molloy said.

It came back to Judith instantly, the re-building of Munich all around her, the sound of cranes, rubble dragged out of the city center by freight cars, wagons, wheelbarrows, the pungency of old plaster and brick, artificial hills that grew on the city's outskirts, to be covered over, swallowed into the city's later growth, strange middens to puzzle archaeologists of the future. The quarrels over how the city should be rebuilt, a persuasive city father arguing successfully, thank God, for recapturing the Bavarian, the baroque, delights of old Munich. Too much of Germany after the war had been rebuilt brutally and on the cheap.

These memories were partly a dream. She hadn't arrived in Munich until the mid-1950s, when the worst of the privations, the rebuilding, was over. "Not hard for us. But for the Europeans, yes. Very hard." She glanced at Inéz, for whom World War II was surely as remote as the Battle of Marathon. "Ancient history." The talk moved on, and Judith turned to back Inéz. "Are you the other local here?"

Other with Benito. Inéz nodded, but her beautiful face had assumed a slight sullenness. Had something happened between her and Molloy before they arrived? Judith tried one last time. "I'm about to bring dinner off the grill. Should I move *la doña* out of the dining room, Inéz?"

"I told you, it's all right." Her petulance belied her words. It was Gabe who, with infinite tact, found a way of talking to Inéz that made her smile, that dazzling smile that illuminated the room. Molloy moved over to talk to some of the other guests, maybe to be lightened of a few dollars by Betty for her infinite number of good causes. Judith stepped back, heard the conversational buzz, and was relieved.

Benito followed her outside to the grill. "Who's the guy?"

"The tycoon I was tutoring. He's bought New Business, so I guess he's my boss too. He may be on the board of the Institute soon. That's his girlfriend."

"The tycoon. His girlfriend." Benito put a hand gently on her shoulder, and she turned to see his wide eyes behind his spectacles blinking unusually hard.

"As you're fond of saying, this is a small town, *querida*. I know her, her family."

In this, Santa Fe Hispaños were wonderfully old fashioned. Everybody was attached to a family; every family had its reputation. An individual stood as part of that reputation, or in opposition to it. *A fine family, a good man. A fine family, but a black sheep. Not a good family; what did you expect?* Inéz's family reputation? Inéz's own? She turned the fish over on the grill. "She bad news, Benitole?"

"*Hija de gata, ratones mata*. The cat's daughter kills mice."

Judith sighed. "Have you heard they've done a second bone marrow transplant for Pete?"

"Oh, God, that poor little kid. Do they bring half of them back from that? Nola must be devastated. I'll call her. She still in Texas? I'd just as soon not talk to Ernie. Let me give you a hand, *amante*."

Local Peaks

For an instant he wishes that Judith and Benito had come back into the house at any time but this. Yet here they are, bearing the fish, the grilled vegetables, just in time to see Inéz making a royal fool of herself. And thus of him. PMS, general bitchiness, God knows; she'd been ragging him already in the car. Who knows why, he assumes he zoned out—the woman does go on—and missed the beginning of all this. If there was an actual beginning, and it's not simply Inéz's all-purpose lamentation.

"Everything measured in dollars. No dollars, you're nothing in this country. Dollars make you something; the more you have, the better you are, you could be a moral monster really." Molloy recalls with no little irony that two days ago she'd been asking for a special donation to the shelter. In dollars.

He sits down, shakes out his napkin, responds gently. "My country. I do believe you were born in the same country. And your parents. It's a bit much, Inéz." This last so quietly that nearly nobody hears him. But Benito hears. Molloy takes a breath, makes an effort to sound benevolent. "But I understand the rage of people who have no money against those who have. Yes, that I do. I've known that rage myself."

Though her smile persists sweetly, it's undercut by the edge in her voice. "Oh, you do love that idea of yourself, that you were born poor, and made yourself rich. A rage against the rich? You're the one who hung around with the German princes—"

"My clients, Inéz, not my friends."

"*Hofjude*," Judith murmurs. Court Jew.

He shoots back fiercely, "*Genau*." Exactly. A nerve plucked. The princes had used Jacko; but Jacko had used the princes. Once understood, a reasonable business arrangement. The boar hunts, much more complicated than slaying the totem animal. In their genes the princes carried knowledge handed down from time out of mind when their ancestors dwelled in huts constructed of mammoth bones: the boar as scavenger, eater of corpses, the beast of death. Who vanquished the beast claimed its tusks as talisman against evil.

"The man trades money," Inéz announces with a grim smile. "Okay, I don't understand this very well, but everyone says that people like this destabilize governments, ruin innocent lives."

"It can't be much fun to be Asian right now," Carter McMahon observes. The Asian currency markets are in great turmoil, watched with apprehension by everyone who concerns themselves with money.

It flows into and suffuses him, the power, the self-control, the signal for combat. He allows himself a small smile, feels a tiny nerve throbbing at his temple, an echo at his jaw line. "Currency traders," he says to the table pleasantly. "We're certainly the demons *du jour*. Revealed truth from editorial writers, columnists, all those self-appointed scolds who offer us the common wisdom. I sell you yen, Singapore dollars, I don't force them on you. If you buy, you obviously believe they have value."

His fingers tented before him, the *sumi* brush eyebrows rise in query. "Who accuses us? Little tinpot tyrants whose cozy games are being spoiled, men with the opportunity to suck their own countries dry who didn't, for a moment, resist. Widows and orphans not their concern. Economic development, code for pocket lining. That sucking sound is, they protest, their historic custom, their national way, their immemorial tribal practice, their ancient ethnic right. Larceny as lifestyle. Here come the global traders to change the order of magnitude, but otherwise it's business as usual, the way they've always done things."

Silence. No one's even eating. "I'll tell you what my colleagues and I did. We looked at all that grand larcency on a national scale and said to ourselves, we bet this can't last. Literally. We placed bets that it couldn't last. We put our money where our mouths were, an option editorial writers, even the most self-righteous, aren't called on to take. Get it wrong on the editorial page, nobody remembers it two days later. Get it wrong in trading, you're handed instant material notice. If it could've sustained itself, all this international squeezing and sucking—nobody would've noticed our bets, much less our losses. But we were right. We won."

"So you profited," Gabe says, helping himself to the plate of grilled Rocky mountain trout that sits like a silver fountain in the center of the table.

"Some of us," Molloy agrees. "Not on the scale of the dictators, but enough to make the betting worthwhile. Now comes perhaps the most interesting part." He leans toward the table, a deft gesture, compelling attention. "Here I am, practicing applied political science, if you will; or to put it more crudely, a kind of whistle-blowing, and what happens?" He looks at each face around the table, even Inéz's, that laserlike focus that Judith has seen at New Business, inviting them to smile with him. They smile. "Am I congratulated for clarifying the matter, exposing this structural rot, this official swindle? Am I praised for risking my own assets to make a point that editorial writers make at no risk whatsoever? Assuming they have the wit to see it at all? I am not. It seems the public would shoot the messenger instead." He pauses. "Of course you can argue that I get paid to take risks."

They're almost laughing; they can't help themselves. He looks down at his plate innocently. "No. What really happened? Without getting too tediously technical, maybe it was just an example of something familiar to people around this table, chaos. The butterfly that sets off this particular catastrophe is a tiny rise—a quarter of a percentage point—in interest rates in the United States that suddenly makes it more attractive to move hot capital back home. A rumor, a month later, that the Thai Central Bank will raise rates—or devalue. The panic begins. One of you experts in chaos theory could trace it nicely." He turns directly to Judith. "To put it more technically, the Asian currency markets were unstable with respect to perturbations of small amplitude." She casts her eyes down, remembering. He turns back to the table, smiles to ease them. "Frankly, I see myself as Dorothy's little black Toto, a scruffy little mutt, no particular pedigree, pulling the curtain aside and exposing the Wizard of Oz in all his chicanery, whether crony capitalists or free-market ideologues. Pay no attention to that man behind the curtain, the voice booms. But of course we must."

"My God, Molloy," Judith laughs. "I'd love to hear you sometime on price-gouging, or market-rigging, or insider trading—"

"Can you think for a moment I'd defend any of those?" It's a soft, most intimate query, as if no one else is at the table. Yes, he sees sadly, she can think such a thing. "I play by the rules," he says intensely. "Scrupulously. But I didn't write those rules. If I had, I'd have done a damn sight better job." He recovers his lightness, helps himself to fish. "Doyne Farmer thinks we could look at the markets as a financial ecology. Suppose speculators are like carnivores in a biological ecology? Suppressing us might have dangerous unintended effects, as it has in biological ecosystems."

Ron, also laughing: "You save us from being overrun by vermin? Have we just heard your next op-ed piece for the *Wall Street Journal*?"

"*Nur Handelsblatt*," Molloy replies with a modesty that might even be genuine.

"*Also*, so be it."

Molloy looks up, around the table, an encompassing smile that invites them all toward him once more. Oh, he's learned a lot dealing with—manipulating—the German princes. "Am I kidding myself? You tell me. I'm watching a few colleagues slowly getting their—" he swallows a vulgarism—"heads handed to them. Americans, betting mostly, but not entirely, American money. The discipline of the market works, even for the rich." He stops. "For weeks those guys have been waking up in the grip of cold sweats you couldn't begin to imagine. When they got to sleep at all." He grins. "Nosebleed leverage. Been there, done that, never again."

"Why don't guys like that just go play on another planet? They're not playing for money; they're playing for—whatever they're playing for. Prestige, ego, twisting off arms and beating the body with bloody stumps." The voice is moderate, but doesn't conceal its challenge. "They're betting the livelihoods, the lives, of real people. Not people they've ever seen or heard of, but ordinary, hardworking folks who never knew what hit them. Wall Street is full of guys who got Ph.D.s in physics, right? Up there on the hill, they used to think they'd blow up the globe. Now they'll settle for blowing up the global economy. To be plain, Molloy, the discipline of the market falls a little harder on the poor than the rich."

Molloy appraises him thoughtfully. The boyfriend. Habitual thoroughness, due diligence, has discovered that while Benito Jiménez is no mediocrity, he certainly isn't in the same league with Madame Genius. Common as they are, such mismatches always have uncommon explanations. Oh well, the dolly, come to that.

It suddenly clicks—for sure he hadn't geared up to combat the negligible dolly; hadn't even thought about an adversary except to note the internal rush to battle stations.

He keeps silent, considering things. In truth, Benito's asking him why there's no justice, and to that question, Molloy has no soothing answer. Luck exists. Sometimes grace. But not justice. He knows how a small dinner in Singapore, simultaneous with an intimate lunch in London, leads to telephone calls among a couple of dozen people, himself included, who later that day will be banging without mercy on some poor currency. Despite what anyone around the table thinks, it's a very old game. In the past, however, the players were governments. At last he replies to Benito obliquely, deferring matters until he has a better sense of the man.

"Many hedge funds speculate, and they're highly leveraged, it's true. You could call what I do speculating, but I do it with my own money, sometimes my clients' money. We don't borrow. We aren't into leverage. For whatever that's worth. But if you want to lay blame, try your friendly bank down the road, the same guys who used to hand out toasters. The real turmoil in the markets is caused by banks, not hedge funds. Compared to banks, people like my brethren and I are noise-level phenomena. We just happen to have faces people recognize. Like the old Greek custom of putting a real face on the statue of an idealized body." He sighs. "It's never been easy to be poor in this world."

Inéz seizes the opportunity. "Come off it, Molloy. You despise the poor. You're just like everyone else who thinks that poverty's like, some kind of personal failure. You're at a board meeting and you go, why is this dumb bitch still on welfare? Off with her welfare, off with her head!" The color flushes Inéz's smooth, tea-colored cheeks as she addresses the rest of the table. "Just after I left—my marriage, I met a man who asked me what business I was in. I say, I'm not working yet, I'm looking. Oh, he goes, you're in the entitlement business. Condescending prick."

No one replies. Inéz seems tone-deaf to the music of this particular evening, and the subject changes. It changes again, the collective mood changing with it, the guests amusing each other, treating whatever topics come up with gentle banter, making each other smile, even laugh. They are not among the poor.

They have a moment to admire the fountain of silver fish rising out of its bed of chiaroscuro vegetables; the spring greens of the salad, the sweet fruits of late summer; the light wine that seems to exhibit (if wine can be said to have such a thing) a sense of humor: it encourages their merriment. Only unconsciously do they register the satisfaction from the heft of good silver in their hands; the comfort of fine linen across their knees; water in heavy crystal goblets to remind them of how precious water really is. This abundant table, a sign of their good fortune in being here tonight, inside and protected from the mountainous desert, where polychrome vegetables and fruits, wines and linens, silver fountains of any kind, do not naturally exist, makes them happy. Tonight connects them, they might sense, with a history of generous tables laid out for guests, among the most ancient of human gestures, coeval with worship, preparing for an afterlife.

Yet as coffee's being served, Molloy begins again, as if intent on explaining something about himself. He's been talking with Carter McMahon, but his voice rises just slightly, and the table obediently falls silent to listen.

"If I seem unsympathetic, it's because I've been intimate with poverty. In no way ennobling. I grew up in a small town in western Pennsylvania. Inéz thinks all-American; okay, upfront street names, River Road, School Street; an Elks Club, a union hall, old bathtubs upended in gardens as grottoes for statues of the Virgin. But the air was so poisoned it chewed the paint off your house. The lining out of your lungs. A kid, I didn't know a single healthy man over forty—that age, they were all crippled in the mills and mines. Or the bars. Fifty they were dead." He reports without bitterness, a matter of fact. His uncle Jack, on the front porch of the two-family house on hot summer evenings, an Iron

City in one hand, a Camel in the other, his belly monumental under his ribbed undershirt. He collapsed two, sometimes three, aluminum frame chairs a season, going down in an explosion of curses, concatenated with verve. Himself, a ten-year-old sprawled on the steps, escaping into Classic Comics, drunk on the ancient Greeks and Romans, infinitely distant from everything around him.

"Hard enough. But the real difficulty—" he hesitates. "They hated anything that might've pulled them out of it, like education; despised, punished somebody with a hunger for more. If I'm unforgiving about anything, I'm unforgiving about that. Completely."

Faces he can read. Benito thinking this is allusion to that streak in New Mexican Hispanic culture that disdains book learning, work without muscle, which might push you above yourself and your people. Ron wondering if Inéz is a kind of project, Molloy undertaking massive reclamation. Inéz wondering when this evening, this endless talk, will ever end. Yeah, well. All of the above. A Schumpeterian kind of guy, Gabe had once joked. Creative destruction. A face he can't read. Madame Genius turning on her bozo filter again?

But she suddenly speaks. "Who was Father Joachim?"

He fails to conceal his surprise. My talent is for asking the right questions, she'd said, and Molloy remembers he'd once quoted Schiller to her, credited Father Joachim for teaching him. "My high school German teacher. Latin too, for that matter." He relaxes. "Poor old Father Yokkie. God was probably as surprised as Yokkie that he ended up teaching Latin and German to the sons of miners and mill workers in such a godforsaken place. Years later, I went to see him in the nursing home for old priests." He chooses his words carefully. "To say thanks for what he'd meant to me. All I did was discover his tragedy." He picks at his dessert, looks up, fork poised, understands that he must go on. "His tragedy. Yes. Simply that he'd survived. He'd taken his vows in the thirties in Germany. As an institution, the Church might've been disgracefully silent, but small obscure orders took in young Jews, baptized them, weren't finicky about their vocation. Protected them. In his old age, Father Yokkie understood he should have been, as he told me on that last visit, a Talmudic scholar, not a teacher to Catholic cretins. A little short in the Christian charity department was Father Yokkie."

"But he was to you as the order had been to him?" Judith is laying it out pointedly, the old man who rescued him, as the old man had once been rescued. He sees the expectant looks around the table, an insight into the mysterious Molloy.

He thinks it over, flinches from genuine self-revelation. "I'm not, in any sense that the Church would recognize, a believer. But sometimes if I find myself in just the right place, the *santuario* at Chimayó, I light a candle to the memory of that poor bastard."

Judith nods, probably trying to imagine Molloy the artistically punctilious in among the plaster saints and lurid lithographs. Side by side with paintings in the old New Mexico tradition. "Chimayó," she says mystifyingly, "is a corruption of the Tewa for obsidian."

A Catastrophe Point

Benito had been listening attentively. Molloy perturbed him, raised his defenses, though the man hadn't uttered anything particularly objectionable. Okay, from a boardroom in Luxembourg it was probably hard to see the peasants and their water buffalo, the real victims of his speculations. But that wasn't it.

"So many of us owe so much to our teachers," Benito said. Even he couldn't have said whether he meant it sincerely or ironically. Memories stirred, questions raised he thought long ago put to rest. He saw his mother standing at the stove not cooking dinner, like all the other moms he knew, but boiling down herbs, extracting essences she used as a *curandera*, an *albolaria*, a folk healer. She'd turn her face to him like a feral animal, not frightened but preternaturally alert. A sixth sense. He sometimes thought he'd inherited it from her. "*Mijo*," Luz would call out, her voice as intense, as healing, as her *remedios*, and he'd run to be hugged, feel her laughter, a bird fluttering in her breast.

She was first to take him to the desert—probably before he could walk—in search of wild herbs whose names and uses she taught him, always a piece of *osha* in their pockets, to repel snakes. How to ask permission of the plants to pick their leaves (preferred to the roots, because taking leaves didn't kill the plant, and leaf tinctures were predictable, more herb-like than drug-like). She'd say aloud how their tinctures would color as she prepared them, how she'd use the medicine.

Luz was first to take him to the pueblos, too, bouncing over the dirt roads in her beat-up old Chevy, to consult with the Native American *curanderas*, exchange dried herbs, learn, teach. Female voices murmuring over coffee, lemonade for him until he squirmed enough to be released out into the dusty plaza with other boys. Thus he'd learned the Tewa dialects. Luz had given him his first Indian pots, not old ones, she'd counseled gently, but holding in their clay old ideas, to be honored for that. She'd taught him that ideas, in words or otherwise, had great power.

Had she been so beautiful, or was that only a little boy's recollection? No, he had photos. A proud woman, amused by the camera, her oblique glance almost haughty. She'd gone her own way, outside the usual paths of Hispanic female subservience. After all, she'd been chosen by God: the proof was her power to heal, clients from all over the Upper Rio Grande.

Later his father also took him out to the desert, taught him to read the landscape, to love the earth in his hands, pull a treat of chewing gum out of the *piñon*'s sap, pine nuts from its cones, but she'd been first. He still had her notebooks, though he hadn't looked at them for a long time. His mother's calling had sometimes been a barrier between him and other children. A whispered *albolaria*, *ambularia*, even *bruja*, witch, large eyes watching him nervously. One of the priests had come to the house to complain about superstition, witchcraft, even—he could hardly believe his ears, hardly say the word—abortion. *"A redo vaya!"* said Luz, deadpan. A young man with much to learn. Luz had taught him.

On the other hand, his family's uniqueness gave them a freedom other children didn't have. Luz and Carlos Jiménez simply assumed that their children would excel, not a common assumption in the village Santa Fe had once been, the last Greyhound bus out of town at ten p.m., and then utter quiet until the roosters started up. His parents waited patiently through his own try-outs in alternative lives, a fling with gangs, his low-rider phase too, though what that silent patience cost them he only realized later.

The Jiménez children had excelled. His brother was a surgeon in San Francisco, his sister a scholar of Asian antiquities, almost always on the road in pursuit of this or that, had given them all a bad time when she insisted on going to Cambodia before it was really safe. He was the only one who remained in the old place (not counting cousins, uncles, aunts, friends of such longstanding that they were family too).

Oh yes, he knew Inéz's family.

"Our country, Inéz, our country—" Benito emphasized it gently "—pioneered the aristocracy of wealth, it's true. The Europeans, your ancestors and mine, mocked the idea of acquiring status instead of being born to it, fixed in the hierarchy from birth. Mocked it. Envied it. After a long time copied it, not without ambivalence." His soft voice from Luz, though nobody knew that. Judith blew him a silent kiss; didn't care who saw. He was gratified, but disquieted.

"Achieving aristocracy instead of inheriting it not only opens doors, admits opportunity to anyone willing to work at it. It also impedes the patron-client system, a problem we still haven't worked out in Santa Fe, have we? Only the stupid Anglos sit through these boring town meetings, zoning laws, rights-of-way. We just go down to City Hall and ask our *compadre* to fix things up. We don't talk about—we don't want to see—that our *compadre* asks our silence in return. No, Inéz, in the beginning, the aristocracy of wealth was fairer than a hereditary aristocracy. It still is. It sometimes rewards luck as much as hard work. But luck comes in different shapes."

The man called Molloy, an aristocrat of wealth, was watching him attentively.

"Excuse me, Benito, this is such bullshit," Inéz retorted. "The client-patron system is still alive and well in Santa Fe, believe it. Except the clients are all Hispaños and the patrons are Anglos." Benito began to object, but Inéz rushed on: "Everybody knows the statistics, in this country most people don't move more than half a class up or half a class down from their parents."

Molloy stopped her. "Everybody doesn't know that for a fact, Inéz, but suppose so. Permit me to explain compound interest. It seldom happens overnight, maybe it takes three or four generations. It never happened at all in the old order."

"It did happen in the old order; I beg to differ," Benito said with great courtesy. "But only because some of Inéz's ancestors and mine came to the New World. Younger sons, no hope at home, had hope in here. A chance, anyway."

Benito's mobile face, which fooled you into thinking you knew what was going on behind those eyeglasses, those violet eyes; in contrast to the opaque visage, the helmet, of Molloy's face. Not adversaries. Not yet. Feeling each other out.

"Benito's got it right. When I was a kid, each little valley in western Pennsylvania belonged to some ethnic group or other, by that time third, even fourth generation. It seems unbelievable to me now. Nobody really learned English, and the politicians exploited it. It's pernicious. It'll hold the Hispanic population down forever if they don't shake it."

"Molloy! It's the rich Anglos—"

He shrugged. "You think I'm insulting your people, Inéz, your poor, put-upon, exploited people, who haven't suffered from the Anglos a fraction of what they inflicted on the folks they found here, but it's a fact. You wouldn't be so pissed at me if it wasn't." This he said with a smile, but it was not benign.

Benito mulled over the dissonances, Molloy saying many right things; a man up and out of another subaltern culture, as the phrase went these days. Molloy with Inéz. Molloy challenging.

Betty and Carter McMahon, who both worked on behalf of Indian causes, let collective breath go. As Judith had told Benito, Betty was not sentimental about such things; could be scathingly funny about Indian artists and their trophy blonde wives. But Betty and Carter had a solid grasp of history; they'd spent their careers untangling old legal documents, whacking away at the knotted roots of chicanery of every kind. In the history of the southwest, they could tell you, nobody's hands were clean. Betty said it aloud.

"Are human hands anywhere? But professional victim-whining makes me want to puke." Molloy shook his head at his own vehemence. "I'm no better at Christian charity than my old hero was, am I? Blessings on you Yokkie, wherever you are."

"Is no one really a victim?" Betty persisted.

"You don't live in Germany in the second half of this century—sure, real victims exist. My eastern European colleagues. They rotted in Communist jails, crippled, body and soul, for the sin of being born the sons and daughters of intellectuals, professionals, class enemies. I know which of them *should've* been in somebody's jail, anybody's. Some just kept their heads down and survived. No, it's victimization as a career I object to. In that regard, Inéz knows how I feel." Inéz, who was pale with fury. Molloy turned calmly to Judith. "Did I mention that my son will be coming out from the east to stay a while with us?"

"I'm not sure I knew you had a son, Molloy," Ron said. "What brings him here?"

"Just out of college. At loose ends. We both thought a little while in Santa Fe might focus him."

We both? Benito thought. He and the furious Inéz? He and his unfocused son? Was this the source of Inéz's rage, an intrusive, unwanted houseguest?

Ron asked, "Where did he go to school, Molloy?"

Inéz threw her fork down. "God, this is so—"

Benito hissed something at her in a Spanish so local that it went completely past the Anglos at the table. But for the first time, Molloy showed his exasperation.

Gabe asked quietly, "Would you rather he didn't come, Inéz?"

"That's hardly the issue," Molloy said.

"Inéz?" Judith, Benito thought, would feel sympathy for this young woman, clearly in over her head with a man like Molloy; would be offended by his bullying. Worry not. If ever a woman could take care of herself.

Inéz was looking fixedly at Molloy. "How can anybody with his advantages be such a spoiled brat?" The rage was deep, but about something else.

"She doesn't even know him," Molloy said in mock surprise. "Spoiled brat. Right."

"I—don't—want—him—here." She looked around, as if finally aware that all this had no place at a table of strangers. "I regret," she began, stopped. "I regret causing pain when I wish to bring only light. But I'm no sunny morning." Her look was warning. "I'm a woman of the long dark wild night. I'll take you from magnificent sunsets to dazzling dawns: ride through the night with me for the mystery and terror that comes with the night. You'll belong to me. I'm telling you, I'm a dark ride.

"I've learned to see in the dark. I learned hiding in the closet when my father was trying to kill my brother. I learned by looking into the nothing where my cousin's face used to be, before the maggots ate it. I learned to see in the dark

"Everyone with something unusual to say is disregarded at first," Benito said, ignoring her implication. "Don't misunderstand me, Inéz Gallegos y Sanchez. I don't go looking for fights. Leave me in peace to my sherds, my dirt, my plumb lines. But sometimes fate sends something your way, you'd never forgive yourself for not rising to the occasion." He looked serenely at Molloy.

"What about the Artificial Anasazi, Benitole? Benito's been working on it with other folks at the Institute."

"A computer simulation of human behavior in small agricultural villages," Benito offered. "It may have to wait."

"It's too important to wait. Not just the southwest, it could have general applications. A rigorous model of how and why humans moved from villages to towns. Sometimes out again."

He started to say that new knowledge had changed that too: maybe the model was too simple. "Then I'll do both, *porque no*? I owe all this to Judith," he confessed to the table. "She's the one who's always saying you should aim to stop the world in its tracks. *Amante?*" He looked over his glasses at her affectionately.

Adaptive Co-Evolution

Inéz wore boredom like a showy costume. "Maybe we should be getting on home," she said to the table, to Molloy. Young, terribly young after all, Judith thought. Had heard a lot of rock lyrics, anyway. When pride had been designated one of the seven deadly sins, surely the good lord meant sanctimonious pride. But the braggadocio was exactly the sign of Inéz's uncertainty. At least Judith hoped so, for Molloy's sake. Otherwise, that stuff would be hard to take.

Molloy got up stiffly, carapaced, completely unreadable. Judith was suddenly enlightened. The easy, charming man he'd been a few hours ago now needed, knew how, to shield himself. In silence Judith walked them outside where moonlight silvered the garden, the walkway, the fountain; intensified the shadows. The house had been cool, and the warmth outside, even late in the evening, was a pleasant surprise.

Her fingertips lightly on Molloy's forearm, she stopped him. Slowly felt the warmth of his flesh, all masculine texture, muscled, hirsute, its vitality a tease under the propriety of starched cotton. A flash of erotic charge, and simultaneously shame for it, self-protection of her own: oh, crone, oh, carrion! That most ludicrous, repellent of figures, the pathetic older woman, mortality embodied, a burlesque of desire, a universal joke. Be mindful of his choices.

Inéz, a lifetime younger, sweet of flesh and soft of head, went on, left the gate open behind her. For him to follow.

Be mindful of his choices. What had they been? The German issue—only chance that had thrown him together with a rootless, German-born priest who honored the mind? What was the money really about? She was hungry to know about Molloy in every way, because she saw that now, she would never know. All that earnest questioning that had formed the greater part of their friendship: it might have been his heart's desire after all to tell her.

He turned to her, still guarded. When had he learned, needed such self-protection? For behind the barricade she also saw a gravity, a melancholy, that touched her. Poor little rich boy. On the outside looking in after all.

She didn't entirely understand Inéz's pain, for pain it surely was; she couldn't decipher Molloy's melancholy; but she did know it was all departing, out through the gate in moments, and for that she wasn't sorry. She had no confidence: her own choices had often been disastrous. The discussion at her table was calling her back.

Molloy waited, but she had nothing to say. He disengaged his arm gently, looked over her shoulder inside where Benito was still talking with animation, rehearsing the arguments he'd be making professionally, while the others, alive to the significance of his finds, pursued him excitedly. They were a serious group, glad to have a meaty topic to chew over, and Inéz's departure had released them. Molloy could see this.

"He's quite wonderful. I understand why—" Molloy shrugged with a touch of embarrassment, looked longingly at Benito pacing, arguing, Ron dubious, Gabe laughing, the McMahons engaged. "Good night, dear Judith, and thanks for dinner."

His longing touched her. "Take her home and come back for coffee. This will go on till late." He kissed her gently on the forehead, began to say something, thought better of it and followed Inéz through the gate.

Much later that night, as she was already in bed, about to put down her book and turn off the light, Judith heard her computer signal from the study that she had e-mail. She knew it was from Molloy. Did she want more of this just before she slept? In a grotesque way, Molloy and Inéz had been entertaining, but also exhausting. She'd been glad to see them off, halt that terrible moment at the gate, get back to the table and talk about archaeology, that human remains might be found, that DNA evidence might redraw the map of human migrations out of Africa and across the Asian steppes. The sweet anodyne of ideas.

At last she got up, pulled her robe on, and sat down at the machine and read.

To: jrg@santafe.edu
From: molloy@newbus.com
September 2, 12:30 a.m.

In some parts of Europe it's considered bad manners to compliment the hostess on a dinner, because it implies she might have served you something awful and luckily didn't. But I'm an American and admire accomplishment of any kind. Dinner was great. Excellent mixture of guests.

Well, fuck this. Sorry. Not what you were expecting, and not what you had a right to expect. I think I will never understand women. She still doesn't see how badly she behaved. Culture clash. Language barrier. God knows. Have I been away from the U.S. too long? Is that kind of behavior actually okay at dinner parties?

Maybe I don't see how badly I behave. I'm bored out of my skull with currency trading, but I do believe I keep doing it just to irritate people with their oh-so-predictable rants against people like me.

Thanks for a good dinner anyway. You're a good woman. You and Benito are a dazzling pair.

Against her better judgment, against her best beliefs about rational behavior, Judith yielded to an overwhelming urge to answer him, reach out to him in return.

To: molloy@newbus.com
From: jrg@santafe.edu

September 2, 12:48 a.m.

We all have our nights of acting stupidly. I've had more than my share. She's an interesting young woman, and heartstoppingly beautiful. It will work out, I think.

She didn't like that. She didn't think it would work out at all. Molloy had been remarkably candid with her for once, and she owed him the same. She amended:

Perhaps it will work out.For whatever it's worth, psychodrama at that level is still unusual, but I'm old-fashioned, with old-fashioned, buttoned-up friends. Nobody took offense. It just raised some questions.

She deleted the last sentence. A May-December romance was an ancient transaction, but each partner had to be clear what the bargain was. Molloy might have snagged himself another magnificent trophy, but this one wasn't to be hung up on the wall in perpetuity. He'd better be prepared for when Inéz grew even more bored and, craving the crises she obviously thrived on, caused them if life didn't offer its own promptly enough. He'd better be prepared to be the endlessly appreciative audience-in-residence to the theatrics of her life. But he was rich and semi-retired; what better way to keep himself amused?

He'd better be prepared to be with her friends, since she wasn't prepared to be with his.

Had she herself known what she was getting with Jonathan? Had he? But there was never intellectual malnourishment with Jonathan, she could say that. When everything else had gone, there was still good talk. Necessary, but not sufficient. Fifteen years afterwards, his rage, his sense of betrayal was as fresh to her as ever. She'd betrayed him. What had once dazzled her, the pantheon around the table, names out of books, had begun to bore her: those famous names now embodied all-too-human weaknesses, repeated themselves, were impervious to novelty, while she longed for new names, new ideas. Then. It must come to her, as it came to nearly everyone, that she would get too lazy, too fixed, for new ideas. Not yet, not yet, please God. As for Jonathan, she'd watched his splendid discrimination slowly degenerate into fussiness, then into querulousness, the great ideas replaced by the dailiness of petty complaints. Had found herself, one Saturday afternoon, murderously pulling up weeds in the garden of their weekend house in Princeton, and crying out in her heart that she wasn't ready for that, no, not yet. She'd betrayed him, first in her heart, and then in the usual way; left him so she could take on the world with an appetite for sensation she'd never known she had, for men mostly, but a woman or two as well. One way or another, she too would be betrayed.

As long as she was with Jonathan, she could not be a real scientist.

After some hesitation, she added to her message.

Benito and I aren't a dazzling pair in any sense of the phrase. We're old, good, very comfortable friends, that's all. I worry about this new find, this new path he'll pursue. I am by now a tough old babe, been through the three stages often enough not to feel the pain (at least hide that I feel it) but he's not tough in any way whatsoever. I had to learn, I guess he will too. Do you know about the three stages? Stage 1 is when nobody believes you. Stage 2 is when they might believe you, but say it's unimportant. Stage 3 is when what you say is so much a part of the common wisdom that nobody remembers you were first to say it.

As for why you do what you do, currency trading or whatever, that's a bit like the question of why we're here. Issues to talk about, not for e-mail. But I tell you this from the bottom of my heart, from hard experience, with every ounce of seriousness I can muster: do nothing boring if you can possibly avoid it. Life is too short.

Tonight I could become a moon-worshipper. Did you see it as you were going home?

Your looney friend, jrg

As she hit *send* another piece of e-mail came, and when she saw it was from Benito and not some petitioner in Budapest or Karachi, she read it.

To: jrg@santafe.edu
From: jimenez@sf.arch.edu
September 2, 1:46 a.m.

A lovely dinner, querida, and thanks. It was good for me to get some of these ideas out into the open, hear the objections, arguments, which I will doubtless be hearing for the rest of my life. I saw it in your face. I'm long in the tooth to be chasing rainbows. But maybe I've just been waiting for the right rainbow all these years.

Your friend Molloy has his hands full, doesn't he. The lady is—well, this is gossip. She has spent her entire life setting booby traps for herself. Three different children by three different fathers, each one of them an irresponsible fool, the fathers not the children, though apples don't fall far from the tree. Two of those men beat her, which explains, I suppose, her chosen work. She is, as they say, in recovery from the hardest stuff. I can't quite see how Molloy fits this pattern, he doesn't seem like a fool or a wife-beater, but we don't know those things, do we? One might very well argue that by choosing Inéz he offers us unassailable evidence of his own foolishness, at the least. He certainly seems like he could be a handful himself.

Inéz has always used her undeniable beauty, her considerable charm, to burden others with the results of those self-detonated booby traps, to suck them into endless sympathy, endless helping her out, endless outpourings of kindness to her. It's tiresome, and those of us who know just keep our distance, charming and lovely as she can be. I admit, I immediately thought less of this man when I saw they were together. You were wise to avoid him.

Wise to avoid him? Oh, Santa Fe, this village! But Benito was right; if a man chose a certain kind of woman, it said something about the man. A pity, but true.

Next week sometime I need to take a run up to see my friend Paco at the Abiquiu morada. Would you like to come along for the ride? I need to talk about this some more. Things I couldn't say at the table tonight. Well, when are you going to be reading this—? I'll phone. Love and kisses and good night, dearest one.

The late summer rains came mercifully each afternoon; the summer lightning storms lit up the ridges. Occasionally, when the rain drove down and filled the arroyos, Judith remembered Molloy and his great house, in danger of melting away if only a tiny part of the wall fissured open to the rain. Unstable with respect to small perturbations. But there was nothing useful left to think about Molloy, his girlfriend, his son, their tribulations. She had luckily avoided what might have been a misery; she was puzzled in a distant way, and the thought fled with the lightning.

Autumn 1997

A Rugged Landscape

"You should fix the shocks in this thing, Benito."

They bounced up Highway 84, which felt like a dirt road in Benito's four-wheel-drive, north from Santa Fe through low, *piñon*-studded hills, recently bedecked with bright ugly billboards for the new Indian casinos, signs only the blind (or blind drunk) could miss. He deliberately looked past, through them to the tilted horizon, the Rockies upthrust, and beyond to the convergence of the Jemez and the Sangre de Cristo ranges, already Colorado's San Juans, a purple band under the Guadalupe blue sky. The land—clawed, gouged, upthrust, scarred—so raw, so unmediated by vegetation, was like history without a point of view.

"But it's a waste, you know? I'm right back out in the field shooting the shocks to hell all over again. A losing battle, *amante*." He grinned at her from under his custom sombrero. She'd got him a handsome beaded hatband for it last Christmas from one of the best Jicarillo Apache bead workers, maybe three teeth in his head.

A satisfying thing, this ride up the valley in companionable silence, summer rains nearly over, the dazzling dry autumn to begin. The Sangres were already snowcapped, deepening the sky's blue. He glanced at Judith's noble profile, fixed on the road ahead. What was she thinking? Always something hidden, withheld from the world. From him. They were alike that way, one reason they got along, that deep respect for each other's untouchable core. Though they'd made love the first afternoon they ever met (after a seminar; her incisive without being bitchy: he liked that at once and she was never to fail him that way) in the ten years they'd been together, they'd slept the entire night together less than a dozen times, at least three of those full nights in tents at a dig he'd brought her to. He'd got used to yanking himself out of a warm bed, hers or his, to go home or make sure she got home. Santa Fe's late-night shadows concealed demons nobody should face on foot.

"I'm a solitude crank," she'd apologized the first time and though he'd never put it into words, he was too. The relationship had grown slowly, no special understandings or commitments, except a tacit one, to make love at least weekly when they were both in town. A private language between them, one part unfinished phrases, one part dance steps—she was the most graceful woman he'd ever led to the dance floor. Or to bed.

A half hour's drive out, the dusty little town of Española behind them, he began. "How much do you know about early humans in the Americas, *querida mia*?"

"Across the Bering Straits from Siberia when the sea was low enough to make a land bridge. The last glaciation. Isn't that it?"

"It's *a* story. The Athabascans—the Inuit, the Navajos—came from Siberia, but late, very late, just a century or so before the Europeans. Others were here well before that. Question is, who? Where did they come from?"

So began his tale of contradictory theories, strange possibilities, new evidence that humans had found the Americas much earlier, and from many other places.

"Then comes the Black Crow site."

"Not evidence, not yet, but it could be. I'm artifacts. I've sent the bones to a specialist; keep me from going off on a toot. Suppose I'm right, my forty-thousand year date holds. Again, I ask you. Where did these people come from?"

The highway had turned into a two-lane blacktop, heading doggedly for the northern high mountains. He gestured toward the scene beyond the windshield. "Think of those mountains covered by glaciers. Before eleven thousand years ago, you couldn't have traveled inland. No ice-free path."

She thought that over. "Humans were pretty good at getting over ice in the distant past, Benitole. Prehistoric people crossed the Norwegian glaciers, the Alps—remember Oetzi, Alpine Man? Frozen on the hoof fifty-four hundred years ago? I hiked in the Oetztal the summer after they found the corpse. Those little villages—how did they deal with the descent of the world press? You know he lost his prick somewhere between discovery and defrosting?"

"What?"

"The frozen Alpine guy."

"I know about Oetzi. I didn't know he lost his prick." She'd tell you the damnedest things.

"Really. Just disappeared. A scientific souvenir hunter unmanned him somewhere between the glacier and the dissecting table. I have this picture in my mind: hey ma, you know that frank in the freezer? I nuked it for lunch yesterday."

"*Querida*!" He was laughing anyway. "Yeah, sure, across mountains and glaciers, but not in numbers needed to populate a couple of continents. Not with women and infants. How else could they get here? The Hopi origin myths say they sailed across the great sea, landed, went north, east and south. Nothing about walking across the Bering Straits. We've always assumed these were folktales. What if they're oral history? What if humans came to the Americas also across the Pacific from Asia or Polynesia in boats? Across the Atlantic from Africa? From Europe? A land or ice bridge across Greenland, Canada? What if the migrants sailed up and down the coasts of the Americas, settling that way?"

"Can you do blood typing, DNA testing, match them up with Asian populations?"

"We don't have any human remains yet. This is all indirect. We don't even have sites that predate thirty-three thousand years, though my Black Crow might. That's the real puzzle. If they came by boat across the southern Pacific, how many came? Migration patterns once they arrived? How? On foot? Coastal boats? Why isn't there more evidence of them? We can speculate, but nothing firm. That Oetzi guy. While you were fixated on his male member—"

"Fixated?"

He laughed, reached over, and squeezed her hand. "Fixated on his male member, the tattoos on his back and legs, most of them lie on classical acupuncture points, spots to relieve back pain. Sure enough, poor guy suffered from lumbar arthrosis. He might've been getting acupuncture treatment for his bad back."

"No kidding."

"The time scale. Acupuncture emerges in China about three thousand BCE. Oetzi is fifty-four hundred years old. Simple arithmetic: acupuncture might've originated in central Europe almost twenty-five hundred years before it shows up in China. For sure there was more back and forth between prehistoric humans than we've thought. Exciting times, hey?" He was ebullient, in no mood to contain himself.

"Never seen you happier, Benito. What's next?"

"I'll take me a trip up to Second Mesa, talk to some of the wise old guys up there. Always wondered why the Hopi put so much effort into their religion, which is also their history—I mean, they spend two-thirds of their time just talking to the spirits. May turn out it was to keep those stories alive until us dumb white guys finally got around to asking the right questions. Then I start making up some stories of my own." The Hopi mesas. You had to remind yourself you were in the United States, not a village in North Africa, remoter parts of Latin America, twenty centuries in the past.

"Benitole. This won't be easy."

"Yeah. Haven't I seen what they do to people who deviate? What the hell. *Querida*, I need to talk to you about the ancient city too. It seems to have colonized my brain."

He began with its puzzles. Ten thousand people crowded together in cell-like dwellings, an astonishing number given the sparse population of the Anatolian plateau nine thousand years ago. This agglomeration, not yet a city (no public buildings—temples, plazas, forums—have been uncovered; no sign that they wait to be found) upends the conventional model of the Neolithic revolution: agriculture produced the surplus that led to large settlements, urban specialization, farmers on the outskirts, close to their crops and livestock. No, these ten thousand souls were mostly foragers. They cultivated a few crops, but gathered most of their food from the river's wetlands: nuts, berries, tubers, and wild grasses. A few domestic animals—sheep, some goats, some cows—but the midden bones say they hunted most meat they ate. At this stage of proto-agriculture it would've been far more practical to spread their dwellings around the landscape, greener, wetter, more fertile then than now. Feeding themselves was more difficult in such proximity, not easier. Why cram themselves together in this colossal hive?

The division of labor supported by agriculture in later cities didn't seem to exist. Families built their own clusters of rooms, carved their own obsidian. Two thousand families in such close proximity, existing almost independently of one another.

Why they clustered is so mysterious, so counter to common sense and material requirements that it may never be known. Not mutual defense. State-of-the-art weapons are bow and arrow, clubs, spears; anyway, no fortifications have been found.

He came to the heart of it and felt his own heart beating faster, the rush from engaging with the hardest questions, the kinds she'd been pushing him toward for ten years, high risk, high payoff. "These people," he said slowly. "Inside the mystery of their clustering is a moment of tremendous cultural transformation, a state of mind, a set of beliefs, that might have preceded the agricultural revolution instead of come as a result of it; a set of beliefs that prepared humans to invent and adapt to agriculture. What were they? The art, fantastic stuff. Maybe that's the clue. But no one knows what it means, why it was made."

She'd listened without interrupting. At last she asked, "Did they know they were part of an aggregation?"

"How could you miss ten thousand other folks all around you, talking, competing for food, building things, piling up trash?"

"Cells don't know they're part of an aggregation."

He mulled that. Suppose they didn't know. What if all that then mattered was mate, children, clan, and clans you might intermarry with? Had she just shot to the core of what human consciousness will become, a subtle dialectic between landscape and settlement, self and other, closeness and separation, self-taming and self-indulgence, compromise, reflexivity, context, multivocality, decentering? "We don't know," he replied at last.

"Do you know why it's colonized your brain, dear Benitole?"

He shrugged, shook his head.

"Could it be that, all laid out for you, is maybe the most gorgeous phase transition we've ever seen? That this is maybe the moment a system, human culture, goes from one phase, which is pre-civilized, to a completely different one, what we now call civilization itself. Our genes don't alter, but *we* do, profoundly. Hey, nail when humans first came to the New World—you change a date, big deal. But elucidate this, the why and how, the tipping point that pushed us from being mere social primates into this complex thing we call human civilization, and you have a magnificent—maybe the major—contribution to understanding who we are, which isn't just biology." She exhaled slowly. "I know enough to be humbled before the sacred." Then, laughing with delight, "Well done, Benitole. You *go!*"

Well done? He hadn't done anything. *Change a date, big deal. But this.* She was right. He'd failed to see it, though it had pushed at him continuously. That she was so innocently pleased at discovering it for him was what made the weight on his heart unbearable.

Only Local Optima

He left the highway for the modest plaza of Abiquiú, an open space of packed-down dirt atop a bluff, on the perimeter, willows and a vegetable garden. What was formerly Georgia O'Keeffe's house lay unmarked, where once, before it was open to the public, Judith had been permitted to visit. Paintings she knew came to life across each threshold. She'd always felt an affinity with the cranky old painter—but what ambitious woman in America hadn't?

The stark and simple Abiquiú *morada*, the fellowship hall of the Penitente brotherhood, stood before them, transformed by O'Keeffe from local subject into international icon. It had been torched a few years ago, with talk about bad luck brought on by all the visitors, by O'Keeffe's paintings themselves, but the brotherhood had patiently rebuilt, was slowly re-gathering artifacts for the interior, *santos* and *retablos*, carvings and paintings in the old style.

Benito swung nimbly out of the car and knocked on the *morada*'s plank door. His friend Paco opened it almost immediately, embraced Benito, then waved her in. She hesitated. *Moradas* were secret places, lodges, not to be entered by strangers, by nonbelievers, above all by women; the ancient hallowed site of male bonding through pain and ecstasy. But Paco was smiling a welcome, and she was ushered courteously out of the dazzling sun.

"Please." Paco motioned to the adobe *banco*, built into the length of the wall. The two men moved off further down the bench to murmur in the local Spanish she couldn't follow, and left her to look around, the satisfying simplicity of the meeting room, freshly plastered white walls, small high windows, altar, packed dirt floor. On the walls were a few *retablos* of the saints in the flat, almost cartoonish local style. Where was the traditional *la doña*? Destroyed in the fire?

Despite the ghosts of flagellation, Holy Week bloodbaths, mock crucifixions that could turn fatal, the *morada* gave her peace. The ancient urge to connect with something beyond herself twined itself around memories of conversations with an old friend from the University of Chicago. "Spirals. Zigzags. Nothing mystical—I'll tell you precisely where in the human brain they originate. Petroglyphs, pottery design, all those universal signs are simply reflections of the universality of the human brain structure." The ultimate reductionist. Quite believable. Simultaneously, she could also quite believe in something beyond the human brain.

The conversation in the car. Humans had always been immigrants, out of Africa, fanning slowly across Europe, Asia, south into the Pacific islands, north across the Bering land bridge, perhaps the webs joining, interweaving on the two American continents. Was the urge to wander as hardwired as yearning for home? As hardwired as spirals and zigzags? Or was moving on just the most adaptive response to a changing environment?

And then the biggest question of all—what had pushed these wandering upright primates into something called humanity?

After an hour they said good-bye to Paco and she asked to go home by way of Chimayó. "To say a prayer for Sophie," she murmured, almost embarrassed. A prayer for myself. "What did you want with Paco, Benito?"

"Nothing special. Keeping the connection open. Someday—well, someday, *quién sabe*." On the drive south they were silent, but now she sensed struggle. Benito's future? His soul?

At Chimayó, a site sacred for the first peoples here (whoever they were), subsequently a shrine for the Indians, then the Spanish, she bought a candle in a little shop near the chapel. They slipped through the churchyard gates, wood polished down to silver grain by the abrasive sun, across the courtyard into the small, stuffy chapel, dark after the afternoon brilliance. The redolence of hundreds of candles was almost oppressive, but Judith yielded to it, settled on one of the wooden benches and bowed her head.

"The laughing Christ." Benito pointed to a bust high up on a windowsill.

Laughing? Agonized? Equivocal, but a comfort to associate Christ with laughter. A strange and sacred day this was turning out to be. To whoever heard the words of her heart, she acknowledged no faith in the magic dirt carried away by the teaspoonful from the chapel's annex as cure or talisman. No comfort from the crutches and braces, the images of *La Virgen de Guadalupe*, lithographs, plaster, home-made repousséed copper, paint on black velvet, even sparkles glued to a mirror, all left by people with petitions or thanks. How young they were, dead in car crashes, of overdoses, dead of mystery. We owed one to the universe.

Chimayó's holiness was simpler. It unfolded most dramatically from the south, after miles of wasteland, bare rock, umber and rose-colored sand, stunted *piñon*. Over a rise and suddenly in the barren embrace of the desert, against all odds, was life: lush willows and cottonwoods, orchards and fields, human habitation; a lovely song defying the silence of death.

In this sacred place, with no idea whom she petitioned (her own hopes, her own brain, the man from Chicago would say) she asked for an easy passage for Sophie. She asked for the wisdom to pick a benevolent and luminous path for herself, conceded she was only one part of a large inscrutable pattern which itself lay within other patterns, larger, interlocking, beyond understanding. Humility before the imponderable was a relief.

All humans were immigrants, pushing across borders. Chimayó was at the border, not part of the desert to the south, nor the mountain forests north and west. On the edge. The border, her natural home. She'd worked for years at the frontiers of science itself, trying to find the present unknown, the forever unknowable. She lived now at the border between life and death, moving closer to one, cherishing the other all the more. The edge of chaos, a place to learn.

One more thing about the frontier. You were always alone.

At last she sat back and studied the large paintings on the side walls, and behind the altar, vegetable pigments fading with muted sweetness. Saints she'd never heard of, not in her Episcopalian girlhood nor her art-passionate adulthood, stood side by side with *bultos*, carved figures, of some she had—St. Raphael, St. Michael, St. James—their images rendered New Mexican style, markedly flat and austere, so long out of the mainstream. She was idly struck by the affinity of this with Ethiopian art she'd seen, wondered if something about the desert, its clear dry air, inspired these unmodeled polychrome figures like cutouts against the sky.

Which said the moment of transcendence was past.

She nodded to Benito, and they came outside, sat on a bench in the small courtyard beside two gravestones, a wife who'd outlasted her husband by half a century. Benito took her hand. "They say the first *Virgen de Guadalupe* was carved by St. Luke himself, black face and all, hidden in Spain for the six hundred years of Moorish rule. The black virgin was the sign of—*querida, amante,* don't cry." He pulled her to him, stroked her hair, his lips butterflying her temple. "Such hard times. It won't get easier, *querida, nunca más fácil.* Sophie first, but more will come. *Querida*—we're all afraid. In our bowels, in our hearts, in every organ, we're afraid. We shouldn't mind confessing it to each other. Maybe we can't face it alone. *Querida,* let's be there for each other."

She nodded slowly.

"Paco. My mother was his teacher. I had to ask him about the dreams. He knew only that they were important. You, of course, knew why. I asked him where in my mother's notebooks—never mind." He pushed her away gently so he could search her face. "Let me be clearer. I want us to get married."

A stupid grin crept across her face, a grin in no way pleased, the rectangular smile, as Sophie herself would've said. An image from—who? Stuart Kauffman?—an agent clambering around a landscape, seeking peaks to scale, when suddenly the landscape turns to a rubber sheet, every step deforming it wildly, a path not to peaks but to chaos.

"Here. We could do it here," he urged. "A lovely place, *querida,* just right for two old soldiers like us. Don't shake your head. Don't say no. Think it over. I wouldn't have—you led me here, right to the very edge. Plunge over to destruction or leap to the heights. Risk everything, right?" He added with mock solemnity, "I hereby promise you great sex and great dancing so long as we both shall live." Not mocking, squeezing her hand hard. "I promise to be there for you."

She looked away, picking through the confusion, trying to find something, the right thing, the best thing to say. She'd loved this man's gentle sweetness, needed the comfort of his friendship. But not husband, all day every day, all night every night, for a lifetime.

Why not?

Benito, a stimulating intellectual partner, a choice lover, who knew every inch of her and wanted her for himself forever. No, not every inch. Not the last few inches inside the deepest core of the human heart, perverse, contrary and trembling. No one had ever been allowed near that.

Don't trap me, she pleaded silently, on some pleasant lower ridge, some middling saddle point, the summit above ever receding. What summit? The impossible, whatever it was. She didn't know. Worse, she didn't know how to express this in a kind way, and she owed Benito kindness above all.

Because she couldn't bear to look at him in this new role of suitor, she continued to look away, summoned him up in her mind, tried to see him afresh, his abundant benevolence a haven she'd fled to often; their erotic pleasures; their ordinary fun together; his new-found professional fire. They'd made love and laughed. Gossiped across the pillow. Danced beautifully together. Sufficient? Not for marriage, that perilous journey, but surely for friendship, which was what she needed from him.

She pulled together her courage, knowing that what she'd say would change the landscape yet again. "No," she said, striving to be gentle. "Marriage isn't for us, you and me, Benitole."

"Marriage is for me," he cried. "Long overdue, my family says. I should've married years ago, had kids, all that. But it never—" Trying to account. "Maybe it's a professional problem? Time gets lost. You're thirty, forty, and then fifty. It's nothing on the time scales you think in all day. And until you, no woman ever moved me enough. *Querida*, my mother comes to me in dreams these nights. I wish you'd known each other. You're alike in so many ways. Until now I thought I had no goal, no quest—what a quaint word, right?—worth offering you. Okay, what I finally thought was good enough, you just—just raised the stakes on. But I'll meet that, *querida*. For you, I'll try."

"I shouldn't have said—"

"If you'd condescended to me, *querida*, treated me like I was—unequal—it would've been impossible." She saw the yearning in his eyes. Ten years of happy friendship. Why rewrite this? Why now? She desperately didn't want things to change. Too bad. Too late. Slowly she withdrew her hand from his. "I'm such a fraud, Benitole. I always want nothing to change—I don't want Sophie to die, I don't want Alijo to grow up, I don't want you and me to change. I want to freeze everything as is. Even when, above all people, I—I know that change must happen. Must." She was silent for a moment. "You find a woman who'll—savor what she might have with you, Benitole. A woman who understands her infinite good fortune. She'll be very lucky, my love."

"Not you, *querida*?" He studied her closely, suddenly masked himself. "Not you? Is there someone else? Did I wait too long?"

She shook her head. Nobody else. No handsome young graduate student who wanted to share her sleeping bag. A kind of blankness where desire lay, a blankness she was too frightened to look beyond, where some fugitive dream came and went.

"Paco said—"

"Paco said?"

"Paco said you're lost to me, *querida*, and you don't even know it yourself yet. That was the bad news."

Her heart contracted. "Was there good news?"

Benito did not conceal his despair. "He said I have Luz's gift. I should use it. Trust my inner sight."

She could say nothing right. She knew that, kept silent.

Avalanches of Extinction

On a Friday night in mid-September, Santa Fe's summer came to an official end with the ritual burning of Zozobra, Old Man Gloom. The ceremony had originated in the 1920s with the *Cinco Pintores*, the Five Painters, easterners who'd discovered the brilliant clarity of the Santa Fe light, who'd invented the idea of Santa Fe, then claimed the city as their own. One had built the first Zozobra effigy, and with his friends, burned it ceremonially to rid the coming winter of troubles and sadness. It became an annual public event, Zozobra growing bigger and more elaborate over the years. Now the effigy was fifty feet high, and the drama drew close to thirty thousand people from all over northern New Mexico.

The artists had appropriated bits and pieces of ancient ceremonies, so that Zozobra's sacrifice seemed a ritual not decades old but millennia, which in some real sense, it was. Zozobra's long white gown recalled the martyrdom of saints and sinners alike; of slaves and philosophers, cattle thieves and monarchs, witches and heretics, all judged, condemned, and dispatched.

Simple, theatrical, it plunged children into nightmares. Adolescents flung themselves into it mindlessly. Adults confident of their own rationality shivered at the primitive human past, lurking just beneath a thin tissue of late second-millennium Christian civilization.

Judith felt bound to see it for exactly those reasons. They acknowledged, she and Ron and Gabe, quietly, half-jokingly, that each of them could have been a Zozobra in the past, burned at the stake for multiple offenses: their learning, their skepticism, their sex, their sexuality. They did not need to say to each other that it could happen again. For them the ceremony was both an act of witness and a memorial.

They walked over from the eastside, picnics in backpacks, through the cordoned downtown, up the small hill from the Federal Oval (once a race course for mules, fit precedent for the Feds, Gabe once observed) to Fort Marcy Park, joining thousands of others streaming into the field. On their picnic blanket they settled down to eat and drink, watch the passing scene. At Zozobra's burning, your blanket was your territory, for the most part respected, but the crowd grew huge enough that soon no space could be found between one blanket and the next. It was a tense and restless horde, having arrived early to get a place, impatient now for the main event. As dusk fell, packs of young males roamed its outskirts; mothers and fathers held their youngsters close; unprotected women suddenly felt uneasy.

Ron surveyed it all. "Think Tyburn Oak was like this?" For it was festive yet menacing: simultaneously a celebration and something dolorous. People were beheaded in the French Terrors in such an atmosphere; prisoners of war brought back in shackles—to anywhere: Rome, Istanbul, Mexico City—to be sacrificed in such a splendidly bloodthirsty air. Mariachi bands on a side-stage struggled to entertain, to calm, but nobody listened, nobody cared. What mattered was the main event.

Darkness at last. Along the foot of the platform where giant Zozobra stood, his arms outspread in supplication, twenty small bonfires suddenly burst simultaneously, magically into flame. In grim and elegant foreplay, lurid colored smoke curled delicately toward the effigy's skirts, his arms, his oversize head. When all the bonfires were fully ablaze, scores of young boys in white robes marched gravely in from the sides, climbed the steps to the platform, approached Zozobra's mighty feet, bowed, and began to dance. Before the towering monster, his white skirts rustling in the evening breeze, the currents of the bonfires, the Glooms looked both unearthly and defenselessly small. It came to Judith sadly that Alejandro and Pete had both been dancing Glooms, their faces in clownwhite, their eye sockets rimmed with black. Time. Oh, time.

Zozobra seemed to concede that he'd perish. He stirred his hydroencephalic head, his arms, shifted in his long white tunic, and began an eerie, piteous groaning that, amplified by loudspeakers, echoed all over the city. The young Glooms fell back.

Up the stairs toward Zozobra danced an adult male, clad only in a loincloth, body oiled, bending sinuously, waving a lighted torch. A signal. Thirty thousand voices cried out in unison: "Burn him! Burn him! Burn him!" This too echoed over the silent town, a counterpoint to the monster's groans.

Judith and her friends kept silent. One year they'd tried joining in, wondering how it would feel to be on the other side. What they felt, they confessed afterwards, was shame, and they never did it again.

The solo dancer moved priest-like around the feet of the monster, bowing, stretching, teasing with his torch, closer and closer to the hem of the monster's robe. The crowd's chant grew frenzied, its collective will a physical thing, fate. The monster groaned louder, more piteously. The dancer paused, torch above his head, arms and legs spread wide, as if waiting for permission from the gods. The crowd was nearly hysterical, possessed by a conviction that its collective voice *was* of the gods, the voice of righteous destruction.

Burn him! Burn him! Burn him!

The high priest, the dancer, yielded to the crowd's will. He collapsed forward, touched the torch to Zozobra's hem—right, then left. Silhouetted by the bonfires, the little Glooms screamed in ecstasy. The crowd screamed back, waved, stomped on the grass in joyous approval, *Yes! Yes! Burn him! Burn him!*

Flames shot up Zozobra's skirts, engulfed his lower half. Reached his torso. His arms flailed, his groans rose to screams. Flames erupted from his eye sockets. The whole puppet was ablaze, a brilliant image of what had once been a solid thing, flames reaching unstoppably to the stars above. His arms waved, his burning head shook in futility, limb parted from fiery limb, a nebula of flame and dust, and was consumed. No sound now but the fire itself, its pitiless roar, smoke reaching even to the back of the field.

The crowd went silent, dwarfed and spent by the immensity, the irrevocability of what it had willed. Flames lingered, licking at supporting structures, but Zozobra was gone, a holocaust too odious to dwell on.

The three friends moved down the hill from Zozobra's remains in silence, pushed by the crowd swarming around them in the dark. Beer-drinkers nearby were threatening to explode; police leaned against patrol cars, top-lights spinning. Down the hill, at the same place by the Masonic Temple every year, fundamentalists harangued the crowd for its paganism, exhorted men to turn to Jesus before it was too late. From inside their own nightmare, they clamored monotonously: "Pagans! Pagans! The Lord God Himself saith ..."

"Like Christians don't have their own history," Ron said, not quietly.

Gabe snorted. "Pagan's the nicest thing I've been called by those folks." Judith said nothing. For the first time since she'd been coming to Zozobra, she had serious gloom to dispel. But it weighed even heavier now. No remedy.

Suddenly she spotted Alejandro in front of the zealots, enthralled as if they were street performers. She struggled through the crowd toward him. "Alijo! Where's your dad?" With a kid's beaver-tooth smile he shrugged. They'd got separated. "Stay with me, guy." But when she grasped his arm, pulled him to her, turned around, somehow Ron and Gabe had also disappeared in the milling crowd, the darkness.

Under her breath she swore.

"Let's go to the plaza," Alejandro begged. "They got a band and everything." So instead of turning on Paseo de Peralta, the natural way home, she stumbled along Washington Avenue, pushed, shoved and carried by strangers toward the plaza. She could already hear amplified bass throbbing. Alejandro squirmed out of her grip, too humiliated to be seen hand in hand with an adult, even in the dark. "Alijo, don't lose me, please." Even as she pleaded, he'd darted off, lost in the mass of people drawn inexorably toward the music.

She was exasperated. He was perfectly capable of walking home by himself, did it most afternoons from the skateboard park by the river, but the crowd's mood felt ugly, and she wished he'd stayed near her.

Behind, a police radio erupted in static. She turned to see a mounted cop dig his spurs into his horse, part the crowd with a yell. She jumped back from the charging horse, heard gunshots. Her heart pounded inside her skull. Alijo? Ron and Gabe?

People had stopped. Somewhere up ahead for the second time this night, cries of fear and horror, running footsteps, back toward her. Panic: people turned, then stampeded, forced her back, shoved her. She feared the ground, being trampled. Feared for a missing boy.

A covered *portal* loomed, and she slipped quickly, gratefully into the shelter of a stout wooden column, held on as if she might drown in that rushing, maddened crowd, forced to part around it. She was breathless from fright and vexation.

Momentarily the flow let up. She put her head out. In the darkness was nothing, people rushing past, but a block away, the plaza was still brilliant. Tentatively, she moved toward the light, searching for Alijo, though futility chilled her.

Beside her, a figure rose out of the darkness, grabbed her shoulders. She screamed in fright.

Linkages

"What you doing here?"

Molloy in black, in the shadows, and she flings herself to him.

"The little kid next door . . . I had his hand. What happened?"

"A shooting. You look—a bit wild." He pulls her back into the protection of the column, makes himself a barrier from the mob, his hands locked to the column on either side of her.

"Wild. Oh God, glad to see a friendly face. Anybody dead?"

"So it seems." He pulls her out of the way, behind the column to wait, the crowd ebbing around them. Suddenly she sees how close she's come to being trampled, begins to shake. Molloy himself is as still as the ponderosa column, only his eyes moving, assessing. "Okay. Now."

She grabs the arm he's taking back. "Please—I've already lost two sets of people tonight."

"You want to call? Maybe the boy's at home?" She can barely punch numbers on his phone. No, Alijo is not home, and Anita curses her husband with a few choice New Mexican epithets; she can't leave the baby alone. "It's okay," Judith says. "I'll find him."

They move toward the plaza hand in hand, upstream past human bodies. He pulls her close so they can hear each other. Where did she last see Alijo? Exactly when, in relation to the shots, the panic? What's he wearing? Patient, methodical questions; he doesn't let go of her hand. At the plaza, already cordoned off with police tape, they ask every officer they can get near. The police are tense,

dismissive: the night's excitement isn't over; gangs are known to retaliate. But this stuff happens down on Agua Fría, Airport Road, not the plaza.

On San Francisco Street ambulance lights flash blue and white, the paramedics are loading a body. "Not him." Molloy pulls her roughly away. "Much older. Now. Where's the closest McDonald's? My kids that age, the first place I looked. How would he walk home?"

"Up Palace. Maybe up Alameda. Up Canyon." But those are car roads. Alijo, born here, will know every back footpath, creek side trail to get him home. At last she agrees to wait, call Anita again in half an hour. He leads her into the Inn of the Anasazi, and orders two double cognacs. "You do drink," she says irrelevantly. The cheerful bar, the corner fire, is comforting. In the giving leather couch, she lets down a little. "Were you at the burning?"

He nods. "Those fundies have it right. Pagan. Oh well. Action art. I got separated too, from Inéz and Stephen. My son." He pulls out his phone again, punches impatiently, turning his head discreetly for conversation, but obviously gets a machine, leaves no message. They stare off into space, mute in their separate anxieties. After a while, he offers the phone to her. Alijo's at home. Relief and gratitude melt Judith down. "Tell him there are three kinds of mathematicians," she says to Anita. "Those who can cope and those who can't."

She hands him back the phone. "A lame little joke for Alijo."

"Let's get you home. Trouble is, we walked, the family and I. My car's at home. Wait here?"

"No," she says decisively. "Do I look like I'm losing it totally? I am. I can't be alone again tonight. I'll walk to your house with you. I'm three-quarters of the way home by then."

"Not even two-thirds," he says.

Palace Avenue near the plaza is almost deserted now, trash-strewn, abandoned sweatshirts and windbreakers. Behind them emergency lights still pulse, play strangely on the smooth brown walls. He takes her hand again, a man accustomed to taking charge.

"It's hard to think of a guy like you at McDonald's."

"I've scarfed down Big Macs at every McDonald's in the world. With

kids you eat at McDonald's. They aren't always up for the local cuisine. Once in Antalya—"

"Which is where?"

"Turkey. The Turquoise Coast, far southern Turkey on the Aegean. Doesn't matter."

"Did you usually travel with your children? Daunting." But it explains something about him, his way of shielding her, as he has.

"School holidays. Their mother wasn't always able—to care for them."

Up Palace, across Paseo de Peralta, past the little fieldstone Episcopal church, forever England amongst the adobe. High walls hide houses and gardens; the sidewalk narrows. She senses he's deliberately slowing down for her, would walk faster alone. They're like a courtly old-fashioned European couple strolling through a park, along a quay; he's taken her right arm, and covered her hand with his own. "Did I thank you properly for dinner the other week? Does e-mail count? Your reply," he stops under a streetlight, face sharply shadowed. "It was nice to get something personal."

"Personal? You're the ultimate private man. I don't know anything about you." Fatigue has hammered her every bone.

Walking in step, him guiding, almost clasping her. "You and Benito aren't lovers."

Not this, not now. "We've slept together a little. More than a little."

"You slammed the door in my face so often these past few months I thought maybe you preferred women," he says softly. "Then I thought, no, the archaeologist. Now I don't even get that consolation." He's smiling in the shadows, making gentle fun of himself. Of her.

She halts. "Molloy, if I've been a bitch—and I have—I apologize." She puts her aching head into his shoulder. The lessons from Sophie: speak clearly. "I wish I could begin *ab initio* with you. I'd do it differently. For my bitchiness, my fearfulness, everything I put between us, I'm sorry. It could've been—memorable." No! Is that Maya's word? "Forgive me, if not now, sometime. I hope we can still be friends."

"Friends? Not enemies, anyway." He moves her along despite her fatigue. Resumes so softly she can barely hear. "Just tell me why. If you know. I offered you such a ragged heart. But it was—" he smiles grimly "—my heart." He stops, studies her curiously, with a detachment that chills her.

The confessional of the long walk. She's told the truth there more often than anywhere. Warns him it's in no particular order.

Maybe, she ventures, it was what Einstein once called the great flight from I and We to the It. Among scientists, an occupational hazard. Maybe it was the bitter taste of a failed marriage, a marriage begun with the same urgent tumult Molloy had also stirred up in her. "I have an orderly life now, Molloy. Not too many big ups, big downs. I cherish that order. Which I remember you once dismissed as overrated." She sees him exhale slowly, thinking they've overheard, remembered each other from the beginning.

A low-rider moves slowly along Palace Avenue, its muffler gurgling. A dog barks back, affronted.

"Then superstitiously, I wondered if the universe had sent you as payback for some very bad behavior. If so, I didn't want that either, okay?"

"Myself as universal tool. No. Just a guy." His voice alters, charged with fury, flashing through his guiding arm, his sheltering hand. "The inevitable unhappy ending. About as sentimental as the inevitable happy ending, right? The real world hands out both."

"What can I say?" She tries to withdraw her arm, but he holds fast. Hurting her now.

"Madame Genius, at a loss for words at last?" His pace quickens; with effort, he recovers his self-control. In profile the nose is straight down from the forehead, helmet-like.

"Don't shout at me, Molloy. It's been a terrible few weeks—"

He spins and smashes an adobe wall with his open palm, nearly knocks her down, a rage that makes her yelp. "Shout at you? You'll know all about it when I'm shouting at you! God, you're an aggravating woman." She hears him struggle with himself, his heavy breathing, regaining his self-control, rubbing the injured hand. "How did the marriage end?"

They stop, not touching at all. "Mine? Badly." Jonathan, weeping, raging. Suffering. Herself indifferent, even to the suffering. Hating herself for that. Hating Jonathan for it too.

"Sichel. Jonathan Sichel. Hard to leave all that prestige?"

"His prestige, not mine." Don't do this to me now, Molloy.

"For sure." Then: "He left you that Chinese bowl."

So he's known Jonathan was more than just a mentor. Hasn't let on. But why has she concealed it? Because she recalls Jonathan best as mentor, and not at their miserable parting, not at his final collapse? "I was surprised. Touched. He knew I loved it. I'd like to think he forgave me in the end. I don't know. Everything else went to the Metropolitan. How did you—?" Silly question.

"He loved you all the way to the inevitable unhappy ending."

"Loved me. Hated me. Both. With cause. I was very young, younger than Inéz." The comparison slips out.

"Older, established, renown, dazzling." Molloy executes a list. "Did you ever love him? Or did you just want the short route to what he had? What he was?"

Her eyes fill. Obediently she summons up what had once been, composes herself. "Proving theorems together can be a real—aphrodisiac. Discovering something together, knowing it, something nobody else in the world knows. Those days, I was, teach me something, I'm yours. Maybe sex isn't the same thing as love—"

"I'm a careful student of all the varieties of desire," he interrupts curtly. "The Athenians believed that thought itself derived from erotic dialogue. Look up the history of metaphysics sometime, Madame Genius. Not tonight. Back to love among the theorems."

"Molloy, I'm no genius. And I don't get you."

"No shit." He's walking again, she hurries to catch up with him. Palace Avenue curves toward the river here, his house up ahead. Over the adobe wall, lights show in the upper story, filtered by willows, cottonwoods, all the old trees that have long ago sunk their deep thirsty roots into the banks of the Santa Fe River. Whether the lights mean people at home, or are simply left on against the night, she doesn't know. He motions to wait while he gets his car.

"I can manage."

He assesses whatever the house lights signify. "No. I want a little more, thank you. I'll even say you owe me that much." Shivering, miserable, she acquiesces.

Error-Correcting Strategies

In fact they drive in silence the few moments it takes to get to the old goat path. Not until he's pulled up beside her wall does he slump back against the car door, observe her. "Go on. Love among the theorems."

"It didn't last. I see now it couldn't."

"Why not?"

"Not because he was singing Gilbert and Sullivan, and I was singing Tom Lehrer. Though that's true." Who deserves the credit? Who deserves the blame? Jonathan, traveling from hotel room to hotel room with a portable digital room thermometer, no longer trusting his senses to tell him whether he was comfortable. He grew obsessed with weather forecasts, listened to them hourly, though about the weather he could do nothing, forecast right or wrong. Recovering from a bad sinus infection, he hung on to the habit of clearing his throat, hawking unconsciously every few moments, as if he were alone in his own bathroom. It nearly drove her mad. He began to emerge from every toilet, private and public, with stains on his trousers, and didn't even think to look, never mind prevent. All the energy he'd once poured into first-rate mathematics was forced now instead into the ordinary: shopping lists, counting out vitamins and other pills, the finicky details of travel plan.

They penetrated her consciousness—young men on airplanes, businessmen as tenderly barbered as choirboys, athletes who stowed backpacks in the overhead bins with their well-toned abs thrust into her face—and provoked rushes of erotic longing. Then others, closer at hand, this time not imagination but flesh. Even in the dark car, she's not prepared to confess this. She tells other truths instead.

"An inequality between us could never be—overcome. I'm not cut out for the role of junior partner. Put it another way. I was very young and ambitious in those days. I could work twenty-four/seven; never feel anything but exhilaration. I was so hungry to make my way. My name. Jonathan's reputation became, well, an ambiguous issue for me. I never took his name, but still. Some people assumed he did the heavy lifting. That nettled me, but I knew the facts, I did my own." She stops, lost in recollection. "Except it undermines you slightly. You need to know if people's perceptions have more truth than you're willing to admit. I got so touchy about all that. I was—" She searches, finds no word, torn as she is between the pain she'd felt then, and her shame for what had come after. She'd left Jonathan to leave all that. She couldn't be a real scientist until she'd left Jonathan once and for all.

"Then something else. Funny, I haven't put this into words before, but Jonathan and I had a fundamental difference about the nature of mathematics. Forgive me, Molloy, this isn't—"

"Go on." The imperative voice.

"Sounds idiotic, it didn't matter at first, but eventually. He loved mathematics for its beauty, *l'art pour l'art*. Applied math was tacky, second-rate. A craft, not an art. If something he'd done had a practical application, fine, but not important. Except to convince a funding agency they should keep supporting his research." She feels disloyal, making him sound hypocritical. In that sense, he had been. It comes to her in this dark night that she's weary of apologizing to Jonathan.

"But I loved—applications to real-world problems. For me, that's where real mathematical beauty lies; the map between the mathematics in my mind and the real world, the way an equation can illuminate the world like—like a good painting. You never see the world the same way again. One of the great flowerings of mathematics began under the Arabs in the ninth century—*they're* the ones who saved civilization—remember that conversation?"

He looks offended. "Every word of it."

"Think of it, mathematicians in a great arc from Spain to India, all speaking Arabic, applied mathematicians every one of them, because it was a holy calling, to find out what God has to teach us about the world. Mathematics as the very language of God." She drops her head exhausted, knows she's babbling.

"Jonathan thought that any joy I took in the applied, the practical, was a female flaw. Thought he could convert me, refine my mathematical taste, but he never did." None of this in words until now. She's chilled to the bone.

"Jonathan sounds like a real asshole."

She starts automatically to defend Jonathan, realizes she's been relieved of that. Dwells in the long silence gratefully.

Molloy at last: "Judith, Judith. How do you mathematicians express the equations of love? What are the limits to knowledge on that one? Some things, she once said, can't be done; some things can never be known. To identify those is my own sweet game."

"Oh, Molloy. If this is gotcha, you won."

He seems weighted with sadness, the anger dissipated. "No. I haven't won anything. Nothing at all."

"Well, then," she whispers, afraid to say it aloud, "come in. Come in now." Fatigue has given way to desire, blunt and hungry. She wants only to be in this man's arms all the night.

He puts his hands over his face for a moment, then drops them; she can see the weariness. "Dear lady, those words would've thrilled me once upon a time. They're still a bit thrilling, to tell the truth. It's not that you don't stir me, Judith." He watches to see that she smiles ruefully. "It's been nice holding your hand tonight. In every sense. But as anyone can plainly see, you're in meltdown. I take it this isn't just the missing boy, or even Zozobra. My God, that's a primitive thing," he adds.

She shakes her head. The landscape a rubber sheet.

"How could I live with myself if I took advantage? Okay, just kidding. A little." He gazes at her thoughtfully. "It's an amazing thing to see you quite so undone."

She starts to speak, reconsiders.

"But here's something serious," he says gently. "I once wanted you—what drew me to you in the beginning was your strength, can you understand that?

I'd spent a lifetime," he pauses, "*constructing*, and I wanted someone who'd appreciate my—most interesting works of art. I thought I was finally entitled to it. Well, entitled to try for it. Yeah, Beatrice to lead me to Paradise, places I'd yearned all my life for, Scheherazade to tell me stories. But some rogue butterfly flapped its wings."

"I'm not what you hoped after all."

No reply.

"Ron once warned me, said you were afraid of me."

"You've always seemed—not quite human. What Ron didn't say is that I scared the shit out of you too, right? No, Ron adores you. In his eyes you're invincible. *Jesus, Judith, why? What were you afraid of? What could be so awful? Where was your courage? If we fused we might explode?"*

Afraid of failure. Afraid to run the risk. Such a penalty if it went bad. If we fused we might explode. Better to do without. *Not quite human.* When did we become human? That will be Benito's great question; she has no answers. A sob, a gasp, but she pulls herself together; even if she can't stop the tears, at least they're silent. He doesn't reach over to comfort her, leaves her to weep in a solitary confinement she could never have imagined, a confinement she's left to understand she's deliberately chosen. An agent of her own destruction.

After a while he shifts, reaches for his wallet, pulls out something papery. "You once asked me why I was in Santa Fe. I said I'd tell you. I came to Santa Fe with this in my pocket." She stares in disbelief at the tattered clipping from a financial newspaper, recollected more than seen in this darkness through her watering, and yes, middle-aged, far-sighted eyes.

"Remember this? A lovely woman, sitting outside in the sunlight, laughing, a concha belt—I now know to call them, didn't then—big skirt, cowboy boots, and a whiz on financial derivatives. It haunted me. Gave me hope at a time I thought all hope was gone. Wasn't sure I'd ever meet you; if so, I'd like you—you me. But I wanted to be where women like that could be found. And there you were, the very first dinner party. Talking about Santa Fe's eroticism, of all the fucking things." He folds the clipping carefully, returns it to his wallet. "Little cause, big result." He lifts her hand to his lips, puts it down. "You get yourself a good night's sleep. Everything will look better in the morning."

So tonight is yet more loss. Not just friends, not the boy, who's safe at home; but something vital, lost through her own carelessness, vanity, faint-heartedness, a peak that might have transformed her. My most indelible—my most poignant—learning experiences are usually failures. However rich the autumn might be, an autumn she's spent her life preparing for, she'll taste that harvest all alone, in the coming cold.

"Everything's changed now," she says slowly.

"Yes."

Lamentation erupts from every cell, a cry that, even with a lifetime's practice at self-control, she barely manages to choke. Uttered, it might have sounded something like *Molloy, my love*, but she ruthlessly silences it, leaves it to die in a back alley of her soul. She's had her chance, wasted it; won't be forgiven. "If we'd met ten years ago."

"We'd have found each other insufferable ten years ago."

Her hand to his cheek, she says a silent farewell to his flesh, to him, what might have been. He's rigid. She thinks of the way they met, moved so tentatively toward the edge of chaos, adapted, resisted, co-evolved and changed each other anyway, always connected, always in relation to each other, a personal history that recombined and gave only the illusion of repeating itself; some chance thrown in; the whole greater than the sum of its parts. But always, in their case, destabilized, far from equilibrium, out of kilter with each other.

"You know," she says, "you're in Santa Fe. Just grow the beard and save yourself a lot of trouble."

That's the first time she hears him laugh. "Dear, dear Judith," he says at last, "only the gods are permitted to have beards." She doesn't get it, and he doesn't explain.

Birth-Death Formalisms

"Can you come over?" The voice was almost inaudible, but Judith knew it at once, thrilled.

"Isn't Ellie there?"

"Yeah. But I need you too." Need. Not a word in Sophie's vocabulary.

"You okay?" The stupid questions that somersaulted out of the mouth. Judith heard her own breath against the mouthpiece.

"Different. But okay. I'd just like for you to be around. If you can."

She took the four-wheel drive for a distance she'd normally walk: before the day was over, she might need to get to a pharmacy or emergency room. Quick apologies on her cell phone to other machines, no lunch, will miss the seminar, emergency, so sorry. A full-body charge from a connection reconnected, a voice that says I need you, from someone who said she didn't.

Through Sophie's gate, the place looked a little seedy. She'd have to see to that. She reached for the front doorknob, then stopped, rang the bell. A signal to Sophie: I've learned something. Ellie let her in, led her to the kitchen.

Surprisingly, Sophie looked unchanged over these weeks, more tired, maybe. She was up and dressed, her corduroy trousers held up with suspenders since she was now too thin for a belt.

"I know you're busy, and I really appreciate it."

"Soph, puh-lease."

Sophie looked too fragile to hug. The little granny voice, "I feel odd, different. Suddenly much weaker." Sophie leaned against a kitchen stool, too bony to sit on it. "Been on this plateau for so long. Not better, okay, but not worse for months. I woke up this morning feeling—" Then, summoning ranch-bred hospitality. "You want some tea?"

"Let me call the hospice nurse and see what she says."

Sophie nodded, alarmingly acquiescent. Judith coaxed her back to bed, but understood what a defeat bed was for her, after the effort of getting up, dressing, sitting around like an ordinary person. Sophie insisted that Ellie undress her; would not let Judith see her skin and bones. "It would gross you out altogether, frankly."

No, she cried in her heart to Sophie: you have no right to be ashamed of your body in front of me. What do you think I am? Remembered how she'd feared to expose herself to Molloy. So she permitted Sophie this, left the bedroom, resolutely pulled herself together. Thought of and dismissed her own shame about her body.

At last Sophie was in her bed, her tee-shirt nightgown. "I wanted to say I'm sorry."

Judith shook her head, put a gentle finger to Sophie's chapped lips. "Enough."

Sophie sighed. "I've envied you, Jay, but I've loved you. Admired you. You know that."

"I know, Soph. I love you too." Sophie lying quietly, chastely, in her nun's cell of a bedroom. You don't know what went on in this bed, Benito had teased. But here, no paintings on the walls, no knickknacks, nothing Sophie had wanted to collect, to please her eye, remind her of other times, nothing but books on shelves, on the floor; since her sickness, the TV moved in.

All the hospice nurse could tell them was that Sophie's blood pressure had sunk. It could be anything. "I'll call back at four," she said, consulting her watch. "Page me if you need me before then."

Judith walked the nurse out to the front door, questions in her eyes alone. The nurse shrugged. An hour from now; a month. "You have the morphine?" Judith nodded, embarrassed to say she was a stranger these days, just presuming.

"So?" Sophie asked.

"She doesn't know. It's not in our hands, love. But the moment you're in pain, tell me. Don't suffer till you can't stand it, all right? Promise?" She took Sophie's light, strangely roughened hand, as if all moisture had been sucked from it. "We may have to get you to the hospital."

"Don't. Please don't," Sophie begged. "I always come away from that place worse than when I went in. Promise me that."

"Soph." This luminous, fragile life in her hands now, her duty to see that Sophie had an easy passage. Each of them making deathbed promises to each other.

"Promise!"

"Yes."

Sophie seemed to shrink with relief. "What's it like out?"

Judith felt Sophie slipping away from her, and suddenly gifted with this last-minute grace, wanted to tether her here before she disappeared altogether. Delicately put chipped ice on Sophie's tongue to help with the thirst. "When did you know you wanted to be a biologist, Soph?"

Sophie looked up at the ceiling, licked her dried lips, spoke sometimes fluidly, sometimes not. "When the vet came to the ranch, I got to help him. We only called him when things were extreme, you know? We were used to doing for ourselves, a lot of animal remedies around. But sometimes we needed an expert." When an animal cost more to replace than to cure. The reality of ranch life.

Sophie drifted into silence. Judith kept the silence with her, watched Sophie's eyelids flicker, hoped she'd sleep, get past the pain. Strange how Sophie had burst with words for the year or two after her diagnosis, and was now back to her former—her normal? her real?—laconic self.

Sophie was walking the ranch very clearly for the first time in years, the barn, the sheds, the vegetable garden, greens with their arms out to the sun. Her brother had it, and she'd never gone back after her mother died. "I loved it, that I'd be the hero to rescue animals that no one else could save. Like a comic book. In college I saw different ways to help. Learn about cells, you could help a million animals, not just the ones . . ." Her eyes closed. She was under the eucalyptus trees at Berkeley, saw Judith in her radiant youth, skin the color of pale but-

terscotch, hair sun-bleached, a swimmer, a mathematics prize-winner, doting family, perfect Judith Greenwood with her ultra-perfect life. Judith of all people at her deathbed. Strange turns life—and death—took.

Sophie stirred, began again. "I'm sorry about—the other day."

Almost two months ago, Soph. "My fault, love. I should've been more."

"Yeah, you really should've." Sophie had opened her eyes wide, was quietly laughing. "As if."

"I love you, Soph, but sometimes I'd like to smack you one. That day was one of those times."

"How would that look in my obit?" She shifted, looked into the distance. "Everyone who comes in tells me this is the most painful kind of cancer, but so far."

"Christ, people are morons. Why do they say such things?"

"To scold. Stupid me, choosing ovarian." Once more she fell silent. "But I'd rather endure—some pain than hallucinate, Jay. No morphine. Not yet. A harpist in town comes in to play and get you through. I wonder how she chooses her music."

"Maybe you get to choose."

"That would be nice, harp music. Not that I believe in the heavenly host. Do you? We've never—"

"Never been pushed to say what I believe in, Soph. Except the laws of science. Even they get amended. I guess I believe in behaving decently, though I—haven't always made the grade. But you're the one in the foxhole."

"No," Sophie said with effort. "A revelation somewhere along the way, a sense of the divine purpose of all this, that would've been welcome. I tried being open to it, really I did. But no. You'd say, of course, that no single element in a complex system understands the pattern, the behavior, of the system it's embedded in. Tough luck. But I say that a sense of the divine purpose would be a help." She looked at Judith directly and smiled. "On the edge of eternity, not chaos. Or maybe it's chaos in fact, hey? That final disorder? I'm the same old skeptic." She shifted on her bed, an enormous, gasping effort for a small turn. "If an old guy appears later and tells me he's God, I'll say—I'll say, hey, just another random event, pal. Too bad I missed out on the small and probably useful delusions."

Was the sacred only an infantile wish made public? No. Judith did not believe that, but was at a loss to know what she believed. "Was it a good life anyway, Soph?"

"A waste. A goddamned waste. Never forget."

The words depressed and wounded her. She'd hoped Sophie had arrived at reconciliation these last few months. Oh, Sophie, let me tell you about waste. The wrong things for the wrong reasons.

Sophie had once been poised as all life is, inside the regime called order but on the edge of chaos, open to change, ready to adapt as things around her changed. But her disease had pushed her downward, at last over the edge, was plunging her into that ultimate disorder called death, where change is forever foreclosed. This call had been Sophie's last vain hope to be hauled back from chaos to order, to life. I can't do it, Soph, she cried in her heart; nobody can. Yet she was sickened by her own failure.

An hour passed, and Judith reconsidered. She'd failed mightily, but she could help in another, smaller way. She'd never accompanied anyone through this descent, had sometimes wondered if she could. Now she knew that for Sophie, she must.

Let me, she prayed to a deity she did not believe in—but to a universe she did—let me do this one right, at least.

At four the hospice nurse called, but Judith could only report no change. No, Sophie had resisted the morphine so far, but because she was not yet in enough pain, or didn't want to hallucinate, who knows. Sophie's doctor actually came over after office hours, checked vital signs.

Judith walked him to the front door too. "Probably a blood clot somewhere, maybe her lungs. She could pull through this, maybe not. If you're a praying woman, pray that she doesn't." Judith looked at him in disbelief. He was experienced, unsentimental about death. "I've seen people go through months of unendurable pain, pain we can't begin to touch. We wouldn't want that for her. Not for anybody, but especially not for her."

Ellie asked about supper. "A little soup if you've got it around, Ellie." *I surrendered completely, again and again, to vegetable soup.* But this soup got cold on the bedside table as Judith watched Sophie sleep. Oh, Sophie! she cried in her heart. Sophie, Sophie! We should've grown old together, old ladies on the porch, at peace at last.

At eight in the evening, Sophie awakened, whispered. "Morphine now."

Oh, Soph. Anyone else would be screaming in pain. The radiance of the last few weeks had gone altogether; Sophie was gray, great sepia shadows under her eyes, her skin falling strangely from the bones in her skull, internal structure slowly collapsing upon itself. Judith struggled with the drops under Sophie's tongue, ashamed for her own clumsiness. "Just fifteen minutes, love, it'll grab hold." Sophie had soiled the bed and was embarrassed, insisted Judith go out so that Ellie could clean up. "I used to think you were lucky to be so loved. But now I see it wasn't luck at all. You were blessed with a gift—"

"Soph, I've blown it big-time." But Sophie was away and didn't care. My heart is broken fifty ways, Soph, and you aren't around to tell me I had it coming. I need you, Soph, how I need you. Need your love, even your scorn. Your envy. Love you, my prickly-pear girlfriend.

The morphine didn't grab hold in fifteen minutes, in half an hour, even an hour. Judith called the doctor, the hospice nurse, suddenly shrunken in her helplessness to do anything for Sophie, who was suffering terribly, tears down her cheeks, though she did not often cry out. We're trying, Soph, she whispered. But so what, if nothing worked?

The hospice nurse brought an injection. Sophie reached for Judith with surprising strength, and childlike, buried her face in Judith's chest, wept a little from pain, not fear. "I am so sorry," she apologized pointlessly. Judith could find no words, was tearful herself. "What time is it? I just want to—see the garden one last time. I think I can do that." Yes, Judith said, yes, you can.

Birds began to call; the sky was gray with the coming dawn. Sophie tossed, whether conscious or not, Judith couldn't tell. Now the outlines of the garden could be seen, the shrubs, the last of the summer petunias leggy in the containers, the new asters looking forward freshly. She should've come over and deadheaded some of those flowers for Sophie, welcome or not. "You can see the garden now, Soph."

Sophie's eyes were wide open, but beheld something else. She groaned, scratched at herself ferociously, to undo her own existence. With enormous energy, she tossed herself beyond Judith's arms, nearly out of bed. The voice had lost its granny timbre, was Sophie's own again, yet not, for the words that came out were hallucinatory, just what she hadn't wanted to endure. Couldn't the hallucinations be generous, offer the specter of a kindly mother, a comforting aunt?

Ellie had heard the sudden thrashing, pushed open the door, shivering in her cotton nightgown. "I'll call the hospice."

But the cries died away, the little body calmed, save a horrible rasping, Sophie still desperate to breathe, determined to live, and failing. The sun shone brightly in the garden now. Judith looked through the window, took in everything about this sunny morning, the hues of the flowers both fresh and dead, chamisa buds like the fists of misers, soon to open into golden largesse, a house finch chattering at its mate; imagined she could transfer the image to Sophie's mind, a substitute for Sophie's seeing it herself.

At last even the breathing failed. Judith felt for the nonexistent pulse, kissed her friend's forehead, released her gently onto the bed, and dropped her own head and sobbed. Relief, exhaustion, grief. Utter desolation. Forlorn, deserted, alone at the border; alone and staring down from order to beckoning chaos. Everything and nothing.

Shape Spaces

Nola sits quietly beside Molloy as he drives up the highway north of Santa Fe, past Española, past the pueblos of the Tesuque, the Pojoaque, the Santa Clara, the San Juan, and also past the trailers, shanties and half-ruined mud huts that speak of the poverty of rural Rio Arriba County.

He appreciates the quiet. Inéz runs a sound track, a narrative that tells him not only what she's doing at any given moment—*there, that's finished; I can hardly reach this, remind me to call Alisa*—but also what she thinks about it—*finished, but not the best job I've ever done, Alisa's so stressed out, but she brings it on herself.* Reading a magazine, she burbles nonstop, responding to whatever passes before her eyes: *Ah! Oh no! Now, really?* He doesn't know if these eruptions are involuntary, or invitations for him to ask what or why. After years of solitude he's found it odd to be summoned so continuously out of his own preoccupations, but not without its charm. Then tedious. Then irritating. Then maddening.

"I don't know what to make of this, not my thing," Nola had confessed on the phone. "Outsider art, folk art. Maybe not for you either. But I thought you'd like to see it, and I trust your eye." He says he's understood that art was on the back burner while Pete was so ill.

"Remission time. A respite. In this brief moment, pay the bills, do the housecleaning, get to think outside your own misery." He hears her silent plea: keep me company along this harrowing path a little while. Her silence in the car is a blessing.

At a turnoff they leave the highway that would have brought them to

O'Keeffe's Abiquiú, and instead cross the Rio Chama, here narrow and well-behaved, its riparian cottonwoods a flamboyant gold in the briefer, cooler autumn days.

"The artist did another one somewhere near Taos, but on public land, it really took a beating. He finally bulldozed it. Worried he'd get sued or something."

"We have such a human urge to be in control," Molloy muses. "Most of the time we can kid ourselves. Then the universe laughs, lays down the law, lets us know who's boss."

"That's it. All out of my control. I do the best I can." Grief has carved the core from her voice.

"No timeline, no deadline." He stops, dismayed by how much the English language refers to death. He's wanted to ask her about the little wooden crosses that appear at the highway's edge, but guesses they're sites of fatal car crashes, the local custom to mark them. Death won't go away because he shuts up. "Maximum stress. It wasn't exactly like that for me. My wife was an adult, and what happened was—avoidable, I guess. That added one kind of burden, lifted another."

They lapse again into silence. From the parking area, the trail leads down into a sandy arroyo, sparse clumps of native grasses, grama and bluestem, poking up beside sagebrush and cactuses, chollas and crimson prickly pears with extravagantly long gray needles. A butte looms above them like a medieval battlement, and this they climb by a side path. Weathered roots poke out of the sand like prehistoric antlers, and strange rock formations lie ahead, always on the verge of suggesting they're something else. They pass stunted cedars and junipers, spiky yucca, mountain mahogany. Little cairns begin to appear on the side of the trail, three, four and five rocks piled upon each other, signs of pilgrims come before them.

At a small shelf on the trail they survey the valley below, volcanic plugs like upended vessels submerged in an ancient seabed. At the center of the valley, cottonwoods conceal the river under autumn foliage. O'Keeffe's Pedernale looms, and the Jemez mountains seem suddenly much higher, darker, more menacing than they looked from Santa Fe.

A narrow trail along a ledge brings them at last to the entrance of the shrine, a strange man-made cave, a pagan temple, quarried out of northern New Mexico's red sandstone. At the entry a bowl-like carving is just the height and shape to be a fount for holy water. They step inside and let their eyes adjust to the roseate dimness; noticeably chillier than the warm afternoon they've left.

"Ronchamps," Molloy murmurs. A child tugging at his hand, fussing for ice cream. Flooded with the tenderness of young fatherhood, he'd given in to her, left the chapel, and though he always meant to, never returned.

This place seems sanctified too, a living thing, with softly rounded columns, smooth and fluid, that rise into the darkness like arteries, organs, mimicking living flesh, from palest pink to deepest shadowy rose. At the same time, its undulations, its carved shells and nautilus chambers, its waves and rays, are a tribute to water, to the sea, in a sere land that has seen no seas for tens of millions of years.

They begin to explore the chambers that lead off in various directions, drawing them ever farther within. Hidden fenestrations softly illuminate the walls and ceilings, the light reflected from concealed mirrors. Small risers lead up and down to adjacent chambers, nooks, crannies, all flowing organically inward; walls fluidly into other walls; these decorated sparingly with bas-relief shells, spirals; at their feet stone plant life that has no botanical equivalent on the earth's surface. Here and there, benches are carved to allow the viewer to sit and contemplate when he finds a place he wants to remain. One, needing a little climb, is more a throne than a bench, and only when they back away do they see some fanciful animal, its mouth wide open, the throne its tongue.

Inside this warm, protective, almost living structure, she follows Molloy in silence, watching him scan, hesitate, touch, and move on. It comes to her slowly that this ancient token of the earth's volcanic core, the earth's heart, pressed and tamed by long-gone seas, is the place where Molloy will open his own heart, break his notorious private silence at last. She's to be entrusted with the secrets, however sorrowful. However squalid. She doesn't want the responsibility, to hear the confession, but Molloy's mute pain saddens her. So when he halts thoughtfully in the middle of a roseate chamber, a ventricle, swirls shadowed on the ceiling, she prompts. "Your wife?"

A businesslike answer. "She died a few years ago. Not a pretty death, and there was nothing I could do about it except mourn."

"Oh, Molloy, I'm sorry. What did she die of?"

He turns to her, considers the sweet earnest innocence of her question. He wishes he had something noble to reply. He hadn't taken Nola seriously at the beginning. She was so perky, so endlessly enthusiastic, so soon made glad. He'd held her idiot of a husband against her. But he's misjudged. Her good will, her kindness, are deep, dear, and very rare. She deals with her own burdens courageously. He senses, at a level he can't put into words, that she's a woman to be trusted.

"My wife overdosed on speed, coke and alcohol. Very eighties. The addictive personality." The last phrase said with an iciness that implies his contempt, not only for the jargon, but also perhaps for the woman herself. "Was it deliberate? Who knows? I thought I knew her better than anyone, and I don't know."

Though his voice has dropped, the stone walls amplify it, an echo that makes the words portentous. "Some people say I drove her to it. You could argue that. The early days, I often left her alone. A strange place. Later I left her alone because—she made it clear she preferred that. You could argue that dying on me was the best retaliation she could've imagined." She damn near destroyed me, he does not add. Exiled me from the human.

He kneels to examine a strange carving at the juncture between floor and wall, neither known plant nor animal. "But then some people would say that robs her of the most responsible act of her life. *If* it was deliberate." He gets up, brushes the pale pink dust off his black trousers. "I can tell you this. I bore it all, the decline, the very long decline, the death, mostly in silence. I covered for her, lied for her. Even when my concern had frayed completely, I was there. Well, pretty much. I was loyal. By then, it was mostly a matter of my self-respect. Old-fashioned boys' school of me, I think now, but then I'm from an old-fashioned boys' school."

He gazes directly at Nola. "I was naive enough to think I'd earned some credit for that loyalty. Not so. Some people thought it was all my fault. Our kids, for instance. That's how my burden is different from yours, Nola. Nobody blames you for Pete. They think you're heroic. So do I."

Something Inéz once said about her clients: *They don't lie to protect the man. They lie to protect themselves. From their own shame.* He covers his eyes and could weep.

"Like I've had a choice." But Nola doesn't want this to be about her or Pete. She's saddened for Molloy, his encumbrances, though she knows sympathy isn't what he seeks. Relief, maybe. Exoneration. The beginning of restoration. On sheer instinct, she pushes ahead. "Did you? Drive her to it?"

"No final answer to that, Nola." He's drawn to a carved spiral, traces the circular groove inward with an index finger. "She had a very unhappy life. She was always fragile. I was many things, God knows, but not fragile. I blame myself for this. I went into the marriage knowing how fragile she was, and then let her down. I wanted to help. Couldn't. Maybe nobody could. All I know is, I couldn't."

The impotence of those years.

"Not that I wasn't capable of driving her to it. I once left a man on a mountainside to die, Nola. He didn't. No thanks to me." Eberhardt, tagging along though he was out of shape, too old; not a technical climb but a glacier scramble, four of them hitched by rope because of the crevasses. Exhausted, Eberhardt fell. Molloy, furious, determined to finish the climb (to show himself he could?) had abandoned him. An unforgivable transgression against the mountain code, Molloy knew, pushed the others on anyway. By the time they came back, found Eberhardt in the snow and got him back to the inn, his toes were frostbitten, and he'd lose two. "In those days I was known as Mackie Messer, German for Mack the Knife. Even I knew it wasn't exactly a compliment. In those days, I didn't give a shit."

Then things changed, as they always do.

His finger retraces the carved spiral outward from its center. "I love this symbol. So universally human. Found everywhere. Native American, Celtic, Cretan, Aurignacian. There's an Egyptian pot at the Metropolitan nearly six thousand years old, decorated with spirals. Just about the time Thoth, the moon god, and also the patron of the sciences, is represented as a baboon."

Nola takes this in with great solemnity. Judith, he thinks with regret, would've rewarded him with a laugh, a tart remark. Maybe even the etymology of baboon. The laughter around the table at Socorro. Genesis.

Nola waits patiently. He's somewhere else, musing. "I've seen ancient German jewelry, necklaces, armbands with spirals. Stones in the Urnfield burial mounds. The Celts borrow the spiral from the Greeks? The Greeks from the Egyptians? Is it hardwired into the human brain? In bronze age Europe, it symbolized change and growth. A place to dance. Great potency, this symbol."

She allows him the respite he needs. "That, and the human hand. *I was here.*"

"I was here," he agrees. "Like the cairns we just saw on the trail. Such a human message."

"Did she know you wanted to help?"

He's puzzled. "I guess so. Knew I was trying. Ineptly, uselessly, not always patiently at the end, never heroically, but I was trying. Why?"

"Knowing that your partner is trying, even if—is, you know, a comfort," she says stiffly. Winks.

Ernie, withdrawn into his skulls, his so-called research. Himself, trading around the clock, tracking the markets across the world, always daytime somewhere. The high from it, the blessed, addictive, anodyne high. Phone calls from airports, from breaks in meetings, rushed, alien languages knitted around his own. She'd been gone for years before he realized his wife had left him.

"He's trying, Nola." Something to say, though he doesn't believe it. He'd spoken to Judith of human failure, the inability to be there for somebody who needed you. Faced his own failure long ago.

"In somebody else's bed, he's trying," she says with sudden bitterness, seizing Molloy's moment after all. "How can he even think about fucking? It's the last thing on my mind, believe me." Molloy doesn't answer. "Did you stray when your wife was—absent?"

He shakes his head slowly. "Lived like a monk. The late seventies, the eighties, yet." He raises the *sumi* eyebrows in mock surprise at himself. Not the whole truth. In Paris he'd once had a three-star dinner with an exquisitely beautiful woman, was still poor boy enough to be affronted that she hardly ate what he was paying good money for. As dinner drew to a close, she shifted gracefully, opened the jacket of a suit that had surely cost more than his entire college education, and revealed a silk blouse; under that, only the most obvious sexual readiness. As he was registering this, she took his hand and put it roughly in her own crotch, to let him know this was going to be an interesting ride home. So it was. He remembered laughing; he hadn't fucked in the back seat of a car since college. His impeccably discreet driver made sure that they only arrived at her apartment—one of the few *hotels particuliers* left in the Marais that wasn't a government building or an advertising agency—at an appropriate moment. Upstairs Molloy saw the first, and for that matter, the only, clit ring he'd ever seen; asked her in three languages if it was for her or for him, but the lady was in no position to answer. Later he found himself staring at her body. Boobs like an L.A. porn queen, standing up even when she was lying down, the heavy-handed prop of silicone. Everything else had been sucked to the bone by the surgeon's vacuum. For a man who loved women's bodies, in paint, marble, or in the flesh, it was grotesque.

A silent driver took him to his hotel at dawn, and he wondered idly what the man had done after all that aural stimulation, possibly fingered himself to relief; remembered he'd heard that drivers of a certain class belonged entirely to the gay community, and traded sex in the dark while they waited around. It seemed downright wholesome by comparison.

Later—earlier?—a wonderful Turkish interpreter who had, in the Turkish style, plucked out all her pubic hair. The infantile mons had both repelled and inflamed him. A *Fürstin* who made it clear that if he wanted her husband's account, she had some business with him first. But that was it. Nothing, nothing at all, compared to the opportunities.

"No special points for me, though." Later, after his wife had died, he'd learned from Ross that lack of libido is a common sign of clinical depression. By that time, he'd been deeply depressed for years. His desire for one woman had died first, then his desire for any woman. Which was worse? To lack desire, or the means to gratify it? He'd lacked both, and it was—bearable. Other signs too. He snorts. "You couldn't say some things out loud in those days. You were barely permitted to say people were drunks. Alcoholics. I—protected—her for a long time."

At his Frankfurt doctor's, he'd got up his courage and asked. "Nothing organic," the doctor said with Teutonic embarrassment, bent over his chart to end the conversation. *I'm forty-two and my sex life is over?* his heart cried.

He looks down to a light-reflecting mirror and sees his own face, studies it glumly. Older, coarser. Worn is the word. "Once, when I was ransacking the mini-bar fridge for chocolate in the Istanbul Hilton, I found a packet of condoms—no, no, that's not the story. Story is they were a brand called *Shakespeare: to be or not to be.* We owe that bit of poetry, of real-time ethics, to Korea, not Turkey. As I saw from the label."

"I'm so very sorry about your wife, Molloy. But—" Her voice takes on a cheer that seems a talisman against excessive sadness. "But somehow you muddle on through, don't you, and get rewarded with the lovely Inéz. You cheer me up, Molloy, give me hope."

"She's certainly lovely," Molloy agrees lightly. He turns abruptly from his own image and moves further into the undulating cave. "How far back does this go?"

Nola follows him. "Ernie and I have our own ways of living with the situation, but we haven't been able to comfort each other. I want to bring it up, but he's just—gone. Blank. He adores Pete, always has. But he's gone from Pete too. Pete needs him. I want to know how he copes. I mean, besides the other woman. If I ask, he'll tell me all about her, and really, I can do without that in my face just now. So I don't ask, he doesn't tell, very nineties; we tiptoe around each other. But he could be there for Pete." A wink for emphasis.

Molloy studies the sculpted spirals, waves, and the seductive corridors that lead off with vague promises into the warm red semi-darkness. Amplified by the caves, his steady breathing becomes a series of sighs. "Here's something from the best advice money could buy at the time. Couples—like all living systems—set a sort of temperature for themselves, their homeostasis point. Most everything they do is to keep themselves inside the tolerable range. Pete's illness has shot your family temperature completely out of whack. You react in a way to control for that. If Ernie's gone, absent, maybe it's protective—of him, of you, of the marriage. But if it's not serving you as well as another way might, you could ask for something different."

"I don't know what I want. I want an end to it, that's what."

"Ernie fooling around? The marriage? Pete's illness?" For the first time, he looks wary.

"Everything. Believe me, I'm good at getting myself over hurdles if I can see the end in sight. Here's no end in sight. Just vigilance, anxiety, dropping everything and getting down to the hospital right now. I say yes to whatever, always knowing I might have to be elsewhere. The worst thing of all is—to wish for an end is to wish for the death of my boy, because that's the only thing that could end it. I will never, never sleep right again, for worry of that kid. The remissions are as agonizing as the flare-ups."

"This has been going on now—?"

"Two years. Molloy, I know parents who've been through it for ten. They're the heroes. Well, tell me what you think of all this."

From a sandstone bench carved into the side of the cave wall he appraises. Runs his eyes, his fingertips over aggregate not ground into sand by geological forces, exposed and curiously decorative stones, jewel-like, rich hues of green, purple, deep reds, black and white in their sandstone matrix. "Raises the usual questions about art, doesn't it? What do the marks we make mean?"

"What's the artist trying to convey?"

"Of course not," he retorts. "I don't have the faintest idea what the artist was trying to convey."

Locally, Not Globally Wise

Molloy has spent much of the last few months driving his Gelaendewagen across the desert, seeking rock art. He's begun with daytrips to sites near Santa Fe—the Galisteo basin (named, he's amused to think, for his ancestors, the Gauls, the Celts). Over to the Pecos; up to Velarde, to Chaco Canyon. The desert's colors—sienna, umber, ochre both raw and burnt, *sandia*, watermelon, a rich pink that's one part mineral, one part a visual trick of the thin dry air—exhilarate him, take him back to Istanbul's spice market, where he once stood transfixed by aromatic cone-shaped mounds of powdered mace, mustard, cinnamon, cardamom, cloves, nutmeg, coriander, cumin, ginger, pepper red, black, and white, inhaling their fragrances, bedazzled by their luscious colors, fixed so long that the spice-sellers had retreated cautiously into their stalls, convinced they had a madman out front.

From New Mexico he's moved on to southern Utah, Colorado, northern Arizona, sometimes solitary, sometimes hiring guides. Nobody knows who made southwestern rock art (ancestors, strangers, gods) or what the images meant. They have no special meaning for him either, but he invites them cordially into his head, a man already high on history.

At home he's deep into books on linguistics, what's known (not much) about the arrival of each of the three great families of American Indian languages, their connections (remote but visible) to other world languages, the evidence they offer (along with DNA and dentition) of tribal migrations. At Judith's dinner that night, he'd pulled himself away reluctantly. So many questions that might've been answered by people at that table. Under the circumstances, he'd been relieved to go. He thought of calling Benito or the McMahons to pursue some issues, then didn't.

But he feels confident enough to take on the rock art by himself. Some images call to him like old friends: the spiral, the swastika (a variation on the spiral known worldwide), the human hands and figures, the signs for clouds and rain, the moon. Other images are new, but none completely strange. All are potent. One of his Navajo guides comes close to convulsions at some petroglyphs he's led Molloy to. Art with such power: eat your hearts out, curators of the world. The guide won't tell Molloy what the images mean to him. Might not even know.

Art begins in the body. Himself a quarter century ago, hair in a ponytail down the middle of his back, alarmed by, then giving over to whatever had seized him in the Louvre, the Uffizi, the Prado, and was making him tremble. Not bad dope but great art. The body's rhythms, opening, closing, expanding, contracting; quickly, slowly; regularly, irregularly; up and down, hard and soft; warm and cold, dark and light, all pushed into representation. The early humans who moved tentatively, then boldly beyond the body, the act of representation—pictures, dances, songs, stories, adornment—something sacred, a way to make the group cohere. Early art making has always fascinated him, and he's considering a tour of the great rock art sites of Europe, the Alps, the northern part of Scandinavia, the British Isles, maybe on to North Africa, his guides the finest scholars.

Then again.

Art, a biologist had said to him sniffily. Just a sexual selection mechanism. You exhibit characteristics—symmetry, precision, coordination, perfect vision, imagination—all to show how fit you are to mate. The human equivalent of a peacock's tail, nothing more. Molloy had permitted himself a courteous but skeptical nod.

This cave, this piece of folk art, that Nola has led him to seems of a piece with the rock art he's spent the summer looking at. A hazy hypothesis has begun to form, that early pictures, sculptures, visual representations of any kind, are the embodiment of something in the physical nature of the human brain. He's tried that intuition out in e-mail with various artist friends, kind enough not to laugh; friends who pass him on to anthropologists and evolutionary biologists pondering the same idea, though with scientific precision. They give it a name, *entoptic* phenomena, what the human brain generates when it's hallucinating.

Art begins with biology, the body, but moves outward. To long for, to express, finally to achieve transcendence, whether by shamanistic trance or sheer flow. That's the meaning of art. The meaning, if meaning exists, of a human life.

Not enough for him. He struggles stubbornly to find the connection between symbols and their meaning. Not what the symbols mean—decoding might eventually be possible—but the nature of meaning. When he looks at the work of the philosophers who've asked these questions, he drops the books in frustration.

D'où venons-nous? Que sommes-nous? Où allons-nous? Why are we here? This is the real mystery he's brought to the sciences of complexity when the philosophers and metaphysicians have failed him: the mystery of representation. He knew before he arrived in Santa Fe that representation is one of the two essential capabilities of complex systems. He knows too that meaning isn't one-to-one, but lies in relationships among elements, the result of a process, a dialectic, shaped by history.

He's been abrupt with Nola, annoyed that an art professional would talk naively about what the artist was trying to convey. He regrets that. Leans against the cool roseate sandstone, resumes.

"Meaning is fundamental to every piece of art I've ever loved. Pictures that are merely pretty." He shrugs. "Still looking for a theory of meaning I can live with. The best, the greatest art is freighted with meaning, just like the great events. But the meaning isn't only in the painting; it's called up in me, the viewer, by the power of the painting. The magic of art turns out to be—another transaction."

"What it calls up in you? You're so many things, Molloy. Your history. Your taste."

"My story, yeah. Not to mention the stories people tell about me. Always changing, dynamic, as they'd say at the Institute. Paintings lose their meaning for me and I get rid of them. But some I've had from the beginning." He runs his hand lovingly over a deep carving. "What does it mean, that I love the spiral, hmmm?" Among some local tribes, the symbol of emergence into this world from another. Elsewhere, a symbol of cyclical eternity, or the complexity of life.

He moves back in the cave toward a small dark room with a modest New Age nameplate: The Luminous Egg Chamber. Enters awkwardly, sits down cross-legged, looking up into the bowl of the egg. Though he can still see Nola in the outer room, he feels strangely distant. "What does it mean that I can stand in a field below the Pedernale out there, and be moved to tears by serpents, fanciful creatures, maybe gods and goddesses of people whose very name is lost to history?" He sighs and is quiet.

Then again: "What does it mean, that my son is shagging my girlfriend?"

Nola gasps. Molloy has spoken as quietly, evenly as if he were still discussing art theory. He can see her trying to make out his face, expecting a terrible rage; at the very least, humiliation, but inside the Luminous Egg Chamber, he knows he's opaque.

"How—?"

"How do I know? Or—how long has this been going on? Or—how come? Or—what does it mean?" In his own ears his voice echoes, hollow and haunting. He emerges, stretches, explores another chamber. "Does it occur to you, Nola, that we only know what we already have the framework, the representational structure to know? At New Business, we're always telling our clients that. All information, data, and interpretations, we tell them, are just opportunities for the reformulation of ideas."

He's told the story to himself enough that it slips out smoothly, the painful edges planed away. "An old guy, let's call him Theseus, vain in his success, woos and wins a gorgeous young creature named Phaedra. Old Theseus gets this gorgeous thing to show off to all the other bulls. A sign of the gods' favors. Not an unimportant message. And also this desirable creature to warm his bed and console him for his past disappointments, his present lapses, his approaching old age. Theseus, they say, loves the wisdom of women, is always trying to appropriate it for himself.

"But. Always a *but*, right? Theseus has a son, younger than Phaedra, but old enough. You know this old story, Nola? Do I have to finish?"

"You too." She barely breathes.

"We're at the end of the twentieth century, not in mythological Greece. Can we think about all these facts differently? Maybe the story can be told another way."

"You've held things together with your bare hands, haven't you? Often."

"Okay, not Theseus but Molloy. Favored by the gods, laurels and showers of gold descend, et cetera. He's known in his world as a warrior of strength and cunning—" he gives Nola a slight smile "—and people don't fuck with him if they can help it.

"But there's another aspect to Molloy. At least as important as the warrior." He stops. "Oh, God. This is asinine." Inéz at Judith's dinner party, mortifying. The performance, the rock-lyric sentiments, the humiliation that he'd heard the same words months earlier in private and imagined something precious was being disclosed, when in fact it was her currency. So he has Greek mythology instead of rock lyrics. Does that make it classier?

He moves closer to Nola. She's removed her enormous glasses, dabs at her eyes with an old-fashioned lace handkerchief. The white lace moves him inexplicably. He lifts her chin, kisses each eyelid. They remain closed. Without haste, he takes her mouth, sweet and soft, savors the desire flowing between them, first comforting, then urgent. She finds his hand, places it ceremoniously on her left breast, moves her pelvis obediently into his, pulls him close. Women and their softness—the silks and gauzes they wear, promise of their fragrant, loamy flesh. A white silk sweater unbuttoned effortlessly. Women and their warmth, their moisture, the fluids of life. All the more precious in the desert. He'd have taken his time, but she's the one in a hurry. The rose-colored chamber. He might be mating with the earth itself.

They lie side by side in the ruby half-light. "I feel," she whispers, "as if I came to this cave and got fucked by a god."

He kisses the hand in his. A life with Nola. An unconsidered possibility. After a while she gets up, arrays some of the pretty disarray as he watches.

He hitches himself up, follows her into yet another chamber. "Look." On the wall is a heart, carved to look like a tongue, the tip of a phallus. She fingers, kisses it. "Asinine, you were saying. No, not asinine. Go on, Molloy. Go on with your story."

But he's told no one and hopes never to speak aloud of this again, though the voices in his head are plenty pressing. "This side of the man longs for something different, an end—the battling is only a means. Oh Jesus, not quite. Molloy gets off on the sight and smell of blood for its own sake, gets high from victory. Anyway—Molloy hungers for something he'd call—" He tastes a word on his tongue, just as he'd tasted her depths. "Tenderness. Not just the tenderness another person might offer him, but a release for all the tenderness he holds, has to offer. Here's the problem. Not just anyone. Someone—" he searches for words, a picky and eloquent man after all despite his long silence. "Coequal, commensurate with him in some important way. If she isn't, then tenderness turns into mere pity. Then impatience. Boredom. He doesn't want to bond with his twin, do you see? He's looking for that complement, that other. All very platonic; the boys' school gave me an excellent classical education."

She takes this as opportunity, opening, still greedy, still needing consolation, desire denied too long. With gentle, meticulous skill, the mouth and fingers of an experienced woman bent on her own satisfaction, she brings him back to eagerness, straddles him and soars, her core pulling him out of himself; then collapses on his chest, sobbing. He's voyeur to this as much as participant, and thinks it's the least of gallantry to say, "Now the goddess has been to me." But she gazes down on him reproachfully at the duty in that utterance.

He strokes her hair, considers the possibilities. Imagines himself into the future, an ever-considerate, courteous lover. Somewhat absent-minded. Dutiful. Distracted. Detached.

Low-Dimensional Chaos

"Tell me," she murmurs languorously, "the rest of your story. You came here for that." She's stretched out on the throne, the beast's tongue, not bothering to array the disarray this time, head cushioned on an arm, breasts and belly exposed, a body that has given birth, suckled, been betrayed, knows its needs.

"And you came here to fuck your brains out," he says gently. Her smile acknowledges it to be so.

I thought, he begins, I'd found that other half. Married her. The woman reaching for the lavender oil at the bathtub's edge. Her laugh. Her lassitude. The invisible injuries clawed across her soul that would never heal, no matter what. He hadn't seen that then, couldn't even be sure he thought of her as his other half, his soul mate. He simply wanted no other.

But time passes, and he longs for something more. Forced to conceal so much. Forced to conceal her weakness, addiction, sickness, call it whatever, from the world. From himself too. Conceals his own tenderness as other men must hide their homosexuality, their deviant politics. From his colleagues he hides his intellectual hunger behind athletics, hunting, above all, making money. He cultivates cheer, optimism, as a willed thing, a discipline, not a natural state of being.

"Lindy. I was stupid. Rage, desperation, some terrible chemical imbalance, I mistook it for strength. Then thought I could fix this too. I couldn't. You know the rest."

Nola sighs. Molloy glances at her, but will rush ahead now regardless, unstoppable.

"So I put the pieces of my life back together, and somehow Santa Fe—land of enchantment, entrapment. Women like I want—seem abundant here. Self-sufficient. A partner I could love, would know enough to love me. When I think I've found her, it doesn't work. So I find another. I think. But the gods love to mock guys like me; it's just a re-run, rage and desperation, not courage."

"What do you really want, Molloy?"

He cries out sharply. "A woman to appreciate one—both—works of art I've made." Then quietly, almost glumly. "To cut to the chase, Nola, if I got home today and found out that Stephen and Inéz had run off together in his pickup, I'd breathe a big sigh of relief and get on with my life. So much for the outraged cuckold."

Nola's sigh turns to something like a kind laugh. "You were Sherman through Georgia last spring."

"A maniac. Libido resurrected with a roar. The gods love paradoxes. That was one of the loneliest times of my life. All that flesh, and—to be or not to be. After Lindy died, I was sorting it out; loneliness wasn't much of an issue. By the time I got here, I thought I understood, had put it behind me, walked around like some silent open wound, hoping for—whatever."

"You have other children?"

"A daughter. Calls herself an artist; it's real shit. Even if I tried, I can't hide that from her."

"That *opinion*," Nola amends mildly.

"She thinks I'm the world's biggest asshole. Among other things, I'm sure. She says, love me, love my art; I say I love you, but I'm not suspending my taste: the art stinks. We are, you might say, estranged. She's still in college; she might improve."

"Couldn't you?" No, she sees that. Imagines a daughter and novice artist, devastated by that unsparing paternal judgment. A daughter without a mother, a daughter without, really, a father. She longs for him to call this nameless daughter, restore harmony, be a father and not an art critic. She tries to reconcile this terrible judgment with the fact of Inéz, who'd come to her at the gallery after all, slides in hand. Nola had examined them, mediocrities, refused them with the kindly excuses she was very good, very practiced, at making. A

painful compassion arises for all the strugglers she knows, artists and scientists, artist and scientist wannabes, parents and children, longing and grieving for each other endlessly. For herself. Her heart may burst. "Nothing is easy with families, is it?" Aware of his gaze, warming in it, she sits up. "But Molloy. One day this daughter will come to you with the knowledge that the collector's eye and the artist's eye are entirely different things. If you've been wise and kind, she'll tell you this wisely and kindly." She puts her feet down on the floor. "If you haven't, she'll tell you this as she slices out your heart."

A cry, strangled. "How will I be wise and kind, Nola?"

"You could begin—you could begin by telling her yourself that you know this."

He doesn't answer.

Desire again. She'll feed it, have him, but this time it'll take tact. She pulls her silk sweater across her bare breasts, brushes off some red sand, buttons it slowly, deliberately, to remind him how easily it comes off. Zippers the jeans, and tucks in the sweater, stretches her bare feet, her whole body humming, finds her shoes. "Why the money? You seem yourself sort of, well, abstemious."

"Abstemious? Don't think I didn't go through my stage of fastest wheels on the Autobahn. I still keep an old Lamborghini in storage down off Second Street, token of the good old days. If I want so much as to roll it out the door, I have to fly a mechanic in from New Jersey, along with a crate of his tools. I have other little luxuries, indeed I do." He's struggling too, though probably not with desire. With the alien nature of self-disclosure? "All those years of sleeping in hotel rooms—my housekeeper has to change my bed every day, the sheets are linen, not cotton, from Europe. See? But it came to me early, that toys don't make me happy. Other things . . . I do the money because I can. Because it's easy. Because it makes for prodigious fortifications. Not always prodigious enough."

He's remembering now; his tongue wags on. "In the seventies, gang warfare was being waged on German businessmen, maybe you remember that. All over Europe. A colleague was kidnapped in broad daylight off the streets of London, held for ransom, somehow escaped. Scotland Yard found three gangs involved—one that kidnapped him, one that held him, and a mastermind group. Eventually the Brits got the first two but the masterminds escaped. So my colleague, a thorough kind of guy, made sure word got out, and in due time, for the right fee, the Syrian secret police took care of the masterminds too. The word got round, he's no one to fuck with. We've all had to do something like that from time to time. I know the word for bribe in thirteen different languages. *Dash. Poongli.*" He allows his mind to wander.

When he resumes, it's a different voice. "My best friend—his wife answered the door one night, found the daughter of an old family friend on the doorstep, a student, invited her in. She's carrying what's supposed to be a bottle of scotch. In fact a bomb. Which she presents to her host, of course." He finishes with difficulty. Jürgen bouncing down the staircase in his tracksuit, on his way to play squash with his best friend Molloy, who'd waited and waited; called and got an odd electronic squeal, cursed Deutsche Telekom; drove to Jürgen's house to find mayhem, the police, the bomb squad, Ute staring into the abyss of hell.

"They took out Jürgen simply because they could. Because the girl seemed one thing and was in fact another. Trying to be. I sometimes wonder what she thinks now, twenty-five years later. What *for*? My God, if there's any justice, that bitch is rotting in the darkest, coldest, dampest cell in all of the *Bundesrepublik*. Jürgen was—" He halts, maybe surprised at his own passion so many years later. Jürgen, he says in memoriam, an exceptional man, good and kind—Jürgen had taken Molloy under his wing when Molloy first arrived in Germany; his wife was kind to Molloy's new bride. Jürgen sitting in a pub doing sidesplitting imitations of their colleagues, their clients. Jürgen had been his friend, his good, good friend. He shakes his head to dispel the old memory, the old pain. "I traveled in an armor-plated car with bodyguards in those days, can you believe it?"

"Were you scared?"

Shakes his head. "An adrenalin rush day in and day out. Some of the best deals I ever cut. I'd come home and play ninety minutes of killer soccer after work just to unwind. People were drawn to that young man. Even I," he hesitates, "even I loved the young man I was then. Sometimes." He's lost in thought. "When Lindy finally died, I went back to Germany to see Jürgen's widow, thinking maybe she'd know what to say, since nobody else had a clue. She'd remarried by then, had a new life. She says, you'll always be in pain. It will let up, but it'll always hurt. Yeah. The woman I came to Santa Fe for—she saw right through to that, wouldn't touch it with a ten-foot pole. Who can blame her?"

Nola wonders who the woman is. Or was. She's never known a man quite like this, his odd mixture of self-deception, vulnerability, pig-headedness, loyalty, courage. He's evaded the abstemious question, why he doesn't live the way rich men can live. Linen sheets. Please. But he's told her more valuable things. She can think all this at the same time she's thinking how to have him once more. She imagines moving toward him, touching him, comforting him for this awful thing, knows instinctively not to. Not yet.

"The money's not negligible, Nola. Not negligible. I do the money because for a long time that's all I was good at. Maybe I can do something worthwhile with it one of these days. But it's not my religion, thank you very much. It's not my addiction, my substitute for—oh, fuck it. And thank you for remaining neutral on the question of whether I'm the world's biggest asshole."

He leans against the cave wall, a man still in torment. "I admire you, Nola, you know that? I admire the way you can offer me kindness when you're the one who needs it, deserves it. People always want something from people like me. You don't."

She's shaking her head. What a damn fool. Draws on a practiced patience. "Eventually—eventually you'll have to do something about the situation at home, won't you?"

"I could always just waste away from boredom; how's that? She's not really stupid; someday she might get over all that derivative crap she spouts, even turn herself into a halfway decent artist. Yeah, I knew. Kind of you not to laugh her out of your gallery." Arms folded against his chest, he's suddenly detached, weary. "But the lovely Inéz hasn't surprised me in months, and what in the hell did I expect? No fool like an old fool, the sages got that one right. I'm sure she's having fun with do the papa, do the son, compare and contrast. Worry not; experience and finesse still triumph over sheer animal horniness. Even my own son's. As for Theseus. Well, poor old Theseus awaits a visit from the Queen of the Amazons. You know that painting, Carpaccio? Theseus a white-haired old man by then. The lovely Inéz—with, God knows, some just grievances—will be released. But not without being made to think twice."

"You deserve that equal, Molloy." Did Theseus ever find his equal? Maybe that's just the wrong myth. Maybe something even more ancient explains all this.

"I've done it wrong every goddamned time. I'm finally learning I can't trust myself ever to do it right. Well, shit. Nola, this wasn't to weep on your shoulder. I'm fine, fine. I'm saying think again about Ernie. Try putting the facts into a different structure, see what happens. That's the way we'll all be thinking in the next century, at least according to Madame Genius—Judith Greenwood. She's probably right. I think you love Ernie very much. Reconsider the situation. We learn because we have to, adapt or die."

Ernie. She's shut the whole world out in this wonderful place. For one afternoon she's looked to herself alone. She nods wearily. "I know what they say about him, Judith and her scientist friends. At least they're polite enough to laugh behind his back. He doesn't suspect. It'd kill him. Maybe he *is* a crackpot. How do I know? But he's my crackpot. We had such a good life, Molloy, before—" She stops. "It's been my task in this life, my path, to love people who were unlovable; that no one else could love. I think we've shared that task, that path, for a little while, you and I." Do you think yourself unlovable? she's asking.

"No path, Nola. A treadmill. I'm going somewhere else now."

"Before we go—"

He's as close as Molloy ever gets to bashful, that apprehensive grin. "Jesus, honey, I'm not seventeen any more."

He puts his hands firmly on her shoulders. "Pete's illness is a fact. I wish I could help you past that one, but nobody on earth can." He pulls her to him, kisses her forehead affectionately. "Let a good thing happen, dear Nola. I wish it for you with all my heart."

"Let a good thing happen," she repeats. "In New Mexico we call this a power spot. A magic place. Leave it to me." And works him over more than makes love to him. Afterwards says slyly: "So tell me, Molloy, what do you think of this? As art?" She's gesturing to the cave, the pagan temple, other meanings unsaid.

He understands, yields. "An installation that turns you inside out has to have something going for it, no?"

Frozen Accidents

Molloy believes his intuition has shaped his life. Trusting it, he's done well. His intuition had drawn him to Father Joachim, away from his uncle Jack, who loved him, who'd stood as a father to him in the absence of his own. But his uncle wanted him to come into the mill, earn good money right away and forevermore into the future, if he was only willing to bend to the shop rules, dirty his hands a little. Against his intuition, to please his uncle, he tried the mill in the summer between high school and college, and knew he'd never go back. His mother, sister to Jack, suffering with a thousand and one unnamed disorders (the family affliction of depression, he saw much later) emerged spectrally from her bedroom, her prison, her tomb, to pack his lunch pail the first night of work, graveyard shift, but said nothing either way. She was nearly a stranger to him, a washed-out woman in a washed-out cotton bathrobe. That she made such an effort on this occasion moved him, but at that age, he couldn't have found the words to tell her. (Though he wondered to Ross many years later, why hadn't she fought harder for him? Why had she handed him over to Char so obediently?)

He liked the physicality of the steel mill: he was a strong, tough boy growing into a strong, tough man, and took pleasure in his body stretching to the unexpected. He liked the company of men. But he hated the exclusions of manual labor. He'd memorized both poetry and conjugations for Father Joachim's German and Latin classes, and it had pleased him, this getting his tongue and mind around new languages. He sensed there was more in life. Worse, he sensed that the mill was the end, not the beginning, and the beginning was where he wanted to be.

He'd begun his fortune building with his intuition, discovered his knack for betting in the markets, nearly all of them. Asked to explain his strategies, he knew he was talking nonsense: he couldn't explain, and became superstitious about trying. Years later, when he saw the artificial stock market project at the Santa Fe Institute, its canniness jolted him—yes, trade at first on the fundamentals, and later on guesses about the behavior of other traders—but he resisted looking at it in detail.

His intuition was the only education he'd ever had in art, and he trusted it completely. By the time he could afford to collect, he exasperated dealers, because he refused scores of paintings for every one he acquired, and made no effort to articulate what he wanted until it was in front of him. Then he knew at once, and seldom made a mistake.

Eight months out of college in his first job on Wall Street, his intuition made him say yes to Germany, an opportunity that should have gone to a more senior man. But Molloy was the only one available in his firm who spoke German (in a schoolroom fashion) and was willing to go. Unencumbered, he was looking for something new. So he stormed the Frankfurter Börse, that pompous piece of late-19th century architecture that might easily be mistaken for the opera house, moved up in the firm quickly. He made friends with other traders and then their bosses. Then their bosses' bosses.

He'd happened to arrive in Frankfurt as the generation that created the *Wirtschaftswunder*, Germany's post-war economic miracle, was retiring, and his intuition told him that the replacement generation was far more timid. They wished merely that money might continue to make further money, at virtually no risk. This he found he could do (though he risked more than they ever knew) and they loved him for it. With such a skill, and lacking the social baggage of a native-born German, he was welcome everywhere. He invented, polished and elevated himself spectacularly, the flatlands of Frankfurt a fitting place to achieve liftoff and earth orbit. The Germans embraced him, saluted him and his New World energy, his New World swagger. Deluded themselves that his ruthlessness was also New World.

Intuition drew him to Jürgen, the best, perhaps the only friend he'd ever make. Jürgen was determined to transform him into a European. Along with instructing him on the finer points of aristocratic precedence, Jürgen spent hours in a municipal park teaching Molloy how to control a soccer ball with his feet, how to shoot with his head, soccer strategies. *What matters is the speed of the breakthrough; attack fast, get it over with*. Like hoops that way. He was never as good as if he'd done it from boyhood, but he made it up in drive; he had quick reflexes, a formidable kick, and on the field, he and Jürgen could read each other's minds. Among the pictures he'd brought to Santa Fe was a photograph, two young men in soccer uniforms with their arms around each other's necks, one dark, one fair, caught in delighted, self-congratulating laughter: their team had just won the amateur league championship.

That day too, Molloy had just put together his first billion-mark deal.

The first important occasion he'd let something overrule his intuition was his marriage. Intuition told him to stay away from Lindy, whose moodiness, so ebulliently up, so harshly down, was trying, yet whose beauty was incandescent and finally unforgettable. They'd been on again, off again; she didn't really want to live in Germany, and he'd forced the issue. Since he could do anything, he knew he'd persuade her, cheer her, protect her from her own demons. He thought she'd love the receptions in palace ballrooms, the opening nights, the men bedecked in white tie, red sashes, medals; the weekends at castles in the same family since Charlemagne. Instead she was frozen with fear, tongue-tied by the language, and put off by everything German. He thought she'd love their first apartment near the zoo, each balcony cheerfully stuffed with with bikes and (a good omen) baby carriages. When she didn't, he was already making enough money to move them to Frankfurt's Westend, a spacious flat in a fine old Bismarck-era house, not far from the American Embassy, the Palmgarten, and not incidentally, a short walk for him to work, and to the main train station.

Much later he wondered if he'd really wanted to be Stephen's son more than Lindy's husband. Lindy's father Stephen was another self-made man, a refugee who'd escaped to America from behind the Iron Curtain—Slovenia, Slovakia, Molloy hardly knew where—with nothing but the clothes on his back. By dint of intelligence, industry, a grasp of art that was innate, he'd become one of New York's premiere dealers in fine prints. Stephen loved Molloy at once without reservation; he recognized their essential affinity, and promised a family love like Molloy had never known. But the year after Lindy and Molloy were married, Stephen died suddenly.

The marriage was a stupendous miscalculation, and Molloy had two children before he admitted how profoundly he'd erred. Lindy had lasted two years in Frankfurt, finding solace only in other American expatriate wives, refusing even to make an effort, he thought. The baby, he reasoned, would make all the difference. He agreed she should go back and stay with her mother until it was born, to have doctors she could talk to. The moment he heard she was in labor, he flew to New York. He was there to hold his newborn son in his arms and make wordless promises to him; to weep with the sheer sweet joy of this tiny creature's existence.

Lindy didn't return with him to Germany, and when he went to fetch her in a couple of months, her postpartum decline stunned him. He finally understood her mother's oblique attempts to prepare him. Nothing could. The physicians told him medications were being tried, had not yet been effective. Something deeper was at work.

So he left his wife and his baby son (named, of course, for Lindy's father) in the hands of Lindy's mother and hired help, went back to Germany, working almost round the clock, phoning daily, beside himself with anxiety. Later, he'd think that he could've at least confided in Jürgen: not to tell Jürgen something he hadn't already guessed, but simply to ease his own heart. But he never did. All this what his own father had run away from. He would not.

Lindy recovered, after a fashion. She took an interest in her baby; could tell him things on the phone. It seemed extravagant but essential to commute long weekends from Frankfurt to be with them, and he was an early adopter of every electronic device to keep him in touch with his office, the markets.

Lindy declared she'd never go back. Still, he put off selling the Frankfurt apartment. Anyway, he needed a place to sleep. He was working by then for a German firm, running the risk arbitrage desk, betting the company every day. He hardly had time to think of anything else.

When Lindy found she was pregnant a second time, his intuition told him—against everything he'd been brought up to believe—to abort this misbegotten child, and he suggested it to her, then asked, then begged, then demanded. Furious, she refused, and of course had her way. For a while he could think she'd been right. No postpartum swoon this time: she was a good and attentive mother, along with help from a housekeeper and a nanny. He was more often present; things held together. If Lindy's once-ravishing beauty had been wrecked by the miseries that seared her (or so he thought) Molloy only let himself notice occasionally. Maybe not the best of husbands, but he tried.

Things held together long enough for his children to reach school age, and then slowly dissolved. The private rehab clinics, blindingly expensive and luxuriantly bucolic, Connecticut, Massachusetts, Long Island, were, he discovered, communications nodes. Clients emerged knowing new connections, new suppliers, new combos of drugs. The second time Lindy was hospitalized for an overdose, he took the children back to Germany with him and put them in an elite boarding school at Überlingen near the Bodensee where he could see them regularly; Christmas and summer holidays the three of them, occasionally even the four of them, together. Struggling to keep it all whole, he told himself he was being stress-tested to the max, as they said in his business, and surviving. He stubbornly refused to notice the wreckage of his own life until Jürgen was murdered, Lindy died, and he had no choice. Then he quarreled with almost everyone, fell out and in and out with his nearly grown children, felt himself a hundred years old.

He wondered later why he hadn't put more effort into finding a U.S. job. By then he had a reputation. A bad bear market, but still. Or why didn't he do what he took up after Jürgen died, after Lindy died? He began consulting independently, fully licensed to trade in the U.S. and in Germany, slipped back and forth between the two continents on his own timetable, tended his investments, investments for a few clients, which evolved into an investment company, a fortune built on the strange and volatile connections among options, stocks, and interest rates. The answers to why, if understandable, saddened him on behalf of the eager and hopeful young man he'd once been.

When he emerged from that period of self-scrutiny, he understood more about himself; could even extend compassion to the young man who'd once made such self-wounding, nearly mortal, blunders, and such Herculean efforts to fix them. Blunders and remedies, all as gratuitous as works of art.

For above all, he understood that he'd attempted two major works of art himself. One was his fortune—not negligible, as he'd told Nola—and one was his life. Maybe the fortune had been a more successful work than the life, but then it was easier. Not in the sense that building it had been easier, though that was true; but anyone could see it, get it, at some level or other. The life, however, was not negligible either. The life had been shaped, stroke by struggling stroke, and when false moves had been made, he'd eventually seen them, patiently backed up, overpainted. The life as a work of art was complex, full of apparent contradictions, apparent unresolved tensions, hidden meanings, expressed in a near-forgotten symbolic language, but on the whole his masterpiece. For better or worse.

In the long, still, Saturday and Sunday afternoons in provincial cities all over Europe and Asia Minor, he'd begun the education that a third-rate college couldn't give him, reading, studying. Music, he began to discover, captured his feeling for the numbers that had made him rich. Number patterns he'd watched so obsessively had movement, antecedent and consequent; they appeared in motives and phrases, with foot and phrase rhythms. He realized that he responded to movements within phrases and movements of phrases with respect to each other; he saw dissonance and waited for consonance; he saw the equivalent of chord progressions and the relationship between cadences. Sometimes the markets were polyphonous; sometimes not; sometimes multiple markets (bonds, equities, commodities) produced what musicians called color; certainly each had its own style.

In Frankfurt he'd had access to the great social circuit of Germanic music—Frankfurt itself, of course, flush with money for all the arts in those years; then Berlin to Bayreuth, Munich to Salzburg and Vienna: the gala openings, the parties on lawns, terraces, beneath baroque ballroom chandeliers. The cults directors and artists formed he observed with amusement, but also with distaste. What was important in the music transcended all that.

One morning in Frankfurt, Molloy opened his newspaper to see himself in white tie, celebrating and celebrated at an opera gala the night previous. He never let it happen again. At the time, radical terrorists were the great threat, but he knew that when they went out of fashion, kidnappers and other perpetual extortionists would still scan the social and business pages. Later he simply cherished his privacy, which was why it was so easy to say no to any involvement in politics.

He sought museums too, not just art, but the other kinds, historical, archaeological, where he was thrilled to discover the centrality of trade to human history. How had he learned to be slightly ashamed of trade? Trade carried things, yes, but more important, trade carried ideas from one part of the planet to another, was the occult and unappreciated lifeblood of civilization—only look at places that hadn't enjoyed its benefits. No, he argued with himself: trade was necessary, but something more was needed too to ensure that an idea traveled, took root, transformed a culture.

So he mused on these long weekends, these evenings alone, forming and re-forming questions, examining the world's central trading cities, the ones that thrived, the ones that crumbled into dust, trying to tease out the principles involved.

Over those continuing dinners with the princelings, at those hunting lodges with the counts and barons, he came to realize that he'd cultivated himself in the European grand manner. He could more than hold his own. It diverted and pleased him how far he'd traveled from a desperate boyhood in a squalid and dying little steel town on the Monongahela River.

He longed, he still longs, and he understands this very well, to present this *chef d'oeuvre*, this self, however imperfect, to somebody with the intelligence, the experience, and the sensitivity to appreciate it. A connoisseur. That's egotism, but that's a fact.

Heeding his intuition once more, he's come to Santa Fe, the last place in the United States where Europe (and what preceded Europe, the ancient history of the world) is still apparent. He's wanted a fresh start with a woman he'd seen in a newspaper. Or her equivalent. He's wanted a woman at peace with herself, a woman with no particular need of him, but who'd simply like him, or maybe, though he'd hardly dared hope for this, love him, not knowing or caring why; just as he loves the right painting the moment he sees it. Presenting himself to her, she'd know at once, explanations unnecessary. Then would surely follow peace, come joy again.

But his intuition, once so foolproof, has finally failed him. It still works in the markets; he's making more money than ever, with another fortune socked away securely in the safest and most sluggish investments, the grownup equivalent of a postal savings account, for the inevitable rainy day. His children are provided for. He can think about starting a foundation, what it might accomplish.

But with the woman his intuition has failed him. The words came out aloud for the first time with Nola. *I've done it wrong every time. I can't trust myself ever to do it right.*

No. As he reflects upon it, his intuition has been better than he could've hoped; commonalities between them exist he hadn't dreamed of. What years they might've had together.

He's been clumsy, yes; decades of cultivation had fissured comically under the strain of his eagerness, how he longed for what she seems to be. But Judith has been stiff-necked; ungenerously unforgiving. Sentimental. It's too late in his life for tragedy, but not for disappointment. Not his intuition but her courage, their courage, has failed them both. What she told him in the car the night Zozobra was burned came as no surprise. It's just come too late.

Information Contagion

Meanwhile, he's mistrusted his intuition and listened to reason. Every wealthy man he knows presses the competitive edge his money gives him, and so he's gone through Santa Fe's eligible women systematically. That wasn't all. He's been an agent, gathering information, moving from cluster to cluster, learning about Santa Fe, storing it for future use.

But arm candy, frozen desserts, the one-night beauty and ego prop, have in fact embarrassed him: to his mind, the real message of these is just the opposite from what they're supposed to convey. Dollies, longer-term trophies, are even worse, and much harder to dispose of. Dollies are not only vacuous, but insist on toys: yachts, planes, summer places, skiing where it's social instead of challenging; insist on other baubles he has no interest in. The cynicism of the transaction depresses him, only reminds him of how much he longs for something more profound.

That longing had first swept over him one winter's dawn in New York. He'd finished an all-nighter, was getting ready for bed, when the rising winter sun was caught by the windows of a building on the New Jersey side of the river. It illuminated a wall in his room, filtered magically through the bare elms across the drive. He stopped to gaze, thought he'd never seen anything more beautiful, the graceful shadow fingers swaying and overlaying each other. At that moment, he understood how much he needed to tell another soul about it; wake her, pull her out of bed to gasp too, for he'd gasped in joy, then been desolate.

He'd slowly freed himself.

First, his firm. Inculcated with the *Rheinische* business model, which held that a firm was not just *for* the stockholders but *of* the community, with multiple obligations, he'd consulted with all the major stakeholders, and finally permitted his personal interests to be bought out for serious money. He'd overseen the unknotting of limited and general partnerships from investment groups and holding companies, from trusts and other legal entities bearing his name. His several hundred former employees gave him a jolly farewell dinner, and he fled. Though he can still watch from afar while an apparition called J. B. Molloy & Co. materializes occasionally in Wall Street mergers, conjuring whatever power yet remains to it, he's been happy to start over with a brotherhood that can collect around an ordinary kitchen table. Trading is now amusement, not obsession; arm wrestling, not global warfare.

The Gulfstream went with the firm, and he isn't sorry, knowing that he doesn't ever want to go anywhere again except for occasional pleasure, which can always be arranged.

Sailing, with all its fussy details, has always irked him: no boat to dispose of. He counts it in Santa Fe's further favor that you can fly-fish some two hundred days a year.

He still loves to drive himself, at least in Santa Fe, so he's kept his cars. Including the Lambo—oh well, the Lambo. No use even trying to explain the Lambo.

He's arrived in Santa Fe with a goal, because that's his nature, but the goal has proved unattainable. At a low point, at a moment of great fatigue, of utter disappointment in himself, in life, in the future, a moment when he thought he might literally die before having a genuine connection with another human being, a woman—more than a dolly, an überdolly—has presented herself to him. She's not vacuous, having a cause to champion; she's uninterested in toys, lacking the imagination for them. So, why not? He isn't getting any younger, and the nights aren't getting any shorter.

For a while the überdolly enchants him, though he concedes that most of that enchantment is hormonal. Then she begins to annoy him. Finally, inevitably, bores him. Surely he bores her. Let him tell Inéz that the Irish, or the Arabs, or trade routes, had saved civilization, and she wouldn't know what the hell he was talking about. "So *serious*, Molloy," she'll say dismissively, when he talks about anything but sports, or her own monomania, the pitiful situation of battered women. He's never laid a hand on a woman himself except in affection, doesn't understand a man who could, but even less does he understand women who endure it, no matter how often he's informed that it's beyond their power to help themselves. She has further answers, but he doesn't understand those either.

He's argued with Inéz at first, asked about the general principles behind rescuing battered women. She responds with anecdotes, examples, not just the women who are thrashed on a drunken Saturday night, but the women who come home from a one-day stay in the maternity ward, only to be raped by partners who feel entitled to sex no matter what tissues have just been ruptured by childbirth; the women who are dying of unspeakable diseases, their organs bleeding raw, but whose mates pound away at them anyway, sobbing no deterrent, maybe a turn-on. "We know about these because they still have the energy to find us. Most we never know about. Ideas? What kind of ideas would you like, Molloy? That most men are shits? Does that work for you? Don't think no one *you* know lives like that. Our clients come to the shelter from all over the city. All over."

He backs off. He's making malicious comparisons, first in his mind and then aloud. Ragging her. The überdolly might not be the brightest light in the world, but he doesn't like himself as bully. He mocks himself. The woman he can buy fancy underwear for doesn't move him; the woman he'd like to buy it for buys her own, thanks.

The long period of self-scrutiny has accustomed him to being honest with himself. Is the major reason he's invited Stephen to Santa Fe, he asks himself with caustic candor, to provide some relief, some stimulation at the dinner table? In that rigorous Bodensee boarding school, Stephen learned to read and talk, could riposte bilingual jokes with trilingual ones, followed the German elections. Alone at the table, Molloy might read, but he can't do that to Inéz. So he simply evades her with what he tells her are business dinners, mostly with Madame Genius. Who can also riposte bilingual jokes, follows the German elections—and, sweet Jesus, uses *ab initio* conversationally. A term of her trade, he hopes.

Or has he called Stephen to take Inéz off his hands effortlessly?

Or all of the above?

He and his son haven't actually seen each other since Thanksgiving, the last one at the New York place—an idiosyncratic dwelling compared to the Fairfield or Westchester County places his colleagues prefer. It isn't even on Park or Fifth or Sutton Place but on Riverside Drive, because, among other things, the Hudson reminds Molloy of European rivers, the Main, the Rhine. In the old days he liked running in Riverside Park, beside him the German shepherd that looked like a family pet—that was—but could gash out a man's throat on command. It wasn't casual muggers Molloy needed to worry about.

Thanksgiving dinner hadn't been planned. It happened that the three of them were in town simultaneously, Molloy to supervise some packing before he went to Santa Fe, Stephen stopping over on the way to a vacation in Mexico, Nikki in town to see shows, shop.

They'd brought friends, and Molloy was gratified to hear the racket of young people downstairs, rock, hip-hop, laughter, sweet argumentative life. When he proposed they all cook Thanksgiving dinner together, they hadn't laughed at him. They'd got into it with zest, braving the lines at Citarella's, at Fairway and Zabar's. He'd called Char (neither husband nor sister-in-law alive now) at her Florida condo and had her coach him through cooking the turkey, her giggling, consulting with her cronies; it had turned out great.

"What you did for your kids, they'll never know how much they owe you. Mom and dad both to them. You're a good man, Jackie." Since her move to Florida, Char's accent had gone from Mon Valley to decided Lawn Guyland.

"Well," he said dubiously. "No more than you, Char."

"I had your uncle Jack alongside. You had nobody else. You and me, we're survivors, Jackie."

"Yeah, Char. That we are."

After dinner, everyone sated, the talk got interesting. How pessimistic his children and their friends were. No hope of ever having what their parents had, not their parents' choices, nor their material goods ("Unless we inherit them, and papa, we wish you a long life," Stephen said, a shade piously to Molloy's ears).

He heard how his generation had been the last to have real freedom: free love, disease-free sex, inventing new music, clean drugs, jobs by the bunch to choose from. Things hadn't looked all that easy when he was younger, trying desperately to evade getting his ass fried in Vietnam, while these days dot-com billionaires under thirty ruled, but he shut up, listened.

If his generation went to the streets for revolution, they'd failed. The world didn't get better, but they got old and made money—lots of it—and stubbornly blocked the routes young people might take. Competition now was a death struggle because resources were so scarce, with so many fighting over them.

Still, he kept quiet. He heard how his generation had divorced as fecklessly as they'd fucked; it was all self-fulfillment, follow your bliss, while the kids paid the price. Blended families, ex-husbands, new wives, half-sibs young enough to be your own babies; the whole rotten thing. People weren't disposable, and that's something his generation never got.

Molloy waited to hear one of his children defend him, at least explain a dad who kept the family together as best he knew how; that the missing mother was dead and not divorced. Neither of them spoke up. It hurt. Years ago, he'd get on a Friday afternoon plane in Frankfurt, arrive in New York still Friday afternoon, go straight home, crawl into bed in just his pajama bottoms, Nikki lodged on his chest under his chin, Stevie in his pit. "You're a tranquilizer for them," said his mother-in-law (the nanny nodding vigorously), "no matter how much they fuss during the week, when you come home, it's snooze and laugh all weekend." Then dragged his ass out for a Sunday night flight so he could go straight to work the next morning in Frankfurt. It seemed to go on for decades, but it couldn't have been more than a few years, all of them breathing each other in, at peace in sweet comfort. Wasn't this lodged somewhere in their primate brains, bonding them all together?

"What should we have done?" he asked on behalf of his fellow-geezers. His son, as deranged-looking as the young Mayakovski, shrugged. Something. Anything. You should've made the world better. Molloy had nodded. "And how will you do it?"

"Equality," Nikki's friend, Marianne, said. "A balance of power. Maybe it's not even about power at all. It's about—being partners. Supporting each other's ambitions."

Robbie, on his way to Mexico with Stephen: "A woman who doesn't need me, just wants me. She does her share, I do mine. We do the kids together."

"And you, papa? What do you want?" Nikki had asked. "I mean, aren't you like, lonely sometimes?"

He looked around this group, all of them waiting for his answer, reached over and picked at what was left of the turkey. "I want exactly what you want. Yes. Very lonely sometimes."

They hadn't believed it, he could see.

Later, he overheard Robbie: "Hey, the Jackster isn't *so* anal." Thank you, Robbie. Thank you *too*, Stephen.

Still, since Stephen's arrival, dinnertime conversation has improved considerably at the old adobe.

Overlapping Generations

On Sunday afternoons Molloy has been going out to a nearby park where, beneath the falling leaves, Latinos play their favorite game, soccer, *el fútbol.* For a few weeks he watches, then gets involved in a dispute. Gradually he's become a trusted referee, his impartiality and precision much valued. He loves these Sunday afternoons, one part nostalgia, one part just the sheer fun of being with male animals at the peak of their vigor. He's flattered to be invited out for beer afterwards, and always gently declines, being to them just some old guy in a sweatshirt who not only knows the rules, but every fouling trick there is; can chase up and down the field with them and not get in the way. One afternoon he forgets himself in the heat of the game, and altogether baffles a young Salvadoran by standing over him, upbraiding him in German.

When he comes home to tell this story to Stephen, to Inéz, he finds the house reeking unmistakably of rut.

All right. A giant hit off the clue bong, as your kids would say, Jacko. You've known; you've pondered; you've even told the ravenous Nola. Now a challenge to do something about it.

He says nothing over dinner except to tell the story of the afternoon's *fútbol.* They laugh too hard, glance knowingly at each other. On top of everything, he's being condescended to, which stings too. Inéz he's dismissed to the margins of his concern a while ago; it's Stephen he wants to know about. What kind of a man is he?

At Stephen's age, Molloy had already earned himself a whole summer's vacation in Europe, was daily screaming himself hoarse in a trading pit, about to go to Germany to live. But he doesn't need his son to be his carbon copy; isn't eager to have him in the mills, if the mills aren't what suits him. What suits him? Stephen has tried a garage band, which fizzled; got hot on computer graphics, thinking he'd be a web site designer, then lost interest; began an on-line 'zine with friends, which sputtered out; talks vaguely of opening a restaurant here in Santa Fe. Acts, in short, like a rich dilettante.

Molloy has always been circumspect about how much his children know of their means. It would do them no good to think they were rich; he's seen too many spoiled brats among his colleagues and their children. So he says no from time to time; has informed them they're comfortable, yes, but not rich, and he himself has lived without ostentation. The paintings, the most apparent sign of his wealth, are known in the family as papa's little hobby, and when his kids got to university and learned that most of papa's painters had worldwide reputations, he could tell them truthfully that he'd recognized the value of the paintings long before the artist's reputation had climbed to such heights, and you didn't see any recent stuff by that guy on the walls, did you? You did not. He didn't need to add that his collection, like his investments, was the result of a joy in being there at the start.

So Stephen is behaving like a dilettante. A fatherly failure somehow, Jacko; father-failure runs in the family. Or, maybe life's too sweet. If Stephen had grown up where the most interesting, the only, challenge was getting into a girl's pants without having to marry her, he too might have been ignited for something more. If he'd been an ambitious poor boy like his father.

Molloy knows that fraternity well. One night in Singapore, he's driven out to a fashionable suburb for dinner. He lounges on a balcony; the evening air reminding him of the Mon Valley in late August (but no worse), waiting while his host tends to drinks. Koh has installed lighting that simulates moonlight, so that forest creatures will approach fearlessly, and Molloy's been urged to wait and see what comes out of the trees.

As his eyes adjust to the demi-light he starts, automatically steps backward. The forest animals are rats. Dozens, hundreds of them, pale, nervous and huge, chattering like birds, swarming over a hillock, their backs rising and falling almost sexually, feeding on—he can't see what, doesn't want to know. The swarm seems itself a unity, living, breathing, and undulating of its own accord.

Koh is silently beside him, hands him an iced gin and tonic. "Yes," he says in his British-inflected, Chinese-colored English. "Yes. Not exactly pets. Reminders. Do you know how rats manage? They feast while you're sleeping, and they're such clever devils, they don't even disturb your sleep. You wake up and the skin on your fingertips, the ends of your toes, is gnawed down just to the point of drawing blood. But not yet bloody. They don't really like blood. You're sore, very sore. It hurts for a long time. It can get infected. Especially if you're malnourished. Now how do they manage that, the clever devils, without waking you? Can you believe this, they blow on your skin as they're chewing, fah, fah, which numbs you. At least until they're finished."

Then to Molloy's unasked question: "Because I made myself stay awake to see it."

Ambitious poor boys, he thinks, are the same the world over.

For Stephen instead, the best of European prep schools, an Ivy League education, and—nothing. Except this.

"So," Molloy says finally.

"Are you trading tonight, papa?" Stephen's try at the casual question is laughably transparent. Your career path will not include negotiator, my boy.

Molloy consults his watch. "It's only five a.m. in Frankfurt. Four in London. But as a matter of fact, no, tonight I'm not trading. I have something else to do." He leans back and observes them both, his face, as he well knows, opaque. In German he murmurs to Stephen: "It's finished here. She's leaving tonight, and you can leave with her. But I expected better from you." A pause. "You could've waited till you inherited her."

Inéz, who understands no German, might guess what's being said, but isn't certain enough to speak. She starts forward, sits back, watching warily. Does she really think he'll slug her? He stifles a smile. Stephen answers, still in German. Meets his father's eyes. Begins to tremble, but meets his father's eyes. "I owe you an apology. Please believe me, I am sorry. There's no excuse. For you she was just—but I—I think for me it's the real thing."

"Oh, I doubt that. Not the überdolly. For your sake, my son, I hope not."

Not another bad marriage, oh please. Nothing you can do about that, Jacko. He analyzes the situation rapidly, upside, downside. He's kept quiet about the trust fund that will kick in when Stephen turns twenty-five: let him think he has to hustle. Above all, let Inéz think so. But—if his son has betrayed him, and he has—he's relieved by Stephen's straightforwardness: relieved too to see that Stephen continues to tremble. Well he might. Well he fucking well might. The beginnings of the sweats showing on his son's brow: so already in his groin, his pits. See you in the men's room, Stevie.

Molloy wants to laugh; wonders what there is to laugh about. If they'd tried to deny it, or promised to go and sin no more, he knows his disgust would've been venomous. But no, he only wants to laugh. He maintains his composure. Too bad about the resort to sentimentality, *the real thing*, but Jacko, you've been known to resort there yourself from time to time.

A glance around his dining room, where he's entertained sweet, and yes, sentimental fantasies of his children and their mates, their children, sitting at the holiday table, babies bawling and needing to be changed, him the contented paterfamilias. He's longed to do vacations European-style, three generations gathered in the formal hotel dining room, little boys wearing their first neckties, little girls in patent leather shoes. He hasn't counted on Inéz being there in any capacity whatsoever.

Stephen speaks to Inéz in English. "My father would like us to leave his house. He's right. We should have left—sooner." He gets up uncertainly, the chair scraping across the terra cotta glazed tiles harsh as a factory whistle.

Out of her chair, Inéz flings herself on Molloy, wailing. "What are you saying? I've loved you so. You've left me so lonely. Forgive me! Only give me a chance, my man!"

"Oh, Christ." Molloy thrusts her from him roughly. What rises in him informs him suddenly why men hit women. In German to a shocked Stephen: "Everything clear?"

Stephen is no longer trembling but shaking. Takes Inéz, who's weeping loudly, by the hand. "She doesn't know what she's saying."

"She knows perfectly well what she's saying," Molloy retorts. The urge to laugh gone, Molloy feels his temper rise, which he'd wanted to avoid. Lets his voice rise instead, now in English: "Both out, right now. And for Christ's sake, Stephen, bag it or jag it—you don't know the half of where this woman's been. She ain't worth dying for. Oh, and ask her where her kids are. She makes your own mother look like the patron saint of motherhood." That last he hasn't meant to say.

He doesn't stir from the table as he hears them putting their belongings together. And yes, Stephen stopping in the can. He doesn't stir as he hears things moving into the bed of the pickup, a door slam.

His son returns, stops, unsure what to say. "Papa." A half-dozen bitter replies spring to Molloy's tongue (how your children can provoke you!) but he swallows them. He has, when all's said and done, set this up. Maybe not with forethought, but still. He doesn't like to think of himself as a manipulative old bastard. He does like to think he's in control. No controlling nonlinear systems, Jacko. Learning experiences all over the map these last few months.

"Papa," Stephen begins again. "We didn't mean for this to happen. We certainly didn't mean to—deceive you. I think I love her very much. But I—also love you, Papa." The voice steady, that young face, his own genes staring back at him; but softer, more earnest than ever he'd been, which was earnest enough. Black Irish like you, Jackie.

Molloy stands, a chair falling backward, and moves toward his son, is saddened to see Stephen back away from him, frightened. He shakes his head, holds out his arms imploringly. He longs to hug his son to him, remembers, inevitably, the little creature he'd once held in his arms, to whom he'd made wordless promises. Tears sting behind his eyes. He says nothing. Reconsiders. "I love you, Stephen. Loved you from the moment I first held you. Always will." Despite effort, his voice breaks. Stephen's head drops. For a horrible instant Molloy wonders if he's forcing his son into something the boy doesn't want; can't handle. No, he's his own man by now—or never. Molloy hopes miserably for the best. "Call me when you're settled."

"Papa!" A rebuke, an embarrassment. An implicit query: am I forgiven?

Not yet. Don't expect miracles.

"For me, Stevie. Call me—for me." This from the place all honesty dwells in his soul. He feels aged and chilled; wants to warm himself. And call me for you, when you're fed up to the teeth with nothing but the plight of battered women and you've heard the dark lady story so often you gag on it.

His son steps back, scrutinizes his father's face. "Are you okay?" Molloy nods, okay. Thanks for having the balls to ask. "Inéz is—she thinks you're going to—" he's embarrassed "—retaliate. I told her you weren't that kind of guy."

"What made you think that?" The bitch has something to worry about comes to his tongue, but he understands how fragile it is between him and his son. He shrugs ambiguously.

Stephen walks out, stops, comes back a final time. "You should know—" This is costing him, Molloy sees. "You should know that you're a tough act to follow."

"Yeah? Would that be in bed or in life?"

Stephen swears, spins on his foot and slams the door after him.

Dumbass Jack-shit, you didn't need to pile it on. The rise and fall and rise yet again of Mackie Messer.

He slumps on a couch. He's relieved that his son has acquitted himself with reasonable grace, no woman-did-tempt-me-and-I-did-eat whine, the perfect gentleman, at least for a man who's been fooling around with his father's girlfriend. For some strange reason he thinks of calling Nikki, who'd greet him coldly, even sarcastically. My God, your children! Great springs of love are theirs to summon and saturate themselves with if only they would. If only—if only they didn't all rub each other the wrong way these days. No, he's too raw to listen to Nikki tonight.

He stands now at the living room fireplace, and though there's no fire, stares contemplatively into it for a long while, reckoning his own part in his children's comings and goings. Long ago he'd seen how he'd underestimated their difficulties: bad enough a crazy mother: worse, to be uprooted and pushed into a boarding school where everything was alien. When he left at the end of a weekend visit, Nikki's sobbing crushed his heart; Stephen turned his back in rage. Just as he did this very night. At the time, Molloy hadn't known what else to do. When they got over it, became polyglot bi-continental citizens, politely voiced their preference to ski with their friends at Gstadd or Vail instead of skiing with dear old dad wherever, he congratulated himself. But somehow they've all avoided talking about it, about Lindy, her illness, her addictions, her death, the aftermath. What is mowed, cut down. Yo, Madame Genius. You've got me doing it. They blamed him, he knew. He'd been too proud to defend himself.

How have I failed? Let me count the ways. As husband, as father, as lover. Just a little dwarf who piled up the Rheingold, supposed to make you lord of the world, and you aren't even lord of your own soul. (But, Ross had once objected dryly, there are two parts to that: he grabbed the ring *and* he had to forswear love. You aren't ready to forswear love. Greedy Jacko.)

Okay, he'll—what? Make friends again with each of them, if only he can. Shut his eyes to the awfulness of Nikki's so-called art; shut his eyes to—well, Stephen might have been more sinned against than sinning, though it's time that kid got a grip and a life. The pater impulse rises up, irrepressible. Stifle it, Jacko. He simply must. If he can mask himself for clients, he can mask himself for his children. And behind the mask? Nothing but nothing.

Now he moves along, the house's silence sad and oppressive. He punches the sound system as he walks by, and suddenly Wagner (who else?) is sweeping him through the rooms, chromatic fevers, recklessness, delirium. Wagner delirious, not him. He doesn't have the energy. He walks slowly, deliberately humiliating himself with his failed dreams, dreams he'd had when he acquired the place. Stephen's room in disarray, an open drawer, a single athletic shoe on the floor. The adjacent bathroom still redolent of fear made physical. Further along the hall, a room for Nikki, who has yet to deign to visit.

But who knows? Eventually the life he's composed, put together, his *chef d'oeuvre*, might be interesting to his children at least. Well, almost as interesting to them as his money.

A guest room, where Inéz had been banished after just a few nights of sharing his own room, on the grounds that he was sleeping badly (which he was), needed to be up and roaming sometimes, lights on, playing music, didn't want to disturb her. Because really it wasn't the überdolly he wanted sleeping beside him. In this room she waited like a concubine, first for him, then for his son.

Finally a large room, sunny in the daylight, that gives out onto an inviting flower-filled patio, beyond that just below, the city of Santa Fe, near enough to see people coming and going. Not the mountain view she's used to, but beautiful in a different way. The walls bare, waiting for her to choose whatever pictures she wanted, bring her own. That skeleton she loved. He's imagined this her study, even her bedroom if she wished that kind of separation, part of their wing, him part of her life. Under his wing. Well, *arschloch*. As she hadn't said but might've, she had no need of that hypothesis. No need of him either: she was said to carry a lipstick-sized vibrator in her purse for emergencies. God, who told him that?

Nola's intelligent face shadowed in the cave, querying. Molloy? What is it you want? A lover? Or an admiring audience? A partner? Or merely a witness? A certain kind of woman might not find this tempting, Jacko; might possibly even object; having a few summits she herself has struggled to the top of, a few painfully-won laurels of her own to exhibit, thank you very much.

So a third task ahead, and this one the hardest of all.

He punches the sound system back into silence. Utterly exhausted, in the bathroom mirror a battered, nubbled face, sunken eyes half-closed with fatigue, the chin in perpetual shadow. No one to complain: he goes to bed unshaved for the first time in months.

Deep and Beautiful Laws

Autumn had made Santa Fe, the royal city, *tierra santa*, both royal and sacred another way. Along the roads, across the rolling stretches of high desert, on the banks of the dry arroyos and the islands in between them, up against the tea-colored walls, the chamisa, a subdued gray-green the rest of the year, had blossomed with brilliant gold, and the wild asters, otherwise unnoticed, burst out with luxurious purple. The lambent blue sky, the golden cottonwoods, the sunset crimsons of the Sangres, all these resplendent colors commanded the attention of even the most distracted mind, and the citizens of Santa Fe mutely thanked the year's cycle for such an offering.

Judith had entered Jill's workroom with that same gratitude in her heart, but melancholy too from the brevity of all this glory. As she stripped she nodded to two small smooth stones on a table, one incised with a spiral, one with a human hand. Another kind of thanksgiving for what transcended even the world's cycles.

Naked now, she lay on the massage table under the quilt, stared up at the muted Russian olive ceiling, the old-fashioned light fixture with its accidental art deco spirals, and felt the kindly warmth of a heating pad beneath her back.

When Jill entered the room, she did what Judith always thought of as diagnostics: asked how she was generally, queried earlier symptoms ("Still clenching your jaw when you sleep? Less? Good.") then moved to the end of the table to hold Judith's bare feet, receive whatever messages they gave her. Above the quilt she ran her hand lightly up the front of Judith's legs, one at a time, felt the hipbones for the paths of energy, their alignment. Meanwhile the two women laughed about local things: a restaurant owner they both knew, the antics at city council.

But gradually talk stopped. Jill seemed transformed into a kind of priestess, Judith a seeker, both of them silenced before powers they could not name, did not wholly understand.

It was a pleasant state for Judith, alert yet detached, hearing the music, Mozart today, the incense, the scent of the rubbing oils in her nose, turning her head from time to time to gaze out at the soothing pale gray-green Russian olive tree.

Jill, slight and wiry, who lived, Judith imagined, on a diet composed of seaweed and wheatgrass, bent over her intently. "During the eclipse last week, I had an out-of-body experience. I've brought back something different for the work."

Out-of-body experience. Judith's skepticism stirred. An eclipse. The moon taking precedence over the sun. Something in that, but it eluded her. Jill spoke softly about the ability of one person to send, to place, their own electromagnetic field into another. Physics or only metaphorical, Judith picked up something different in Jill's touch—it was stronger, deeper, more concentrated.

As the intensity grew, Judith's very grounded, practical side asserted itself. "No short-circuit in the heating pad?" Jill's eyes met hers, laughing, no.

So she let herself feel this electrical agitation, energy, whatever it was, flowing out from her lower spine, her sacrum (the same root as sacred, she'd once told Jill, the sacrificial bone) her solar plexus, stronger and stronger. It glided upward from her center, neither pleasure nor pain, but sheer, flavorless intensity. Suddenly it filled her chest. Distinctly not pain, distinctly not pleasure either, but perhaps the most sustained sensation she'd ever known. An orgasm would eventually have ebbed; pain, and she would have fainted, but it was neither. Some part of her was wary, fearful; mostly she yielded over to it.

Faces she'd known throughout her life came in a slow (maybe swift) montage: not people she was close to, but acquaintances, former office-mates, fellow committee members, people who'd come to work around the house. A vast wave of sympathy swept over her, empathy, compassion. How hard it was just to be human on this planet, get through the day, doing the best you could, trying to learn your lessons, hoping to avoid pain, which, in the end, was your legacy. The human condition seemed so unbearably sad, so hopeless; even the lucky ones suffered. Great tears filled her eyes.

Time stopped.

The parade of people continued, joined now by unknown faces, old and young, every color and shape. She ached for them all, their lot on earth, the difficulty of lessons they must learn, the inevitability of their grief. Her chest seemed alive with power that might split her open, (but deeply benign, she knew that) neither pleasure nor pain, but transparent intensity. As it subsided, she mourned it like a dissolving dream.

"From the moon?" she murmured stupidly. Jill shrugged. Maybe.

She was depleted. But at peace, reconciled. Struggle ended in failure, and still you must struggle. Love was evanescent, pained as often as it magnified. Still you must love. Jill bent over her, gently kissed her temple, still wet. "That was your heart chakra, just busting open. Enlightened ones feel that compassion all the time."

Home, a solitary dinner to reflect. How far away she was from being able to bear that degree of spiritual enlightenment, impersonal yet profound. Another lifetime. A different woman. Halfway through the night she woke, the right side of her body at ease, the left side in agony, as if she'd suffered physical blows, was having a heart attack. An image of the sacred mountain came to her, the distant indigo peak supine under a sky that it seemed to illuminate. She could see it every day from her study window, far across the Rio Grande Valley, curiously bisected half the year with one dazzling snowy face and one brooding dark face, natural motley, until the summer suns finally melted away the ice and made the mountain monochrome again. Now in the darkest part of the dark night she wept for the people she loved intimately, here and no longer here, saw their faces in painful detail, longed to hold them once more.

Benito. A stiff little e-mail from him a few weeks ago. He was taking a teaching post for a year in Arizona; he'd leased his house, she shouldn't be surprised to see a strange car parked there. He wished her the best. And concluded:

I'm going because I can no longer bear my own dreams.

Ron. Whose sheltering arms she'd fled to, needed again and again; her own history lodged in Ron's neurons, his in hers. They dreamed about each other, lived out the missing part of each other's lives.

Sophie. Who'd left everything to her, savings, stocks, insurance, house, a legacy born of bitterly disappointed dreams.

Molloy. Who'd virtually disappeared from New Business, taken up, it was said, with venture capitalists, bringing out an IPO for the firm, involved with some other project too. Papers had come to her for options that she'd signed numbly, unseeingly. She didn't know if he dreamed at all.

Finally, she wept for herself and the dreams she'd put aside, those she'd failed. The dreams that had failed her. Then she slept.

Forever Expanding into the Adjacent Possible

In honor of the formal inauguration of the J. B. Molloy Foundation, a party would be held at Sol y Sombra, a fine old estate southeast of town on the Old Santa Fe Trail. Sol y Sombra had once been a rich family's toy, had even been Georgia O'Keeffe's home when she was too frail to remain in Abiquiú, but in the last decade, it had been reborn as a center for study and experiment under the care of its wealthy and visionary new owners. Some twenty acres of Sol y Sombra been reclaimed from the desert, healed, restored to vitality, thousands of plants lovingly placed and already producing food, conserving water, sheltering wildlife. It served as a conference center, offering its lessons to visitors from all over the world.

As the guests arrived this mid-November evening, they were greeted and guided to parking by men and women from the Huichol tribe of southern Mexico, arrayed in their festival wear, extravagantly lacy white cotton skirts or trousers, all elaborately embroidered. Huichol came up regularly from Mexico to Sol y Sombra: in return for learning about land restoration, they offered their spiritual wisdom to the studies of community and the conservation of indigenous cultures, another part of Sol y Sombra's mission.

In the lodge, a low pueblo-style building, food had been laid out, wine was being poured near the central fountain, and a guitarist played lovely Andalusian airs. The warm twilight, last gift of the dying autumn, called guests outdoors one last time to enjoy the superb gardens, the rising moon, like a tusk to be found in a Hong Kong curio shop, carved layers of busy miniature activity, cold and inaccessible.

A phone call had delayed Judith, and parking was tight, making her later yet. At the Lodge the crowd seemed impenetrable, though these were people she worked with every day, their husbands and wives, their friends. The distance was in her own head she knew, but the feeling was acute: outsider, alone, and always would be.

A few conversations where she was received politely, even warmly, but her sense of separation from all this would not dissipate. She waved to Maya, had a brief conversation with Nola, now gaunt with wear and worry, shrinking, it seemed, behind her giant spectacles, and searched without success for Ron and Gabe. She wanted to ask them about the mega-bookstore that was said to be opening downtown—how would they deal with that? Eventually she gave up and wandered over the grass to the wetlands, four terraced ponds that began as black sewage, collecting all Sol y Sombra's human and animal wastes, and converted them, pond by pond, into clear, life-giving water. Behind her came the murmur of the party, gentle and happy.

The moon was still on the rise. She pulled her shawl over her shoulders, wondered if she could wait long enough to see it reflected in the blackest pond.

How long she stood there she didn't know.

"Praise the moon," said a voice behind her. "A goddess you can look straight in the eye without being blinded." Then: "You missed my brilliant speech."

The satyr emerging from the woods, intent on mischief. She didn't turn. "Congrats. I know you'll do great things with this foundation." She meant it, but even in her own ears it sounded pro forma. "All this and the IPO too. High-energy guy."

"Worse, you missed Paul's ludicrously flattering introduction. You'll never know what he said unless you call him, because modesty forbids. But it would've been nice to think you'd heard it. It would have been a small fix to the problem of hardly knowing me."

"Don't tease, Molloy. Please."

"Judith?"

"Sorry. A phone call before I came here. May I confide, you'll pretend I didn't? I've been offered a post at the Max Planck Institute's new headquarters in Munich. It's tempting. Very."

She sensed him stepping aside, behind her, concealing himself completely. He seemed to consider before he spoke. "Santa Fe, this *tierra santa*, would miss you." He'd learned to say the city's name the way the locals said it, a Spanish *a*, a real *t*, not a *d*. Sahn-ta Fe.

"I'd miss Santa Fe. Home now in so many ways. But bits and pieces of it keep crumbling. A new place, a new space, might be just the thing. Job offers won't come my way forever—at my age."

"A job offer." He knew of this particular installation, recalled the bond offering from the Bavarian government to fund its construction. An administrative office. In effect, she'd give up research, the den of the metaphysician no pretty place to labor.

"Has it got so difficult?"

For a long time she didn't answer. "I am so—empty. So tired."

Not yet, he thought. Exhausted, yes; desperate for a long restorative holiday, overdue to be pampered, cosseted, indulged; but no, not yet ready to quit. The ordinary rhythms of extraordinary lives. He could have said all this, but didn't. Instead he teased. "All your friends getting e-mail: send green chile stew by the next FedEx." He stepped close, slipped his arms around her waist. They'd once stood this way at El Bosque, keeping each other warm. "You think Germany has twelve-step programs for capsicum?"

She shrugged, felt his arms tighten slightly against any getaway. "Last time I was at the *Viktualienmarkt* in Munich, I saw a stand selling chiles. Red chiles, from Hungary, but can green be far behind? There was even a bar called Santa Fe up behind the Gasteig." She put her hands on his at her waist, felt their texture, the hands of Esau. Remembered touching his forearm once in her garden, the potency of that moment. Hair like that all over his body. A satyr, but the most civilized of men. "Does that pelt keep you slightly warmer than the rest of us?"

"I don't know," he said lightly. "I've never been the rest of us." Then, almost irrelevantly: "I think—I think this is one of my favorite places in all of Santa Fe. What Charles and Beth have done here—the regeneration of the desert. It gives you hope."

"Tall timbers, high grasslands until us. Sheep and goats finished off what logging hadn't. These poor runty *piñon* are what's left. Desert. The absence of. From the Latin, *desetere*, to forsake." She stopped. "Sophie's dead, you know that."

"I heard. I'm sorry. Sorry I never knew her." He could have meant it.

"We quarreled before she died. That's really what was eating me the night of Zozobra. It was so stupid. Correction: I was so stupid. I should've just pushed right back into her life. We made it up; I was there the night she died, all the way to the end. But we wasted a lot of time."

"Ah," he said. "Can I take it you no longer think the boundary between living and non-living is meaningless?"

She was weak with mortification. All this time, he'd been waiting for her to catch up. Almost to herself: "Why are we here?"

Behind her, he warmed her in what was quickly becoming the desert nighttime chill, sharpened now with the coming winter. Pulled her closer. She struggled gently, laughing a bit. "We're professional colleagues now, Molloy. You mustn't do that."

"Will you litigate?" He dropped his head to her shoulder, an intimacy; his scent, musky and troubling. Something new.

"You grew the beard. Let me see." But he held her tight, refused to let her turn. "You win. We'll watch the moon." She leaned against him, grateful not only for the warmth, but for his strength. The web, she said silently. The web, he agreed. Who took part? she asked. Who didn't? he replied.

Aloud, she said, "Our moon was such a contingent event. It could've happened otherwise. But it didn't. Remember asking me once what life is?"

"Of course I remember. I even remember what you said. More or less. And Judith, my darling Amazon." My beloved goddess. "Shut the fuck up."

Water trickled over the rocks to the dark ponds below. The moon's reflection was magical, the ponds an ethereal silver that everywhere humans had ever lived had caused poets to commit poetry.

You, Inanna,
Foremost in Heaven and Earth
Lady riding a beast,
You rained fire on the heads of men.

"Don't go to Germany, dear lady," he murmured. "Stay here where you belong. I don't know why we're here, but we are. Don't forsake Santa Fe." In German he added: "We could always visit Munich together, be there for Christmas. We'd check in at the Fier Jahreszeiten, then go off to the Hax'nbauer, eat würst and beer and red cabbage till it came out of our ears. Stand awestruck in front of the Dürers at the Alte Pinakotek. I'd love you to see that virtuoso self-portrait with me, a thirty-year-old genius at the top of his form, a show-off kid. You could tell me what you were like at thirty. I'd tell you about me. We've never really told our stories to anyone, you and I, have we?" Her eyes began to fill. The story she never told Sophie. She hardly told herself. Maybe now. At last. He's still murmuring. "Come with me to Düsseldorf where the art auctions are great fun, *viel Spass*. We'll see the new Berlin. *Die Fledermaus* on New Year's Eve. I'm thinking of a grand tour of the European petroglyphs, Scandinavia to Anatolia. Maybe beyond. You need a rest, that's all."

"An agreeable fantasy." Agreeable. We offer each other grace. According to our pleasure. She was on the precipice, the edge of chaos, drew back fearfully. Behind her, he held her fast. This isn't going to be easy, she warned him silently. It's never been easy, she heard him reply.

Against her second-lowest chakra she felt a distinct warmth, spreading out from the end of her spine to warm all of her pelvis, creeping up and out, life-giving, regenerating. Felt it mix with her own desire.

"Scorpio rising," Molloy said. "My apologies."

"Never apologize for that," she said. "Never." He released her so that she could turn to kiss him. Such life in that soft mouth and tongue, hidden in its new hairy nest. She pulled away for a moment, felt her own tears, laughed in delight, as if she'd received an unexpected gift. The obsidian eyes laughing back at her now. *Molloy, my love.* They stood together drawing in each other's breath, uttering little cries, each other's name, that neither of them heard. She led him then from the top pond, dark and mysterious, down the switchback path among bulrushes and cattails, the frogs singing to each other, past the second, the third, and finally to the last pond in the terraced chain, holding water clear as diamonds, clean enough to scoop up and drink.

The Huichol night watchman, passing by later, silent as a shadow, saw that a couple had strayed from the party, and lay content in each other's arms, half-naked under the moon. He permitted himself the thought that some deities had chosen to emerge onto the earth and make love on this lovely night. In his own tongue, a gift, he believed, from heaven, he blessed them in his heart before he moved on.

Acknowledgements

Sitting down to have a conversation with a writer is like leaving your jewelry out on the windowsill: she's a jackdaw, and eventually you'll find your own words woven into her nest, no longer quite recognizable as yours. For such rich conversations, I owe thanks to the following: Dieter Baumeister, Harold Cohen, Doyne Farmer, Jill Fineberg, Shannon Gilligan, Joe Griego, George Gumerman, Stuart Kauffman, Chris Langton, Benito Martinez, the late Robert K. Merton, Cindy Lou Myers, Donna Odierna, Maxine Rockoff, Enrique Sanabria, Celeste Winterland, and a handful of traders in currencies and commodities who prefer anonymity, but who led me to their trading rooms and showed me how it was done. Judith Greenwood's research in the limits to science is borrowed from a period of research pursued by my husband, Joseph Traub, who also corrected my mathematics when necessary. Joe is always there for me in more ways than I can gratefully begin to name.

Since it's my woven nest, none of them is responsible for my errors or emphases. *Abrazos y gracias.*

Study Guide to *The Edge of Chaos*

1. Each of the principal characters in this novel is on a quest, or even a set of quests. What is the nature of those quests, and how successful is each character in attaining his or her goal?

2. Though the main characters live very much at the end of the twentieth century, they often call on ancient mythology to explain themselves. What are some of these myths? Do implicit, unnamed myths also animate the characters? Is Molloy right when he tells Nola that it's possible—perhaps even necessary—to reinterpret the old myths?

3. Each of the principal characters has a personal encounter with death, though the nature of each encounter is somewhat different. Explore these differences. Do similarities exist also?

4. Likewise, each of the principal characters has erotic encounters, ranging from the playful to the sordid to the search for the divine. What do you think these erotic encounters signify?

5. From its title, *The Edge of Chaos*, to the conversations between characters, to descriptions of the landscape, the motif of edges, borders, frontiers, and margins often recurs. What do you think this means?

6. The city of Santa Fe is almost a character in its own right. Why is it so significant? Might the novel have been set in another city?

7. Judith tells her young neighbor, Alejandro, that his generation might be the first to understand that random events happen, something Sophie also refers to. What does randomness mean in this book, and why is randomness so difficult for humans to deal with?

8. The novel is pervaded by the sense of transition: the century and the millennium are about to change; the point of view represented by the sciences of complexity is already changing how both science and business are conducted. The edge of chaos is said to be where a system is open to change, to learning, but where catastrophe can also follow—chaos, or frozen order. In your opinion, which of the characters learn and change, which do not?

9. The prejudice against women in science is real and well documented. Is Judith right when she tells Sophie that what really underlies that prejudice is a woman scientist's declaration that she will not serve (*non serviam*) in any socially conventional way?

10. Molloy is deeply affected by both art and music. Judith is a mathematician. Are there similarities between art and music, on the one hand, and mathematics on the other? How would you describe the similarities, as embodied by these characters? The differences? What do you think this signifies?

11. Nearly all the principal characters attend the burning of Zozobra, a ceremony that indeed takes place annually in Santa Fe. What does this strange ceremony seem to mean?

12. Molloy and Nola make a significant visit to a man-made cave, a work of art. What meanings do you attribute to that episode? Does it remind you of other caves that have appeared in the Western canon?

13. Language is vital to these talkative characters. As Sophie is dying, she begins an uncharacteristic talking streak. Molloy compares talking to the act of mutual grooming, practiced by all primates. Judith and Ron have little language contests, and elsewhere, Judith compares mathematics to discovering the language of God. What do you think this is all this about?

14. The novel's chapter titles refer to concepts used regularly by scientists who explore complexity. Without knowing exactly what they mean, do you begin to see some of the issues that complexity raises? Can you see the connection between the chapter titles and their content?

Printed in the United States
93435LV00004B/109-114/A